Eulogies II:
Tales from the Cellar

Edited by Christopher Jones
Nanci Kalanta
Tony Tremblay

HW Press

ဆ 2013 03

Cover art © 2013 Deena Warner
Interior Art © 2013 Keith Minnion
Interior Layout by Nanci Kalanta
ISBN-10 0979234654
ISBN-13 9780979234651

HW Press
Website: www.horrorworld.org/e2

CONTENTS

ACKNOWLEDGEMENTS

Christopher Jones

Thanks to Nanci Kalanta and Tony Tremblay—great editors, better friends.

Sincere thanks to Deena Warner, Elizabeth Massie, Keith Minnion, Jack Ketchum, Kurt Criscione, and Fran Friel for your contributions. This book is better because of you.

Extra special thanks to all the writers who submitted stories.

For Jazmin and Aaron—the little monsters in my cellar.

Nanci Kalanta

Thanks to Chris Jones for coming up with the idea for Eulogies II and for suggesting that the proceeds go to helping Tom and Michelle Piccirilli. I'm eternally grateful to Tony Tremblay for stepping up and helping dig through the slush pile and for helping keep *Eulogies II* on track and on time.

Thank you to Jack Ketchum, Elizabeth Massie, Keith Minnion, Deena Warner, and all the authors who submitted stories.

Finally, to the Cellar Dwellers for keeping the Horror World Message Boards alive in this day of Facebook and Twitter.

Tony Tremblay

Many thanks to all of the authors who have contributed to this anthology. The work between these pages is often breathtaking and always brilliant; I continue to be in awe of all your talent.

I would also like to thank Deena Warner, Elizabeth Massie, Kurt Criscione, Keith Minnion, and Jack Ketchum. Their contributions to this anthology are like icing on a cake; they have made a great book even better.

Especially warm thanks goes out to all the members of Horror World; you guys are the absolute best.

I would also like to thank my wife (who never complained once about my involvement or the time I put into this anthology), and my son and daughter for their encouragement. While I'm on the personal side of these acknowledgements, I would also like to smile and nod my head at my neighbor Doug Doster for his encouragement and for spreading the word around town about this anthology, and to my writing group, The Blank Page, located in Goffstown, New Hampshire, for being there for me when I needed them.

I am grateful beyond words to my coeditors Chris Jones and Nanci Kalanta. If I could give bear hugs like the great James A. Moore, I think both would have been crushed to death by now. My respect for Chris and Nanci has grown enormously over the course of this anthology; not only did I learn a lot from them, they made the learning a hell of a lot of fun.

Finally, if there is a supreme being, I want to thank him for giving Tom Piccirilli the opportunity to read this anthology.

Introduction
Elizabeth Massie

Shakespeare said, "All the world's a stage, and all the men and women merely players." The contributors to *Eulogies II* seem to be saying, "All the world's a cellar, and one only need pull open the bulkhead doors to catch a whiff of the stench, or to walk down the damp, crumbling concrete steps to brave an encounter with what creeps, crawls, or festers in the darkness." In most cultures, hell is known as a place underneath, down below, in the dark where it is either unbearably hot or unbearably cold, where terrible circumstances overwhelm or even destroy those who wander there. Hell is the ultimate cellar. So it's no wonder the idea of going down stirs up such a sense of dread. And our life experience is filled with cellars.

Cellars of place. Cellars of time. Cellars of circumstance. They can all hold dark, horrifying, and unseemly secrets.

This anthology is chocked full of dark, horrifying, and unseemly secrets from the cellars of our beings. We read them. We shiver. We relate. As you read these tales you will find that they touch something personal. That's the mark of a good story. In particular, a good horror story. It feels creepily familiar somehow, no matter how strange. It reminds you of something deep, something hidden, something painful. And yet you let yourself go there, anyway.

Cellars of Place ...

When I was young, my family would visit my grandparents' house every so often. They lived in a stately old mansion made of bricks imported from Europe and boasting a lovely front porch with white columns, countless rooms, and furniture that smelled of polish and elegance. But then there was the cellar. The wooden stairs led down to a main room with small, grubby, ceiling-high windows. In this room was old furniture that sagged, a water-warped radio that didn't work, a dart board where my father had been stabbed once in the arm by a mis-throw, and a "toy bag" for the grandkids, full of dolls and puppets that smelled like old biscuits. In the far wall was a narrow door and behind the narrow door was an even narrower hallway. A hallway with a low ceiling and a naked light bulb hanging from it like a fat, legless spider. There were several small rooms off this subterranean hallway. Only one had its own source of light. The others were illuminated only by the hall light when the doors were opened. The first dark, dirt-floored room was home to a single old crutch with a stained cloth padding. I never knew who'd used the crutch, or worse, what the stain was. I never went into that room but only gazed in horrified wonder at the crutch from the hallway. The second and third rooms were storage, and the fourth had a naked lightbulb in the ceiling. It had been the "maid's room." It was the farthest from the main basement room, as if they didn't want the maid anywhere near the family when she wasn't cleaning. It had a tiny bed, a sink, a dresser. The family hadn't had a maid for many years, but the room sat as she had left it, stinking of despair and loneliness. This literal cellar of place haunted my childhood nightmares and colored those of my adulthood.

Eulogies II will haunt your nightmares with numerous glimpses into the dingy, disturbing cellars of place. "A Serving of Nomu Sashimi" by Eric J. Guignard serves up a cringe-worthy, surreal dining establishment. Matthew Warner's "Muralistic" takes us into an ordinary library where omens reach out to take us by the throat. "The Second Carriage" by

Jonathan Templar forces us into an attic of the darkest secrets imaginable. And there are many more dark places to explore here.

Cellars of Time ...

We all have learned of strange, troubling, or terrifying things from the past. Whoever longs for the "good old days" longs in a fog of ignorance and denial. Sometimes these terrifying things emerge from our very own pasts. I doubt there is a person walking this earth who doesn't have, somewhere in his or her ancestral line, a thief or an arsonist or a murderer or rapist or hateful abuser of people or animals. Such discoveries are unnerving at best and nightmare-inducing at worst. Several years ago, I found out that my great-great-grandfather James Aaron Moon, a Civil War veteran and disowned Quaker, killed himself in 1876 with a homemade guillotine in a room at the Lahr Hotel in Layfayette, Indiana, leaving his wife and four children behind. Pity and horror merged as this cellar of time opened its doors for me and dragged me backward into the vivid mental image of a blood-soaked hotel floor, a burned-out candle, and a severed head beneath a chair. And it's not just the past. There are also frightening things awaiting us in the future. Whoever longs for the golden years that lie ahead need only look at history to know there has never been a golden time and most likely never will be. Terror is timeless. As long as humans walk the earth, fear will walk beside them.

The anthology in your hands presents powerful tales from the cellars of time. Stories that reach out from years gone by or beckon with bony fingers from years ahead. A small sampling include "Footnotes" by Magda Knight, a time-twisting terror rooted in a bizarre past, "On the Hooks" by Keith Minnion, a chilling step forward into the future, and David Schembri's "The Black Father of the Night," which hangs in its own time, a new, gut-punching look at a classic legend.

Cellars of Circumstance ...

When someone believes he or she is going to die, that person most likely experiences one of life's greatest rushes of fear. Just ask Anne Boleyn, if she could come back around and talk. "What was it like the seconds before the sword met its mark, Anne?" Or ask someone whose car has plunged off a bridge and he or she struggles to open the car door or window as the vehicle plunges to the murky depths. "Are you scared?" Answer, most likely, will be in the affirmative, something along the lines of, "Are you fucking stupid? Of course I'm scared!"

Panic. Horror. Dread. It's all part of the survival response as we struggle to keep from happening what seems to be happening. Now, I've not died. Obviously. But I remember one winter day hitting a patch of black ice in my car, the car spinning and slamming into a telephone pole that broke off at the base. In those few seconds my heart slammed like a jackhammer against my ribs, my breath locked in my lungs, and all I could think was, *I'm going to die! And it's going to hurt like hell!* Life's circumstances, be they death or illness or loss or danger, swoop down, scoop us up, and throttle us senseless.

This terrifying anthology offers many tales set in the cellars of circumstance. "Loneliness Makes the Loudest Noise" by Monica J. O'Rourke is a labyrinthine cellar of overwhelming and evil circumstance. Then there is the comically dark and introspective "Neck Bolt Lynch Pin" by Steve Vernon. Religious zeal and control at their worst are explored in Lucy Snyder's "Spare the Rod." And there can't be a more dreadful, realistic, and heartbreaking cellar of circumstance than Maurice Broaddus's "Awaiting Redemption." Those are just a few. More await you, sitting patiently, fangs bared.

All these cellars—place, time, and circumstance—meld into one vast and particularly dark cellar within the pages of *Eulogies II: Tales from the Cellar.* And that is The Cellar of the Mind. Where fear is born. Where terror thrives.

And so here, for your enjoyment, are thirty-two terrific tomes of horror, thirty-two trips into the Cellar of the Mind by way of time, place, and circumstance. Don't bother taking a candle with you. These authors will cheerfully blow it out for you and then watch for you in the darkness.

—Elizabeth Massie, 2013

The Thing with Nothing to Give and Nothing to Lose
Tom Piccirilli

I'm sitting across the bar looking at myself, the me I was a couple of years back. Holding on by my teeth, the stress and strain apparent in every line of my face, slugging down glass after glass of scotch on the rocks. Eyes skittering all over the place, checking out the chicks, angry with the guys in better suits, with better looks, better haircuts, better cars, more cash in their pockets. They've got no wives at home, no kids, no debts, no mortgage. Despair seeps from him like sewage from a busted toilet.

He doesn't understand the wonders and relief of letting go, the way I do now. And I can't teach him, and I can't tell him. No matter what I say he won't listen, and he won't believe. He still thinks things are going to get better. He still has faith. He believes in miracles. He might hit the lottery. He might have a rich uncle he's never met who suddenly croaks and writes him into the will for a few mill. It's no wonder he's about to lose his job. It's no wonder they're going to foreclose on his house.

It's no wonder the wife is cheating, the kids are ungrateful and stupid, the car is about to die.

I am the man he will soon become after everything is gone. I am the man who no longer believes in consequences. I am the man who can do what others cannot do. I can talk back. I can punch the boss in the head. I can demand justice. I can hold the bank manager hostage for three hours on a sunny May day and then cut his throat with his own letter opener. I pillage. I take. I swallow no shit. I give killer glare. I offer charming smile. I lay who I want. I don't feel guilt. I felt guilty too much of my life even when I did nothing wrong. I always played by rules. I always did right. I always lent a helping hand.

Now I am fist. Now I am fire. Now I am theft. Now I am alone, receded in shadow, a taker, a biter, a knifer, a drinker, a laugher, a howler. Like the me I'm staring at, like him over there, I never used to laugh. I nodded and chuckled and looked on yearningly. I wanted. I lusted. I glanced up sadly. I wept. I moaned. I drank. I begged. I prayed. Now they beg me. Now they pray to me.

That's what happens when you consign everything and they still try to take even more from you. You become a different thing. You become the thing with nothing to give and nothing to lose.

I watch myself, knowing myself, understanding. The other me glances at me, afraid to make eye contact, afraid to offend, afraid to look in his wallet, afraid to call the wife, afraid to have an affair, afraid to quit the job, afraid to move on, afraid to stay. He is a statue without a heart, carved from terror.

I was once carved from terror. Now I carve terror. I have nothing, but I do something. I teach. I am a teacher.

I step around the bar and take the other me's arm. I tug him toward the door. He is afraid to fight. He almost whimpers. He almost calls out for help. He almost resists, but that's impossible for him. He tries to speak but can't. He can never speak when it matters most. He can only speak when it doesn't. He pleads and whines. He leaves many messages on many voice mails because he is afraid of confrontation. I will teach him differently.

The bartender barks about the bill. I throw money down to cover it. The bartender continues barking. I pick up a stool and hurl it at him.

The other me cannot make words. He makes sounds and noises. He groans. He thinks, deep inside him, the thing he has always thought his entire life. That he deserves all the pain he receives. He deserves betrayal. He deserves trauma. He deserves disease. He deserves loneliness. He deserves attack. He deserves loss. He deserves the death of dreams. He deserves humiliation. It is no wonder, even to himself, that he receives all that he believes he deserves. He calls down the lightning. He calls down the storm. He accepts the pain.

I am the storm. I survived the storms only because I became one of them. He will understand this. He has no choice. I have no choice. The storm has no choice.

I drag him out the door. I recognize his car instantly because I used to drive it. I take him to it. I have already parked beside it. Rain begins to fall. He holds his face up and the rain drips into his eyes and mouth and awakens him from his slumber.

I get behind the wheel of my car. I tell him to get in. He does. He's impressed. Of course he's impressed. He's everything I was a few years ago. This is the car he's always wanted but could never afford and would never buy even if he could. It has muscle. It has power. He is a man afraid of power. But power will come to him the same way it came to me. He's almost there.

He asks who I am. He is a fool. He sees but doesn't recognize. We drive together down the road. It's a road he has traveled many times before. It's a road he has never traveled before. The storm lashes down. His phone rings but he doesn't answer. It is only more pain. It is always more pain. It is nagging. It is debt. It is argument. It is butchery. It is government. It is banking. It is church. He rolls down the window and throws the phone. He begins to laugh. It is the first real laugh he has had in months, years, perhaps ever. Thunder roars in the sky, in the engine, in his belly. The journey begins.

The police are waiting ahead. The police are always waiting ahead. There has been an accident. Red flares melt in the distance. The road is full of white-capped waves. The ambulances are too late, always too late. The bodies are covered and carried and put in back. He says he thinks he sees a dead child.

Of course he sees a dead child. There's always dead children. There's always been dead children. The storm demands sacrifice. Becoming the storm demands sacrifice.

The flares light the dark interior of the car with a wash of fiery blood. He looks like he wants to get out and help, but the dead are beyond his help, and the living don't want it. I reach out and grab him and hold him in place. He doesn't understand that the time for help is long past. It has always been long past.

Chain lightning ignites the dark clouds overhead. We watch the sky burn for a hundred miles in every direction. I turn on the radio. He likes music. He finds solace in music, and in books, and in films, and in other things that truly do not offer solace or peace or power. His devotion is always mislaid. He prays at the wrong altars, to the wrong gods.

"It's not so bad," I tell him.

"What's not?"

"Letting go."

"Letting go of what?"

"Of everything. Not paying your taxes. Not paying the mortgage. Telling the boss to go fuck himself. Throwing the bills in the trash. Kicking your wife out. The worst consequences you think you'll face involve prison and embarrassment and loneliness. But you're already caged up and you're already humiliated and you're already alone. Letting go is the best thing for you."

"I can't just give up."

"You've already given up."

"Who the hell are you?"

"I'm what you're about to become."

"You don't even know me."

"I know everything about you."

"What's my name?"

"Your name doesn't matter. It's never mattered and it's about to matter even less. It's like you. It's meaningless. It's colorless and transparent."

He stares at the police in the rain as if they can help him. They have never helped him. They will never help him. They can't help him and he can't help himself.

The only thing they might do for him, and it'll be a relief if it ever happens, is put a bullet through his head the day he barricades himself inside his house after taking some smug-smiled prick banker from the mortgage company hostage.

"Where are we going?" he asks.

It's a question he's asked himself many times before. He's never gotten an answer before. So I give him one.

"I'm showing you freedom."

I take him to the water. I take him past the high school. I take him to the cemetery, where our father is buried. I take him to the places where I died by inches and was reborn. I take him to spot where he proposed to his wife. I drive by the motel where she and her lover met every afternoon while I ate shit, gunpowder, and plutonium at the office.

He stares at the side of my face as if he's beginning to recognize me. I turn and stare. He sees my eyes and knows them. He reaches out and touches the dashboard with the proper reverence. This is the car he's always wanted. This is the car he will soon have. He smiles, sensing this, understanding this, somewhere deep inside himself, where he still has dreams, where he still has a name.

"Do you love?" he asks.

"Do I love?"

"Yes, do you know love?"

"No. Love is loss. Loss is pain. I have nothing to lose. I can no longer be hurt."

"You expect me to become like you."

"It's not an expectation. It's a realization. A self-actualization."

"I don't know what the hell you're talking about."

"Yes, you do."

"Why did you pick me?"

"I didn't pick you. I am you. I was you."

He reaches into his pocket. I know what's there. He's got a gun. Something small, something to stick in his ear, stick in his mouth, that won't be too frightening at that last moment, thinking of his skull shattered, his brains spattered, his soul released. He's never fired it before. He kept it in his night stand, then moved it to his bottom desk drawer, then a box in the closet, and then he just started carrying it all the time, like a toy for the son he doesn't have. Something he can use up close on the boss, on the office workers, on the wife, on the lover, on the random fool who crosses his path. He considers shooting me, probably in the groin or the leg, at least until we're past the accident area. He wants to run. He wants to join the storm. He doesn't understand he's already joined it, that it's inside him, that it is me. Whether he kills me or kills himself or kills anyone else is as worthless and pointless as his name and his next breath.

The wreck on the road is a bad one. Kids. Some punk showing off for his girlfriend and a bunch of his friends and their girlfriends too. Five or six teenagers spread out across the highway from shoulder to railing, the cops and the EMTs picking up the pieces. Thing is, they'll never get them all. A month from now, some prisoner in a jumpsuit will be cleaning the median and find a finger or an ear or something worse.

"So seeing that doesn't bother you?" he asks.

"It bothers me," I tell him. "About as much as it bothers you."

His eyes are bleary, I see, in the flare light and the refracted headlights, and the red and blue lights of the ambulances and cop cars. The shadows of the rain falling across the windshield drip across his face, but none of it fools me into thinking that he's crying or even profoundly hurt by the scene before us. He's too wrapped up in his own fear and pain. He's thinking of his bank account, the promotion he didn't get, the secretary he wants a piece of but can't have.

The kid parts are gory but not as gory as our parts. We're out there someplace too, smashed up, torn to shreds, traffic slowing around our corpses, rubberneckers gawking. It happened to me. It'll happen to him soon. What else is the gun for if not that? He glances at me and I know he sees the fiery flare glowing in my features. So it makes me demonic. Is that where his imagination is leading him? Does he think I'm the devil here to take him on a short ride to hell? He really is an idiot, still holding on to some notion of God and sin and consequence.

"There is no redemption," I say. "There's no need for redemption."

"Why are you saying these things?"

"They're the things you need to know. I'm trying to help you."

"Why?"

"Because I remember what it was like. And I remember wanting someone to help me."

"I don't want your help. Your kind of help."

"A .32 isn't going to help you either."

"It's a .22."

"Even less. Put it against your temple, and all it will do is scramble your brains. It won't even kill you. The bullet doesn't have enough velocity to break through your skull. It just ricochets around and around."

"You're an evil son of a bitch."

"No, I'm not."

He thinks about shouting to the police again. He stares. He tries to make subtle motions to attract attention. Like cops in the rain surrounded by dead teens might notice his scaredy cat face pressed to the cold passenger window glass. He's ludicrous, the same way I was. I think about reaching past him, opening the door, and throwing him out. But that serves no purpose at all.

One of the decapitated bodies is a cheerleader with tremendous tits. She's got her cheer sweater on, wet, her nipples proudly displayed even in death. They wheel the gurney over to the body and gently lift it and place it on the pillows. They are kinder to the dead than the living. They are kinder to the hot dead girls than the live ugly ones.

He can't help watching the rain-soaked torso, thinking of teenage cleavage. He will hate himself for this as he hates himself for everything. But he's no different than me, no different from any of the hundreds of middle-aged men driving by at this hour. All of them gray and beaten, all of them thinking about their daughters and mistresses and porn star goddess dreams. They are the same. We are all the same.

I'm not evil, I'm simply honest. My lies and my pride and my hopes were all seared away in the great revelatory light and blast of my own undoing. It will happen to him too, perhaps tonight.

"If you're going to try to rob me, I don't have any money."

"I know that," I say. "I paid for your drinks, remember?"

"What happened to you?"

"The same thing that's happening to you."

He looks at the cheerleader trying not to appear lecherous in front of me. He fails. He is a pig even unto himself. It's the truth of us, of all of us, of any of us. He has no idea how much better it is when you stop fighting everything you are, everything you want to do, everything you feel. He is in conflict over every moment, every motion. Whether to smoke, whether to sneak a glance, whether to kiss, whether to forgive, whether to fuck, whether to strike, whether to scream. I know the agony of being torn apart. I was once in more pieces than these children.

"Where are we going?"

The answer is self-evident. I say nothing. He looks at his watch as if there is something waiting for him, someone, some reason to care about the passing of hours. There isn't. There never has been. He realizes this inside himself, or he soon will.

Two lanes are merged into one beyond the accident. The guy across the broken white line from me stares, knowing my thoughts, knowing who I am. He is me, the me I am now. His passenger is the other me, the old me, practically screaming in his seat, clawing at the fogged glass like a terrified cat. I slow and the driver maneuvers ahead of me, rear right tire barely missing a pool of blood on the black glistening road. It's a muscle car too. It's got Detroit steel, hard-earned miles, horsepower to burn. Our treads will be thick with blood for months, maybe years, to come. And for once it's not our blood. And for once it's not the blood of men who are like us or will be like us.

The other me sits up, a touch wary now. He saw the other passenger and knows his face, sees the same pain and horror in the passenger. He leans forward, peering through the windshield, wanting to see into the fogged back window of the car ahead. He swipes his hand across the glass. He snakes his hand into the dash to move the defogger fan switch up another notch but it's already up as far as it will go. The other

passenger stares in the side mirror, his eyes fiery with a new
and profound understanding. He's at the edge of the big ledge.
He's going over. He wants to be saved without fully realizing
that his salvation lies at the bottom of the abyss. He's already
halfway there. The other me learns something by watching
him. He relaxes and sits back and sighs. He knows the fight is
almost over. I know the sound of the sigh. He's leaping
himself, finally.

It's a quieter undoing than my own was. He doesn't go for
the gun. He doesn't go for the wheel. He doesn't weep. He
doesn't call the wife. He doesn't call the therapist. He doesn't
call the secretary. He doesn't call the cops. He saw himself in
the other passenger and decided he no longer wished to be that
terrorized cat wanting out, out, out. The never-ending stress
and fear alive even in his sleep, the nightmares following into
day, day after day after day. His fantasies failing, his reality
failing, his marriage failing, the job dying, the boss openly
antagonistic, the friends disappearing, the dog dying, the bank
always calling, the credit card companies bitching, bankruptcy
looming, his dead father's voice loud in his skull. The
disappointment in the man's dark eyes and darker voice so
much more alive than he ever was.

The doctor requests to meet in the hospital. The blood
pressure, bad. The blood sugar, bad. The cholesterol, bad. The
knees, bad. The back, bad. The teeth, bad. The sinuses, bad.

He still fidgets with the gun. Maybe to feel like a man
again, for a moment. Maybe to feel powerful, dangerous.
Maybe to fire it out the window, a signal to the other
passenger. Maybe a call to others become things with nothing
to give and nothing to lose.

"I don't want to be like you," he whines. The whine
offends him. The whine humiliates him.

We follow the other muscle car and take the next exit. We
wind up on an empty road that leads to the cemetery. A
cemetery where a kid murdered another kid last year, and then
brought all his friends around to see the remains. A cemetery
where they hang cats and then pretend to be Satanists, hunting
power, hunting knowledge, hoping to sell their souls, as if their
souls had any worth to anyone, even God or the devil.

The driver ahead slows in the downpour. I bump his fender lightly. Both cars swerve wildly. Both passengers cry out. It's the last time they ever will. From now on their silence will be part of their armor. They will feel nothing to make them cry. They have nothing to give and nothing to lose, but soon they will understand it. We pass the cemetery gates.

He asks, "Why have you brought me here?"

"I haven't."

"My mother is buried here. And my father."

"That doesn't matter."

"It matters to me."

"Soon it won't."

"Like hell."

"Yes, like hell."

The other driver parks. I pull to the side of the road. The other me climbs out and steps into a puddle. He curses his luck. In the distance, the graves of his parents stand out the same way they did the day his mother and father were buried. They stand like temples. They stand like gods in the night sky.

The other passenger climbs out and steps into a puddle. He doesn't curse his luck. He's closer to his ruination and rebirth than the other me. We all get to the end in our own good time.

The other driver gets out too. So do I. We close the distance between us. We openly appraise each other. Thunder erupts in the distance. It fills our chests. It reminds us of what we once were, as children, as men, as husbands and fathers and house owners, as creatures of social convention. We've left all that behind but the thunder, like a pulse, like the never-ending headache, remains. The passengers mill together seeking comfort. They introduce themselves. They state their names. The other driver laughs. I laugh too. Even when you are the thing with nothing to give and nothing to lose, you can still laugh. It's another reason to become what we've become. To become what the others are becoming.

The passengers reach for their cell phones. They have wives to call. They have promises to keep. They have work that still needs to be done. They have the bank manager on voice mail. They have friends who murmur regrets. They have brothers who can no longer lend any more money. They have boss's complaining about shoddy work. They have secretaries clamoring for their time, for their promises. They are supposed to be in ten other places.

I walk among the dead. The other driver walks with me. Mud doesn't disturb us. Cold and rain doesn't bother us. The call of the dead is loud enough to drown out any other commitments. You just have to listen. You just have to be ready.

Music coasts over the lawns and mounds, emitted from one of the vaults. The sound of glass breaking makes the other me jump. The four of us walk to the vault. The stone door is ajar, inviting. A girl's laughter leaks through. The music is harsh, ugly. The kids are playing Satanic Panic. They read from the Bible, backward. They make up prayers to call down the black fates. A small fire burns in the center of the crypt. They are seeking purpose in the world, and they've found it.

I move to the girl. She screams. He draws his .22. He tells me to leave her alone. Of course I'm leaving her alone. I leave everyone alone, even him. He is trying to be fatherly, respectable still. His voice is an offense. He is trying not to imagine fucking her, he's trying not to imagine being a boy again and doing everything right the next time around. Move left instead of right, try harder, be smarter, choose better, pay more attention. His face is full of regret and dream. The other driver stands before one of the boys and presents himself. We are object lessons to be learned. We are examples well-set. We are revelation.

The kids scatter and flee into the night. The Bible's pages flip in the wind. The other me reaches for the girl asking if she's all right. She is for now, but soon she might be dead on the highway with her perfect but lifeless tits pressing against a tight sweater. The other passenger stares into the fire looking for answers.

He hasn't hit the bottom of the abyss yet, which is a sad state to be in. Halfway between slavery and freedom. He senses he is falling, that he has fallen, but can't do anything to speed it along. I put my hand on his arm and he turns slowly to look into my face. He's surprised at what he sees there. He didn't know we'd all look so much alike. He almost shrugs me off, almost takes a step back, almost jumps into the fire, almost chases the girl out into the rain. He wants to do all of these things and instead does what he does best. Nothing. He has become what I became. The relief is so powerful he drops to his knees like a penitent. The dark gods shine down upon him. His heart is purified. His phone rings and he doesn't care. I fall to my knees beside him. The others do the same. The fire dims and I throw the Bible onto it. The flames rear and crackle and spit as if they're choking on the gospels. Each of us is in control, master of our fate. The girl returns. She doesn't know what to say. She disrobes. We take her in turns. It is the purest love any of us has ever known. We thank her. She thanks us. She is the bearer of light and life. The storm lashes the world. The dead are content. So is she. So are we.

Tom Piccirilli is the author of more than twenty-five novels. He's the winner of four Bram Stoker Awards, two Thrillers, and has been nominated for the Edgar and the World Fantasy Award.

What Was Once Bone
Gary A. Braunbeck

Or I will wrap the(e) up in such a terrible fathers curse that thou shalt feel worms in thy marrow creeping thro thy bones ...

—William Blake, *Tiriel*

It was a little after four in the morning when the man in the apartment next door started beating his wife again.

There was nothing loud at first, nothing to suggest the ferocity of the violence about to occur, only a slight, muffled bump, as if someone had stumbled their way into a darkened bathroom.

William Baker lay in his bed, listening, hoping it wasn't going to start once again. This was the first time in two weeks that Michelle had been able to spend the night, and the last thing he wanted was for her to experience the constricting helplessness that always overtook him. Sure, he had done his concerned citizen bit the first few times, but when the police arrived, the woman always—

—a glass flew against the wall and shattered. William gripped the sheet in his hands and held his breath. Why did it seem that the man always picked this same time to begin his brutality?

William blinked at the prick of the memory.

Papa always seemed to reach his breaking point about four in the morning; then it was up the stairs to jerk Mom out of bed and make her fix him something to eat, or clean up the mess he had made getting sick, or countless other drunken reasons that were so similar in William's mind they became interchangeable over the years, all of them screamed in a sick, intoxicated slur.

Next door a woman's muffled whimpering crept under the cracks in the wall and emerged next to William's head. The voice was thin and terrified, and William always cursed himself for the pictures that slipped into his mind at times like this: there was the man, standing over the bed, taking his wife by the hair and yanking her awake, pulling her face up to his, spitting fetid breath into her face, perhaps his other, free hand found its way to private, delicate parts of her body where it grabbed and twisted, making her yelp like some wounded animal and then, yes, of course, he would lower his voice to a menacing whisper, threatening to make the pain worse if she didn't quiet down.

Pay attention, boy, Papa would say, still drunk, always drunk, stumbling through the debris of his last rampage, *and don't you say nothin' back to me—you tell anyone what happened to your mom and I'll pound you down into the ground where people bury their dead and you'll live the rest of your life surrounded by rot and stink and the touch of cold, sticky, dead meat. You'll feel all them squiggly little maggots crawling over your face, slitherin' into your nose and mouth, maybe slip down your throat and choke you, yessir—and you'd deserve it, too, boy, for talking out of turn about your old man and—I said you don't talk! Goddammit, here's a little—don't you pull away from me, you little shit—*

William tasted something coppery in his mouth and realized he had bitten into his lower lip. Reaching up, he touched the lip, pulled his fingers away, and saw the trickles of blood splashed across his fingertips.

A sharp *crack!* echoed through the walls, and he tried to rise quietly so as not to disturb Michelle. Maybe it wouldn't get

so loud tonight, maybe the man just needed to make a show of
power, maybe—

—something heavy slammed against the wall, followed by
another shattering glass and a shriek that broke through the
floorboards and shook Michelle by the shoulders until she
came awake like a small child from its first real nightmare.

Pulling herself up into the sitting position, she asked,
"What the hell was that?"

"Next door," said William, resigned not to lie about it. If
things went the usual way, she would know well enough in a
few moments.

It didn't take long.

The sounds that erupted from beyond the bedroom wall
were inhuman: screaming, thrashing, cracking, breaking, wet
slapping noises, whimpers that rose into shrieks which
escalated into cries silenced by something heavy being
walloped into the far wall and tumbling down the stairs, filling
William's bedroom with a cold blanket of impotence.

(I'll teach the both of you a lesson, by God …)

Before he could even rise from the bed, Michelle was on
her feet and heading toward the phone.

"Don't," he said. "They won't come."

Michelle whirled around and stared at him. "How would
you know?"

He crossed to her and took her gently by the arms. "This
has been going on for the last couple of weeks. I've called the
police four times, and every single time the woman comes to
the door and tells them nothing's wrong."

"Maybe they'll think differently if the call is *from* a
woman." She ran into the next room and made the call.

Ten minutes later the police car pulled up and two
uniformed officers went to the door.

William and Michelle stood next to the bedroom window,
peeking out from behind the curtains and listening to the
woman's voice; weak, hollow, hoarse from screaming and
crying.

She told the police there was nothing wrong.

William shook his head in disgust, stormed over to the
bed, and sat down.

As the police car pulled away, Michelle turned from the window and whispered, "Is that it?"

"What the fuck did you expect?" he said. "I told you not to call, didn't I? She tells them the same goddamn thing every time, and they just go away. The last time I called the cops, they didn't even show up!" He exhaled heavily and rubbed his eyes, looking at the clock. Four in the morning. He thought about that line from F. Scott Fitzgerald, about how in the dark night of the soul it was always four in the morning. He looked up at Michelle, who was gathering up her clothes and getting dressed.

"What more can you do?" he asked.

"I can't believe that you'd have just sat there and done nothing about it!"

"The cops can't do anything unless she presses charges, and she won't. Outside of going over there and killing the guy, I'm hard-pressed to think of what else to do. What goes on in a person's house is their private business, regardless of how much it might offend someone else."

"God! You sound like all those people they talked to after Kitty Genovese was killed: 'I didn't think it was any of my business.' I don't … I mean, how can you … ?"

"I know what it must be like," he whispered. "I spent the better part of my childhood sitting through things like this. I've told you about my father, the way he became after the plant shut down. I watched a decent man, a loving man, turn into a monster that wanted to destroy everything around it in slow degrees. I was eleven years old. Once I even thought about killing him but I lost my nerve because Mom did love him for … whatever pitiful goddamn reason. I don't know how many times I snuck downstairs after he was finished and found her crying in the bathroom. I always hugged her and helped her clean her cuts and told her that I loved her and it never seemed to help. She'd just pull her ratty old bathrobe around her so I couldn't see the bruises and ask me if I wanted to have a cup of hot chocolate before I went back to bed." He looked straight into Michelle's eyes. "So don't look at me with such disgust. What the man is doing to his wife sickens me, but I am powerless to do anything about it. So save your theories and passionate lectures for your sociology professors."

"I'm leaving."

"That'll accomplish a whole lot, won't it?" He didn't know why he was getting so nasty with her; they hardly found time to be together anymore, what with him working days and final exams taking up all her evenings.

"I just can't believe you think you've done all you can do," said Michelle, staring down at the floor. She wiped something from one of her eyes, sighed, and then looked at him as if she were about to say something more, and in that moment William knew that their relationship was over; in that moment, he saw what would become of her, what eventually became of most women who were unfortunate enough to be born and raised in places like Cedar Hill: she would complete her education, perhaps even, for a while, find a teaching position at one of the local schools, but then would come marriage, the growing ten pounds heavier with each passing year, having the children who wouldn't much respect her, a husband who wouldn't much like her, and one day she'd awaken to realize that she was forty-five years old and there was more of her life behind her than there was ahead, and she'd settle into the not-quite-sad but far from happy mindset of thinking that her life was good enough.

Good enough.

But never great.

No one who lived in Cedar Hill had a life that was great; in places like this, greatness of that sort was something you envied in those who didn't live here.

He took a breath and stood up, ready to apologize, but before he could say anything she finished dressing and stormed out of the bedroom, down the stairs, and out the door to her car.

William grabbed his pants, put them on, and got outside just in time to see her car vanish around the corner. As he turned to go back inside he froze at the sight which met him.

The woman stood in the doorway of her apartment, wiping her bruised and swollen face with a wet towel. Her eyes were red and puffy. Her hair hung around her shattered features like cobwebs covering a piece of old furniture someone had forgotten about.

(… live the rest of your life surrounded by rot and stink and the touch of cold, sticky, dead meat …)

William tried to find something to say, but no words came out. A throbbing pressure in the back of his throat rendered his tongue useless.

They looked directly into one another's eyes for a moment, long enough for William to notice the line of scratch marks and bruises that began on the left side of her neck and ran down, vanishing in the material of her torn bathrobe. William knew that she probably had nothing else to wear, had probably owned this same robe since the day she was married, and would never, ever own another.

She pulled the robe around her so he could not see the marks and closed the door. Gently. Quietly. Without malice. Shamefully. Helplessly.

William stood alone and stared at the door, wondering what must be going on behind it. Perhaps the man was almost in tears now, blubbering through a pathetic apology, begging her forgiveness. And she would give that absolution, freely and with all the love she held in her battered soul.

The glare from the single streetlight suddenly felt like the stare of a million disapproving eyes to William, so he lowered his head and went inside, the ache in his throat spreading fast.

He sat in silence on his bed, staring at the far wall, listening for any sounds. In the back of his head he could hear the rustlings of his father, deep in a drunken sleep. He could hear the shallow, terrified breathing of his mother as she tried to find rest, afraid that she'd embrace the comfort of a night's dreaming only to be ripped awake and faced with the fury of a beast that was once her kind and loving husband, before the sadness came and found him easy to defeat.

He looked up toward the ceiling. It was a blackboard sky where the faces from his childhood were drawn in red chalk that dripped blood from the corners and into his eyes. He wiped the images away but not their sounds, their voices, their whimpers and words. He saw the clock; still four a.m. He could still taste the blood in his mouth from the cut on his lip.

(Damn lucky that's all I did, boy …)

He found himself staring at the crack in the wall near the floorboards. It seemed to have grown larger, higher, as if the wall were a safety curtain on a stage, rising now so the show could begin for his entertainment.

He didn't know why he felt so compelled to make his neighbor's troubles his business. What could he do to help? The woman obviously didn't want it …

… her face. He couldn't have seen that face on her. But that face, maybe it was trying to give him a clue as to why he couldn't sleep, why he couldn't think straight, why he had been so nasty to Michelle, why Papa had turned into such a monster before he died, leaving William and his mother with little more than tainted memories, memories that sucked and chewed at his mother's spirit until she died a lonely, joyless, broken woman. He remembered standing over her coffin, thinking the morticians had done a nice job, covering up the scars and marks like they had. And he didn't even get the chance to hug her and tell her how much he loved her.

He had wanted to run out and find her waiting at home for him, all her sadness gone, making hot chocolate for the two of them, and while they drank it they would talk about going out to a movie or something because she never got out and wouldn't it be nice to leave the house just for a little while and do something?

God, the things he wished he had done.

And what use was regret now? What possible good was his guilt and self-pity going to do that poor woman next door? He could sit here and feel bad till the flesh decayed and dropped from his bones in slick, greasy clumps; maybe he'd do that, just lie here and embrace helplessness as if it were his lover, lay here until he was nothing but bone, and then what once was bone would itself degenerate, would crumble away, would fall into the earth and fossilize, becoming just an ancient sliver to be dug up one day and examined … yeah, he could just lay here, but that wasn't going to change anything for the woman next door, not one bit.

He opened his eyes and pulled back, his breath coming in short, desperate gasps. After a moment he was able to clear his vision and slow his heart down to a normal rate.

A sound came from beyond the wall.

The woman's voice, tired and soft, whispering.

An image came to him then; the woman clutching the neck of her ratty bathrobe, kneeling on all fours, pushing her words through the crack.

"Help me," said the voice.

William did not hesitate. He jumped to his feet, scrambled into the hallway, bolted down the stairs, out the door, and over to the next apartment. Sprinting up the three concrete steps to the door, he grabbed the handle and pushed, flinging the door open and bursting inside.

The place was a shambles; broken lamps, pieces of shattered glassware, a few splotches of drying blood on the stairway banister, overturned chairs, a pile of broken record albums, and a wedding photo album that someone had taken a lighter to.

Something shuffled at the top of the stairs. William grabbed a wooden leg from one of the broken chairs and, holding it like a baseball bat, started up toward the sound.

The woman, still bleeding and crying, met him at the landing.

He froze as he looked into her face and recognized her. Outside, when she had been standing in the door, the glare of the streetlight had made it difficult to see her features clearly. But now he saw, and felt his grip weaken on his weapon.

She reached out and took the leg from his hand, smiling at him. Then she gently took his arm and led him toward the bedroom.

He saw the familiar form lying on the bed, deep in a drunken sleep. He shambled over and stared down, thinking to himself how true it was that booze could perform plastic surgery on your features, given enough time.

He remembered how Papa had told him that, before the plant shutdown, he had never had a drink in his life.

William felt his chest begin to heave as he stood staring down into his own face, a face that was years older, sagging and discolored by drink and sadness and impotence.

He turned to face Michelle.

"Help me," he said.

Her answer was a brief smile before she kissed him.

He turned over and looked at the clock.

Four in the morning.

He felt the sweat clinging to his back like a thick layer of mucus. He took a deep breath and felt it catch in his chest.

A shuffling sound. Something bumping.

Any time now.

For what seemed an eternity he lay there listening to the whimpering and screams that accompanied the violence.

Then it ended.

More thumping and muffled cursing as the drunken monster fell into its bed.

William reached up and rubbed his eyes as he heard the soft crying.

He rose from his bed and put on his new slippers, snuck out into the hall and down the stairs.

He found her hunched over the bathroom sink, weeping, trying to choke back the noise so as not to wake the beast. William crossed over and hugged her. The terrible feeling was still snapping at his heels.

His mother embraced him and told him how much she loved him and how he shouldn't hate his papa, who was having such a rotten time of it right now but it would pass.

Eleven-year-old William knew exactly what it would pass into.

He drank some hot chocolate while his mother put her face back together, and then he rose to go back to bed.

But on the way up he stopped to get something.

He crept into his papa's room and climbed gently onto the bed. He looked down at the sleeping face and remembered the way he loved his papa, but Papa wasn't there anymore; Papa had died of sadness and left this thing in his place. And Papa had always promised them he'd never leave.

The beast on the bed opened its eyes and saw William.

"Help me," it whispered. Its voice was a breeze from between the cracks of the floorboards.

William raised the butcher knife high over the beast's head and saw the reflection cast in the gleaming blade.

He saw a man behind him, an older man who was not Papa, sitting at the foot of the bed. William knew how this man felt; he felt like a helpless little boy.

William stared into the reflection of the man's eyes.

The man looked into William's gaze, and both of them smiled.

The child with the knife looked at the clock.

Still four a.m.

He wondered which of them was dreaming.

But it didn't matter. The woman who had met him at the top of the stairs would forgive them both.

It seemed like it was always four in the morning.

But not for long.

He gripped the handle of the knife with both his hands and plunged down.

In the back of his head, the woman's screaming stopped.

He pulled the knife out and plunged in again and again and again, the warm, splattering wetness drenching his pajamas.

(I'll pound you down into the ground where people bury their dead …)

When it was done he crept softly from the room, threw the knife and his pajamas into the clothes hamper, and went to bed.

Looking at the clock, he smiled.

It was almost five.

He closed his eyes and felt himself beginning to slip away. Peacefully.

He wondered how old he would be when he woke up.

He opened his eyes and saw the little boy sitting on the edge of his bed, crying.

William wanted to reach out and embrace the boy, tell him everything was going to be all right, but when he tried to move his torso filled with fire.

"I'm sorry," said the little boy. "I was only trying to help."

"Listen," said William, feeling the blade push in deeper as he tried to roll over. "The screaming's stopped."

"She'll feel better now," said the little boy.

William felt the blood as it seeped from his body and covered the mattress. He hoped Michelle would not be the one to find him.

"I don't feel so good," said the little boy.

"You can lay here next to me," William said. The little boy nestled into the crook of his arm and soon both closed their eyes.

William smiled. The violence was over.

He turned his head and softly kissed the little boy's cheek.

He wondered which of them was dreaming.

And then he saw the time.

 Gary A. Braunbeck is the author of twenty-four published books, evenly split between novels and short-story collections, and two books of non-fiction. His work has garnered six Bram Stoker Awards, three Shocklines "Shocker" Awards, A Black Quill Award, and a World Fantasy Award nomination. He lives in Columbus, Ohio, where no one has heard of him. If you think his *stories* are bleak and disturbing … try spending an hour with him. G'head—try …

Spare the Rod
Lucy A. Snyder

Jake Blevins was finishing his third mug of Budweiser when he finally confessed to his brother: "I'm gettin' real worried about Ricky. I found him in his ma's makeup case the other day. He painted his toes pink. *Pink*."

Sam set down his own mug and gave Jake a concerned frown. "Did you discipline him proper?"

"I ... I did my best." He took another swig of brew to quench his suddenly dry mouth. His hand shook, he hoped not so badly that Sam could see. "I yelled at him and slapped the box outta his hands—broke the hinge, I got an earful about that later from his ma—and made him take the paint off with turpentine in the garage."

"But did you spank him?"

The question made bile and beer rise in Jake's throat. For a moment he thought he might puke right there on the cigarette-burned Formica table. Maybe talking to Sam about this was a bad idea. But who else did he have to go to besides his brother? He knew what his father would say if the old man were still alive. He knew what the parish priest would say; hell, Father Walton would probably offer to punish the boy himself.

His wife had made it clear she didn't approve of spankings, ever, but she was just a woman. It wasn't her place to boss him, and it wasn't his place to listen to her. He was the *paterfamilias*, and discipline was his responsibility.

"I yelled at him for a long time, and he seemed plenty scared when I was done," Jake replied.

Sam shook his head, his frown deepening into a scowl. "That ain't good enough."

"I don't think he'll do it again—"

"Are you tryin' to raise up a Goddamned faggot?" Sam slammed down his mug, but the bar jukebox was too loud for anyone to pay any attention. He looked horrified and furious. "You want your boy's soul to burn in everlastin' hell because you didn't have the stomach for good discipline?"

Jake felt as though he'd been slapped in the face. "No, of course I don't."

"You know as well as I do that a boy who plays around with makeup is well on the road to faggotry. You gotta nip that in the bud! Today it's painted toes, tomorrow he'll be into his mother's unmentionables dressin' up like a queer … you gotta beat some man into him. Spare the rod and spoil the child."

"But he's only seven."

"Seven?" Sam snorted. "That's plenty old enough for a spanking. I was eight when Pa gave me my first. My boys were six. And you was seven, though I reckon you don't remember too much 'bout that."

For just a moment, Jake felt as though he were back in his old room at the farmhouse, his father grabbing him by the back of his neck and throwing him down on the bed. It was all happening because Jake had cried and refused to help his father and uncles slaughter the calves. He'd been taking care of one calf since she was born, and he loved her like he loved his puppy Rufus. He couldn't bear to put the knife to her throat.

"If you ain't willin' to do man's work, that makes you a goddamn *girl*, and I ain't raisin' no girls in this house," his father had thundered as he pulled Jake's jeans and underwear down around his ankles. "You wanna be a girl, boy? I'll show you what's it's like to be a girl!"

His own blood was a freight train in Jake's ears, the remembered agony and terror and his shame at not being able to take his punishment like a man almost overwhelming, and he wished for the ten thousandth time since he was seven that the earth would open up and swallow him and leave no trace behind.

"Pa spanked the devil out of you." Sam paused to drain his own mug in a single gulp. "I reckon Ma was sure you'd bleed to death, and she finally got Uncle Eustace to take you to the county hospital. Sheriff Andy came by and gave Pa a talking-to. Almost hauled him in. You recollect any of that?"

Jake shook his head numbly. Bits and pieces of the spanking and his hospital stay circled like sharks through his nightmares, but he couldn't be sure what was a real memory and what was just a figment of his imagination.

Sam laughed with a good-times humor that didn't match the darkness in his eyes and slapped Jake on the shoulder. "Don't matter if you remember it … the important thing is you butched right up and flew straight! Wasn't a boy in the whole state more eager to help with the slaughters than you! Pa didn't have to spank you but a few times after that to keep you in line, did he?"

"Three," Jake replied.

He seldom dared to remember his Pa's fourth attempt. He was fifteen. Sam was off in the Army by then. Jake had crashed the tractor when he hit an unseen sinkhole; after he got himself out from under the hulk he'd run to the barn to escape the old man's wrath. When his Pa came after him, he grabbed a rusty scythe … and he didn't remember much more after that but coming to and seeing the blood and entrails dark against the straw and the whitewashed walls. His Ma found him out there, and she held him for a while and helped him clean everything up. Nobody ever found the place by the creek where they planted his Pa.

Jake still blacked out sometimes, and came awake in his car or standing in an alley someplace with blood on his clothes and hands. He never went looking to see where it had come from. Once he found a severed finger in his pocket. He threw away all his knives after that. Still, sometimes he'd find blood under his fingernails or in the treads of his work boots and have no idea what had happened.

"He spanked me three times in my whole life," Jake said.

"Three times, and you turned out just fine!" Sam gave him another shoulder slap.

Then he leaned forward across the baskets of chewed-up gristle and discarded chicken bones and spoke to Jake more softly: "Look, I know you don't want to hurt your boy, but pain is good for a young man. It builds character. Pa spanked me twice, and yeah, I hated him for it.

"But he was preparin' me for the world, Jake. If he hadn't given me proper discipline, I'd of never survived what the Serbs did to me when they captured my squad. The pain Pa put me through was a gift that kept me strong, kept my mind clear, and when I had my chance I got free and killed every last one of those sonsabitches with my bare hands. And then me and my boys went down to the nearest village and gave 'em all a taste of good ol' American payback. I kept some baby teeth as souvenirs; I knew Sarge would have confiscated anything else once we were back on base."

Sam paused, looking as serious as Jake had ever seen him. "Do right by your son, brother. Don't let him grow up to be some God-forsaken faggot. Make sure he grows up strong like us."

Jake poured the rest of their pitcher into his mug. Maybe Sam's advice was solid. Maybe spankings were like vitamins; too much or too little made you sick and weak. Maybe if he just spanked his son once, and didn't do it so hard or for so long that the boy passed out and couldn't remember it clearly afterward, he'd never have to do it again.

"Okay," Jake said. "You're right."

"I'm glad you're seein' things more clearly." Sam nodded grimly and raised his mug in a salute. "Sometimes it's hard to spank a boy the first time, and there ain't no shame in that; I got some little blue pills that'll help if you think ya need 'em. And make sure you use some lard. Not too much, or it won't hurt enough."

"I will," Jake promised. "I will."

Lucy A. Snyder is the Bram Stoker Award-winning author of the novels *Spellbent, Shotgun Sorceress, Switchblade Goddess*, and the collections *Sparks and Shadows, Chimeric Machines*, and *Installing Linux on a Dead Badger*. Her writing has appeared in publications such as *Strange Horizons, Weird Tales, Hellbound Hearts, Dark Faith, Chiaroscuro, GUD*, and *Lady Churchill's Rosebud Wristlet*. She currently lives in Worthington, Ohio, with her husband and occasional coauthor Gary A. Braunbeck. You can learn more about her at www.lucysnyder.com.

Born Again
Michael Boatman

There were good days now. More days when Joshua
Belton thought he could at least glimpse the possibility that he
was free; that the Hard Man had left him for good. Sometimes
an entire hour would pass without him once thinking about the
children, and the things that had happened to them.

Sometimes whole days would pass without him thinking of
the blood and the tears, and the secret, creeping contentment
he now despised. At those times he could even think about
Cody and remember the good times. Like now. The sun was
shining; it was pleasantly warm for late October, and he was
just another father, sitting in the park watching the children
play.

"I'm better," he whispered. "I've been redeemed."

"What did you say?"

The man with the little redhead was standing over him,
glaring down at him with the suspicion Joshua had come to
know too well. That was all right too. He understood. He was
one of them. After so many years spent looking in, like a wolf
separated from a pasture by a fence too high to ever climb, he
was on the inside.

One of the sheep.

Joshua winced. It had been a while since last he'd heard the Hard Man's voice, snarling at him in his dreams; roaring at him when he ignored its demands. But fifteen years ago, another voice had entered the echoing chamber inside his head. A powerful voice.

The voice that whispered and defeated the whirlwind.

It was the voice that had spoken from the torment of Golgotha and saved the world entire; The Voice, whose merest whisper could drown out the Hard Man's screams.

"'It is finished.'"

"Sorry? Excuse me … but are you here with anyone?"

The redhead's father. Joshua opened his eyes to find him there, still glaring, expecting, no *demanding* an answer. As if he had the right. Joshua took a deep breath and went to the special room that the Lord had prepared in his heart. He turned the key and let the light of salvation shine.

"Sorry," he said. "I was just enjoying the day. It's so stuffy at work. They keep the windows closed, even on really hot days. Herb … my boss … is trying to save on cooling costs. But it gets pretty uncomfortable when it's …"

The redhead's father flapped his hand as if to wave away the need to hear the rest of Joshua's statement. "It's just that … well some of the parents over there were wondering. This neighborhood is pretty self-contained; we all pretty much know each other and … well … nobody in our group seems to know *you*. And since you're not attached to any of the kids … we just thought …"

"I understand," Joshua said, standing. He wiped his hands on the cloth napkin Rose always provided in his lunch, and extended his right hand. "Josh Belton. I work at the radio station, over at the college. My family and I moved here from Illinois last year. My wife works at the hospital. She's an RN."

Joshua could see the tension straining across the man's face, the overused smile, the one that never touches the eyes, beginning to fracture as he understood that Joshua was actually *engaging* him. Behind him, Joshua could see the other concerned parents, all women, watching their interaction like hawks watching a rabbit hutch. That was okay. They were smart to be concerned. No one understood that better than him.

"When I got the job—I'm an engineer—we understood that the Lord had opened a door for us. I usually eat lunch in the cafeteria. I can see this park from my table and it always looks so peaceful, with the kids playing and everything. I've been complaining *forever* to my wife about the stuffiness. She's been telling me to get out and see more of the town ever since we got here. Today I promised her I'd get some fresh air."

"I … umm … I see," the redhead's father said, shifting his weight uncomfortably from his left foot to his right and back again. Joshua suspected he had to force himself to keep from looking at his watch.

"See, Rose and I … we lost our son two years ago."

The redhead's father's façade cracked, just enough for Joshua to see the frightened parent underneath.

"Oh my God. I'm so *sorry*."

"Thanks. We left Moline—that's a few hours west of Chicago—Rosie … she's a traveling nurse … well she got a contract over at the hospital. And then those fools at the college actually gave me the best job I've ever had. The rest is history … as they say."

The redhead's father seemed to retract into himself. He'd come over with his chest stuck out and his fists clenched, as if he meant to batter Joshua with his suspicions. Now he looked confused. Vulnerable.

"This is the kind of place—the park I mean—the kind of place my Cody would have loved. The trees and the tall slides. He would have been all over that jungle gym. I called him my little monkey-boy."

The redhead was picking her nose; a habit Joshua despised. She had clearly grown bored with the conversation. Now she was tugging at her father's grip.

"Daaaddddyyyyy …"

"I *know*, sweetie. Just a second, okay? Sorry, Josh. How old was your son when he …?"

"Oh, Cody was nine. He was struck by a hit and run driver before the Lord called him home. I guess the real reason I came here today was just to try to feel close to him again. You know?"

"Of course. Oh God, I can't even imagine what you and your wife must feel."

47

Joshua smiled. The smile felt genuine. He felt the compassion for this man glowing like clean sunshine at the core of his soul. He could *feel* their connection.

"We have our daughter, Candace. She's fourteen. She's the reason we were able to go on. When you have kids, sometimes you have to pick yourself up and keep moving, you know? Just for them."

"I can't imagine."

"Well, we also had our faith," Joshua said. "Without the Lord's guidance we never would have made it through."

The redhead's father stepped closer and extended his right hand. Joshua accepted it. Gladly. At the same time, the redhead broke away and ran back to join the other kids on the playground.

"I'm sorry to have questioned you like that," the man said. "You enjoy your lunch. Not that you need my permission of course. I mean you've got every right to be here ... just as much as anybody else. I mean ..."

Then he did it. He actually glanced at his watch.

"Wow. I've got to get Shannon to our Daddy/Daughter class."

Joshua nodded and smiled, brimming with grace.

"No problem. I gotta get back to work myself. What was your name?"

"Oh. Sorry! Keith. Keith Alderson. Shannon, the redhead who's currently cruising for a major timeout, is mine."

"Oh I know." Joshua nodded, easing into it now. He'd connected every kid in the park to a corresponding adult before he'd finished the first half of his tuna sandwich. "She's a real heartbreaker."

"Thanks. Well, Joshua, it was great talking to you. Maybe we'll see you again sometime."

Joshua grinned.

"You bet."

He was still feeling good when he walked through the front door of the quaint little two-story Colonial they'd rented for almost a year to the day of their arrival. He closed the door, shut out the wind and the bluster that had blown through town earlier that afternoon. Indeed, the euphoria he'd felt after defeating Satan in the park had nearly been overshadowed by the rumble of thunder. By the time he'd made it back to the radio station he was drenched. But even that wasn't enough to dampen his spirits. He'd surpassed this latest trial. He'd forced himself to walk into that park and face the Hard Man down, and he'd felt nothing. He was a blank slate. He was clean.

"Rosie? I'm home, babe."

Sausage, their two-year-old schnauzer, barked furiously from the living room.

Probably needs to be let out of his kennel.

But why hadn't Rose or Candace taken him out? Other than Sausage's barking, the silence was odd. Rosie worked the night shift at St. John the Divine Presbyterian. She usually slept in the mornings, ran whatever errands she needed in the afternoons before coming back home to catch a quick nap before dinner. His wife of fifteen years still slept most of her days away even two years after Cody's death. She'd spent those first terrible months entombed in a kind of stunned grief, a black cloud that attended her waking moments like an invisible shroud. They'd come together in the wake of the accident that had robbed them of their greatest joy, but for a while, Joshua had walked along the edge of the abyss. That was when the visits to the parks and playgrounds had taken on a greater urgency. Because the Hard Man, what he thought of as his *old* self, had never spoken to him more clearly.

He'd rediscovered the Bible during his trial. At the urging of the prison chaplain, he'd taken up his own cross, truly borne its weight, and finally understood the dark power it wielded over him. In that very moment he'd accepted a new savior. He'd forsaken the Hard Man and been changed in the blinking of an eye. That resurrection had redeemed him. So much so that when he was acquitted it seemed that the Lord was leading him away from his old life, exchanging his devotion for a better one. He'd moved away, met Rose at his new church and married her. Candace had come along a year later, and Cody four years after that. It was all working as the chaplain had promised. He'd been born again.

He was so excited to tell Rose about his trip to the park that when he turned the corner into their living room, at first he didn't grasp what he was seeing. The room was dark, which was also strange. Rose hated to be in alone in the dark.

"Rose? What's going on around here?"

He reached for the wall switch and flipped it. Light pierced the darkness and illuminated the objects in the center of the room.

Rose, *his* Rose, was tied into one of the heavy dining room chairs they'd bought at Bed Bath & Beyond last year. Her face was streaked with mascara, her lipstick smeared, as if by rough hands, across her mouth and lower jaw. A sock, or some white cloth, had been forced into her mouth and secured with black duct tape, distorting her features even more.

Candace, their fourteen-year old, was tied to the chair next to her. Her hands, feet, and mouth had been similarly bound, her lower face covered with duct tape. Both were crying; Candace's eyes begged, pleaded silently for him.

On the floor at Rose's feet, half a dozen open newspapers lay spread across the floor.

"Rosie? What is this? What ... what ...?"

"I imagine your wife must be thinking the questions anyone would be thinking at moments like this."

The shape that emerged from the shadows near the French doors coalesced and became a man. A man holding a gun. "How are you, Mr. Belton?"

Joshua stared, frozen, as the man stepped into the soft yellow light from the front hall. Keeping the gun trained on Joshua, he reached down and switched on the lamp at the table next to the chair which held Rose, and his features flooded into clarity. He was old, maybe in his seventies. But his jaw line was firm, his shoulders straight. He was tall, long-limbed, his head framed by a cap of snow-white hair. He was smiling. But no, that wasn't it. Half of his face was paralyzed, the right side as immobile as statuary.

"Sit down, Joshua."

"Who are you? What do you want?"

The shot, when it came, was a sharp bark, followed by the sound of breaking glass. Inches from Joshua's right hand, a vase shattered and fell to the floor in pieces. Joshua felt a burning lash across the back of his hand, and a sudden wetness, but the horror on Rose's face demanded his full attention.

"Just so you understand the way this is going to run," the old man said. "I'll give you an order and you'll do it. Every time you fail in this, I will destroy something you love. Do you understand, Mr. Belton?"

Joshua nodded. The gun ... the old man was holding the barrel next to Rose's head.

"Please ... please don't hurt her."

"Sit down, Mr. Belton. I won't tell you again."

Joshua sat down.

"Just so we're all on the same page, Josh ... you should understand that I'm calling the shots. If you move before I tell you to, or try anything silly, I will shoot your wife ... I'm sorry, dear. It's Rosemary, right?"

Rose nodded, her eyes bright. Her terror tore at something in Joshua's chest.

"Very good, Rosemary," the old man said. He reached into the front pocket of his tan windbreaker and then raised his left hand and showed Joshua a pair of handcuffs. "There'll be no need for any dramatics as long as we all behave ourselves."

Moving quickly, the old man ordered Joshua to raise his left hand, all the while keeping the gun trained on his face. With a practiced economy of motion, he hooked one handcuff around the armrest of the chair and snapped the other one shut around Joshua's wrist.

"Now, I'm going to undo the strip of tape around Mrs. Belton's mouth. It's quite easy. I can pull the tape with one hand. Your good lady has a question she'd like to ask you, and I want you to answer her. And a word of advice, Belton: I know the truth."

The old man pulled the tape away from Rose's mouth. She shook the last of it free, the thickest strip tearing a lock of hair from the side of her head with an audible rip.

"Who are you?"

Joshua shook his head, uncomprehending. "What?"

"Answer truthfully, Belton," the old man warned. "Tell the truth or she dies."

"But ... I don't know what's going on!"

The old man pivoted and fired into Sausage's cage. The dog fell to the floor of the kennel, dead. Candace screamed, the sound muffled beneath her half-mask of duct tape.

Someone will hear, Joshua thought. *Someone will come.*

But they'd selected the little house specifically with an eye toward privacy: it sat at the end of a long private driveway, set well back from Rte 118, the rural highway that ran past their house on its way out of town. They'd often joked about it being their own piece of heaven. The perfect little hideaway. The nearest neighbors were the Mayfields, nearly a quarter mile down the road. No one would hear. No matter how loudly they screamed.

The man with the gun spoke softly in the gloom. "Ask him again, Mrs. Belton. I think you'll find him in a more truthful mood."

"Please don't hurt my daughter," Rose said. "Whatever he's done, she doesn't deserve this!"

The old man pointed the gun at Candace and fired. The shot, though muffled, was still loud enough to evoke another scream from Rose.

But Candace was still alive, her eyes wide, stunned, but alive.

"I'm an excellent shot, missy. I earned high marks in the Marine Corps. Fought in Korea. You'll find that slug buried in the wall a few inches to the left of where your daughter is sitting. Now, Mrs. Belton, please ask your husband the question again. I promise you, I won't miss a second time."

Rose was crying, shaking her head, her dark hair obscuring most of her face. But Joshua could see her eyes glimmering through her dark strands. He saw the hatred building there.

"Who are you, you *bastard?*"

Joshua looked toward the door to his left. It led upstairs to the master bedroom and his office. If he could make it across the room, even dragging the chair behind him … it was only a matter of seven or eight steps …

"You'll never make it to the stairs," the old man said. "And even if you broke out of that chair and made it outside, you'd be leaving me here with these two lovely ladies. I know you're accustomed to abandoning injured women, but I assure you your escaping will end badly for them."

Joshua nodded. "Okay. I understand. Please …"

"This doesn't have to get ugly, *Josh,*" the old man said. "All I want is for you to answer a few simple questions. When I get what I came for I'll be on my way."

"Answer me, Josh," Rose hissed. *"Who are you?"*

"Stephen Campbell. My name is Stephen Campbell."

"Good," the old man said. "Now we're getting somewhere."

"Please let them go," Joshua said. "They didn't do anything."

"That may be true," the old man said. "Sometimes bad things happen to innocent people. Bad people do *unspeakable* things to innocent people for no reason at all. Isn't that also true, Stephen?"

Joshua nodded.

"Aloud please."

"Yes! Bad things happen to innocent people."

"Good. We're cookin' with gas now, aren't we, Rose? You don't mind if I call you Rose, do you?"

Rose glared at Joshua, her eyes shining.

"I can explain, Rose. I can explain everything."

"Who is Jessie Waverly?" she asked.

Joshua's eyes flicked toward Candace, who was staring at him now, shaking her head as if to beg him, *No. Don't let it be true.*

"Rose ... don't ..."

"Who is Jessie Waverly?"

"Rose ... please don't listen to him."

"It's not me she's listening to, Campbell," the old man said. "It's you who's lived a lie all these years. You who's been holding back."

"Answer the question, Josh," Rose cried. "Answer or he'll kill us!"

"She's the last one."

"The last ... *what?*"

"The last of my victims."

"All right," the old man said. "All right then."

Joshua speed-searched through his mental Rolodex of alibis and excuses, built up over two lifetimes. But the betrayal in Rose's eyes held him in stasis. He couldn't think. And trapped beneath the glaring illumination of her pain, he couldn't lie.

"So it's true? You hurt ... you *raped* all those girls?"

"Rose, you have to listen to me …"

"Six girls?" Rose said, her voicing rising like the cry of an avenging angel. "Children? You *did* that?"

The newspaper clippings, some yellowed with age, lay scattered about Rose's feet. On one of them he could even see his picture, the clip taken by an ambitious photographer the day he walked out of court a free man. The man had been insistent as Stephen Campbell was ushered into a waiting car by his attorney. As they'd moved through the press and the screaming mob, the photographer had slipped across the police barricade and thrust his camera toward Campbell's face. There he sat, one hand upraised as if warding off a blow, while his lawyer shoved the photographer away. The shot had been plastered all over the news later that day, along with headlines declaring the mistrial and subsequent dismissal of charges. Something about the way the detectives gathered evidence, the way the witnesses were led to identify him. The case against him was flimsy at best: Stephen Campbell wore gloves and used condoms and a mask when he committed his crimes. It was his voice that damned him, some of the girls claimed; a resonant baritone that all of them remembered.

An actor's voice. A preacher's voice.

"You disappeared after the trial,' the old man said. "I tracked you for years, kept up with you, waiting … dreaming about how I would make you understand. When you moved, I was able to follow you through the predator registration websites. An old friend in the Dayton police department provided me with the information I needed. Everyone understood that they'd screwed up, and so they were only too happy to help. But then you disappeared. I searched for you for five years but I couldn't find you. You changed your name, forged documents … a whole new life."

"Why are you doing this?" Rose said. "He did what you wanted. Can't you let us go?"

The old man shook his head. He reached into the pocket of his jacket and produced a single cigarette. He raised a Zippo lighter and flicked the wheel.

"I'm a little nervous, folks," he said. "I haven't smoked in thirty years. But since this is a special occasion I thought it appropriate. I hope you don't mind too much."

Joshua strained against the handcuff, but it held fast. Even now, as he struggled to find a way out, he was confident that if he could only draw Rose's attention he could assure her that he had changed; Stephen Campbell had died the day he walked out of prison. It was God's will. He had been born again. For her.

"You've built a beautiful life, Campbell. A family. A lovely home. It's almost perfect." The old man exhaled a long streamer of smoke into the air and coughed, a wet rumble that built in the depths of his chest and rattled up through his throat.

"Excuse me," he said, clearing his throat. "That's one thing no one tells you about growing old—the things that happen to your body while time marches forward. No one tells you about the goddamned cruelty of it all."

"Please," Rose said. "We won't tell anyone. Just let us go."

"I'm afraid I can't do that, Rose. Not until I tell you exactly what my Jessica endured at your husband's hands."

He licked his thumb and forefinger, pinched out the lit cigarette, and shoved the remainder into his jacket pocket.

"While you were building this new life, did you ever stop to consider what was happening to your victims, Campbell? The lives you ruined? Their families?"

The old man reached into his pocket and produced a single, wallet-sized photo. He held it up to allow Joshua to see it.

But in the deepening gloom Joshua could only see a shape, a glimmer of blonde hair, a flash of faded colors; green, red …

"My granddaughter was sixteen years old—not much older than your girl is now—when you raped her: Up 'til then she'd been a straight-A student. She wanted to go to college and be a veterinarian. Can you imagine that? Sometimes she stayed up so late with her homework my wife and I worried about her. But she never wavered. Never *faltered*."

Moving slowly, Joshua pulled, straining, against the handcuff. And something deep in the body of the chair began to give way.

"After my daughter died bringing her into this world, Jessie was our only connection to her. Her dad abandoned her before she was born so it was just the three of us. But we were making do. Then you crawled through her bedroom window."

The old man studied the picture, his eyes focused on the small square of paper in his hand. Joshua felt the arm of the chair yield the slightest bit. In the quiet, the sound of wood splintering seemed as loud as a train whistle.

Be quiet. Be careful.

Hope flooded his veins with adrenaline and he remembered that the chair looked solid but was actually quite flimsy. He recalled lamenting the poor workmanship the day they bought it.

Someday, when we're in a better place, I'm gonna burn this cheap garbage.

It's fine, Josh.

You deserve better.

I've got *better.*

Now the chair's cheap construction gave Joshua hope. The old man had cuffed his wrist to the chair's weakest point; the spot where the underside of the armrest met the post that had been glued into a hole in the seat. He pulled harder and felt it give a little more.

"My wife, Hilda, we were married fifty years. When our daughter died … Christ, it almost killed her. Then the doctor handed us our beautiful little girl. Jessie almost didn't make it; she was so small. But she came through. Hilda and I raised her, cared for her like she was our own little miracle. Like a promise from God."

The old man, still lost in his memories, had allowed the barrel of gun to drop toward the floor. He spoke softly, as if to an audience only he could see.

"When you did … what you did, it changed her. When they caught you, I promised her: now you'll understand. Now we'll get justice. And when you walked away … it was like you raped her all over her again. She slipped off the honor roll that same year. Stopped caring about school, grades … The drugs came next. She dropped out in the middle of her senior year. Started running around with a bad crowd and got pregnant. She thought she could keep the baby. Hilda and I even offered to help her, on the condition that she go back and get her diploma. But she'd lost hope by then. Four years ago, she tried to end it. I found her in the bathroom with vomit all over her face. But she'd only killed the baby. After that, she took to the streets."

The old man looked up at Rose. "Do you understand what it is to mourn for a child who yet lives, Mrs. Belton? To wake up to a cop on your front step telling you your gift from God whores herself for heroin? Can you possibly understand what that feels like?"

"I'm sorry," Rose whispered. "I'm sorry for your family."

The old man smiled; a grimace. "Thank you. Yes, I think you must be a compassionate woman, Rose. I can't for the life of me imagine how you ended up here."

Joshua worked the armrest, using his forearm to push it back and forth inside the hole in the seat, carefully, moving in short jerks, trying to break the glue seal and rock it free.

"Jessie died six months ago of a heroin overdose. She left the women's shelter and prostituted herself to buy what she needed. Then she came home. Hilda and I were at our bible study class. We'd kept her room for her, in the hope that she would come back to us. Only I think she was really returning to the place where she'd already died. April twenty-third, the anniversary of the day she met you, Campbell. Fifteen years to the very day. I'll never forget the sound Hilda made when I opened that bedroom door. I *can't* forget. Hilda died last month. Her doctor said it was her heart, but I know that she lost the will to live. That was when I decided to pay you a visit."

The old man's teeth bared in a feral snarl. Then he lunged across the room and struck Joshua across the face with the butt of his gun. Once. Twice. Three times. Joshua felt teeth shatter in his right jaw and his vision went white as a bomb-blast of agony detonated in his head.

When his vision cleared, he saw the old man place the barrel of the gun against the side of Candace's head.

"Do you understand, Campbell? Do you understand what you stole from me?"

"I understand!" Joshua gasped, fighting to stay conscious. "Cody ... we lost ... my son!"

"Yes," the old man said. "I know."

"Then you know," Joshua said. "You know how God can give you a second chance."

"A second chance."

"Yes! After Cody died ... I met with our pastor. He told me that I could be delivered."

"Delivered?"

"Yes, that's right. I believed him. After my trial I knew I'd never make a life, never find peace. So I left."

Now he was speaking as much to Rose as he was to the old man, trying to explain, to help them understand the way things were.

"It was wrong to hurt those girls. Your Jessie. I ... I know that. But I was forgiven. Rosie ... *you* helped me understand that."

"A good woman of the church," the old man said. "Her faith helped transform your life."

"*God* transformed my life."

The old man seemed to consider Campbell's plea. Even through the pain in his face, his mouth, Joshua sensed this weakening of his captor's will: God was handing him an opportunity. The armrest creaked softly. He felt the wooden chair crack beneath his left hand.

"Are you ... are you a believer?"

The old man started, as if jolted from his memories. "How's that?"

"A believer? You know ... a Christian?"

The old man squinted, his eyes narrowed to thin slits. But he nodded. "Yes. Of course I am."

"You go to church, yes?"

"Hilda and I attended Holy Name Presbyterian, over in Brainerd," the old man said. "We've worshipped there for nearly forty years."

"Good," Joshua said. Lights were flashing in his eyes. His tongue felt too thick for his mouth. But the old man wasn't shooting. He was *listening*. "Then you know the power of God's grace. How that power can change you into something better. You know what it means to forgive."

"I believe in redemption," the old man whispered. The gun dipped lower, the barrel aimed at the floor. "But I don't believe in you."

The old man looked down at Candace. "I'm truly sorry you had to be a party to this, young lady. You look like a girl who might be going places. Smart. Pretty as a picture. So much like our Jessie. Isn't that right, Hill?"

Candace's eyebrows knitted, her mascara, which Rose had only recently allowed her to use, had left twin tracks along her cheeks. "I'm Candace," she said, simply. "My name … it's Candace."

The thunder of the shot tore the air in the living room. Then Candace's head slumped forward. Joshua saw a gout of blood erupt from her temple and spatter the wall behind her.

Rose, *his* Rose, screamed; a wailing shriek, singeing the air with horror.

"Your girl's in a better place, Missus," the old man said gently. "She's with my Jessie now, wrapped in the arms of our Savior. I believed your husband when he said you were a woman of faith. I think, in time, you'll come to understand what I mean."

The old man reached out with his empty left hand as if to touch Rose's hair. Rose screamed, gnashing her teeth even as she wept and raged.

With something like sorrow in his eyes, the old man turned to Joshua. "I expect we'll meet again, Campbell. A final reckoning, as they say in the movies. I suppose, now that we're members of the same club, that only makes sense."

The old man set the gun on the coffee table, walked toward the French doors, and opened them. He stood in the doorway, outlined in silver moonlight, a mere silhouette.

"He didn't die right away. Your boy. It took him a while. After I hit him I circled the block, parked the car, and walked back. He lay there in the street, breathing, heavy-like. The people who came, they tried to help, but by then it was too late. One lady said she was a nurse. She held his hand while he died. He wasn't alone. Like my Jessie."

The old man hitched in a breath, as if stifling a sob.

"I wanted you to know that, Campbell. He wasn't alone."

Then he was gone.

It took him five minutes to break the chair. When he had freed himself, he stood up and faced Rose, seeing her with new eyes.

Old eyes, the voice in his head advised. *True eyes.*

"Call 911, Joshua!" Rose snarled. "She's still alive! Candace ... *she's still alive!*"

Campbell looked and saw that Candace was moving, shuddering in her restraints. A slow runnel of blood leaked from the wound in her temple.

Right again, Rosie.

"Why are you just standing there? Call 911, Josh!"

Campbell took two steps toward Rose.

"No! Don't worry about me! Call the police! Call 911! She's alive!"

He wrapped his hands around Rose's throat and began to squeeze. It had been a while, years in fact. He'd strangled the others too; throttled them until they lost consciousness. A few times he'd been tempted to finish the job just to know what it felt like, but something, some shred of compassion, had always stopped him short. Now it felt familiar, like riding a bicycle. It felt *real.* Rose fought him, spitting and straining against the tape that bound her wrists and ankles, but in the end, she couldn't win. He watched the lights go out in her, watched the blood vessels in her eyes burst like blood-soaked fireworks until the whites turned red and then black. And when he'd made sure she was dead, he picked up the gun the old bastard had left on the coffee table and shot his daughter in the head.

He'd suffered too much, worked too hard to create his new life. There was no way Rose would let him move forward into that bright future now that she'd learned his secrets. He stood in the center of the living room where they'd danced and made love and said his good-byes. Then he went to bed. He had a long day ahead of him and he needed his sleep.

He waited until the next night to burn the house. That morning he'd called in to work to tell them he wouldn't be in for a while. A family emergency out of town. He'd called in for Rose and told her supervisor that she'd gone to visit her ailing mother in Phoenix. He'd assured the woman that her prayers were appreciated and that he'd pass them along. After that he'd called Candace's school to tell them she'd gone with her mother. That would give him enough time to get out of town. He'd gone to the bank and closed out their life savings, withdrawing the money he'd need to make his way until he could begin again.

As he watched the flames engulf the immaculate little Colonial, he gripped the gym bag that contained the things he'd need on his journey: cash, about twenty-thousand dollars in large and small bills. He'd left Campbell's passport and any other identifying documents to burn with the house; he wouldn't need them anymore. He'd created a new life for himself once before, after the acquittal. He could do it again.

He checked the pistol the old man had left behind, and he wondered, briefly, if this moment had been destined for him all along—God's way of pointing him in the direction he should go. The old man had given him just enough information. He remembered the girl, Jessie, a petite blonde with freckles, whose nose was crooked from having been broken and badly reset. She'd cried silently, begging him not to hurt her family, promising not to tell, until he'd finished. He remembered watching the whites of her eyes turn first red and then black, as he choked her. He remembered the little house where they'd met; the immaculate Tudor situated in the center of Jessie's block. He knew the old man's church; had even attended a funeral there, a lifetime ago, with friends who'd ultimately abandoned him. The old man had given him just enough information to find him and send him to hell.

He knew this was right—

God's will.

—could feel the *rightness* of it in his bones, and the ancient rage the old man's attack had resurrected in his soul. He would visit the old man, tie up those loose ends, and then head north, possibly to Canada. Yes, all the answers were laid out for him, shining before him like a road paved with gold, the way his mother had always insisted that the streets of heaven were paved with gold. Yes. He would travel God's road until he found his new home. A new life. He was free.

Born again.

Michael Boatman acts for a living and writes for sanity. He is the author of the horror-comedy novel *Revenant Road* (DarkFuse 2013), his short story collection *God Laughs When You Die: Mean Little Stories from the Wrong Side of the Tracks*, 2007. His fiction has appeared in *Weird Tales, Horror Garage,* and *Red Scream* magazines, and in anthologies such as *Dark Dreams II: Voices from the Other Side, Dark Dreams III; Sick Things: Tales of Creature Horror; Lords of Justice;* and *Dark Delicacies 3: Haunted.* His short story *The Flinch* was given an Honorable Mention by Ellen Datlow in her *2010's Year's Best Horror.* He's written essays for AOL's Black Voices and Parent Dish websites, and blogs at his website. By day, he pretends to be other people. He's costarred in television series such as ABC's *Spin City,* HBO's *ARLISS,* and the Vietnam drama *China Beach.* Currently he appears *on* the FX comedy series *Anger Management* and costars in the upcoming Nick at Nite comedy *Instant Mom.* He lives in New York with his wife, four kids, two dogs, and several species of opinionated owls. Visit him on Twitter, Facebook, and his website Michaelboatman.us.

A Serving of Nomu Sashimi
Eric J. Guignard

Terry ran his sales report for the fifth time that night. It was 7:00 p.m. on a Friday, and he knew he should go home, relax, watch a movie with Shannon. But then he looked at the sales report again; compared to his coworkers, his numbers were low. Too low. The amount of business he brought in should have surpassed every other sales representative on the floor but, instead, he was down. Again. Low performing reps didn't last long in commission-driven careers. He'd been working at Global Bank for a year and had never busted his hump so hard, but he could never catch up with the others.

The door to Dean Kleggman's office opened and the others poured out, laughing and high-fiving each other. Dean, Brett, and Marc Burns, the top three sales reps in the company.

"—so then I told Bitzy Carole if the players were reversed, he'd be driving a *hatchback*!" Dean bellowed laughter and Marc fist-pumped the air.

"And wait until you see the swing!" Brett added. They doubled over in hysterics.

Dean, Brett, and Marc had ridden the top three spots since Terry started working at Global. He couldn't come close to producing the volume of any one of them, and it drove him half-insane with frustration.

"Yo, T-Man," Brett called across the floor to Terry. "What're you still doing here this late? Working hard or hardly working?"

They guffawed with a sound like belching turkeys.

Terry made a face that he hoped looked like good-natured sincerity. "Gotta put in the extra hours to catch you boys."

His remark made them laugh even harder.

"It'll never happen, buddy." Marc said.

Terry's fake-smile faltered. "I'll find my way into your ranks. I don't give up."

Dean winked at Marc. "Sure. You'll get real far with tenacity and low numbers."

Brett shook his head. "I don't know, maybe it's time Terry came out with us. Learn how to close some *big* biz."

"What're you saying?" Dean asked. He punched Brett in the shoulder. "I thought we agreed not to tell anyone else."

"It's okay. Terry's a good guy, and I think we could use another top earner around here to pump up the investors' confidence." He paused. "You can keep a secret, can't you T-man?"

Terry nearly leapt from his cubicle chair. He knew that sales reps kept to a hierarchy within the company, and the elite associated with each other after hours; success mingled with success. Shannon might be a little upset that he was going out—probably to drink—but this might be the opportunity he'd been waiting for, a chance to bump up his numbers.

"Of course I can keep a secret."

"C'mon then," Brett said. "We're going out for sushi."

Twenty minutes later, Terry sat in Marc's Mercedes with the others. They sped through a labyrinth of city streets.

Dean chattered from the front as they drove. "You think you've had sushi before, but this isn't like anything you've ever eaten."

"It's not *really* sushi cause it's not from the sea," Marc said.

"True. But sushi's the closest comparison." Dean turned back in the seat to look directly at Terry. "It's exclusive."

"Really exclusive," Brett added. "If not for us, you wouldn't get in."

"And if there are any problems, you won't be coming back."

Terry nodded. He felt nervous and wondered if he should have stayed back at the office. He wanted to improve his presence on the sales floor, though he personally couldn't stand any of these blowhards. "You're talking to me like a kid," he said. "I can handle anything you bring."

"Sure, just like the Constance deal, right?"

Terry grimaced. Last month his biggest project collapsed and his commission went into arrears.

"Don't worry," Brett said. "After tonight, those things won't happen to you anymore. Just stick with us."

"*If* he can handle it." Marc said. "Remember Lance Thompson?"

"If he turns into another Lance, I'm finding a new restaurant."

The name sounded familiar to Terry. He thought back to when he first started working at Global Bank and realized with a sense of dread that he was hired as Lance Thompson's replacement.

The car slowed, and for the first time Terry looked where they were driving, past neon marquee bulbs that flashed pink and white. Each shop doorway and window announced specialties on placards in languages he couldn't understand, though the pictures left no doubt as to what unsavory specialties lay within. They were deep in neighborhoods he normally tried to avoid, and the dread that coiled in his gut grew stronger.

Marc parked in the shadows of an alley, and the four of them made their way to a plain metal door embedded in a brick wall.

Dean pounded on the door and an eye slot opened. "We're here for Yuki," he said and stuffed a pile of bills through the slot.

The door opened and they entered. To Terry, inside appeared like another world.

The interior was red. He saw gold trimming on the bar and frames of menu boards, and there were hints of black and white, but otherwise it was all red; the walls, floor, even the furniture and glowing fluorescent bulbs. *Red as hell*, Terry thought. The red lights were dim, and the room was filled with clouds of haze that circled the red tables, so everything appeared distant and lost in shadows.

The doorman led them to a private booth. Across the floor, other tables were filled with boisterous men in business suits, smoking and playing cards, or eating slices of meat between chopsticks. In the distance, Terry saw a long glass terrarium that stretched alongside one end of the bar. Trapped inside were little creatures with humanoid appearance, each no taller than half a foot. Some banged on the glass and seemed to shout, others ran from side to side in their confines. Most just sat, forlorn, with head in hands.

The other sales reps chatted excitedly around him though Terry didn't pay attention to their words until Marc slapped him on the back. He asked, "You ever eat Fugu Sashimi?"

"If I have, nobody's told me," Terry replied. This brought laughter from the others.

"You'd know if you ate it. Fugu is pufferfish. The Japanese consume it to gain fortitude and sexual virility. Real masculine food, y'know? Shows how brave you are."

"I remember now," Terry said. "The news runs stories sometimes about businessmen dying when it's not prepared right."

"Fugu's for pussies," Dean interrupted.

They laughed again, and Terry felt further out of place, glancing at each of their braying faces in turn, tinted red by the lighting.

"We're eating gnome," Dean said.

"Say again?"

"*Nomu Sashimi*," Brett explained. "Right here's the only place in the city you can get it."

An elderly Asian man wearing a white tuxedo jacket approached their table and smiled wide. "Welcome, gentlemen."

"Yuki, my man," Marc said. He slipped some bills into Yuki's pudgy hands then nodded to Terry. "We brought a newbie."

Yuki narrowed his eyes and seemed to appraise Terry, as if contemplating his privilege to dine in the restaurant. He rubbed the sparse gray hairs sprouting from his chin and then carefully nodded. "Very good. Nomu for four?"

"Only your best," Dean said.

"Always the best," Yuki replied. He began to depart and then turned to face them. "In the spirit of full disclosure, we have a new chef this evening. Though he does come highly recommended for his skills of preparation."

"If he's good enough for you, then he's good enough for us," Marc said. Yuki walked away, disappearing through red shadows.

Terry frowned. "We're eating *gnome*? I don't even know what that means."

"Gnomes, buddy," Brett said. "You know, little people who live in the forest. They have white beards and pointy red hats and talk to the animals."

"What's the punch line?" Terry asked.

In the smoky distance, he saw a man in a white chef's hat open the top of the long aquarium and reach inside with metal tongs. The little creatures ran in disarray, and he thought he heard their faint screams echo across the room. Terry felt a queasy sensation in his guts like the beginning of sea-sickness as he watched them flail against the glass. They clearly moved like people, but only in diminutive scale, and he thought of small children fed to villainous ogres in the dark fairy tales of his youth. These were no fairy tales though; they were little men and women and children, naked but for scraps of bright blue cloth hanging from their pale bodies.

"No joke," Marc said. "They're mythical creatures for a reason; Gnomes have magic. It's part of their flesh the way DNA is part of us. Every gnome is different, but their magic—that *power*—is absorbed by anyone who eats them."

"You *absorb* magic?" Terry blanched.

"Not too much, or you'll get poisoned," Dean said. "But just a little goes a long way. Your wishes come true, Terry. Why do you think we close the big accounts, month after month? I used to sell newspapers before eating the gnome. Now I make twenty thousand a month at Global and bang every chick I want. You can't make wishes that you couldn't normally do in life—I can't say I want to be the king of Spain or anything. But the magic makes happen what otherwise might have been offset by the potential for failure."

"Nomu Sashimi has to be served just right," Brett added. "The preparation takes a very steady hand. The meat must be sliced in the right direction, thin, and not tainted by the gnome's toxins. They're boiled in hot water, like lobster, seasoned and served. *Voila!*"

A tuxedoed waiter approached through the haze bearing a tray of drinks. He appeared as a wraith, shifting soundlessly, until he spoke as he set a collection of bottles in front of them. "Shots."

When he spoke, the waiter smiled, and Terry saw his teeth were plated in silver. He had a dragon tattoo that climbed up the side of his neck. *Yakuza, the Japanese mafia.*

"Sake bombs!" Marc shouted.

They drank and pounded the table. Terry noticed there were no women in the room. Marc must have read the expression on his face.

"This is a men's only club. Very old traditions here."

The others fell silent and watched Terry's reaction.

"So, you in on this, T-Man?" Brett asked.

Terry's mind fired through a dozen different scenarios, each ending with his co-workers laughing at him. If this was some sort of twisted orientation or hazing, he would do it. He was ready to try anything to get into their good graces, though he was loathe at the notion of being dubbed a sucker.

"Sure, I can do anything you boys can," he said.

"My man!" Marc exclaimed. "More shots!"

They drank. Several rounds later, Terry started to laugh like the others, fist-pumping and mirroring their animalistic cackles with jokes and business tales of his own.

Brett reached over and punched Terry in the arm. "By the way, don't ever accept Gnome prepared by a one-handed chef."

This caused another round of raucous laughter. Terry joined in, nodding his head in agreement, though he had no idea what that meant.

"Nomu Sashimi's not for everybody, but it's worth the risks. Men die from eating gnome much more often than the puffer fish, but their deaths don't ever reach the news. However, Yuki's a legend—his chefs are immaculate in their preparation."

"Except in Lance's case," Dean said.

They nodded and drank. Terry wanted someone to explain that remark, but thought asking outright would be an admission of his ignorance, a reminder that he wasn't *really* one of them yet.

Again, Marc seemed to read his mind. "You hear what happened to Lance Thompson, right?"

"He got drunk and rolled his car off a cliff last year," Terry replied.

"And you heard they never found his body?"

"Guess it was incinerated or something."

"There *was* no body 'cause Lance didn't roll his car," Dean said. "He ate the gnome and got Nomu Sashimi poisoning."

"But he survived," Brett added. "Though he wasn't Lance anymore."

"What does that even mean?" Terry asked.

"The toxins changed him," Marc said. "The chef didn't prepare it right, and instead of enhancing, the gnome magic *infected* him. Yuki cut off the chef's hand as punishment."

"That's why you never accept gnome prepared by a one-handed chef. It means he's a flop."

Laughter again. Terry gritted his teeth, thinking that hell couldn't be any worse than listening to these three laugh at each other's jokes. Marc was short and the other two tall, but each of them had the same gel-spiked hair, wore the same gold-and-diamond watches, slapped each other on the back the same way, and pointed at themselves when they wanted attention.

He knew, too, he was going out to buy his own matching gold-and-diamond watch this weekend. He joined in their laughter as he stood up.

"I'll be back boys. Gotta take a leak."

"Knock yourself out," Mark said.

Terry walked across the tile floor toward the restrooms, following an aisle that curved past the aquarium. He told himself not to, but he couldn't resist peering in close to the condemned inhabitants. Up-close, their expressions were unmistakable; heart-breaking sorrow and the hopeless fear of someone fitted to a short noose. The gnomes were only as tall as the length of his forearm, though pudgy for their size, with round bellies poking over squat thighs. Their faces were rosy and, under happier circumstances, would surely be filled with mirth in song and laughter. Here, however, they only wept. There appeared to be families amongst the gnomes, as men and women clutched each other and trembling elders held tightly to small infants. It was Gnome holocaust. Terry envisioned himself gripping the glass enclosure and overturning it with a mighty bellow. *Run, little people, run for your lives …*

But for what purpose? Terry didn't know how gnomes could exist in the modern world, or how they were brought here in the first place. They would probably just be quickly gathered up again. And, if this was a Yakuza joint, he would be killed, no questions. Just taken out back and executed. No, best to just play along and ride easy-street with the top sales reps.

When Terry returned, the waiter was back at their table, hunched over a serving tray. The alcohol was beginning to make everything fuzzy and slow for Terry, and the room looked surreal and tinted, like the sepia-toned photograph of a thirties speakeasy.

He sat, and a plate was placed before each of them. Thin ribbons of pink meat lay delicately atop a bed of rice and mint leaves. The meat looked like shavings of tissue paper. One tapered off at an angle as if sliced from a leg.

"Enjoy," the waiter said and flashed his silver smile.

"May the devil look past us another night!" Marc exclaimed. He pinched his chopsticks together around a slice of the Nomu and popped it in his mouth. "Mm-mm!"

Brett and Dean ate their portions in quick gulps, making slurping sounds like sucking up wet noodles.

"Good stuff, tender cut," Brett said.

Terry lifted up the first slice to his mouth and hesitated, looking at it.

"What's the matter," Brett asked. "Is there still some white beard on it?"

He and Marc laughed.

Suddenly, Dean gripped the table with both hands. He groaned, his eyes bulged, and he leaned forward, shaking. He threw his head back as if trying to escape something clawing at his face.

Terry jerked away. "He's sick!"

Dean sat up quickly with a shriek of laughter. Food flicked from his mouth, and he punched Terry in the shoulder. "I got you, dude! You thought I was poisoned."

The sales reps all laughed again, an ear-splitting peal that sounded in unison. Terry wondered if they practiced together at home, like a garage band. He was ready to slug the next one in the face who punched his shoulder. He popped the Nomu Sashimi in his mouth.

Actually tastes pretty good, he thought. Sweet, not like the salty sapidity of regular sushi. Doesn't taste like chicken, as most exotic meats do. More like cooked peaches in a cobbler.

"Not bad," Terry said and nodded.

"Not bad," Marc mimicked. "Wait until you *feel* it. Takes a few moments for the magic to absorb into you, but you'll know when it does. It's like an orgasm while doing a line of coke. We've got a lot to teach you, buddy."

"More shots!" Brett shouted.

Terry raised his glass, and then something curled inside his guts, like a white-hot snake. He groaned and gripped the edges of the table, and black dots flickered in his vision. He wondered for a moment if the alcohol had caught up to him and then his body bloated.

Brett waved at Terry in dismissal. "Dude, Dean already played that gag."

Terry felt as if his skin caught fire. He jumped from the table and tried to pull off his jacket, but his hands didn't work as they should. They swelled and fat bubbles pulsed at the knuckles.

"I don't think he's faking," Marc whispered.

The sensation of the curling snake bit through his stomach and Terry screamed.

"He's got the gnome poison!" Dean shouted.

Terry doubled over from the splitting, tearing pain that seared his guts. He screamed again, then belched, and black vomit spewed out like a geyser of oil.

The other sales reps screamed, too. Yuki and several waiters appeared in a rush through the smoke and dim red light.

Terry puked more across the table, the oily expulsion filled with pulsating shapes, like bulging worms. He collapsed to the floor and convulsed, and things seemed to move under his clothes as if parts of his body had broken free and scurried to join other parts of his body. He felt himself lifted through the air by Yuki, and the world turned dark. The last thing he saw were the gnomes watching him, upside down, as he was carried past.

Terry woke inside a cell within a larger room that echoed as if it were underground. Every part of him ached, and he gasped for breath, but it felt that when he breathed there was a weight on his chest, so he could only inhale shallow pants. He sat up and immediately felt his neck twist and sag and realized with surging dread that he looked *backward* across his confines.

The back of the cell was iron-gray bars, like an animal's cage. Terry turned his head around so that it faced forward—a motion that should have been physically impossible—and saw that the front of the cell was the same as the back, framed in iron bars, though a locked door was mounted on that side. His body felt much too heavy and coated in secretion like the residue of fruit jelly. He turned his head in a complete circle and saw with increasing visibility that there were other cells in that underground room and other motionless *things* contained within.

Outside the cell, Yuki stared in at him, holding a silver platter. His white tuxedo jacket still gleamed. Behind him stood men with guns.

Terry wondered how long they had watched him, how much time passed since he became ill.

"I'm sorry for your unfortunate dining experience last week," Yuki said. "I hope you will find comfort in knowing the chef will never make that mistake again."

He lifted the lid of the silver tray and presented it to Terry. A severed hand lay on top, its fingers loose and curled inwards, like a great bug that died and turned upside down. "Satisfaction has been made on your behalf. I wish I could do more."

Terry tried to shout, wanting to curse Yuki with threats of what his lawyers would do on behalf of gaining *real* satisfaction. His mouth opened, but no words came out, only garbled clicks and gasps as if his throat filled with marbles.

"I *wish*," Yuki said, "this could be undone. However, the

magic of Nomu Sashimi does not work like that. I can only wish for something to happen quicker and more definitely than it otherwise would."

Terry lurched toward them. Air seeped from his lungs and it became more difficult to replace exhaled breaths with fresh inhalations. He brought his hands to his face and saw in horror that there were more than two. The fingers were dark and gnarled with green buds, like baby leaves, that sprouted from the tips.

"The magic turned you. Your body absorbed it, but not like the others. You are changing, and you are dying. I can only wish for you to die quicker."

The men behind him brought up their guns.

"Do you ever wonder where gnomes come from?" Yuki asked.

His stomach grew and things were inside, pushing out.

"*Hahaoya Nomu.* Mother Gnome."

Terry shook his head, and it simply flopped from side to side.

"That is you, Hahaoya Nomu. My supply was running low, so I wished for more. You were transformed, and I cannot let your magic go to waste. Some men die immediately, while others are *fertilized.* It is a slow death, but also one of great blessing. I will not let you suffer any more than you must."

Terry's stomach split, and the first baby gnome erupted, cartwheeling to the floor like a tumbling dandelion. One of the men grabbed it up with a pair of tongs and placed it into a pail.

"Hahaoya Nomu, we honor you!" Yuki said, and his men repeated in solemn chant.

Terry convulsed and more black oil shot from his mouth. A wave of baby gnomes poured from the tearing fissure in his belly.

Yuki motioned for the men to fire. "Hahaoya Nomu, we honor you!"

 Eric J. Guignard writes dark and speculative fiction from his office in Los Angeles. He has over fifty publishing credits for stories and articles in magazines, journals, and anthologies. He's a member of the Horror Writer's Association, the Greater Los Angeles Writer's Society, and is the Horror Genre Correspondent for *Men's Confidence* Magazine. He's also an anthology editor, including *Dark Tales of Lost Civilizations* (2012, Dark Moon Books), which was nominated for a Bram Stoker Award, and this year's critically acclaimed release *After Death ...* (2013, Dark Moon Books). His novella *Baggage of Eternal Night* is scheduled for release in September 2013 (JournalStone Publishing). Visit Eric at www.ericjguignard.com or at his blog: www.ericjguignard.blogspot.com.

Latchkey Child
V. M. Zito

"Damn it," Davis griped as he crumpled backward in his chair. From the wall in his home office, a rude bang answered him.

A pause.

Then another bang.

He glared at the wall, half-expecting to find cracks in the blue plaster. The kid in the apartment next door was doing a goddamn job over there, punching or beating the wall from the other side, a smack like a hammer every fifteen seconds. On a shelf above the desk, leather-bound art journals wriggled with each blow, spitting dust into the air. Davis had bought the books at a flea market last year, charmed by the scholarly brown spines, but hadn't touched them since. Now he cupped a hand over his coffee mug.

If that shelf crashes down, he thought, *I will kill that freakin' boy.*

With a sigh he set his notepad atop the mug like a lid to keep the dust out. *Not today, of all days.* Piled on the desk were his notes for the Advocate article, solemn and ready for a hard night of writing to meet tomorrow's deadline. Tonight was going to suck already—worse now with this crap from the kid.

"Damn it," he said again.

Deadlines didn't ordinarily shake him. As a freelance journalist he had a knack for these crazy-ass turnarounds—hell, it was the only reason Mark Herder had even called last night, an editor he hadn't heard from in months. *Hey, Davis.* Herder's voice crackling through a bad cell connection. *That casino piece you pitched last month ... got it? We're short this week. Get it to me Thursday, it's in.*

"No problem," Davis had promised, though it wasn't halfway written.

Now the wall rocked once more with a loud blast. The epicenter seemed two feet to the left, a bit higher than where he sat; the kid was definitely hitting the wall from the other side, sending shockwaves into Davis's head that two Tylenols so far hadn't calmed. He could hear the television over there, too, blaring through the thin walls in this low-rent building. He and Marcy had been here a whole damn year now, hoping for him to sell some work to a big paper like *The Advocate*. Then maybe he'd land a permanent job. Move from this dump to a good neighborhood.

Shit, he needed this article.

Another bang on the wall startled him. He pushed his hands against his ears, hiding in the sound of his own skin; he could hear his blood sizzling below the surface. He listened for a few beats then released his ears and, turning to his Mac, ran a word count on the article. No surprise there. He'd written twenty-four words since the pounding started. He listened to it. "BaHUM," he typed. The sound the wall made.

BaHUM. BaHUM.

Every fifteen seconds. How the *hell* could he write with that crap going on? Jesus, he hated freelance, but at least the apartment was his alone while Marcy worked downtown until six. Peace and quiet, on a normal day. Perfect for writing.

But the kid had ruined that.

The kid and his goddamn pounding—every day after school this week.

BaHUM. Davis stabbed the delete key with his finger and erased the nonsense words mucking up his article. Then he stood and stared at the wall, deliberating. *Not today.* Let the kid bang all he wanted tomorrow. By then Mark Herder would have the article, and Davis would have his check. But today

Davis needed quiet. He brought his coffee to the kitchen and dumped it, then found his shoes. His fingers fumbled with the laces. He counseled himself to take deep breaths, the way Marcy always suggested.

A minute later, he was in the hallway outside Apartment 203.

He felt sure the kid was in there alone. The parents both worked; Davis rarely saw them. A few times he'd passed the mother or the father in the stairwell as they returned home for the night. The woman, he recalled, was blond, ugly, small eyes pinching the bridge of her nose. The man was bald and pale, always with a look of exhaustion.

The kid, though, arrived home before them at three o'clock. Each day the school bus flashed Davis a yellow warning as it groaned to a stop, half a block from his window, and ejected the boy from its double doors. Even the sight of the kid was an annoyance. Eleven or twelve, tall already, dragging his green backpack behind him on the sidewalk. His wardrobe consisted mainly of baggy hooded sweatshirts and jeans that were too loose and bunched at the ankles. And always a baseball cap. Davis never saw him without a hat, a different hat every day, all different colors. A minute later the stairwell door would slam, and Davis heard the kid in the hallway, letting himself in next door.

A "latchkey child." That's what kids like this were called, Davis remembered, years back when schoolchildren coming home to empty houses had been a fashionable concern in the media, piling guilt onto working parents. Reason number eighty-five why Davis never wanted kids of his own screwing up his career, his life. *But nobody seems to care about latchkeys anymore,* he thought. *Too much other shit to worry about.*

And so the boy was over there alone, no supervision. Free to do as he pleased. Pound the wall, play the loud television, the loud music—afternoons had transformed into full-out assaults on Davis' concentration, breaking his thoughts like bones.

But now here he was, outside the gray metal door of the kid's apartment, planning his counterattack. He could still hear the pounding within, although it was muffled and less intrusive. *Maybe I should work here in the hall,* he thought humorlessly. Below the peephole on the door was the round black doorbell; he pushed it, grimacing at the obnoxious buzz it produced. He couldn't remember the last time anyone had rung the bell at his own apartment. He and Marcy never had guests, not in this crummy place.

The pounding stopped. He waited a full minute, but nothing else happened.

Then the pounding began again.

"Goddamn it," he said and pressed the bell harder.

This time he immediately heard the kid's voice inside the apartment, shouting far beyond the door. *"Come in!"* Annoyed, impatient.

Come in? Not what Davis was expecting. He rubbed his face and then hesitantly tried the knob of the metal door. To his surprise, it was unlocked; apparently the kid didn't heed all those safety lectures in school. Davis glanced up and down the long hallway, self-conscious that another neighbor might be watching him. He didn't want anyone to get the wrong idea, that he was some kind of creep preying on kids.

He opened the door and entered.

The entryway to Apartment 203 was dark, but he instantly recognized the unit's layout as the same as his own. First the foyer, then the kitchen to the left, and then a short hallway leading to what would be the living room, with another hallway branching off from there to two bedrooms. A blue haze emanated from around the corner. In the living room, still out of sight, the glowing television was turned to high volume—some awful rap music he didn't recognize. Behind him the door sidled shut. He took a cautious step toward the blue glow and paused. "Hello," he called.

"Yeah," a rubbery pubescent voice squawked back.

Davis sniffed. The apartment smelled, a sharp pinch in the air like body odor. Or maybe some old food going bad in the kitchen trash. Either the kid didn't take baths or didn't do his chores after school. Probably both.

He poked another few steps to the entrance of the living room. The kid was there, sitting on a long sofa, face turned toward the television on the far wall. The wall Davis shared with his office. As he approached, the boy didn't move; Davis saw only the back of the kid's head, still covered by a dirty red baseball cap. The kid's sneakered feet were propped on a glass coffee table that had been dragged closer to the sofa.

"Hello," Davis repeated. "I'm Richard Davis from next door. Maybe you've seen me around the building. Or my wife."

"Uh huh." The kid still didn't turn to look at him, as though the introduction wasn't important enough to bother with. Davis bristled.

"I'm sorry to come when your parents aren't around," Davis said, and then silently chided himself. *Sorry? Don't say you're sorry.* "But the problem is, see, I work at home, and you probably don't realize it, but I can hear you every time you ..."

The kid's head half-turned.

Davis hesitated and then finished. "Every time you hit that wall. Or whatever you're doing. My office is right on the other side there."

On the television a music video chanted hip-hop lyrics, and a man atop a car hood waved a gun. The boy abruptly raised his hand to show Davis something he was holding—an old tennis ball with nearly all the green fuzz worn away. "You mean this," the kid said. He cocked his arm back and hurled the ball across the living room; it slammed hard off a blackened patch of paint on the wall, a few feet to the side of the television.

BaHUM.

Davis winced. The ball ricocheted once off the floor, and the kid caught it again as it sailed toward the sofa. "Bull's-eye," the kid said.

"Don't do that," Davis sputtered, astonished. He goggled at the spot on the wall where the ball had struck, a mass of dirty smudges, and just as Davis had imagined earlier, cracks in the paint. Indentations in the plaster from the force of the ball. The kid's parents *had* to notice damage like this. How could they not, after a whole week?

"I can throw it harder," the kid said and drew his arm back again.

"Don't," Davis warned, regaining his composure. The authority in his voice surprised him—pleased him even. He didn't have much experience with children.

His command seemed to work. The boy froze.

For a long moment, the kid's arm remained back in a

throwing position over his shoulder, as if he were posing for a Little League photo. The music video ended; the kid lowered his arm and, for the first time, turned completely around to face Davis.

Holy Christ, Davis thought.

The kid's eyes radiated aggression, like two blue jets of gaslight, hot and threatening, too close to the bone of his nose. By comparison, his eyelashes were so faint that he appeared to have none, and the rest of his face had a washed-out, faded look; he was pale, far paler than his father. He breathed through his mouth, two gummy lips heaving on top of overlapping teeth, badly in need of braces.

Ugly as hell.

Whatever flicker of confidence Davis had enjoyed moments before suddenly vanished. He'd spoken too sharply, he realized. His face reddened; he was self-conscious now, like a small animal that had attracted a predator's attention. The boy studied him while balancing the ball up and down in one hand, as if weighing it.

"Why not?" the kid asked.

A challenge. Davis took another deep breath to cool the heat creeping up his neck. He wished Marcy were here. She was better at things like this; she had the instincts that would've made her a good mother, if he'd ever agreed to a family.

"Because it's not good for the wall," he said. "See, you're breaking it." He gestured at the cracked plaster, but the boy's eyes remained on Davis.

Unsteadily Davis continued. "And like I said, it's very loud. I can hear it back in my apartment. Maybe your parents don't mind, but—but I'm asking you to stop." *Blah blah blah,* he thought. He felt foolish, the model of a boring adult. *Wrap it up.*

"If I have to, I'll come back," he concluded. "I'll talk to your parents when they get home from work." *There,* he figured. That should fix the kid.

Instead, the boy shrugged. "My parents aren't at work," he said. "So … see ya, I guess." He returned his attention to the television and raised the volume.

Not at work? Davis was damned if he'd let the boy win on a technicality. *Okay, fine.* "Home from wherever they are, then, I'll come back—"

"They're home now."

Davis stopped mid-sentence. He blinked, then turned, half-prepared to find the mother and father standing behind him. The thought creeped him out.

"Yeah," the kid continued. "In that closet. I'm keeping them in there. They're dead." Without looking, he pointed over his shoulder to a closed white door a few feet away, where the hallway led deeper into the apartment.

An electric jolt seemed to surge up Davis's back. He discharged it with a single sharp breath out his nose before speaking. "Oh, really."

The boy shrugged again. "Seriously, dude," he said. He sounded bored. "They're in there. Wasted 'em, stuck 'em in a few days ago. Go see if you don't believe me."

Another challenge, Davis thought. The kid was fucking with him now, trying to startle him into looking like an idiot. The best thing to do was *not* give the boy the reaction he wanted. Not be shocked by anything he said.

"Yeah, whatever," Davis remarked. "They're in there."

That strange rancid garbage smell. The pounding all week long. The black dents in the living room wall that had gone unpunished.

Casually he surveyed the closed closet door. It looked normal, perfectly serene. What did he expect? Blood leaking from the hinges? Weak cries for help? If he went over there and opened that door, he'd be the world's biggest idiot, discovering nothing but shelves of clean towels and sheets while the kid sat on the couch and got his rocks off over the whole joke. *Asshole kid.*

Davis turned to leave. He was done playing along. "Just stop throwing the ball," he called, returning to the foyer. "I mean it."

BaHUM.

Davis flinched. His hands curled into two tight fists, and he had to resist an urge to lash out and knock a hole in the hallway wall. Instead he exhaled with a long hiss, smoldering, and debated whether he should return to the living room and confront the kid again. But he knew that would be useless.

Better to just go back to his apartment, squeeze out whatever he could on the article and then return later and complain when the parents were around.

They're in the closet, he thought, annoyed with himself.

Annoyed too for feeling shaken. He couldn't help it. He just wanted to get out, away from the kid. Those lashless burning eyes—the same eyes that continued to watch him from a painted portrait hanging here in the dim hallway, the kid and his parents posing formally in front of a scarlet satin backdrop. Davis had never seen them all together before. The paint made their skin look waxy and fake. Like cadavers.

Stuck them in a few days ago.

"Hey," the kid shouted from the living room. "Still there?"

Davis hesitated, listening to himself breathe. "Yes."

"I have the key to your apartment."

Davis felt the heat drain from his head, momentarily dizzying him. He gazed at the kid in the portrait. "My apartment," he said.

"Yeah."

He's fucking with you again. Davis patted his front pants pocket and found instant reassurance in the hard outline of his keychain. He pulled it out for confirmation and cleared his throat. "Nice try. My key's right here," he said; he caught himself speaking to the painting on the wall. The thing was godawful, but hard to look away from.

"I have my own set," the kid in the portrait said, his lips unmoving. "I have keys for the whole building. I stole them from the maintenance guy."

Latchkey child, Davis thought.

Was that possible? No way. Just more bullshit. Davis thrust his keychain back into his pocket and wrenched his eyes from the painting. Enough. He didn't have time for this crap. He had to write. He had to leave.

"I'm going," he announced and hastened to the front door. He yanked it open, hoping to get out before the kid said another word. He almost succeeded. As the door closed behind him, he heard the boy call out.

"See you later!"

Davis stood alone in the outer hallway. The words resounded in his head.

See you later ...

Back in his office, he sat moping. He wished desperately he hadn't gone next door. The pounding on the wall continued another hour, as he fell further and further behind on *The Advocate* article. He didn't care. He didn't even want to finish it. Instead he leaned back in his chair and shuddered as dust from the shelf sprinkled over him.

He thought about the kid and the parents. The portrait.

Hard to keep a family together these days, he thought.

Unless you keep them in the closet.

Around five o'clock, he heard the lock on the front door of his apartment click open. He hoped it was Marcy home early from work.

V. M. Zito lives in Connecticut, where he spends his weekdays writing advertising copy and his weekends trail-running and tripping over rocks. He is a lifelong horror fan and an active member of the Horror Writers Association. His novel *The Return Man* is available online and in bookstores. For a free chapter, visit TheReturnMan.com.

By the Throat
Wesley Southard

Roman shuddered as her nails found the small of his back. *This is it*, he thought, cringing. *She's touching me again.*

In a terrible lapse of memory, he'd forgotten to wear his shirt to bed, the one with the high collar. It was the only thing that saved him from her touch ... her needs. But with his bare back now exposed—and his own needs to eventually be satisfied—he wasn't sure if he'd have the strength to stop her.

Goddamn her, he didn't want it. Not tonight. If given the choice, not ever again. After their last time, he was finished with his wife's foreplay, her rambunctious love making, and her unruly hands.

In moments, her fingers slinked up his back like the delicate legs of a spider, forcing Roman to tremble—

Oh Christ, she's almost there!

—then abruptly gag.

"Goddamn it, Roman!" Gail yelled. Roman nearly cried tears of joy when her fingers left him. He curled up, shuddering at the thoughts of what could have been.

"You weak piece of shit!" Tossing aside the covers, Gail threw herself out of bed, as angry as he'd ever heard her. "This is absolutely ridiculous, do you hear me? *Ridiculous!*"

Roman wanted to scream, to lash out. She knew better. She knew his weakness from day one—but did that ever stop her?

Had it ever stopped anyone from touching his throat?

Doctors called it *Pnigophobia*, the fear of suffocation and choking. Roman called it his ruin. But his trepidation of rough fingers around his throat was not unwarranted. There was a time in his life where a much younger Roman spent his days playing records and kicking bullfrogs around the creek behind his house. The sun seemed much brighter back then, and the nights far more peaceful. The nights before Cammi, his adopted sister, used his neck as a stress reliever. For years his older sister tortured him, bringing him closer to death than the night before. Even now, years after she died from a brain aneurism, the memory of her voice still brought him to tears.

How long can you hold your breath?

Does that hurt? Does it?

Don't scream, little boy, don't you dare fucking scream.

That was only the beginning.

What his older sister had started, Roman found no end. As a child, he was constantly terrified for his life, overly aware of the space between his chest and head. He had trouble sleeping, for fear of Cammi's hands, and to have his head lying back, neck exposed, was completely out of the question. Everyday actions like hugging and kissing became a struggle. Girls never stuck around. Friends left him. His parents, blissfully unaware of Cammi's cruelty, had thought of their son as moody and unhappy, though his frequent outbursts did little to help their views.

Roman wanted to believe marriage would change him, but it only intensified his fear. The act of love-making proved to be nearly impossible, continually straining his relationship with Gail. Lucky for him, Gail wouldn't quit easily. For years she attempted to help him, was supportive, even accepting of his phobia. Still, love couldn't conquer all. With the birth of his twins, Scott and Harrison, a whole new set of challenges emerged. Children with their tiny hands. Always *pick me up, hold me, hug me*. Why couldn't they just leave him be?

"Are you even listening to me?"

Gail smacked at the bed, snapping Roman back to reality.

"*Listen to me, you stupid bastard!*" With a quick jerk, she ripped the comforter from the bed, exposing Roman to a room constricting with her anger. He groaned, curling tighter into himself.

"I've had it, Roman," she growled, crawling up behind him. Her breath was hot against his back. "I've put up with your nonsense for thirteen years. *Thirteen years!* Every single day I've been patient with you. I've listened to your whining, gave you alone time, space when you needed it. I've even managed to distance your children from you, so—God forbid—they wouldn't touch or kiss you, or do anything that might resemble some sort of *normal* relationship. And for what? Just so you can stay inside your little fear-filled bubble. All by your lonesome. Well, I've had it!"

Gail climbed off the bed. "How does it feel? Knowing that you've driven your own children away from you? That your parents don't even speak to you anymore? You're a goddamn stranger in your own house—in your own life! And all because of that neck of yours … pathetic."

Roman was disgusted with her words. But even more disgusted with himself. How long had it been since he'd spoken to his parents? Been invited to a party? Had he really been that selfish? *My little boys*, he thought. They were growing up so fast. Not long before they were old enough to start forming their own opinions.

What will they say about their old man?

Gail searched for her slippers. "This is the last straw. I thought—hey, maybe I would try one last time and help you forget your problem and maybe we could beat this thing, but obviously I was wrong. I guess we were all wrong to help." She located her shoes and sat on the bed corner to slip them on. She laughed harshly. "Well don't you worry my loving husband. We'll all be gone shortly."

Shivering, Roman broke from his paralysis and rolled over toward his wife. He was surprised to find her nude. He stared, taking her in as though he'd not seen her in years. She was still beautiful. Though her patience had been stretched to its limit, Gail remained as attractive as the day they'd met. Maybe a few pounds heavier, with stretch marks she still complained about.

Her blonde hair had grayed some. And those wrinkles—had he caused those?

She stood up and slipped on her pink robe. "I should've listened to everyone. They told me to never marry that—that *freak!* I'm sure I can find someone else. A real man to satisfy me."

Roman cringed, her words burning his core. Was she really going to leave him? The contemplation of her not sharing their bed was terrifying, but the thought of her sharing someone else's, in someone else's arms …

Gail stomped toward the door.

"Wait!" Roman quickly sat up.

Gail stopped and slowly faced him. Her eyes spoke in volumes. "No. This is done. We're through! I may never get these last thirteen years of my life back, but I'll be damned if you're going to waste another minute of my time!" She moved for the door.

Roman lunged and snatched her wrist, pulling her back onto the bed.

"Let me go," she screamed, punching his chest. "Let me go, damn you!"

He snagged her other wrist, and held them both away from him. "Please don't leave me!"

"*Please don't leave me!*" she mocked, twisting in his grip. "You're ridiculous."

"I'm sorry, Gail. I'll do whatever you want—you name it! I'll get help, I swear. I'll do anything. Just don't leave me!"

Another of her harsh laughs flattened him. "Help? We've been trying to help you for years, and all you do is collapse deeper into yourself. Face it—you're helpless!"

Roman panicked. He had to think of something—anything to keep her from leaving. Who else would have stayed this long?

"There has to be something I can do? Something to make you believe in me again?"

Gail sneered. "Roman, there's nothing in this world—"

Before he could turn back, Roman quickly lifted her hands and placed them around his neck. Gail gasped and immediately stopped struggling. Dropping his grip, Roman's eyes stayed tightly shut, wondering, *What have I just done?* His entire body quaked, stomach clenched, neck bobbing. Several seconds passed before he finally managed to breathe. Though his eyes were shut, he could only imagine Gail's stunned expression. Keep breathing, keep breathing! He counted every finger around his throat, from one to ten then back again, over and over—

But nothing happened.

For the first time in his adult life, Roman felt something strange. Something like happiness. True elation at his revelation. She wasn't there to hurt him. Maybe … maybe no one was. Roman sighed and slowly relaxed against her hands. Though his fears were far from over, this was surely the beginning of something wonderful. The first big step to the start of a new life. Things could only get better from here. After this, no one could hurt him.

Roman opened his eyes. Tears fell down his cheeks.

Gail's wide stare was glued to her hands, her mouth in a small o. Almost lovingly, her thumbs stroked his Adam's apple. She was just as surprised as him, he knew it.

He managed a shaky grin.

Gail looked up. Then her eyes narrowed as she gave small, wry smile—

And began to squeeze.

 Wesley Southard is the author of several short stories, which appear in *Big Book of New Short Horror, Daily Flash 2012, Cover of Darkness Magazine, Eulogies II: Tales from the Cellar, Grindhouse,* and *Fresh Ground-Coffee House Flash Fiction V3.* When not watching numerous hours of hockey, he spends his free time reading, finishing his first novel, and drinking copious amounts of local green soda. He is also a graduate of the Atlanta Institute of Music, and he currently lives in Southwestern Indiana. Visit him online at www.wesleysouthard.wordpress.com.

Loneliness Makes the Loudest Noise
Monica J. O'Rourke

It is loneliness that makes the loudest noise.—Eric Hoffer

Jess knows how to do this because she's tried before, but it seems someone's always watching. As if someone always suspects, waits in the wings with bated breath, knows she's about to do something monumentally stupid.

Only Jess doesn't think it's stupid. What she believes is stupid is slowly watching your feeble life slip away because you're too incapable of doing anything worthwhile with it.

She lays in a bathtub and relaxes back, rests her head on a small inflatable pillow. The utility knife feels natural, an extension of her fingers.

She quickly runs the blade across her wrist—one clean slice, deep, maybe half an inch, not as deep as it should have been. The blood pools around the fresh wound, slick and so damned richly red, bright and pretty and almost purple ... so thick and pulpy. She stares, fascinated ... her life pouring out of her wrist. And there is no pain, just blood, just—

And then the air hits the fresh wound and *fuck*! there's pain! No pain, the website had promised, just bliss ... you'll feel lightheaded and then you'll slip peacefully into a euphoric state right before the motherfucking angels grab you in their toxic wings and drag your sorry ass to hell.

She discovers the water is conducive to clotting and healing, not bleeding out.

Fuck!

She squeezes the wound to reopen it, sending fresh bolts of pain through her arm and into her brain. She tries to slice her other arm but can't cut herself again.

She leans back against that pillow and closes her eyes. Her wrist hurts like a mother but now she feels lightheaded … feels herself wavering between awake and unconscious. She tries to lift her arm but has no strength …she manages to crack her eyes. The water is shockingly red. She had expected swirls of color, fruit-on-the-bottom yogurt, not a bath of solid Kool-Aid.

She suddenly remembers she forgot to leave her mother a note. For a moment there's a twinge of guilt, but her mother understands Jess's profound loneliness, her severe agoraphobia and bipolar disorder and PTSS and myriad other mental disorders that have plagued her most of her life. She'll understand. Not that it matters.

Close now … her life's blood pooling in the tub … and moments later there's a splashing sound as water cascades over the edge and she remembers she left the tap running. She tries to lift her foot to turn off the tap but can't move. So tired …

Then a pounding at the door and Mom saying, "Jess? You okay?" and then more urgently, "Jess?" and then frantically, "Jess? Open the door!" and Mom wailing on the door, and a pounding sound as Mom throws herself against it, more screaming and yelling for Jess to get up—

And then silence.

Jess sat in Dr. Fields's office wearing nothing but a cotton gown that didn't cover much of anything and cotton slippers with no-skid bottoms.

He studied her chart, and from the amount of paperwork splayed out on his desk, he'd probably called anyone who'd ever treated her to acquire her records.

He rattled off a litany of meds, his fingers trailing the page as if reading Braille. "You've been on everything. Haven't you?"

"I've tried everything. I have—" She shrugged. Clearly he knew how to read. "It's all there."

Fields tapped his pen against his bottom lip. He stuck his nose in her chart, read bits and pieces aloud. "First diagnosed age eight … psychotic breakdown age twelve … permanently mentally disabled at seventeen." He shrugged. "It's funny what a person can get used to. What she learns to accept."

"What?"

But he ignored her, continued reading, occasionally jotted notes.

She peered at him through strings of hair that fell into her eyes and tried to read his handwriting upside down. "I hate getting up. Hate being awake all day." She wiped the back of her hand across her dry lips. "I can't talk to anyone. It's not that I don't want to …" She leaned forward and hugged her knees. "I, it's … I can't. Except for this trip to ye olde psych ward, I haven't left my house in years."

He ignored her again for an excessive amount of time until she wondered if she had become invisible.

"This is all treatable, Jessica."

She leaned her head back. The ceiling was a Rorschach of badly stained tiles. "It isn't treatable." She sighed. "I've tried everything. Do you know how much it all just sucks?"

"Tell me," he muttered.

She sat up and stared at him, tried to see past his indifference. *Really?* she wondered, staring at her shrink, wondering if he heard a word she was saying. "There is no treatment for what I have. Why does every doctor think he can cure me?"

Fields scribbled something on his legal pad. He sighed and turned away, his disdain apparent.

Terrific. She didn't feel like looking at his blurry carp eyes and big fat glasses that dangled off his nose anyway.

She tried again. "Even when I'm with people, it's like I'm alone, like I'm the last person alive. I drown everyone out, even when I don't want to. The pain I feel becomes its own voice. It screams to end the pain, and there's only one way to end it: end you."

He rested his chin in his palm for a moment before responding. "What about now? You're not drowning me out."

"Sure I am. I can be thinking about something else, like what I want to watch on TV tonight, or what I might have for lunch. This isn't real. And soon you'll drift away, become a smoky puff of air." She waved her fingers. "Not real people. Just ... ghosts. Clouds. No substance."

He reached across his desk, struggled across it, actually, slid over the blotter like a well-fed boa constrictor, and took her wrist. "Listen to me," he said, sounding somewhat excited.

Jessica shrank back, tried to pull free. The last thing she wanted was physical contact. Her skin itched where he touched her. And she really didn't want to hear his rush of adrenaline-addled upbeat psychobabble.

"I can help you," he said, clearly excited, struggling to slide his girth back into his chair.

Her left eyebrow cocked involuntarily. "No offense, but you can't imagine how many times—"

His chair groaned as he eased back into it, oozing into the leather like a puddle. At least he'd let go of her hand. "Listen to me. Clearly you're not cognizant enough to make decisions for yourself; you've proven that by your suicide attempt."

She swallowed, turning her head away, her cheeks reddening.

He opened her chart, skimmed the pages but didn't seem to be reading anything. "You've been isolated your entire life. You have just a mother who takes care of you. I can cure you," he snapped. "Why are you trying to make this so difficult?"

"What?" she whispered, growing angry at his empty promise. Why was he throwing around the word *cure*? If a cure existed, she would have known about it. She would have tried it by now.

Fields swiveled in his leather chair and unlocked the metal cabinet behind him. He removed a small kit. "I want to help you," he said, turning back to face her. "You have to trust me."

"No."

"No?"

"How do I know what's in there? You might try to kill me."

"Isn't that what you want? You already tried to kill yourself."

Hard to argue with that convoluted logic. Hard, but not impossible. "No ..." She shook her head, turned away. "I'm not a guinea pig."

But then he was beside her, touching her face, so goddamned invasive and she wondered if she should scream because his behavior was not appropriate, she knew her rights, she knew he wasn't supposed to treat her without her permission, never mind lay his clammy palms on her face. She stiffened, her breath growing shallow, her chest hurting, feeling pressure, as if he was sitting on her. Deer-in-headlights now. He could do whatever the hell he wanted and she'd be unable to fight him off. Her body and mind chose the most inopportune times to shut down.

"This works," he muttered. "It has to ... do you understand me? Just ... trust me. I know what I'm doing. I'm the doctor here, not you."

He leaned in closer, but Jess had all but shut him out by now. She could hear his words, but they made little sense.

"I'm giving you your life back." He stared into her eyes, and it seemed an eternity before he spoke again. "Don't you see? Stop being so difficult." He glanced over his shoulder as if someone had sneaked up on him. He looked past her toward the closed door, focusing on it before bringing his gaze back to settle on her.

He leaned in, so close to her face now ... his breath warm on her cheek, on her eyelid, on the bridge of her nose. His breath smelled like coffee and mints, and Jess wanted to sit back, tried to sit back, to move away from him but froze instead, something she was used to but hated. The lack of control was something she would never fully accept, but she had no choice. One of those necessary evils she'd learned to live with.

"Your life doesn't have to be this way," he said, finally moving back a few inches. "You can have a normal life."

Again he stared, as if she'd be able to converse with him. "At first ..." He sighed and quickly drew his hand down his chin as if wiping away invisible crumbs. "It might seem strange." He leaned in. "I know you can hear me ..."

Just could barely make out the movement of him licking his lips, but the sound of his tongue running over his sandpapery lips was like the creak of a hangman's noose to her sensitive ears.

"This could work," he said, his voice cracking. He sniffed hard. "And I'm not just doing this for the Nobel!" He smiled. "I really want to help you. There's no reason—"

He shook his head and grinned, a rather unsettling smile that reminded her of that stupid monkey toy with the symbols. "This is going to sound immensely narcissistic, and for that I apologize, but you *have* to do well. You *have* to ... I need this. I'm too goddamned good at what I do for you to squander this."

She eyed the kit he'd laid out on the coffee table: the gauze pads, bandages, syringes, small vial containing a bondi-blue liquid, other vials filled with what looked like jaundice.

"Don't screw this up, Jessica." He led her to the sofa. "Don't be scared. After this you'll never be lonely again. Trust me."

Trust him. She wondered where in the Caribbean he'd gotten his medical degree.

He swabbed her arm with an alcohol pad and injected the contents of the first syringe into her arm. He followed with another shot, and another.

"Rest a few minutes," he said.

Then he left her.

This was unfair, what he'd done. No, not unfair. Criminal. Left her alone, pumped full of unknown meds. Defenseless. She tried to will herself unafraid but her efforts made it worse. She threw her head back against the sofa cushions and tried to breathe. Every muscle tensed. She tried to concentrate, picked something to concentrate on, created a mantra: Fields dying. Fields drowning, face pressed beneath a thick layer of ice, desperately trying to find a small air hole as the oxygen slowly leaked out of his lungs. Fields with his throat cut, like a new grin had been etched into his neck. Fields in a cornfield, a makeshift scarecrow burning to death.

And then, as if a dirty window had been wiped clean: a moment of clarity. Fully aware, in focus. Attached to reality. And more bizarre: not terrified.

Fields returned moments later. "I." She shook her head. The room began to spin and she relaxed against the sofa cushions. "I don't understand."

"Listen," he said, sitting beside her. "We'll need to talk tomorrow. After the meds—after you've had time to adjust. You're not finished with treatment yet."

He brought her to her private room. Beneath the covers she felt safer. Could hide better, could pull the blanket over her head if she needed to.

But she didn't need to. This was new territory for her. If she hadn't been so exhausted, she would have celebrated her newfound clarity.

Elated—possibly for the first time in her life—she closed her eyes, and sleep came easily.

And behold, the woman meets him, dressed as a prostitute, wily of heart.

"What?" Jess's voice was muffled. Still tired, still waking. She sat up, looked around the empty room. Head still, eyes darting, expecting to see people falling from the shadowy corners, creep out from beneath the bed.

They want to hurt us, want to kill us ...!

"What?" Her heart smashed against her ribs, as if trying to find a way out of her body. So many voices cackling and chortling and snickering ...

Sobbing didn't help but she couldn't stop. She threw her hands over her ears and pressed hard.

I will show you the judgment of the great harlot that sits upon many waters ...

She tried to understand. Tried to hear ...

... with whom the kings of the earth have committed adultery and the inhabitants of the earth were made drunk with the wine of her adulteries.

"What?" she choked out yet again, frustrated by her lack of understanding.

But the voices became an endless cacophony ... virtually impossible to understand what they were saying ... blending together, but mixing like oil and water, mixing awkwardly, as if trying to separate, a nasty salad of words and syllables.

The blood is beautiful ... tepid and comforting, oh so comforting, like soaking in a pool of warmth, feel the sensation ... sharp ... feel its power

... you control it ... part of you ... wants to be part of you forever ... metal light glinting off metal ... it's hypnotic. See how the blood glistens like red pearls on the shiny, shiny blade ... you know you love it. You want it.

But it was never that simple. If she just concentrated she could distinguish a voice, could make out the drooling lunacy flooding her head ... but mostly it was a crowd vying for her attention.

And then all at once, voices she'd never heard before were making horrible, raspy guttural noises like sucking in oxygen and then vomiting it back up.

Ugly! You can't do anything right, you wretched sow. Why don't — Blood! ... Oh, taste the ... bite it off! Bite it and— Touch it ... touch it, it's so soft ... he won't hurt— I know you want to die. Next time try harder. Try harder next time. Next time. Next time. Swallow pills. Hide so they won't find you— Beautiful girls! Everywhere are beautiful— Ugly! Hideous! Your own mother thinks you're a pig. You can't do anything right! Why don't you just— Die! Liar! You're like the others!

"Talk to them." That voice she recognized: Fields.

"Help me!" she screamed, falling out of the bed, feet tangled in the sheets in her rush to crawl to her doctor.

He grabbed her shoulders, lifted her from the floor, and shook her until she had no choice but to look at him, head craning back on her shoulders. "Calm down."

"What's wrong with me?" she shrieked. Amid the endless chatter in her head was Fields's voice. She strained to hear what he was saying.

"Let me explain—"

Liar! He lies! He wants to fuck you! He wants—The pens are free at the bank. You can take as many—Why you're not dead. He wants to kill you. Are you blind and stupid?

"—treatment—"

He wants us dead.

"—and the meds will help you if—"

Jessica planted her head in her palms and sank to the floor. "Oh, God," she moaned. "Take them out. Get them out of my head!"

"Pay attention." He hunkered down beside her. "Concentrate on my voice."

And the smoke of their torment goes up forever and ever, and they have no rest, day or night, these worshipers of the beast and its image, and whoever receives the mark of its name—They're coming for you, Jessica.

"What did you do?" She wiped away her tears. It had to have been Fields. It had to have been whatever he'd doped her up with.

"I used a cocktail, a combo of meds. It's amazing, really. I should win the Nobel prize in medicine for this. I used L-Dopa, which converts into dopamine—"

He poisoned us! Look at what he's done!

"—bromocriptine stimulates dopamine release—"

Poison!

"—excess dopamine. Dopamine is a neurotransmitter. It's similar to adrenaline. This is why you—"

Don't listen! Kill him!

"Shut up!" she screamed. She looked at Fields imploringly. "Trying to hear you ... but they won't shut the fuck up."

"You'll get used to them, Jessica." After that she could see his mouth working, knew he was further explaining how he'd poisoned her, but she could barely hear another word.

From him, anyway.

Die, Jessica. Why don't you kill yourself? You're a liar! Pretty razors ... pretty knives ... pretty barbed wire ... see how pretty? It's so nice and neat and doesn't hurt, not like when water touches the hurt, it feels so good ... you close your eyes and feel so warm and fuzzy, like wrapped in a giant terrycloth towel—

"The final medication is called—"

She tried to concentrate, wanted to block the incessant noise in her head but the voices were loud and unrelenting, made it so hard to concentrate.

Don't trust him; he wants your pain!

"—entine. It's what gave you schizophrenia."

Wait. He gave her schizophrenia? Was this some kind of fucked up joke? "The voices—" she groaned.

They responded as if she'd addressed them.

Die. The rabbit is loose! It's going to eat you. Liar! The beast lies.

"You'll get used to them. And you'll never be lonely again."

Lonely? Was he out of his fucking mind? This was his way of curing her? This nonstop screaming and badgering was a thousand times worse than any medical condition she was already suffering from.

Already her brain started imagining new and interesting ways to commit suicide.

She fought to hear him, focused so intently on his voice her head ached.

"Make friends with them. Talk to them. This is designer schizophrenia, Jessica. You'll be able to control the voices and live with them. You just need to practice. You'll be famous! And so will I."

On her own.

More or less.

Mom was there, as always, but what did that matter? No matter what Jess said, she knew her mother thought she was a basket case. Still, she tried. When Fields released her, Jess had no choice but to return home. And fighting with the voices—fighting over the voices—trying to make sense of the goddamn voices—it wasn't a pleasant experience, but it sure as hell kept her busy. Which seemed to make Fields one happy fat fuck.

Struggling now to get the words out … Mom staring intently, as if trying to understand what Jess was saying and Jess knowing Mom was full of shit, knowing her mother had long since truly stopped caring about what was rattling around inside her daughter's ridiculously dysfunctional brain.

"What is it, Jess?" she asked wearily. "What is it now?"

"H-he … did this …" she stammered, fighting for each syllable, each breath. Sometimes distinguishing between her words and theirs was impossible, and she found herself repeating them.

"He who?"

"Fuh-fuh … piece of …"

"You want pizza?"

"No!" Fields! Fields, goddammit! Jess leaned forward, press her fist against the space between her eyebrows. "I … I … God!" She tried to quiet them. Tried to squeeze out a few of her own words, tried to drown out the endless cocktail-party chatter floating in her brain.

Hates you … feel the warmth, a forever rest … so peaceful … no more pain and no more voices, won't that be beautiful? Dog died because you were bad. Bad! When you touch yourself, it makes God angry and —

100

God hates you hates you and wants you to burn in hell! And in the river you drown your baby and you know your mother hates you. You stole her life. She wants you dead so why don't you—

"Jess? What are you—"

She sucked in a huge breath and said, "Fields did this!"

Her mother nodded. "Did what?"

"This!" Jess sobbed, waving her arms in the air, indicating herself as if it was apparent what she was talking about.

"Oh, Jess …" She patted her daughter's hands. "He saved your life. Remember? You tried to kill yourself? You were in the hospital."

She wasn't getting it, and Jess didn't know how to explain. Even writing was impossible. *They* wouldn't let her write more than a word at a time.

She gave up.

Fields had told her to live with the voices. He said they would keep her company, would always be there for her. They were part of her now, part of her mind and life and everyday functions.

And when he saw her in therapy and she couldn't share with him because they just wouldn't shut the fuck up! he still insisted this was such a wonderful thing for her … that he had cured her profound loneliness, but she wanted to ask one question, just one damned question, but they would never let her.

Why did you even bother? she wanted to ask. *This didn't make my life better.*

And he would spend the better part of her fifty-minute session telling her how far she'd come, and still she couldn't understand. Nothing had gotten better—she was still homebound, still trapped—what exactly did he consider an improvement?

But even his words blended with the voices, so if he was trying to explain himself, words were lost in the din.

"Out," she said, trying to say "Get them out of me!" but "out" was followed by, "Out rain and it cleans, it makes a puddle," and she rocked in frustration, feeling utterly useless.

"It's raining in there?" he asked in a rare moment of interest in anything she had to say.

"No." But that was it. That was all they would allow her

today.

"You're doing great!" but she didn't think he knew whatsoever what he was talking about. And the look on his face told her everything she had assumed all along: she was a test case, a subject, and he didn't give a damn what was actually happening to her. He continued injecting her with his bondi-blue and jaundice-yellow concoctions, and she remained helpless to stop him, helpless to cry out for help to a single damned person. Her own mother was oblivious.

Hates you! She carried an umbrella and stabbed the horse with it ... you look the other way ... she knows you're dead ... but eyes in the dark glow and stare and know your thoughts, they know— Pictures! He hid the pictures because you were bad—ugly cow! No one loves you! Death is the only way out. Death will— And you plug up the tailpipe, it's so easy, so painless ... no one will miss you. No one will care when you're dead— But the baby ate too much and now it's throwing up— The cat ran away with the spoon and it's your fault your fault your fault! You are so ugly even God won't look at you. Ugly, disgusting, you have worms crawling under your skin.

"Honestly," her mother said, crossing Jess's bedroom to deposit a tray of food on the dresser. "Sometimes I can't help but wonder—"

And then the voices drowned her mother out again, and Jess struggled to hear the rest. "What?" she asked wearily.

Her mother carried a plate to the bed. "Why are—" The rest was muffled, replaced with *I hate apples. She wants to poison us.*

No apples on the plate. Sandwich only. Suddenly her mother was gone, but just for a split second ... and when she returned, her head was... different ... somehow bigger... kind of bulging at parts, as if studded with tumors. Her mother had sprouted a demon head.

"God!" Jess shrieked, dropping the sandwich. She dipped her head low, refusing to look up, to look at the monster her mother had become. But as she stared at the sheets draped across her legs, she was horrified to discover they were crawling with maggots. She threw back the covers and flew toward the headboard, trying desperately to escape.

Her mother/monster looked angry ... hands on hips, shaking her head. "Honestly!" she said again.

"Help me!" she cried, digging her nails into her palms and biting the inside of her cheek.

"Help you what?" Mom/monster snapped. "Honestly, I'm at my wit's end. You're almost thirty, Jessica. How much more of this do you think I can take?"

Mom/monster picked up the sandwich. Jess stared at it … at the mass of wriggling, angry maggots falling off the bread, at the decaying stench of whatever rotten meat her mom/monster was trying to feed her … a nasty, mealy, earthy odor like mildewed dirt, like swampy vase water when flowers have died and decayed and been thoughtlessly neglected.

Her mom/monster licked her lips and slowly nodded. "I'm tired, Jessica. I thought by now you would …" She started to waver again, as if she was made of light, of clouds and fog … as if made of heat shimmers you see on asphalt on an oppressively hot summer day, but then she was whole again. The monster head had somehow transformed, made complete, but now it was the head of a bull, with huge brown eyes and nose ring and two horns on the top of its head.

"Please get out," Jess cried, not wanting to see this creature her mother was becoming. She looked away.

"Why aren't you better by now?" her mother demanded— only it wasn't her mother. The voice was deep, muffled, the words forced between snorts, loud bursts of air from the bull's mouth.

Her mom/monster finally left, finally left her alone.

Left behind was a bowl of soup and a handful of crackers, which she looked at with disdain. Why would her mother give her a bowl of blood? It wasn't even disguised well. It was supposed to be tomato soup, but Jess knew better. She wasn't stupid.

The bowl of soup parted like the Red Sea. Just stared at it in awe. "Who did that?" she asked the miracle soup.

I parted the soup!

And Jess knew it was the voice of God.

But the voices wouldn't stay quiet and tried to overtalk God. Jess strained to hear God's voice. *They used to call— She wants you dead! Vitamins and nutrients and there will be no bugs— She hates you she said you're sick sick sicksicksicksicksicksicksicksicksicksicksicksicksick sick and you'll get sicker and sicker and sicker and then you'll die and she'll dance on your grave! She will try to kill you. You can't let her kill you.*

And Jess heard him, heard his voice over the others'. But he was wrong. Her mother loved her! "No …" She shook her head. "You're wrong."

But God was never wrong. The voices told her that. Or maybe God told her.

She covered her ears with her wrists. "Shut up!" She couldn't listen to this … if only she could drown them out—if only they'd shut up for five minutes!

The rainbows are gray, they look like shit and they smother you in your sleep— And the robots said not to say another word, you moron! She told me yesterday she wants you dead we can show you such an easy way to die.

Yes, die. Maybe they were right. It's not as if Jess hasn't attempted suicide before. Though despite her mother's complaints, Jess doesn't really believe her mother wants her dead. Or …?

What had her mother said just a short while earlier? *I thought you'd be better by now—so why aren't you dead?* Yes, the voices told her; that's exactly what her mother had said. But she clearly sucked at suicide. The voices promised to help. Maybe they knew better.

Sometimes they were a mass of voices fighting for her attention, all stage-whispers and forced words vying simultaneously.

Tonight the voices were loud and strong and at times singular, as if they had banded together and were all of like mind. Tonight they seem to want to make her listen, to understand, to discover. Tonight they had a lesson they needed Jessica to learn.

Jess's mind raced, trying to follow their orders. Think, think! they told her.

But think what? There were a million things she could think about. What did they mean?

Blades. You need a blade. But not like a razor. You need something big, something beautiful and powerful. Something that dances on candlelight, something all at once dangerous and oh so wonderful, like kitten fur, silky and comforting.

Kitchen.

A magnetic strip along the length of the wall behind the butcher block station held an assortment of knives. She didn't know their names for the most part because cooking had never interested her. But she knew the chef's knife, the one with a blade that reminded her of a three-quarter moon, and between her forefinger and thumb she gripped the pearl handle almost reverently. The knife beckoned in a way the voices said would happen ... once again they were right. She trusted them now, though it was sometimes hard to live with them, sometimes the incessant noise drove her to near insanity. She knew they loved her and gave her wonderful advice, and they meant nothing but good things for her.

They wanted her free from her pain.

She climbed back up the stairs, knife held almost seductively in her palm.

She had just reached her bedroom door when she nearly collided with her mom coming from the bathroom.

Her mother gasped and then laughed nervously, her hands fluttering to her throat. "You scared me!" She smiled but quickly grew serious. "Are you okay? Is anything wrong?"

But the voices chimed in, told her what to say. In her own mind, her words made perfect sense: *Go back to bed, Mother. I'm fine. I needed some juice.*

What she said was, "Dirty ... dirty ... it's not safe. It has to be identified."

"Come on, Jess ..." Her mother took Jess's wrist and gently pulled.

Jess slammed herself against the wall. *Don't! She wants you dead!*

Her mother's hand transformed into a claw, something gnarled and withered, the nails brittle and black and cracked, aged monstrosities, witch's fingernails, sharp and pointy.

Run, run, get away from her! Don't let her hurt you. Run! But her mother wouldn't let go. Her face had gone green, the color of sharp, twisting blades of grass, dipped in poison, in rat poison, in chemicals they spray on the weeds, and those poison fingernails tried to scratch Jess's wrist, tried to stab that poison into her arm.

The voices had told her not to trust anyone. How could she not have seen?

Jess collapsed to the floor, sobbing, still trying to pull away from her hideous, toxic mother … the evil witch trying to poison her … *make her go away!* she begged, watching the hallway walls expand and contract, pulsing with a life of their own, closing in on her …

Jess lashed out at them, wildly swinging the butcher knife, aiming for the walls. And suddenly, the witch lay at her feet, blood gushing from some unseen wound.

Die. It's time to die.

She realized she had just fought for her life, but only because she didn't want to be murdered in some horribly painful way.

The walls began to pulse again, closing in on her, trying to strangle her … ghosts and demons flying up and down the corridor, scared, angry, pinched faces, banshees with mouths formed in wide circles, releasing their screams … shrieking in her ears, filling her head with their shrill cries of hatred and wrath, and she pressed her palms against her ears to drown out the madness.

No more! No more noise, no more hatred and horror, please, no more, no more!

She brought the butcher knife up to her ear and slowly moved the tip of the blade in, the only way to expunge the voices. If only she could get them to shut up, maybe she would know peace again. Maybe … if only … if only she could dig out the eardrums. She trusted the voices, but she no longer wanted to live with them. The sensation of warmth washed over her neck and shoulder and brought comfort but also great pain. The knife was too big and making an unholy mess of her ear and she could still hear every damn thing, every voice, every sound, every fucking breath, and the ghosts still flew, and the demons still taunted until Jess collapsed unconscious to the floor.

Across from Fields, head in her hands, squeezing as if trying to keep her brains from spilling out. Restrained in the chair, limited movement. She certainly couldn't get up if she wanted to. She was lucky they let her move her hands.

"Jessica—"

"Out …" she moaned. "Them … out … pleeeeessssse

… "

"Jessica, listen to me. They can't come out."

Her head spasmed, arm jerked as if shooing away insects. "Noooooo …" she moaned quietly, as if learning the word for the first time. She stared down at her arm and wondered why she couldn't control it. It jerked again. She stared, fascinated. Had the voices learned to control her movements?

Freak! Loser. Die! The voices seemed rather focused these days.

He nodded, and she thought he looked empathetic for a change. More than a pathetic scientist. He obviously noticed her arms with a mind of their own. "You have tardive dyskinesia. From the L-Dopa," he explained, and she tried to hear over the roar of voices. "Involuntary movement. A side effect of the medication."

She nodded, but only because it felt right, not because she gave a shit what he was saying or understood him in any way. Somewhere his words made sense, but not in her mind. She heard "side effect" and just didn't give a damn. Her whole life had turned into a side effect.

"Muh-" she said, just a sound, just something one of the voices forced out of her, but this idiot scientist was still under the bizarre impression she was trying to communicate with him. He responded with something about her mother, something she couldn't follow. The voices drowned him out as usual.

"Your mother was taken to—" *And we went hunting for candy but the clown hid it all, so we reached—* "Where they say she'll have to undergo—" *And they want to shave your head and you can let them if you want, it makes—* "Can't blame yourself, Jessica." *What is in your hand anyway? You never showed me—* "Can you hear me?"

And in a moment of lucidity, which came after weeks of profound concentration, of fixating on the words she desperately wanted to communicate, as she ignored the screaming, leering, twisted, nasty assholes running around her head, she squeaked, "Cure … me …"

Fields stopped moving, stopped rocking, stopped his incessant babbling and stared at Jess. "What?"

She stared back, unsure she could get out another understandable word, waiting for him to pick up on her cues.

"It's not that simple."

Tears poured down her cheeks as she realized the futility of trying to get him to understand.

But whatever he'd done to her, he had to know how it was affecting her. Had to. She knew he knew … and if she could communicate with him for real, she wouldn't ask for her cure. If she could share her thoughts with him, she would tell him to go to hell.

He knelt beside her and touched the back of her hand. "I understand," he whispered. "I know you want them out." He brushed the hair back beside her ear, and she could feel the bulkiness of the bandages there.

She strained to hear him, trying to shove the voices back, trying to make them understand she needed to hear his voice.

Die, she thought. *I want to die...*

Yes, die! Die! Die!

He unfastened her restraints and wrapped his arms around her, carrying her to the sofa.

She curled up, trembling, limbs spastic, head pounding from the unrelenting screams. "N-nuh no …" she murmured.

Fields knelt beside her. "I'll make it better."

She nodded, wiped her nose with the back of her hand. "Jessica?"

Too tired to say another word … to care. Wanted to sleep, rest forever, close her eyes and make the voices disappear. *Please make them stop …*

She watched him fill a syringe.

"Everything will be better now. I promise. No more pain."

Sunlight blinded her, warmed her, healed her. A meadow of fragrant wildflowers and tall grass, surrounded by smells of sunbaked earth.

Near her, several people rested in the shade beneath a tree.

"Jessica," one said. She recognized the voice.

Nothing for miles, it seemed. Endless trees, greenery. A living Monet.

"What is this place?" Jessica stood, shielded her eyes with the edge of her hand. Miles and miles of foliage, nothing but.

And, she realized, there was nothing but blessed silence.

They pointed. Behind her.

She turned to see what they were pointing at. Lying in what appeared to be a hospital bed was Jessica. Everything around the body was sterile, white. She was hooked up to machinery, monitors listing her vitals.

"What did he do to me?" she whispered. She reached out to touch herself, and her hand passed through flesh. Was it the body in front of her that was unreal? Or was she?

Fields was there moments later, followed by a small group of medical students.

"Jessica Carlyle. A former patient of mine. Primary diagnoses are on the chart. Also diagnosed with schizophrenia and later displayed signs of chorea dyskonesia. Treated with Risperdal and Seroquel. Patient susceptible to neuroleptic malignant syndrome, which resulted in coma. There is active brain activity."

The students leaned in and studied her face as if she were about to speak.

"Onset of schizophrenia? At her age?" one asked.

"Late onset," Fields said. "Though at twenty-eight, schizophrenia is not unheard of. Just not as common."

The students left, but Fields stayed with Jessica. "I know you can hear me," he whispered, his mouth beside her ear. "The meds I used are undetectable, so don't worry, no one will revive you. Enjoy your new freedom, Jessica."

"Wait. *Wait!*" But he didn't seem to hear. "Don't leave me here. Wait!" She glanced back at her body: useless, but alive because of machines. And Fields was gone.

The voices that had remained silent began to speak at once, yelling at her, cursing, their faces contorting into snarls and smirks, fingers raised and pointing and accusing. She knew them all, knew their hateful cries. Knew how much they hated her. And now they were here, in front of her, faces now matching the voices.

Jessica wondered how she would be able to kill herself.

 Monica J. O'Rourke has published more than one hundred short stories in magazines such as *Postscripts, Nasty Piece of Work, Fangoria, Flesh & Blood, Nemonymous,* and *Brutarian* and anthologies such as *Horror for Good* (charity anthology), The *Mammoth Book of the Kama Sutra,* and *The Best of Horrorfind.* She is the author of *Poisoning Eros I and II,* written with Wrath James White, *Suffer the Flesh,* and the new collection *In the End, Only Darkness.* Watch for her new novel *What Happens in the Darkness* later this year from Sinister Grin Press. She works as a freelance editor, proofreader, and book coach. Her website is an ongoing and seemingly endless work in progress, so find her on www.facebook.com/MonicaJORourke in the meantime.

Footnotes
Magda Knight

We secrete ourselves in Petticoat Lane, hats pulled low to hide our faces. Victorion's rain-slicked and cobbled main streets are all aglow with moon-green mushroom lamps, the egg sacs of Leviathans farmed off the Cornish coast; here in the alleyway there is only inky darkness and the feeling of things to come.

We have night-work to attend to. Revels, indeed.

The first to pass through our alley is a brassy gentleman. Those mincing automatons—they never carry money. Nor do they have blood to spill. I can't take my knife to them, make their one into a zero—they were never a one to begin with.

Moses sticks a leg out and the thing veers aside in a clanking protestation of gears. I shake my head in disdain. Save for a shared interest in night-work, I do not see much in the Nichol Boys. What must they see in me?

The next passerby is more promising: a cane-twirling mark in a fine coat of excellently sober cut, unlike himself. We step out of our shadows and surround him like the petals of a dark flower. There is no spirit in him. He falls in seconds to our bricks and sticks, and never even makes a sound.

The Nichol Boys help themselves to his fob watch, heavy

pipe, the twelve pounds and fifteen shillings in his purse that could pay a man's rent for a year.

I let them take all that. I want only a few shillings for a trip to the barber. I have been doing some solitary night-work of late: A pinchcock called Emma Smith, just outside the trade entrance of the cocoa factory. My most recent attempt to make this town form a neater equation, to shift it from a one to a zero. It was a messy affair, novel enough to be featured in the *Illustrated Police News*. My own fault. I may have had a blunt stick to hand at the time, and done things I shouldn't. And perhaps I didn't do enough, for she survived long enough to talk of what she'd seen before she gasped her last in London hospital, Whitechapel. And now the East End is riddled with Great Scotland Yard 'wanted' posters bearing the illustration of a face not entirely unlike mine.

And now I need new hair, and my beard close-shaven. I need a barber.

But the City Gent carries something else in his satchel; its bulk catches my eye.

Before I can reach for it, Moses draws a business card from the gentleman's inner coat pocket and wordlessly passes it over, for I am the only one of us who knows what letters do. Making out the curlicue script, I keep my voice low:

"Someone important, I think. Thomas Babcock. One of Her Majesty's engineers."

Moses lets out a long drawn-out whistle and lets it hang in the air. "A man of royal influence? It's a fine fish we've caught tonight, Jacob."

"Not Jacob. *Never* Jacob. Jack." Moses can think what he likes, but I am linked to these men in spilled blood only, not the stuff in our veins. I am of no chosen tribe. I choose myself.

Another of our gang, Big Ben, shakes his head in disgust. "The coppers will have us for this. There'll be posters with our faces on before the night is out."

Moses spits phlegm. "Only for those that lose their nerve. Me? I say there'll be spread legs and silk handkerchiefs for all."

Ignoring this endless stream of word-piss I reach into the satchel lying by our bruised and battered mark and pull out the object within. It feels heavier than it should. Heavier than anything that size should feel, unless formed of solid gold.

Which I'm pretty sure it ain't.

The thing has an ebb and tide to it. I get an inspiration, sometimes, that rises in my belly when I'm carving a carcass or walking down a street safe in the knowledge that no one could hurt me as much as I could hurt them. It's as though I can tell the future, and am at one with all things. Right now, my bones fizz with the surety that this block in all its mystery is worth more to me than even twelve pounds and fifteen shillings.

Peeling off the wrappings I soon reveal what I think I always knew it would be. A book. It is not as heavy as I first thought, but ... the heft. The shape. The very *being* of it. As they cradle the book my hands look watery in comparison, the hands of ghosts. I feel the heavy touch of Moses' hand on my shoulder, but as I look up his face floats as substantial as the vaguest of memories.

Then I blink and he seems solid again; a trick of the light. Though my belly warns me that it is no trick. Not of light and shadow, anyways.

We should be making a speedy exit by now, but I flick through the pages and try to ignore Moses breathing in my ear. Just words. No pictures, even. No glow, no whirr, no punch-carded mechanics.

There is nothing special about this book, yet it belongs to a Royal engineer—a man who shapes our Nation. And ... the *being* of it.

The World's History: 3rd Edition. Never heard of it.

It is not special, this book. But it is.

"You half in love with that thing, Jacob? Must be a pocket-book on losing your virginity, the way you're carrying on." Moses cranes over.

"An interesting title. It's called *Mind Your Own Business.*"

There is a flash in Moses' eyes. With something approaching a thrill, I realize: he would do me harm if he could. But the moment is gone, and I shove the book beneath my topcoat.

"Let's away." I stand up.

There is nothing much left to say to each other, so with handshakes and slaps on the back—on their part, for I never touch the Nichol Boys nor anyone else if I can help it—we go our separate ways, making no plans to meet again, though we know we will. For we always do. It may take a month, or a week, or only a matter of days before the exhilaration passes and our fingers throb with the need to clasp something and use it. Like the sea, night-work has its own pull.

I head for the main streets and start the long walk home under the moon-glow of mushroom street lamps, their long tendrils brushing my face with unspeakable enticements. And yet this is the first time I have ever walked the streets back to my flat with one eye over my shoulder. That flash I saw in Moses' eye … I wonder if one day I might walk into an empty alleyway, all safe and snug, only to find my friends stepping out of the shadows to surround me with metal glistening in their closed fists. I will think on what to do should that day ever come.

But it is not today. I reach my flat without any mishap, fumble for the key to unlock the door, creep up the stairs, light a candle and throw my clothes upon the floor, for I am exhausted tonight. Too weary to boil up a pot of tea, I struggle into a nightshirt and crawl into bed—then stare long and hard at the wrapped book lying on the floor.

The candle stump by my bedside is scarcely higher than a thumb-knuckle and the money earned tonight must go towards a barber, not beeswax. No matter; I cross the bare wooden floorboards and bring the book into bed with me, drawing my knees up beneath the bedclothes as if I were a little lad. Tonight, until my candle flickers down to nothing, I will read.

I wake in the cold hours of dawn in a shivering sweat; nightmares just behind my eyes. The book lies closed beside me, its over-solid pages throbbing with rude health. The bed and floorboards seem most hazy in comparison

Is this book a fake? I think not. I know with every bone in my body that it is most certainly 1888, and that my life is real, though the dates within this book say otherwise. If this thing were a jest it would have to be engineered by an entire school of men, each as great a genius as Drake, Brunel, Newton, Darwin, or Nobel.

I do not think the book is a jest.

Ignoring the cold, I carry the book over to the window and kneel beneath its sash so that no one from the building opposite can see me. It's an awkward position that bathes me in the sporous glow of the mushroom lamps in the street, but it cannot be helped. My nightmare shivers subside as I take hold of the book and open it. It is nearly day, now. Nearly time to open up the shop. A brief glimpse ...

1887. A man I've never heard of called Tesla discovers something that proves to be very useful called an *X-ray*. A year ago. Perhaps it was in the newspapers and I missed it.

1905. A remarkably interesting fellow called Einstein has a busy year. He publishes a paper on the conversion of matter to energy by humans and in the cosmos. It is called *nuclear energy*. He also proves that something remarkably tiny exists called an *atom*, which is the basis of all things. The other scientific advancements he achieves in this year I do my best to absorb, but even after repeated readings I cannot begin to understand what he is talking about.

1909. I am very excited to learn that an American businessman invents the disposable razor blade.

1945. Powered by *liquid oxygen* (whatever that is) and gasoline, a contraption is built that will allow man to go to the moon. An oddity, for this has already been achieved, and progress to Mars also: Victorion's newspapers constantly sound the trumpets on how our green brethren will be the saving of us. Which I doubt, for them Cydonians seem a ramshackle lot to me. Yet the history book in my hands discusses the matter in not only technically astute but convincingly dry and colorless terms. I am more inclined to believe it—*that life, that weight*—than the blarings of Victorion's penny-papers.

1945. A uranium gun-type device levels a city in Japan. The name of the device is *Little Boy*. I am somewhat less impressed to learn that, in the same year, a children's toy is invented that serves no purpose save to fall haphazardly down stairs. It is called a *slinky*.

And so on and so forth.

I skip back a few pages and almost turn over the part that gave me nightmares, but force myself to stop and address its salient dates once more. A city leveled in one swoop is a neat equation, I think all would agree. But this business ... millions in *concentration camps* shrinking, puking, swung against walls, clutching at their throats over time ... such a long time ... this business with the Jews discomforts me. Six whole years? And not even a clean resolution, a simple goal achieved? This is a messy business. Too ornate, too Rococo. Give me ones and zeros, but no half-numbers. Please. This Hitler, with all his fancy symbols and uniforms and swirling promises and unfinished business ... he is a half-number if ever I saw one.

I am more like *Little Boy*. This Hitler, he is not like me.

If I am honest, I am disturbed not only by the untidiness, but by my dreams: Last night, I was one of them, numbers seared into my arm, shuffling, waiting. I do not want to be made a part of something. I am not Jacob. I am *Jack*.

I see rather than hear a soft flurry of fur, and look down to see a mouse taking interest in a husk of bread by the skirting board. Day-old, it looks like. I flick at the mouse; it moves before I am anywhere close to it, and then I eat the bread.

Someone has added a side note to one of the pages in a neat curlicue script. The gentleman we met in the alley last night? That Thomas Babcock, the engineer? Yes, I think so. The script is in his hand.

1862. A Victorion engineer invents the microchip.

Ah. That explains it, I think. He has been playing skulls and daggers, this Babcock. But ... I never much liked brassy gentlemen, nor any other of this Nation's punch-carded fancies. This does give me half an idea, however.

I look around for something to write with and recall a pen down in the shop for writing sums and purchases into the shop ledger. I hurriedly dress and run downstairs, the book tucked into my satchel. I jump half out of my skin when the bell rings—it is the delivery man with his cabette full of meat. My working day is begun, whether I like it or not. His iron horse champs and clacks its alloy hooves on the cobbles, platinum nostrils steaming the air, and I realize I am late to open up the shop, but I politely bid the man wait with a gesture then pull down the door-blind so he cannot see within.

Where is the ledger? It must be here somewhere. Ah— where it always is. On the marble work top, still stained with yesterday's juices of pork and tripe and mutton, next to the till. And there is the pen beside it.

With hands that do not shake I open the page where Babcock scrawled his piece, and where he wrote *A Victorion engineer invents the microchip* I cross it out and write underneath, in my best handwriting, though it is a little hurried, *no he don't.*

And as the ink spills from the pen onto the printed page of *The World's History: 3rd Edition,* it gets so rich and black and dark and inky like a cthonian abyss that I can hardly bear to look at it, and then I get the urge to lick it up, that ink, to get that oily black richness on my tongue and savor it and take it inside me and make me real and whole.

And then the bell jangles again, and I quickly blow on the ink to dry it then thrust the book into its satchel and hide it under the worktop. And then I open the door to bid welcome to the delivery man, and ...

He is very jolly, this morning, and doesn't seem to mind that I've kept him waiting. His little cart is piled high with crates of meat, good and fresh, and his mangy old shire horse has done a shit on the cobbles right outside my shop. Maybe horse dung *is* a good fertilizer, good for strawberries and what-not, but this is the East End. There ain't no strawberries round here.

"Might you help me unload, Sir? Near broke me back attending to a barn roof yesterday."

I step carefully around the dung and reach out for a crate before remembering I should really put on my butcher's apron, for the day has started, and like any other working day it will be filled with juice and blood. And then I remember that this jolly chap never had a shire horse. He ...

I look up in time to see the electric streetlights wink off one by one as dawn turns to day proper. There is no mushroom glow. The light of the lamps is warmly yellow, free of tendrils and enticements. Overhead I hear nothing save the squawk of a pigeon or two. No rumbling airships passing from London to Manchester.

There are no iron horses attached to the delivery man's cabette. His horse is made of sweat and meat and earth, and its ribs show through its stick-thin belly, and its nostrils are no longer fashioned from platinum, and it shits.

It is the book. I have undone Babcock's madness.

It is true, then. This world need not be as solid as it feels.

Two worlds? Which came first? I doubt they have a book of ours. We are but their footnotes.

I turn to the delivery man, who has unloaded all the meat without my help, and without any fuss. I follow him into my shop, note down the day's delivery in the ledger, and pay him his dues. With my butcher's tools arranged so neat and proper on the hooks above and behind my head, a notion comes to me that I could grab any knife, my favorite knife, and set to work on this jolly man; I could do a little night work in the full light of day, and jotting down a line or two in my book would make it as safe as a Sunday walk in a park to feed the ducks.

I don't, though, because this business is too much to take in all at once, and I've a shop to run.

The day drips as slow as treacle, full of mouths making noise. Everyone and everything seems so pallid. It is only when I am slicing meat and bone and twining it into parcels that I feel anything like awake. Finally, with a sigh of relief, I witness the electric—electric!—street lights come on, and then I allow myself to close shop a little early, swabbing down and removing my apron. For the hundredth time today I nudge the satchel under the worktop with my foot: It is still there.

Upstairs I settle down over a nice plate of kidneys, not too burnt with a refreshingly pissy tang, and read my favorite part in the history book. The part about me.

So. It seems that tonight, and again in twelve days' time, I'll go about my business once more. A tasty bit of night-work, by all accounts. Though he sticks to desiccated fact, it's clear the author struggles somewhat against a base urge to revel in the squirming and mewing, the pleas and the raising of the knife, the flinging of sheared skin over a butchered shoulder. Dark Annie and Long Liz, their names are, followed by Catherine Eddowes. It even tells me where to find them, and what time the coppers make their rounds so I can make good my escape. It's interesting to discover I apparently develop a modus operandi, I think the police call it. A signature to my work. I've certainly not stuck to a formula as of now. So long as the cuts are clean and the one is made into a zero, I haven't really thought about it. But this book says I have.

Another thing I like: No mention of Jacob. In this other world, I am always Jack.

My brow furrows—I can feel it—as I read the letter I'm meant to write to the police. It don't sound like me. But then again—in this book, life goes better for Jack. There are no police illustrated posters bearing a face not entirely unlike his own. He does his night-business and gets away with it, and probably sings as merrily as the day is long, and life is all roast duck in plum brandy. So I decide I had best stick to the script and buckle down and write the letter. Just to be sure.

Locating the pen from the shop I find some crumpled writing paper in my room and, in my very best hand—for it is after all a letter to Authority—I write:

Dear Boss,

I keep hearing that the police have caught me but they won't fix me just yet. I am down on the whores and I shant quit ripping them till I do get buckled. Grand work the last job was. I gave the lady no time to squeal. I love my work and want to start again. You will soon hear of me with my funny little games. I saved some of the proper red stuff in a ginger beer bottle over the last job to write with but it went thick like glue and I can't use it. Red ink is fit enough I hope ha ha. The next job I do I shall clip the lady's ears off and send to the police officers just for jolly wouldn't you.

Yours truly, Jack

They say I'm a doctor now ha ha.

On the whole it is a good letter, though he's got some spellings wrong, their Jack. I curse when I realize the ink I used was black. I will have to write it all again.

Once I'm done it's five in the morning and as something of an experiment I open the history book and draw a little line portrait of a man in the entry about me, and underneath I scrawl: *They say he looks like this. That's what they say.*

Does this book understand pictures as well as words? I think it might. It is a very clever item, and you never know your luck.

I'm interrupted by the insistent jingle-jangle of the shop bell downstairs, cutting sharp and loud through the early morning noises of the street. I carefully edge my way to the bedroom window and look out, tucking aside the lace curtain with as much movement as I dare. Surely not the police? They cannot have found me already?

I see five men below, all wearing hats tucked down low. There is something of a sameness to them for all their different raggedy suits, and I realize it is the Nichol Boys, Moses at their fore.

"Come on, you bugger." Moses cranes his neck to look up at my window and I dart back. I hope he has not seen me.

"He ain't there, Moses. We'll get him another day. You'll see."

I hear a thump on the shop door—it sounds like frustration, like defeat. Peering out I see Moses and his lot slink away, muttering. I would love to know what they are saying. There is a darkness in their huddle, and whatever their words are, accentuated by jabbing fingers, I do not think they bode well for me.

I had best stay out their way. But there is night-work to be done. The book tells me so, and I aim to be ready.

Packing my satchel with the book and a selection of fine sharp knives (from bone slicers to ones more suitable for detailed work) I put my butcher's leather apron on under my overcoat, and set out for the backyard of 29 Hanbury Street. That fat old whore Dark Annie will be waiting for me there, though she don't yet know it.

Now, I happen to know—for the Nichol Boys are proud to tell me of their sexual encounters, knowing how sick it makes me—that the front door of No. 29 opens into a narrow passageway that leads through the house to a small back yard beyond. That's where I'll find Annie, with her black skirt and red and white striped stockings. And she won't like it when I do.

And my, how I do laugh in the manner of a free man when I walk past a Great Scotland Yard poster and it's no longer my face on it, but Moses' ugly mug.

I'm quiet as a mouse as I slip into that back yard in Hanbury Street, and the shadows seem thick, somehow. Which is odd, because I've almost got used to how insipid this world looks now I've seen the book. Like a sepia watercolor when it used to be an oil painting. But the shadows look thick.

No matter. There's Annie, all drooped with age and bitter with it, squatting down to have a morning piss. Quiet as can be, I select a knife and have at her. It only takes a few minutes, but so much can be done in a minute or two if you've a mind to it. I see her insides, of course, and so does she before I'm done. Afterwards, I consult the book and do as it bids me with her body. I also tear three brass rings from her fingers and lay some of her womanly possessions near her body: Namely some pennies, two farthings and a comb. She won't need them no more.

And then them shadows move, and five figures unfurl from them like the petals of a dark flower, and all I can do is curse my ill fortune.

"Hello, Jacob," says Moses. Dawn light glints on his eyes and teeth. I may be covered in Annie's blood, but even so I offer my hand to shake like a gentleman. He don't take it, and I don't like the look of it hanging in empty space, so I put it away.

"Followed me, did you?"

"It wasn't so hard," says Moses. "I saw you had yourself a good laugh at my poster up there on the wall. Funny, wasn't it? Seeing as it used to be … yours?"

Ah. Now there's a pretty turn-out. A whole day at work, and not one customer remarked upon how their whole world had changed, with no more brassy gentlemen or iron horses or what-not. But Moses … He saw the book too, didn't he? He saw the writing. Even if he can't read.

"I been thinking," says Moses. "What happened last night, eh? A gentleman cuffed down in an alley, nothing new there. But he was a Royal engineer, see. Them's the world changers. And *my* world's gone and bloody changed, that's for sure. Why's my mug all over town where yours used to hang? You been ratting to the coppers? Telling tales?"

"What's in it for me?" I ask. "They'd hang me soon as see me."

But then Moses' attention is drawn to my satchel, and he looks hungry.

"What's in there?"

"Nothing."

"A book called *Mind Your Own Business*, is it?" he sneers. "Show it, then."

"Come and get it."

And then the Nichol Boys leap on me, but I am no longer there. I am on the other side of the back yard, spinning and flashing, a knife in each hand. That history book thought I was left-handed, but—here at least—I have full use of both my hands.

Let's not forget I taught these boys. With four raggedy men against one butcher strong and well-fed on meat every day, it's an ugly dance but I make short work of them.

At this rate, Great Scotland Yard will barely be able to find Annie Chapman's body in all the mess.

Moses is still alive. A little bit. He's got child's eyes now, not those of a man. I've seen this before in the death-moments. They go a little bit like a baby, a little bit like an animal. Not adult any more. Regressing. Shrinking from a one to a zero.

"Please," he whispers. "Please, Jack."

A bit late for that, ain't it, Moses?

"I'm not Jack," I say very kindly and warmly, like I'm teaching a young baby a new word, and my knife rises and falls one more time. "I'm Little Boy".

In a little while I'll kill two more women. Elizabeth Stride and Catherine Eddowes. And on a wall beside a doorway in Goulston Street I'll chalk the words:

The Juwes are / The men That / Will not / Be blamed / For nothing

But I don't see the point of it really. For one thing, I know how to spell 'Jews'. For another, what is this charade? Why am I bothering with this fancy rigmarole, this merry dance round Great Scotland Yard? All to kill a few women, not even a baker's dozen of them? Seems to me about as useful as what this Hitler chap set out to do, and no more clean and finished than the way he set about things. It seems to me that if you set out to do a job, you do it *right*.

This clever book is all it takes. With no pen to hand, I dip my finger in the blood of the nearest fallen body—man or woman? Hard to tell—and scrawl today's date and two words into the back pages of the history book.

Two little words. So nice and pure. The cleanest ones I know, and I've this book to thank for teaching them to me.

The book works fast, so on the very last letter I take my time in tracing its redness, and as my finger approaches the final curve I draw a deep breath and shut my eyes.

I am Jack. I am Little Boy. I am Zero.

Magda Knight is the founder of Mookychick Online, a UK feminist hub for alternative women. She writes horror and speculative fiction for assorted children, adults, and changelings. For what it's worth, she suspects "Saucy Jack" was probably a bootleg organ donor racket, but, you know, she doesn't lose sleep over it. She tweets and trills at @MagdaKnight, and discusses horror and YA in equal measure at http://www.magdaknight.com. When she grows up she would like to be a sword or a bear.

Chuck
Eric Dimbleby

Most nights Dusty got rip-roaring drunk and spoke to
Chuck. It was easy enough to do, since Chuck hung out on
Dusty's wall twenty four hours a day. There was no need to
travel or worry about a Hail Mary journey home from the bar.
There was nothing better than a bottle of merlot and some
palaver with ol' Chuck ... nothing better on a Monday night,
or a Tuesday night, or any night for that matter.

When they had first met, he called him Charlie. As in
*Charlie's in the trees, Charlie blew up half the guys in my platoon,
Charlie's got blood all over his pajamas, Charlie's behind me, Charlie's in
front of me, Charlie's every-fuckin'-where.*

But nowadays he was known only as Chuck. Conversation
flowed easier that way, when two grown men dispensed with
formality and adhered to nicknames.

"You think you must have enough, Dusty?" Chuck asked
in his broken English, lighting up another hand-rolled cigarette
and basking in the white plume of smoke that encircled his
conical coolie hat. Dusty hated his ridiculous hat.

Dusty slurped down the last inch of his warm merlot,
smiling with the reddened lips of a court jester. He placed the

glass on his kitchen table and pushed it away. He glowered at Chuck, noting, "You lost the right to have an opinion on me a long time ago, Chuck. You killed Mikey and Jawbone and all the rest of them. You slaughtered their asses right in front of me, and now you're monitoring my drinking? If I wanted that, I would have gotten *married* decades ago. Asshole."

Chuck grimaced, shrugging. This was their usual indulgence, spilling over with hatred and love … but mostly hatred. "I just don't want you to get as ugly as last night, Mr. Dusty. Let's go bed."

"I'll go to bed when I damn well please, you rice-eating motherfucker." Dusty's jaw flexed.

He had another bottle of wine, this one a chardonnay, in the basement. Dusty always kept backups. He drank wine on most evenings because beer made him belch and booze caused him to pass out early. Wine was the perfect medium. In addition, *classy* people drank wine. Not drunkards. Drunkards never really drank wine, especially ones who had served Uncle Sam's unappreciative ass in the 'Nam.

"You had enough," Chuck reminded him a second time. An ember flitted from the end of his cigarette. Chuck had been distracted while rolling it and had done a piss-poor job.

Dusty offered no response, turning and trudging down the steps of the basement for more wine. "Don't make me get the paint thinner," he mumbled as he fought to keep his balance.

"Oh, Dusty. You think you only one who suffer?"

When morning came again, Chuck fell silent, snoozing for a spell on Dusty's kitchen wall.

"I hope you like it, Dusty. I've got one just like it at my house. The artist is a vet, too."

"I see," Dusty replied, rubbing his red-speckled beard as he studied the birthday present. He hadn't expected visitors, but lo and behold, Hank had showed up at his door, just like he did every year. It wouldn't have been so bad if Dusty had enough consideration to return Hank the kindly favor on his own birthday. Hank wasn't that type though—he never did anything with hopes of reciprocity.

"The guy that did it lives in upstate New York. Made like four or five of these things last year. Sometimes it makes the nightmares worse, but most of the time I just like lookin' at it … you know, remembering how good it felt to shoot one of these grimy bastards in the face. Hear me knockin'?" Hank asked as Dusty pulled the bright blue wrapping paper from the gift.

It was a painting of a Vietnamese man, smoking a cigarette and squinting.

A tiny patch of thin white facial hair jutted out from the point of his gaunt chin. The hairs looked so real that Dusty wanted to grab a comb and straighten them out.

"I don't know, Hank."

Hank groaned. "Listen. Just hang it up. If it creeps you out too much, throw it on eBay. Or throw it in the trash for all I care. It only cost me fifteen bucks, so don't sweat it," Hank reasoned, grinning from ear to ear.

Dusty was fairly certain Vietnam hadn't inflicted the same sort of impression upon Hank as it had the rest of the guys he had served with. Hank acted almost as if he had never been there at all—like it was something that had occurred in a video game or a in a motion picture that he had once viewed.

Dusty nodded, studying the painting with a scrutinizing eye.

It was damn good. The realistic details were divine, he had to admit. The artist really knew his shit and flaunted it with every stroke of his brush.

The Vietnamese man (or *gook*, as Dusty was more than happy to employ in casual conversation, often drawing glares from strangers) was turned to the left hand side of the three foot by three foot painting. It was a side view of the S.O.B. and Dusty could not help but think that it would have been a perfect angle to put a bullet through the guy's head, from one ear to the other. *Pop-pop-pop-pop.* The man in the painting looked unsuspecting, his eyes squinting as he lit his cigarette. Dusty wondered if it was tobacco or cannabis. Charlie was known to indulge in cannabis on rare occasions, but he generally preferred the quick and easy high of chewing on Betel nuts.

Dusty ran his fingertips over the surface of the painting, noting the thick strokes with which the artist had employed his brush. The background was ashen colored, gradients of light and dark intermingling around the brim of his coolie hat. The bright orange ember at the end of his cigarette glowed and a subtle hint of smoke drifted between his emaciated fingers. The man looked as if he hadn't eaten in days. His lengthy wrinkles and serene eyes told Dusty that the man wasn't a war-worn soldier but a farmer who was well past his prime. He may have been a soldier in his earlier days, but he was more likely to hold a rake than a gun these days.

"What's the artist's name? This is so damn good," Dusty stated, suddenly realizing that he was mesmerized by the painting. It embarrassed him to be so taken away, but that didn't matter around Hank. They had been to hell and back together. A bit of spacey behavior was nothing to shy away from with a brother of that magnitude.

Hank snickered. "You're gonna love this one. Guy's name is Charles Gavin. But his friend's call him Charlie."

Dusty could not help but grin, still running his hand along the rough patterns of paint. "Thanks, Hank. This is something else. Really, I appreciate it."

"I see that you're enjoying it. Makes me glad," Hank replied, patting his former war buddy on the shoulder and joining him in careful observation of the artwork. Hank was always ready to change the conversation to areas that Dusty was unwilling to go most days. "You ever think about what our lives might have been like? You know, if we had snuck into Canada like the rest of those pussies."

"Every grunt thinks about that," Dusty said, unable to remove his eyes from the Vietnamese man's stricken face. He could almost smell the smoke of the cigarette wafting through his nose. The man was so real that the painting could barely hold on to his presence any longer.

Hank nodded, rubbing Dusty's shoulder. "We do, don't we? Every last one of us. It's what we do after the last shell casing hits the dirt. That shit defines us. You believe that much?"

Dusty didn't answer.

"You speak real good English, Chuck. Where did you pick that up?" Dusty asked, his speech slurring already. He didn't feel drunk, but he could hear his voice changing to a different octave. His inhibitions were dying small deaths in his swelling stomach.

"From mother. *You* mother."

Dusty threw his head back in laughter, spilling a dribble of wine on to the table. Red stains adorned the surface of the formerly white surface. Nowadays, it was closer to pink than anything else. If you didn't scrub out red wine right away, it was there for good, no matter what the surface was composed of.

"If you wanna talk about mothers, Chuck, then sure … let's go. Know what I did to your mother? I clubbed her in the forehead with my rifle. I stepped on her teeth until she was beggin' for her worthless life through red gums. I took her soul, Chuckie. I took her soul and I put it on wheat toast and shat it out the next day. How you like that?" he asked, standing up from the table, wine glass still clutched in his fist. He swayed and drew closer to the painting.

"You so angry," Chuck observed, igniting a fresh smoke. Chuck was forever lighting up … it was his primary vice. It wasn't as if paintings could get lung cancer, so there was never any reason not to. Dusty had cut out the cigarettes in the early nineties and subsequently informed people that he was as fit as a fiddle. He never mentioned the wine because that wasn't really a drawback to his health. Wine came from grapes and grapes were fruit. If you were going to judge every wine connoisseur, you would also have to walk around the playground and slap the box of grape juice out of every child's chubby little hands as well.

"Can't you just go back to hiding in the damn trees like you're supposed to? Leave me alone. I never asked for you in my life and you just showed up. *Twice.*" Dusty blinked slowly, and he felt his world starting to spin. That meant it was time to slow down and get his white pajamas on.

"Call children, Dusty. They miss you," Chuck said, tilting his head to the side so he could make eye contact with his human counterpart. Dusty hated direct eye contact, but every now and then Chuck employed that strategy, and it never ceased to drive a wedge into his stomach. The bastard had ugly eyes, to say the least. Not to mention that Dusty had no interest in emotionally connecting with the pajama-wearing murderer of stand-up Americans.

"Go to hell," he snarled back at the askew painting on his wall.

"We already there."

Dusty's forehead thudded against the pinkish surface of his kitchen table.

He dreamed of gunshots, screams, rustling jungles, and gaping wounds that spilled blood until there was no more blood to be spilled.

When Dusty woke the following morning he wiped the drool away from his chin and plodded into the kitchen. He turned on the coffee pot, which he had forgotten to preprogram the night before. Dishes were stacked in the sink and there were no clean ones to be found. He cooked his eggs in the skillet and planned to eat them from that vessel as well, which was far easier than washing all the dishes. When the coffee was done brewing, he poured himself a tall mug and glared at the empty wine bottles on top of his counter. They never seemed to go away—always waiting for him when morning came. He could hardly ever remember them coming into his house, but he could always remember them leaving, swinging in shopping bags at his sides and being dumped into the recycling bin.

Making his way back to the kitchen table, he wiped away food particles from some mystery meal he had eaten the night before. With a steaming coffee and lukewarm eggs before him, Dusty sighed and said a prayer, pressing his hands together at his chest.

He opened his eyes, swigged his coffee, and looked up at Chuck, ready to enjoy the silence of another hot summer day.

But Chuck wasn't there.

"Chuck?" he asked, his eyes affixed to the bland ashen paints on the devoid canvas. The initials of the artist still remained in the corner, the only sure sign that the painting had not been swapped out by Hank while Dusty slept. Even still, it was possible. Hank had never been much of a prankster, but he would have been the only one slick enough to pull it off. For that matter, Hank was just about the only human being Dusty ever associated with anymore.

The bathroom sink turned on for a moment and then turned off again.

"Chuck?" he called out again, his coffee cup jittering in his hand. He felt as if he would drop it at any moment. He put it down on the table with fear of the mess he might make.

From the corner of his eye, a shadow lurched across the kitchen. By the time Dusty's eyeballs caught up with the shape it was gone again, slipping somewhere behind the stove. Dusty stood up from his chair and approached the stove, pulling it back from the wall. He glanced over the top of it, but found only dust bunnies and a tea bag he had dropped several months earlier. "Are you back there, Chuck?"

Chuck said not a word, but another shadow danced across Dusty's peripheral vision, this time moving into the living room with swift determination.

Dusty followed behind, trembling at the thought that Chuck had escaped from his painting.

Was he still drunk? He didn't feel drunk, but it was possible that he had finally pickled his brain. He always knew that it would happen, and that it was just a question of *when*. "Get back in the painting, Chuck!" he shouted, his head throbbing from such an exertion at such an early hour.

Dusty looked behind the couch.

Behind the television.

Behind the rocking chair.

Every time he pulled out a new piece of furniture, Chuck moved to another spot at the corner of Dusty's eyeball, taunting him in silence.

"I'm gonna blow your goddamned head off, Chuck. You watch me."

Chuck remained silent.

"Say something, you son-of-a-bitch gook!"

The days and months and years passed and Chuck never returned to his painting.

The children left messages on Dusty's answering machine, but he had no intention of returning their calls. He could barely remember what they looked like, and he suspected that if one more year went by he might forget their names altogether. Donnie was a plumber. Trish was a ... he wasn't quite sure what Trish did these days. Whatever it was, he was certain that she was well accomplished because she had always been a good girl.

Nobody mattered now.

Only Chuck.

Dusty quit drinking in July, hoping that Chuck would return to his home and stop haunting his every waking hour, but it didn't work. Chuck actually turned sneakier without the red wine swimming around in Dusty's skull. By August, he was drinking the stuff again, white and red alike. By September, he gave up his classy ploy and turned back to vodka as his staple. It had served him well during his youth, and it would serve him well in his final years. His liver cried out in pain but he could not hear those cries, for he was too numb to the real world.

One morning, while chasing Chuck around the second floor, Dusty stopped dead in his tracks, vomiting red slime on to the unkempt carpet. He hadn't imbibed any red wine in more than a week (*vodka*, only rotgut *vodka*), so he knew what it was. He was bleeding on the inside. *But aren't we all?* he asked himself as he pondered the fact that he was about to meet his maker.

On his hands and knees, he cried out to Chuck, "See what you did to me, you rice-munching prick?"

And that was the moment when Chuck stopped running and hiding and lurking and spying.

Chuck rubbed Dusty's back, the farmer's thin fingers sending chills through his spine. "You kill my family, Dusty."

"Eat shit and die." Dusty rubbed the collar of his bathrobe against his chin, hoping to absorb some of the blood. It was a mess.

The bony hand caressed Dusty's spine as he blurted out another wave of crimson on to the carpet. He looked up at Chuck, at the old geezer's wrinkled face, and wondered if he could kill him. It wouldn't take much to strangle Chuck, not at his age. He made a gesture toward grabbing his archenemy but fell short.

"Cannot hurt me, Dusty. Already did. You kill my family and now I watch you die."

Dusty rolled on to his side, wiping the blood from his mouth. "And I bet you want forgiveness for what I did? I did what I was ordered to. You would have done it to me first, if you'd had the chance."

Chuck nodded. "You right."

"So where the hell does that leave us, Chuck?" Dusty queried, glaring up at the bag of phantom bones before him. Why couldn't he have just stayed in the goddamned painting like he was supposed to?

"That leave us here. Two old men in pajamas."

Dusty couldn't help but smile. It felt good to smile.

Good ol' Chuck was back.

Dusty's heart skipped a beat before it stopped.

Chuck slithered back into his painting.

Eric Dimbleby lives in Brunswick, Maine, with his wife and three children. He has published three novels since 2011 and has been published in more than twenty-five anthologies. To learn more about his collected works and of upcoming events, please visit www.ericdimbleby.com.

Chiyoung and Dongsun's Song
T. T. Zuma

An English Translation of the Korean Folk Tale

As was the custom in the sixteenth century, the villagers of
Hahoe, Korea, were busy making festival preparations for
Solnal, the ceremonial holiday that ushered in the New Year.
The three-day celebration called for much work; the men
gathered food for the great feast while the women joined
circles to weave decorations for the celebratory dance held on
the final day.

But on this late afternoon, as the men harvested the grain
and the women worked the straw, Lee Chiyoung and Kim
Dongsun were not among them.

Chiyoung was the pretty and precocious daughter of one
of the more honored clans in the village and Dongsun was the
hard-working son of a farming family. It was Chiyoung who
had suggested a meeting at the clearing in the forest bordering
their village and Dongsun all too willingly agreed.

Dongsun, barely able to contain his excitement, had
slipped away from his work group and arrived early.

He leaned back against a large boulder in the middle of the
clearing, loosened the *jeogori* that draped his upper body, and
waited anxiously for Chiyoung. He had dreamt of her often,

spending many an evening on his cot with a hand slipped into his *baji* while fondling himself. Earlier that morning, when she teasingly offered to meet him in the woods, Dongsun believed his fantasies had come true.

Though Dongsun believed he truly loved Chiyoung, he was no fool. It was no secret that Chiyoung delighted in exploiting her desirability, often meeting with the other boys in the village, sometimes even the men. For his part, Dongsun understood he was merely one of many apples on a tree waiting to be picked. However, Dongsun had hoped that after this meeting his love for Chiyoung would be requited, that she would forsake her ways and chose him as her life partner.

Dongsun's thoughts turned from her promiscuity to her emerald eyes, her full lips, and her large breasts. His anticipation grew.

While Dongsun waited impatiently for her arrival, Chiyoung stood before a long reflecting glass inspecting her features. As an only child, Chiyoung was fortunate enough to have her own private area and, as the grandchild of a village elder, she was blessed with many gifts. Adornments for her long braided hair and colors for her face were the most common and she put some of these to use knowing with certainty that they would assist with her seduction. Believing she could not improve upon her facial beauty, she lowered her head and focused on her clothing.

She inspected her *jeogori*. The blouse clung tightly and she was satisfied with the way it highlighted her breasts. Then, Chiyoung spun around rapidly causing the *chima* hanging from her waist to swish about, exposing her legs suggestively. Chiyoung reached back and moved her braid so it hung before her, and then she caressed it with both hands as she gazed at herself in the glass. Chiyoung smiled approvingly at her reflection. She hoped that Dongsun was worth all the effort. Content with her appearance, Chiyoung quickly draped on a *durumagi* to provide some warmth and then stealthily made her way through the village and to the clearing.

Eagerly, Dongsun watched as Chiyoung emerged from the wooded path. As she strode toward him his heart leapt, and when she smiled, everything else vanished except her face.

"I don't have much time," Chiyoung whispered as she approached, and then she drew him near.

Their arms swiftly encircled one another and they bent their heads forward until their lips touched. Dongsun parted his teeth slightly when he felt her probing tongue.

Suddenly, they both paused and stood rigid. A rustling of branches somewhere close by drew their attention. They broke apart nervously, surveying the area for onlookers. They saw no one.

Dongsun, eager to continue embracing, proclaimed it a deer and that there was nothing to fear. With a laugh, Chiyoung responded, "It might be a Dokkaebi. He's a trickster and we'd best be careful."

Dongsun knew the lore of the Dokkaebi, as did every child who grew up in the village. He had always dismissed it as an old women's folk tale. The Dokkaebi were imps who would grant a wish for a favor given, but the wish was not always granted in the way one had hoped for. It was the generosity of the favor and the whim of the Dokkaebi that determined the outcome.

But the last thing Dongsun wanted to be thinking about right now was of imaginary imps, so he once again embraced Chiyoung. To his relief, she allowed herself to be held and relaxed in his grip.

Chiyoung surrendered herself, but not because it was Dongsun holding her. It could have been any boy and she would have done the same.

It was soon after her first bleeding when she found herself craving the touch of a boy. She had gone out of her way to initiate physical contact with them, sometimes to the point of making them feel uncomfortable. As time passed those cravings grew, and a young girl's yearnings for affection were replaced with a woman's desire for more.

Chiyoung broke from Dongsun's embrace, and then, seductively, lowered herself until she was on her knees. With practiced fingers she slid her hands to the top seam of his *baji* and untied its drawstring. Chiyoung folded her fingers around his waist and pulled the *baji* down around Dongsun's ankles.

All afternoon Dongsun had thought of nothing else but this encounter. Even though he had fantasized that Chiyoung would use her mouth on him, he was unprepared for the amount of sexual tension he was experiencing. He had to concentrate very hard to keep his seed from spilling as Chiyoung lowered his baji.

What Dongsun hadn't anticipated however, was Chiyoung's abrupt halt of all activity after his manhood was exposed. She knelt before him unmoving, without sound.

Confused, he waited.

After a moment, Chiyoung rose from her kneeling position. With a deep frown etched on her face she made quick eye contact with Dongsun and then looked away.

Dongsun's concern about spilling his seed evaporated.

"I am sorry, Dongsun," Chiyoung explained coldly, "but you are too small. I need something larger to satisfy me. You should try with some of the other girls in the village who have not been with boys yet. They may be suitable for someone of your size."

Abruptly, Chiyoung turned from him and then hurried down the path back to the village.

Dongsun's confusion turned to shock, and then disappointment, and finally embarrassment. Still standing against the boulder with his baji draped around his ankles, he did the only thing he could think to do. Dongsun cried.

And that's when a Dokkaebi made its appearance.

The imp, dressed lightly for the season and carrying a small club, sprinted from the path and walked directly up to Dongsun. "I saw what happened, boy, and I will say that you have made my day a good one as I admit to being amused."

Dongsun wiped his tears away with the back of his hand and gaped at the creature, until finally, curiosity got the best of him. Dongsun asked the creature if the tales he had heard as a child about the Dokkaebi were true.

"They are true young man. I will grant you your wish, but I will need a favor to my liking."

"I want to be the one she desires," Dongsun sobbed.

"And what can you give me in trade?" the imp asked.

Dongsun had nothing of value to offer the Dokkaebi and despair gripped him. Then, looking at the creature, he noticed that the imp was poorly dressed for the cold.

"I will give you my *jeogori*," Dongsun offered.

The Dokkaebi frowned. "That is the deal then?"

"Yes, it is all I have to offer."

The last thing Dongsun remembered before the world turned black was the imp rushing at him with his club held high.

Chiyoung woke from an uneasy sleep.

After abandoning the tryst with Dongsun, she hurried back home and lay on her mattress. Then, using the images of a man who had once satisfied her, she administered the relief she had so desperately sought from Dongsun. Finally sated she napped, but instead of a restful slumber she tossed and turned. Chiyoung's dreams were of Dongsun and the horrible way she had treated him.

It was the music from the festivities that woke her. The rhythm of drums and the reedy sounds of wind instruments had invaded her dreams, and slowly, sleep broke its claim on her. As she awoke, Chiyoung felt odd, different somehow. As she tried to determine the nature of the change she noticed an unusual pressure on her thigh. Believing it to be an insect, she absent mindedly reached down to lift her *chima* and remove the object, but when her fingers brushed it, she gasped. Startled, she jumped up and ran to the reflective glass and then tore her *chima* from around her waist. She stared wide-eyed at her reflection. She inhaled deeply and then held her breath. Her reflection stunned and scared her.

Hanging down and making contact with her thigh was a penis. A very large penis. And it was attached to her groin.

On the verge of panic, she reached down and moved the penis slightly to the side. She noticed a large, bulging sack of flesh drooping low behind it. Cupping the sack with her hand, she slowly lifted it, feeling the relief of a small amount of weight between her legs. She also felt the swell of two, round objects nestling in her palm.

Chiyoung was in denial. This couldn't be possible! She

removed her hand from the testicles and gripped the penis, angling it up toward her for a better look.

Then she screamed.

There was a face on the tip of the penis.

It was Dongsun's.

As she peered at it in horror, Chiyoung heard squeaking. She froze momentarily with the realization that the face was talking to her. In a daze, she bent down to hear his voice.

"Do you love me now Chiyoung?" he asked timidly.

Somehow, Chiyoung understood. Tears flowed down her cheeks as she gazed at Dongsun. One of them landed on his face and she used her fingers to wipe him dry. Then she stroked him gently, comforting him.

Dongsun began to rise toward her.

Chiyoung thought about the life ahead of her and how it would be different. She realized that somehow this was all her fault. Maybe it was penance for her sinful ways.

But those thoughts soon vanished as Dongsun, now fully erect and smiling, stared at her with eyes that begged for acceptance.

And, he felt so good.

Chiyoung grinned, wiped away her remaining tears with one hand and answered his question. "Yes Dongsun," she moaned as she stroked him harder, "I think I do love you."

Not too far away, standing by a boulder in the woods, a Dokkaebi, wearing a *jeogori* that was much too large for him, laughed like the devil.

Anthony Tremblay writes reviews for Horror World and Cemetery Dance under the pen name T. T. Zuma. Anthony has only recently begun writing horror with *An Alabama Christmas,* his first professionally published story. He has published technical papers, has written one novel, and has other stories currently on shortlists with two anthologies.

On the Hooks
Keith Minnion

Mal usually ended his hunts by sunrise, after the juiciest game had retreated to their burrows and dens to sleep away the heat of the day. This hunt, this dawn, he found himself farther from the Nest than he had ever been before. He paused under trees edging an open ridge, the smooth stone loose in his hand, and watched the sun slowly clear the skeletal silhouette of a huge, kudzu-choked wheel in the ruined amusement park across the valley below. He was just old enough to remember …

Ahh. Enough. The past was just old stories told by old men and women around the community pot, after all. It was something his father had clung to, but it wasn't for him. Not now; not here; not living through *this*. The stone fit his hand perfectly; all of his hunting stones did. He pocketed it, bent and gathered up his kills, then his sack of trinkets, and made his way back to the Nest.

He didn't see any of the sentries in the outer ring, but then, he wasn't supposed to. He did see Sam, however, one of the inner ring sentries, standing as still as the tree beside her. He nodded as he passed.

"Traveling light today, Mal," she called after him. "Getting too old for this shit, eh?"

"The elk is right behind me," he shot back over his shoulder.

Sam's quick laughter echoed through the big trees.

His boots left the carpet of dead leaves to scattered, and then broken asphalt, and the stockade wall of the Nest emerged through the new growth of trees and the remains of the town that had once existed in this place. He hailed the gatekeeper, who cranked the gate open just wide enough for him to slip through. The Commons beyond was alive with morning activity, and all eyes fell on him, on what was in his hands and hanging from his belt. Only three today, Mal? the eyes said, and scrawny vermin at that?

He gave the two woodchucks to Mary in the smoky day-kitchen. "Huh," she said, giving the opossum on his belt a hard look. The large iron hooks hanging from the beam behind her were all empty. There had been no big game kills, no captures, no deaths for almost a week. The hunger in the Nest was almost palpable.

"I'll send over the leftovers with Gwen," he said. "Keeping the pelt, though."

"Huh," she said again.

Spoils of the hunt, he thought; screw her.

His father's house—strike that—*his* house now, was near the center of the Nest, next to the Hall. Its brick walls were still solid, its roof well patched, and the fireplace worked. He blinked as he entered the flickering light and shadow, and held up his kill.

"A fat one," his sister said, wiping her forehead as she turned from the hearth fire.

"I told Mary you'd put what's left into the pots."

"And I'll make sure it actually goes into a pot instead of into *her*." Gwen winked as she took the opossum from him, and went outside to skin and gut it.

"Da! Da!"

He went into the next room, smiling. His daughter Dorothy's little bed was tucked up near the warm chimney bricks, and in the middle of the gathered blankets the tiny four-year-old raised her thin arms. "You're back," she cried. "You're back!"

"And when haven't I?" Mal crouched, buried his nose in her chestnut hair, and gave her his most tender hug. "And I always bring supper with me, don't I? Today it's Mr. Possum."

"I think I can eat today," she said.

"Of course you can, of course you can." He settled on the side of her bed. "So how is my little Dot this morning?"

She gave a quick shriek of laughter at the familiar joke. "I'm not a dot! I'm Dorothy!"

"Dorothy?" At first he looked dubious, but then he grinned. "Why of course you are! Did I ever tell you that Dorothy is my very favorite name?"

She nodded vigorously. "It was Mamma's name too."

"Yes it was." He straightened her top blanket. "Yes it was." Then he pointed. "Do you have to …?"

"I went potty before. I don't have to go now."

"Good for you." He brushed her soft cheek with a cracked, callused finger.

"Where's your bag?"

"In the other room."

"Did you find anything new?"

"Besides Mr. Possum?"

"Oh, Da! You know what I mean!"

He nodded. "Three things. Three thing-a-jings worth taking to the engineers."

"Important thing-jings?"

"I think there's copper in them. Copper's always important."

"Can I see them?"

"They're dirty, Sweet-pea."

"I don't care. I promise I won't even touch them."

He hesitated.

"Please, Da?"

He heaved himself upright, went and retrieved the sack from the outer room. Settling on his daughter's bed again, he pulled the things out and arranged them on the floor at his feet.

Dorothy looked at them with wide eyes. "Can we play the game? Can we?"

"That was Grandpa's game, Sweet-pea. I'm not very good

at it."

"You're good! You can try! Please?" She pointed. "What's this one?"

He held it up. It seemed complete, but the glass was cracked. "It is an electronic screen," he said. "A kind of computer, I think." He scratched away some dried mud to reveal the design on the back. "Yes," he said, "a kind of computer."

"What'd it do?"

"It told stories."

"How?"

"With pictures. Probably with sounds too." He tapped the broken screen surface. "Here."

"Needs lec—lec—"

"Electricity. Yes indeed. From a big battery inside. The engineers will like getting that too, I think."

She pointed to the next item her father had scavenged from the woods. "What's this?"

"I'm not sure." He picked it up by its handle. It was made of glossy, lavender-colored plastic, had a motor of some kind in a round housing—good copper wire in there, for sure. The handle had a trigger, and a short, wide tube came out the other end.

"It's a pretty color, Da."

"I know. That's one reason why I picked it. I knew you'd like the color."

"If the engeers don't need the pretty part, can I have it?"

"I'll ask them."

She pointed to the third item. "What's this one?"

Ahh. A safe one. He knew what this one did. "That, my darling girl, is a cooking pot, a …" and then the word came, unbidden, long forgotten until he said it, "a crock pot."

She hooted with laughter. "A crocked pot?"

"A nice one too."

"What'd it do?"

"It cooked nice stews."

"With lectricy? Not with a fire?"

"Oh no. With a cord that plugged right into the wall."

"Like there?" She pointed to an old plastic outlet box in the wall near her bed; empty of course, the metals scavenged long ago.

"Yes indeed. Just like there."

"Aunty makes stews, but she's not plugged in the wall!"

He chuckled dutifully. "No," he said, "she's not."

His daughter lay back then, and he saw she was starting to get tired. "Did you say you caught something for Aunty's stew, Da?"

"Yes I did, Sweet-pea. One of my stones knocked Old Mr. Possum right on the head, and I invited him to supper."

"Is he like Old Mr. Squirrel?"

"Hmm. Cousins, I think. Just as tasty, anyway." He rubbed his belly. "Makes me hungry, just like you."

Dorothy nodded seriously, almost frowning. "I think I will be. I hope so. Aunty Gwen found some big onions. She showed me."

"Onions make the stew!" He paused. "Game over?"

She nodded. "I'm sleepy now. Thanks for playing with me, Da."

He reached out, moved a stray lock of hair off her cheek, and hooked it behind her ear. Even in the half-light he could see the circles under her eyes. They were like bruises. "You want to take a nap now, baby?"

Her voice was soft. "I'm not a baby."

"Of course not."

"I'm a big girl."

"Of course you are. How about just a short nap, then? Aunty Gwen's making you that stew, remember."

"Maybe later?" An expression of hope smoothed her forehead, for just a moment. "Maybe I'll be hungry later."

Mal continued stroking her hair, knowing she loved it. Her eyes closed, a faint smile on her lips. When he finally got up from her little bed, her breathing was regular, and the smile remained.

In the other room, Gwen said, "Sleeping again?"

"Yeah."

"Best thing for her. You should rest too. You've been out all night."

"Yeah," he said.

Nightfall.

Mal went out into the cool evening, hunting stones in his pockets, blade in its belt sheath, empty sack over his shoulder, doing his best to ignore the small crowd at the day-kitchen pots waiting for their share of the communal supper, such as it was. The hooks behind them were still empty.

"Something big tonight, Mal," an old, reedy voice called as he passed. "Something with meat on the bone."

Another old voice cut in: "Oh shut up, you old witch! He's doing his best. They all are."

Mal lowered his head and strode through the gate.

The moon was high and nearly full, which was both a blessing and a curse. It was only blind luck, a few hours in, that sent a stupid tabby cat bounding into the open within range, and his first throw neatly caught and crushed its skull. Cat meat was no one's first choice, but flesh was flesh, food was food. He carried that carcass alone on his belt for the next three fruitless hours as the moon tracked slowly across the sky to the west, and a faint smudge of violet showed on the horizon in the opposite side of the sky.

He stood again on the exposed ridge as he had the previous day, looking out at the ruins of the amusement park in the valley, and the great wheel standing stark against the pre-dawn sky. What had it been called? Ferris? Ferris Wheel. And that huge decayed structure to the right of it ... rolling something. Roller coasting. Roller coaster. They should get a retrieval team together, see if there was anything worthwhile in the park that hadn't already been scavenged by other Nests. Dangerous, though. Everything was dangerous, this far out.

Mal hesitated as the paling horizon grew. God only knew what lived down there, in the valley. One scrawny cat on his belt, his trinket sack empty ...

"Fuck it," he muttered. Maybe he would get something on the way home. He turned abruptly, back to the trees.

A quick breath of air touched his cheek at the same instant he saw something flash past, and then there was an arrow buried in a tree trunk just beyond him. He dropped to his stomach without even thinking, into the cover of the tall weeds. He crawled to the tree, reached up to pull the arrow free, and then—thunk!—there was another arrow, no more than an inch from his outstretched hand, quivering in the tree bark beside its twin.

Screw this.

He took off in a crouching, dodging run, concentrating on putting as many solid tree trunks as possible between his back and the open air of the ridge. At some point his boot caught the edge of an old foundation and he tumbled in a bruising sprawl into prickle-bushes and broken concrete. That was when, not even an arm's reach from his face, he saw the half-buried baby.

It took him a moment to realize it wasn't a real baby. It was a toy, a life-sized doll, nothing more than pink plastic under the grime and dried mud. Its hair had once been blond; one blue eye was open, the other closed, winking at him. He rolled onto his knees, worked the doll free from the muck, and was reaching for his sack when he heard someone suddenly sprinting through the woods behind him.

He rose, pivoted, and pulled his blade free in one fluid movement. He met the onrushing figure with a full body block, knocking the attacker's blade arm aside with his left as he buried his own blade into the attacker's belly, lifting him, making his gut cut rip, and using the attacker's forward momentum to throw him aside, onto the broken concrete. As he straddled him he continued cutting, up under the ribs, piercing the heart to stop the struggling and blood spray. Blood was too valuable to waste.

He stood finally, listened, and scanned the woods for another one. For more than one. But no one came. After a silent interval, a bird warbled a short song, and another answered.

Mal looked down at his kill. It was a boy of ten or twelve, wearing nothing but a pair of ratty pants ripped off at mid-thigh. His face, chest and arms were tattooed in red geometric patterns, a darker red than his open gut. He was thin, but there was enough meat on him. More than enough.

He debated following the track back, find the bow and quiver the boy must have stashed along the way, maybe even get the two arrows in the tree on the ridge. A prize like that was more valuable than the meat. The dawn continued to unfold. If he was to do it, it had to be now. He put the doll baby in his sack, laid it beside the body, and covered them both with leaves. Then he turned to retrace the boy's track and disappeared into the woods.

Everyone ended up on the hooks eventually, either from battle, or the hunt, or natural death.

Everyone.

Mary hung Mal's eviscerated kill by its sternum, with a pan underneath to catch anything that hadn't already drained. Several people stood nearby, whispering.

One of them, one of the old hunters, slapped Mal on the back. "Good work," he said.

Mary pointed to the cat still hanging on Mal's belt. "That too, or are you taking it home?"

He untied it and handed it over. Mary took a sniff, wrinkling her nose. "Have to boil this one," she said.

The old hunter said, "Gil in the Armory says you brought in a hardwood bow and near full quiver of arrows."

"Yeah," Mal said. "I got lucky."

The old hunter nodded to the body on the hook. "Was his?"

"Yeah."

"He missed, then."

"Yeah." Mal looked at him briefly. "Twice."

From the inner room his daughter called, "Is that Da, Aunty? Is that Da?"

Mal touched his sister's arm. "She sounds stronger. Did she eat?"

Gwen's eyes fairly glowed. "Full bowl of porridge. I put some bits of meat in it. She finished it all." She gestured to his sack. "You bring anything back besides that big kill I saw on the hook?"

Mal had cleaned the doll in a stream; it looked almost new. He hadn't felt this feeling—what was it? Excitement? Joy?—in a long time, a very long time. "Yeah," he said. "I got something."

"Good. She wants to play Dad's game again."

He smiled. "Me too," he said. "Me too."

 Keith Minnion sold his first short story to *Asimov's SF Adventure Magazine* in 1979. Although not exactly the world's most prolific writer, he has sold well more than a dozen stories and novelettes since and has a novel called *The Boneyard* coming out from Bad Moon Books this autumn. Keith has illustrated for various magazine and book publishers since the early 1990s and has done extensive graphic design work for the Department of Defense. He is a former schoolteacher and officer in the US Navy and currently spends his days drawing, painting, and writing.

Jasmine and Opium
Rebecca L. Brown

Lick her. Bite her. Gnaw her, if you like. The world is full of women just like her, all waiting to be tasted …

It was the way they smelled that made him feel that way, the delicious blending of skin and perfume that made his mouth water. Sandalwood and rose or tropical breeze—there was nothing Gray wanted more than to press his teeth into their soft-scented bodies.

Was her hair blonde? He would never remember afterward. She was a midnight feast of jasmine and opium—a hint of detergent clung to her clothes. He could tell that she drank red wine—had done so recently. Perhaps a few stray droplets still clung to her lips …

Gray followed her—he had to. The texture of her in the air caught at him like hooks. Along Cathedral road and onto the High Street. It hurt too much to pull himself away.

He almost lost her in the crowd—the intermingling of sour sweat and boredom flooded out his senses, sending him reeling.

A woman who had pleasured herself—the scent still clung to her fingers.

An unwashed man with crumpled clothes, and the stubbed-out end of a cigarette cradled in one hand.

Jasmine and opium—she turned toward the castle and Gray followed her.

Following.

Always following.

Did she slow a little as they passed through the worst of the crowd?

She wants me, Gray thought. *This is what she wants.*

There was a freshness to her which he had missed before, as if she was freshly stepped from a shower. Spring rain in Autumn. An unexpected delight. Gray walked a little faster, no longer caring if she noticed him. She didn't seem to—or, if she did, she didn't care. If anything, she slowed a little more.

Come closer—the clit-clat of her shoes on the pavement.

Devour me—the heady blend of opium and jasmine.

She was so close that Gray could taste the texture of her hair—each separate strand, all rough-rubbing over and around one other. There were flowers in her shopping bag—or else there had been. The sap from the stems had soaked into the fabric, souring in the heat. Decay and decline. The subtlest of undertones. Gray allowed himself a moment to enjoy the contrast.

… And then he tasted her.

He hadn't meant to. Not really. Had not even meant to follow her as such.

Their steps matched. He pressed his face against her neck.

His breath.

His lips.

His tongue.

He felt the tendons tense inside her neck then ease. Slowly—almost as if she could relax them consciously, one at a time. The ends of her hair tickled his cheek, curling into the scoop of his throat.

Delicious. She was more than he could ever have hoped for. He wanted more. *Needed* more.

Come home with me. You feel so cold. Let me taste you. Enjoy you. That was what Gray wanted to tell her.

She held him there. Not by force—in fact, she barely moved. Where his lips and tongue had touched her, they seemed to stick. Flesh fixed onto ice cold metal. It hurt too much to pull away.

When she started to walk again, he went with her. Where else could he go? Where else was there?

She didn't speak. He could feel her smiling.

He could taste her as they walked. Smell her too—and only her. The scents of jasmine and opium—and, underneath them, something darker.

Rebecca L. Brown is a British writer, businesswoman, and model based in Cardiff. Her vampire trilogy, starting with *Fever in the Blood*, is available on Amazon.com. For more news and updates on Rebecca's writing, why not visit her blog: rebeccalbrownupdates.wordpress.com.

The Bore
John McIlveen

Munroe Dolan sensed his wife's frustration even through a buffer of sleep. Rising from soporific depths, he opened his right eye and regarded Mekisha Dolan's subtle profile through a hazy curtain. Backlit by the alarm clock, which glowed 2:47 in jaundiced numerals, the side of her face nearest to him was mostly in shadows. He saw an open eye staring at the ceiling.

"You all right?" Munroe asked.

Mekisha released an exasperated sigh, glanced at her husband, and quickly returned her focus to the ceiling.

"Yeah," she replied. "Work issues on my mind; they're giving me insomnia."

Mekisha had become a freelance photographer four years earlier. She had quit her job at the *Boston Herald* after her first photography book *Love Is in the Air*—a collection of gorgeous nude men and women posed in evocatively compromising positions while suspended in free air—garnered generous praise and some *supposedly* revered and unpronounceable photography award Munroe could never recall for the life of him. Two similar flesh-laden books later, Mekisha demanded and received a handsome advance from one of the *big* publishing houses, whose name also eluded Munroe. Was it Abrams or Little, Brown? He was never sure.

A slow but perpetual flow of admirers—most he felt were unsavory men who probably had hairy palms and were proud of their rankings on the "sexual offenders list"—phoned or appeared on the doorsteps toting copies of Mekisha's work, breathlessly soliciting inscriptions.

First printings of *Love Is in the Air*, especially signed, brought in insane bids on eBay, sometimes nearly half his weekly take-home. Not bad, considering it was released at $49.95, and was still found at certain remainder houses for $9.99. Go figure.

The notoriety of being a celebrated photographer offered Mekisha a hectic but enviable lifestyle, clicking glasses with the elite and rubbing elbows with the famous. Her latest endeavor, cleverly titled *In the Jeans*, was a collection of beautiful, denim-clad rich and famous relatives, ranging from risqué to ridiculous.

Munroe, on the other hand, was just an accountant. This pretty much summed up his career ... if you'll pardon the pun.

"What's the disaster du jour?" he asked Mekisha.

"Oh, two problems actually," she sighed again. "In three days we have a cover shoot for *In the Jeans* with Goldie Hawn and Kate Hudson. I have to order a cloth backdrop and can't decide whether to go with black or red."

"Black," Munroe suggested.

"Why?"

"Because they're all light-haired and -skinned; they'll stand out more."

"But red is a sensual color," Mekisha said.

"Then go with red."

Mekisha sighed yet again.

"The other problem?" Monroe asked.

"We don't know whether to go with the Hilton or the Olsen sisters on the back cover."

"The Olsen sisters! Wouldn't that be like child porn?"

"They're well over twenty!"

"No shit," he said. "Still, I'd go with the Paris and Nicky Hilton; you expect to see them nude. Mary-Kate and Ashley may stir negative press."

"Yeah, but sell a million," Mekisha said.

"Then put them on the front cover."

"You're not helping," she said.

They were silent few a few moments.

"God, I'm wired!" said Mekisha.

Another long silence followed. When she looked at Munroe he was eyeing her appraisingly.

"What?" she guardedly said.

"Maybe we can do something to tucker you out," he said.

"Are you suggesting sex?" she asked, as if the mere thought were unimaginable.

"Uh, yeah, I was."

"Didn't we just ..."

"It's been nearly four months," Munroe nearly whined.

She seemed to contemplate this for a while, weighing the pros and cons of a little game of sink the pink. He could almost see the wheels spinning.

"I doubt if it will help me get to sleep," she complained, "but go ahead."

Inspired by her willingness, Munroe slid a hand under her nightshirt and cupped a small breast. Mekisha had unusually plump and long nipples compared to most women, well ... most magazine women, Playmates, Pets, and such. Mekisha and "Melissa the Sistah," a lady he'd employed on numerous occasions before he met Mekisha, were the only women whose nipples he'd ever experienced first-hand.

Mekisha's were nearly red, looking like they were freshly manipulated and moistened; they stuck out like large clam necks and begged to be bitten. Munroe restrained the urge knowing Mekisha didn't enjoy it; in fact despised having them bitten, chewed, or in any other way abused.

Munroe rolled on top of his wife and almost lost it when her legs parted freely, though she may well have been avoiding injury from his bony knees. He jabbed blindly and entered immediately, unhindered into her overly moist warmth.

Munroe sucked on Mekisha's neck, shoulders, and nipples. He gently bit her earlobe and her breasts, thrusting rhythmically, and trying to get a sexual response, hoping to hear her breathing increase, feel her rock in unison with him. Christ, even a soft moan would be nice!

He moved his lips from her downy cheek to her soft lips, trying to part them with his darting tongue, and then he noticed her clouded eyes staring at the ceiling.

"Maybe I should use green," she said.

"Huh?" Munroe grunted.

"For the backdrop."

Munroe stopped, starting to dwindle. "For fuck's sake, Mekisha, could you at least pretend to be part of this?" he complained.

Her eyes met Munroe's. "Oh, I'm sorry. I'm stressed. Keep going," she instructed.

Munroe held her eyes, piqued, daring her to wander mentally again. He slowly resumed his motion and soon he felt a crescendo start building, warmth starting at the base of his dick and spreading outward. Mekisha's eyes were now closed and pleasantly serene, enjoying the lovemaking … until he heard the snoring. At this point he didn't care, the urgency called. He continued, rocked spastically, pulled out and blasted nearly four months of buildup over Mekisha's belly, tits, and under her chin. She didn't stir a bit.

Munroe rolled over feeling a mixture of indignation and relief, but before long was drifting off, wrapped in the comfortable arms of slumber.

When Munroe woke, Mekisha was still asleep, lying face down with her cheek distorted and half-sunken into her pillow, her sandy hair splayed around her head like the clouds of a tempest. He watched her in silence, wondering what odd glitch in reality had mated him with someone as dynamic as Mekisha Coralline Jutras. She was not a ravishing Catherine Zeta-Jones-type beauty, but she was very sexy in a Sheryl Crow kind of way, and she had a ton of charisma.

While Munroe was in no way an ogre or repulsive, he was squirrelly at best, barely moving the scales at a paltry 135 pounds. His nondescript physique, receding hairline—though not terrible for thirty-eight years—and insipidly plain face all added up to something as unexceptional as clay.

Mekisha's eyes snapped open, levered by either a dream or an intuitive awareness of Munroe's study. Startled, she regarded him and her brow furrowed questioningly. "What?" she asked.

"Nothing," he said, rising. "I need to shower."

"Me first," said Mekisha, pushing herself up. The fitted sheet rose with her, adhered to her from chin to chin by Munroe's discharge.

"Ewww, what the hell!" she complained.

"Sorry, I had a little built up."

"We had sex?" she asked, gingerly pulling herself free of the sheet.

We? Munroe thought bitterly, *I did … you were present, but not there.*

"It appears that," he said.

"This is *so* disgusting," she whined. Finally free of the sheet. She pulled it from the bed, balled it up and tossed it to the floor near the bedroom door.

"You could have swallowed it," he suggested, admiring her well-formed ass as she made for the bathroom.

"That's unthinkable!" she said with revulsion.

"You make it sound like it's venomous," he said, feeling annoyed and rejected.

"It may as well be. I don't see how *anyone* can swallow that stuff."

He looked down at his manhood. It could have been in a dictionary under the *common human penis*. Like everything else about him … typical, average, run-of-the-mill Munroe.

"What time do you want to leave for your reunion tonight," Mekisha said from the bathroom, elevating her voice above the running shower.

Munroe closed his eyes and let out a breath. He had zero desire to dredge up memories of high school. There wouldn't be anyone there he wanted to see, and he was quite certain no one there would want to see him, no less remember him. His high school years were generally spent trying to be invisible, avoiding those whose only use for him was for their own entertainment.

"I don't want to go," he protested.

"Of course you do. Anyway, I've already paid for the meal tickets. It'll be fun."

Fun at my expense and humiliation. "I won't know anyone there. Jesus Christ, I only had two high school friends; one's dead, and Jared Gault lives on the west coast."

"You went there for four years and you're telling me you won't know anyone?" She emerged from the bathroom briskly toweling her hair. Munroe admired the way her firm little tits responded to the motion. "What about that girl you dated?"

"Oh my god, Tara Jean Beyer? She was a fluke!" He walked passed Mekisha and into the bathroom. Tara Jean was the Salem High School sweetheart and beauty. Everyone in school knew her name, and every guy, girl, and possibly teacher wanted to either be her or *do* her. Why she had come on to him, he never knew, though she only dated him for a week. "She came to her senses soon enough," he said to Mekisha and climbed into the shower.

He didn't understand why Mekisha was with him, either. He figured he was her retreat after her somewhat legendary furious and promiscuous adolescent phase.

Munroe arrived at work forty minutes late. He was usually prompt—Mr. Seven-on-the-button—and the few times he was late no one seemed to notice anyway, so today he grabbed a coffee.

When he settled at his desk it was ten past eight. He switched on his monitor and clicked on his calendar to see the day's itinerary. The first thing on his schedule was an appointment with his shrink at eight thirty. He switched off his monitor, rose, grabbed his briefcase and left work. He was sure no one would miss him.

"I apologize for the delay," said Dr. Shamus Henderson in a smooth, sleepy voice. As usual, the psychologist was fifteen minutes late opening his door for Munroe.

He seemed to move in a vacuum, as if his motion could stir no air. Dr. Henderson was not a large man, but Munroe found him imposing. Munroe wasn't certain if it was because of the man's black-as-night skin, his Hannibal Lecter sophistication, or his long, stick-like fingers, but Shamus

Henderson positively scared the hell out of him. Munroe followed him into the office and reclined onto the couch, which was a change for him, he usually preferred sitting up.

"How have you been since we last met?" asked the doctor as he settled into his seat at the head of the couch. Munroe heard the quick shuffle of papers and felt sure the doctor was looking for a name to jog his memory.

Munroe shrugged. "Same as ever," he said.

"Ah! Yes," said the psychiatrist, verifying Munroe's suspicions. "So, do you still think your existence is of no importance to anyone?"

"No."

"No?"

"No, I know my existence is of no importance to anyone."

"Why do you feel that?"

"Why?" "Because last night my wife fell asleep during sex … again."

"Does this happen often?"

"Very seldom; about three times a year. In fact, only when we have sex."

"Hmm," said Dr. Henderson. "Maybe the problem is with your wife, not you."

"Hardly! When I left work to come here, I didn't tell anyone."

"How did that make you feel? Do you feel it was a responsible action?" asked the doctor.

"It doesn't matter. They won't notice I'm gone. Wait, check this out!" Munroe pulled a folded piece of paper from his front pocket and passed it to the doctor.

"What is this?"

"My rejection letter. You know the six hundred page thriller I've been writing for the last four years?"

"Yes," said the psychiatrist, but Monroe could tell he hadn't the faintest idea what he was talking about. Munroe waited until the doctor passed the paper back to him.

"How does this make you feel?" asked Shamus Henderson.

"Like shit! Didn't you read it! That's my seventeenth rejection! Dear Mr. Mundane Doldrums, they called me! My fucking name's Munroe Dolan. Don't try to tell me that was a typo!"

Munroe rubbed his hands through his thinning hair. "They said I should not write. They called it 'hapless drivel, less exciting and less tasteful than paste and drier than parchment. We've read instruction manuals and calculus text books that were more exciting,'" he quoted in a mocking, singsong whine. He sat up on the couch and swiveled toward Dr. Henderson. "Christ! They said they were being kind!"

He looked at the doctor, who was bent in half, his head nearly touching his knees. Drool had pooled on his pant leg and he snored lightly. Munroe stared at the sleeping psychologist and felt an intense urge to kick him in the forehead, but true to form, a resigned Munroe got up and walked out of the office. He noticed a pretty, young woman sitting alone in the waiting room.

"The doctor will see you now," he said to her.

The thought of returning to work appalled him. Munroe had had his share of humiliation for one day without willingly throwing himself back into the line of fire. He'd simply tell them that he had told them he was leaving for the day, if it became an issue. He was sure they'd find the possibility of not hearing or seeing him believable. Hell, they did it daily.

With thoughts of avoiding the balmy summer air and lying around the house for the rest of the day, Munroe started his Ford Focus, backed out of his parking spot, and headed for home.

He wasn't surprised to see Mekisha's BMW in the driveway even though she said she had business in Boston all day. He wasn't even surprised to see the shiny black Chevy Silverado. The idea of Mekisha having an affair wasn't unthinkable. Shit, he'd cheat on himself if he were in the same situation. What *did* surprise him was the volume of Mekisha's voice, clearly lost in the throes of passion, trumpeting from the backyard. This was not like her, Mekisha did not get *passionate*, but the voice with the telltale smoker's rasp was inarguably hers. Disappointed yet morbidly intrigued, Munroe rounded the side of the house readying for a confrontation he didn't feel like having. He pictured Mekisha and one of her physically perfect male models entangled in the pool.

"Oh! Bite them harder," she implored. "Oh, fuck yes! Make them bleed! Ow! Yes! Goddammit! *Yes!*"

Munroe stopped short at the gate, mesmerized by the sight of Mekisha lying spread eagle on the gym mats she stored on the patio.

Aerobics, my ass! he thought bitterly.

Kneeling near Mekisha's nimble body, to Munroe's disdain, were two of her physically perfect male models, one black and one white. Each had a nipple clenched between his teeth, and they both gnawed like puppies on chew toys. Mekisha writhed in ecstasy, her hips thrusting her sex toward Munroe as if in ridicule.

The screen door slammed, and yet a third man came into view. He was about six-foot-three, copper-red haired, and NFL worthy. His erect dick was impossibly long, maybe a foot and as thick as Munroe's wrist, and it bobbed like a dowsing rod as he walked to Mekisha. Black Dude and White Guy knelt, exposing their own generous packages, though not as imposing as Big Red's.

The redheaded giant knelt near Mekisha, grabbed her by the hips and flipped her onto her hands and knees as easily as if she were a stuffed toy. Her remarkably large nipples now stuck downward like blood-soaked thumbs.

Munroe watched unwillingly, transfixed by disbelief and horror, as Big Red drove his horse-like rod deep into Mekisha, eliciting from her a shriek of pain, and even more so, pleasure.

"Oh my fucking god," she gasped, repeating the litany again and again in rhythm with the red man's wild thrusting.

Black Dude knelt in front of her and pinned her orally as well. To Munroe, Mekisha looked like a convulsing pig impaled on an agitating spit.

After an indeterminable amount of time, Big Red's face darkened two shades, looking about to burst. "Grarghhh!" he roared.

"In my mouth!" Mekisha cried, urgently pulling free of Black Dude and engulfing Big Red. White Guy immediately filled in behind Mekisha where Big Red left off.

"Oh, you like the taste, bitch?" asked Black Dude.

"Mmm-hmmm, mmm-hmmm," Mekisha nodded convulsively, which drove Big Red over the edge. With a grizzly roar, he held the sides of Mekisha's head in his mitts and exploded.

Spent, Big Red fell onto his back. Mekisha swallowed heavily and licked her bottom lip, retrieving a rivulet of Big Red's juice that tried to escape.

"You want to taste some more?" asked Black Dude, rubbing himself with increased need.

"I want to taste you all," said Mekisha, drawing him to her swollen lips and gorging on him as if she were frantic and starving.

Monroe couldn't watch any longer. Disgusted, immensely betrayed, and maybe a little turned on, he retreated. He could hear the animalistic fury of Black Dude's release as Monroe climbed into his car.

By the time Mekisha called Munroe on his cell phone, he had been sitting in Donut Delight for nearly six hours. The servers had stopped looking at him suspiciously about three hours earlier and now shot him quick glances he could only read as pity. They probably thought this poor pathetic bastard was a loner, or some loser in the world of love. *Boy, were they right*, he thought.

"Yeah," he answered into the phone.

"Where the hell are you? We're going to miss the reunion," she said.

Mekisha loved parties and most public events for evidently self-serving reasons. She got a high from being recognized, praised, hounded, and ultimately, envied.

"How'd your meeting go today?" he asked objectively.

"Fine," she said. "Same as usual."

Yeah, I'm sure, he thought. As if she would give him an honest answer. *Why, I had a gang-bang with three guys today, and you shoulda seen it, I didn't even fall asleep once! Not just that, one had a fence post for a dick. Oh, and you know how I won't swallow for you? Hell, I practically chug-a-lug it for them, and I let them chew on my nipples as if they were beef jerky.*

Munroe's anger had encompassed him such that Mekisha had to yell into the phone to get through to him. "I know you're still there, I can hear the registers."

No wonder her nipples were always so red and tender. No

wonder she hated them touched; they were always recovering!

"Listen," she kept on. "I know you don't want to go, but trust me, you'll have a blast."

He sighed heavily, and Mekisha took it as a yes.

"Good! Get your ass home so we can go have some fun," she said, sounding like the pep rally princess. "It's an hour drive, so we should leave by six at the absolute latest.

"I'll be there in ten minutes," Munroe said. He knew it was over for him and Mekisha; he didn't have much to offer in the *interesting* department, and he bored her to tears in practically every facet of their marriage. What it came down to, the proof was evident in all walks of Munroe's life, was he was an utter, downright, one-hundred-percent, USDA, grade-A dullard.

He bought a final cup of hazelnut coffee—his fourth— and walked out to his run-of-the-mill car.

Not an intellect, but not daft; not handsome, yet not homely; Munroe was the epitome of middle-of-the-road. He didn't know why he was so lackluster. It was an integral part of him that, after years of trying to remedy with conferences, shrinks, and how-to books, refused to be exorcised.

On the positive side, he had always been unbendingly honest, loyal, and respectful, but it was now clear to him that morality accounted for little.

During his drive home a pissed off and vengeful Munroe vowed he *would* have fun tonight, but at Mekisha's expense for a change. Since her image management was so vital to her, Munroe decided a little public indignity was *long* overdue. Munroe wished he had divorce papers already drafted up so he could overtly serve them to her over a PA system. That'd bring her down a few notches, he thought self-righteously.

As they drove, Munroe took in the buildings flanking both sides of Salem's Rockingham Boulevard. He had seldom set foot in New Hampshire for more than twenty years, and as far as he was concerned, he would have been content never to enter the state again.

A lot had changed in his absence. Rockingham Boulevard, otherwise known as Route 28, was still a two-mile stretch of strip malls, specialty stores, and other commercial hullabaloo, but far more thickly settled. Some stores remained, some buildings were razed, and many more were raised, but it was still, well … Salem. It wasn't a bad town by any means, but there were no good memories … neutral and middle ground, par for the course in Munroe's view.

He steered Mekisha's BMW into the valet parking lane at the Holiday Inn hotel and hopped out of the running car, leaving his door wide open. He grabbed a number from the attendant and headed for the hotel doorway, chancing a quick look over his shoulder. Mekisha sat in the passenger's seat looking put out by Munroe's blatant snubbing to open her door as he usually did.

Get used to it, he thought.

One of the valets opened Mekisha's door and she emerged, adopting her stuffily friendly, pseudo-humble demeanor for her show tonight. That's what Munroe now considered her public forays, her pitiable groveling for recognition and acceptance.

He entered the main lobby of the hotel where people flowed like dust motes from one place to another, asking directions, dragging luggage, and talking too loudly with friends, family, and long absent acquaintances. A banner sporting the old school colors of blue and white hung on the right wall of the lobby, welcoming the Salem High School Class of '92. Faces passed in a flux, a few of which Munroe recognized, but none who seemed to recognize him.

Mekisha appeared beside him and snapped, "You could wait for me, Mr. Courteous."

Munroe barely acknowledged her. He turned and followed the flow of the crowd towards the ballrooms. Mekisha frowned but followed.

The main ballroom was nice in its own right, with large contemporary doors and adornments, and a coatroom flanking it to the right. A trio of women sat behind an eight-foot long table accepting tickets, looking at a list and checking off names. He recognized two of the three women. Gianna Reed, who must have a different last name by now judging by the boulder on her left ring finger, was still pretty and shapely, and the years were kind to her. Janet Beauregard, on the other hand, was now a wreck. Her tiny frame now carried at least sixty extra pounds, and her once long light-brown hair was traded for a bobbed bottle blonde, bordering on yellow. What hadn't changed was her effervescent personality; she giggled, tittered, and flirted, and rekindled memory sparks in many eyes.

Munroe and Mekisha moved forward, and Gianna looked up and beamed her talk-show host smile.

"Hi," she said, her greeting directed at Mekisha. "I'm sorry. You look really familiar, but your name slips me by twenty years."

"*He's* the alumni," Mekisha said, jabbing a thumb toward Munroe. Gianna looked at Munroe as if she hadn't noticed him there.

"Oh, okay," she displayed dazzling teeth. "And your name is?"

"Munroe Dolan, also known as Mundane Doldrums, but you can call me Inane Boredom. All that is for certain is that you don't remember me."

Gianna's award winning smile faltered like a brownout, but returned before it lost power. She unconsciously slid a large pair of scissors away from Munroe.

Figures, he thought.

"Well, you're right," she agreed. "But with sixteen hundred students, many of us didn't cross paths."

"Until twenty years later."

"Right!" she said perking up, as if what Monroe had said was strikingly profound. She located their names on the list, fished two name badges from an index box and handed them to Mekisha.

"Have a great night!" she wished as Munroe and Mekisha walked away.

"That was totally humiliating," Mekisha complained.

"What? That they didn't recognize the famous photographer?" he asked.

"No. What you said back there."

"The truth can be humbling."

"Self-debasing isn't attractive," she said.

"Why should I start being attractive now?" he said, barely restraining a sneer.

"What's gotten into you today?"

Munroe stopped and regarded her. "What's got into me today? *Me?*" He spun on a heel and started across the ballroom, heading for the bar.

He felt Mekisha thoughtfully watching his receding back as he walked away from her. She'd never seen him like this before. He wondered if she finally felt some respect for him. He doubted it. Mekisha followed.

Munroe ordered a double scotch on the rocks and kicked back the whole thing in two gulps. His face contorted as the fiery liquid burnt its course. He regained composure and ordered another.

"What are you doing?" Mekisha asked. "You don't drink."

"I don't?"

"No."

"Well, meet the new me," he said.

Mekisha eyed him warily. "What's going on?"

"You wanted to be here, so we're here," he said with a forced vibrancy edged with nastiness. "Let's have some fun."

He took off again, heading for the building crowd. "Let's see how much of an impression I left on Salem High School, my alma mater." He thumped his slender chest emotively with a balled fist.

Munroe approached a group of men and woman standing as if around a campfire. He extended his hand to a tall, rugged man with vivid blue eyes.

"Hi Peter Couture," Munroe said with the effervescence of a talk show host. "Star forward of the Salem Hurricane's basketball team. I'm Munroe Dolan," Munroe pointed to Mekisha. "This is my wife Mekisha, she's a slut."

He included the rest of the group with a sweep of his arm, not acknowledging the gasps from the woman or the mortified look on Mekisha's face.

"Inquiring minds would like to know, do any of you remember *me* from our years at Salem High School?"

They all regarded him with a mixture of expressions from horror to amusement. Some did not respond, some shook their heads, and Peter Couture answered, not without a fair display of haughtiness, "No, am I supposed to know you?"

"Hell, no!" Munroe said with mock horror, as if the question were preposterous. Mekisha tried to pull him away from the crowd, but he yanked free and continued. "You see, I am *The Ultimate Bore*—have been all my life. My wife, who happens to be a noted photographer and likes to gangbang her male models while I'm at work, thought I'd have fun tonight with a bunch of schoolmates who never knew I existed, or couldn't have given a shit if I were dead or alive."

Humiliated and offended, Mekisha started to walk quickly away. Munroe grabbed her arm. "Stupid bitch, thinking that way, huh?" he said—to the crowd or Mekisha, it was hard to tell.

He pulled Mekisha behind him, leading her haphazardly through the ballroom while she tried to maintain a semblance of poise. Finding his quarry, Munroe stopped beside a very attractive woman with Cherokee features.

"Ah," shouted Munroe, causing the woman to start. "Tara Jean Beyer!"

"It's Norway, now," she corrected.

"So you married ol' Danny after all! I'm Munroe Dolan, Dean of Drab, Duke of Dismal, and Master of Monotony." He offered his hand as Dan Norway walked up and handed Tara Jean a mixed drink. "I was wondering, do you, by some glitch in the cosmos, remember me?"

She looked between Munroe and Mekisha, uncertainty and unease knitting her brow.

"I think the name sounds familiar, but I don't think so." She turned to Dan Norway. "Dan, do you remember a Munroe Dolan?"

Mekisha tried to remove her hand from Munroe's again, but he held tight. Dan seemed to search his memory for a while and his eyes brightened.

"Wasn't he that pathetic little worm I dared you to date for a week so we could win a bet?" he said.

"Correct!" Munroe blurted, pointing at both of them.

"Oh, that was you?" Tara Jean asked, reddening.

"It sure was, and I'm *still* pathetic!"

Mekisha yanked again, and Munroe yanked back. "Oh, I'm sorry," he said with syrupy mockery, "This is my wife Mekisha. She likes to drink cum like water, but never mine. She hates mine. But I'm sure she'd love yours!" he said to Dan Norway.

"Okay, buddy," Dan warned. "I think that's enough."

"Oh, I don't think so," said Munroe. "Hey, you know what else she likes *other* guys to do, but never me?" He pulled open the front of Mekisha's dress, exposing two large and distinct nipples. "Nipple chewing!"

Mekisha thrashed at Monroe, but he grabbed a nipple hard between two fingers and pulled her to him. Before anyone could react, Munroe drew out the scissors he secreted from the ticket table and quickly snipped off Mekisha's left nipple. It was actually harder than he expected, her flesh resisting the blades until the final freeing *snip*.

Mekisha shrieked and backed away, covering herself. When the pain hit her, she collapsed to the floor, sobbing, while blood pooled onto her lap.

People, overcome by curiosity, closed in. Dan Norway advanced on Munroe, who smiled at him, popped Mekisha's nipple in his mouth, and stared chewing ardently as if it were a big chunk of Hubba Bubba bubblegum. Munroe raised the scissors threateningly while Salem High alumni watched, some silent, some crying. Two more men moved toward Munroe, nearly catching him from behind. He dove after Tara Jean Norway, grabbing a handful of her silky black hair. Wrapping an arm around her neck, he held the scissors to her temple and backed away from his dumbstruck classmates.

"You owe me one," he said into her ear as they backed toward a corner of the ballroom. Munroe sat at a table, his back to a wall, pulled down his fly, and pushed Tara's face to him. "You know what to do," he said, pushing the point of the scissors against her jugular.

Munroe watched his peers watching him, awarding intimidating glares to anyone who looked ready to act.

Tara Jean's head bobbed on Munroe's lap, working her way around the sobs and coughs, which only intensified the pleasure for him. He looked at Mekisha, still doubled over in pain, but now standing. Her tear-streaked face was now ashen and devoid of emotion.

A commotion arose to Munroe's right as a cop, gun raised, emerged from a service entrance, another from his left. Munroe shot his load just before the bullet hit him.

Munroe rested his arms on the crossbar of his prison cell and looked at the worn smoothness of the floor outside. Because of crowding, there were now four inmates in cells originally intended for two, and the nearness could get a little cloying, if not downright smelly. The crossbar started to hurt under his elbow; he shifted.

He'd been in for two years of a six-year reduced sentence. Attempted murder charges were dropped due to his actions being not deemed as premeditated and from mental duress by Mekisha's blatant infidelity was accepted as a trigger. At first, her accusation of betrayal was considered speculation, but Munroe's lawyer, via a good detective was able to provide proof that Mekisha was unable to resist the carnal lure and submitted pictures of a bandaged Mekisha in sexual suspension between a red-haired giant and two other men.

Munroe heard Kenny say, "Hold him still."

Two men secured Munroe's arms to cell bars, and he felt the ripping pain of Kenny's dick jamming up his ass. He felt like a baseball bat today, and the bitch of it was, Munroe was getting used to it. He rested his head against the bars, trying to lose himself elsewhere while Kenny plunged like a giant piston.

We don't use any KY here, nosiree Bob.

Kenny clenched, withholding the telltale noises of a muffled guttural release, and slammed inside for one last paroxysm, driving Munroe's head soundly against the bars. Kenny withdrew, freeing a torrent of warm liquid to cascade down Monroe's inner thighs. Whether it was cum or blood Munroe wasn't sure; he just waited for the end. Boomer released Munroe's right arm, unzipping as he moved. After him was Carlos.

It wasn't lost on Munroe that there were three men, just like Mekisha's triad. Call it irony, call it poetic justice, hell, call it chicken-fucking-soup, he still felt she—as usual—got the better deal. She lost a nipple. Big freaking deal! They couldn't sew it back on seeing as he swallowed it when the bullet hit him, but at least she still got to choose which dicks entered her. He was the loyal and moral one and she gets the spoils. *There's* justice for you.

"It blows my mind," Kenny said, "that you did what you did 'cause you felt like you was boring."

"That's what I said." Munroe stayed where he was; he knew the circumstances ended much more favorably if he didn't resist.

171

"Hell, we don't find you boring at all," Boomer said and soundly slapped Munroe's ass. "Don't we boys?"

The trio laughed raucously.

Munroe couldn't fight the little smile that touched his lips. He gripped onto the bars and waited for Boomer to shove fire up his ass.

 John McIlveen is an author and a technical writer. His fiction has been published in *Twisted Magazine, Deathrealm Magazine, Metromoms Magazine, Horror on the Installment Plan*, at BuzzyMag.com, and has had stories in *Borderlands 5* (a.k.a. *From the Borderlands*), *The Monster's, Corner* (2011 St. Martin's), *Epitaphs* (2011 Shroud), *Under the Bed* (2012 Sirens Call) , *21st Century Dead* (2012 St. Martin's), *Suffer the Little Children* (2013 Cruentus Libri), and *Eulogies II* (2013 HW Press). He is the author of the collection *Jerks and Other Tales from a Perfect Man*, and his first novel, *Hannahwhere*, is finished and en route to a good home. He is well into his second and third novels, *Going North* and *Corruption*.

He is the father of five lovely daughters, and the O&M/MEP liaison at MIT's Lincoln Laboratory. He lives in Marlborough, Massachusetts, with Roberta Colasanti, whom he finds incredibly smart and beautiful.

The River Acheron
(A Movement of Blood-Destiny)
Arthur Crow

It is a place where life ends and love begins..
It is the river where lovers meet
~ A river forged in deepest scarlet.

Lost in the silence of blackened candles,
clad in silhouettes of poison—I seek love

In the song of a ravaged dawn I hath drowned
Deep in the flesh of the underworld I bathe in
the nectar of requiem
O' father, caress my untamed wounds with
your dread, lest I wander among angels
Dark'n dreary the river's sorrow, as shadows
spill from mine eyes unto gardens of ebony
—where my ache forever sails in portraits
of scarlet & decayed dreams

Dearest love,
Under a blood-filled sky, I shall undress you
in the abyss of my dead soul
The wilderness of your lips I will ordain in
temples of melancholy as you lust and wither
Ash and sanguine bespeaks in the mists of
my sable carriage as haste I night's garnish
Surrender thee to eudemon horizons—for

thou hath become the audience of
my eternal darkness
Bequeath your soul to the hunger of
the River Styx and watch my blood cast
swift into waters hallowed

Covet my love in the elixir of sacrifice
and lay we among wilting thorns and seed
brook with dark fable
Bewail I deeper to the thrust of dagger,
yet knowest you not the tempest of my soul!
Alas I drink whispers of the dead, haunted in
stygian lore & entombed civilizations
Hither the netherworld sow Acheronian winds
and salivate in mortal heartbeat forlorn
For thee, I shall forever bleed until the river
has drowned Moon and stars …
for my blood is without end—a sky of wine
So sweet the flavor bereft upon my lips

Across the dark banks I gaze..
bouquets of death swirl in a tapestry of
passion caressing our naked skin

Adrift in the nocturnal rapture of black roses,
our souls entwine … as the river arcs in
bloodscapes of hadean-fusion
Glistening in obsidian fires, I stagger
thru the timbre of windswept voices,
held captive in incantations of woe
Breathe me deeper my love; for
the ravenous landscapes of my soul await
thine tears of sweet crimson
I am gothic rain upon breast of thy thirst
—drink me deep

The River Acheron bleeds in the exodus
of dreams fallen …
Beware the Crow poised in your
mortal soul

Where the Crows Bleed
Arthur Crow

Silhouettes of scarlet whisper
among the bones..
Forsaken beneath earth and stone, I am
bejeweled in the River's dread

Trees clad in sanguine
salivate in the abyss of sorrow
The perfume of blood seduces the sky
—*incantations of the netherworld*
Ebon ghosts shimmer in falling ash,
where love decays evermore
I undress in the lust of darkness; my soul
bequeathed to oblivion seeds the wind
with poisoned tongue flickering
Upon banks of obsidian I gaze
haunted in a tempest of necromancy
I render my ache in shadow-fire,
—deep in the dark flow
Behold! The River Acheron!

In the syrup of dreams
crimson fields burn in my eye
Bleeding in the silence of dark ether,
I seek your lips..
The song of afterlife covets our love

Kisses blush upon a blade of rusted steel
Corvid screams bathe in Death's lullaby
Vistas of requiem caress our flesh,
as the River seethes deep in my veins
Unto my brethren do I bask—
among black wings wicked n' dreary
Like pitch cast over hallowed waters,
we feast in the primeval wine
of dead-love befallen

Ravenous shadows slither
Beyond the realm of the supernatural—
treasures of eudemon lore bespeak!
I am the elixir of sacrifice
—drink me deep ...

Translucent in bloodscapes,
my thoughts ebb in dark solitude
Talons weave thru the ink of night
into the spice of Acheronian mists
Elegiac hues weep in the trees
as blood drips from the vine of love
Hallucinogenic thorns beckon our kiss
In the wilderness of crimson rain
I will embrace you
Brooding in gothic ambience, *angels*
of death make haste
Seek you me in the river's dread
and sail in the eternal rapture
of my dead soul

Betwixt worlds Hadean spirits sojourn
Where dark dreams rain and flow—
forever the Crows bleed ...

Ghosts of the Sun
Arthur Crow

Solar winds unveil dimensions Betwixt duel suns I remember the future as the desert sands cascade like dreams embalmed in deep space Truth seekers meditate in the spice of universal consciousness My blood shimmers in synchromysticism DNA-serpents weave crystalline evolution Incantations of Jupiter covet the rise of ghosts forlorn—slaves of eternity, morphing in sacred geometry star-crested Siren's undress upon the tip of my tongue as I sow fabled constellations Astral-shamans linger; they thirst among silhouettes of love Cosmic wine flows into the sea of hyper-space Witches burn in Lemurian civilizations Eyes stare thru the mists of Alpha Centauri, translucent in Reptilian architecture Lunar deities paint alien whispers in the dawn of indigenous rhythms Hallucinogenic nebulas bejewel minds.... Undressed deep in the cosmic tree folding stars into dreams, I sojourn in virgin skies Emperors of the galactic kingdom seed lore in cosmic rain Swimming in the golden ether of magnetic portals between distant Suns, I drink the elixir of a thousand worlds Dragon scales fuse into ambient fields Obsidian winds bespeak The breath of extraterrestrial delirium haunts the ethos of mountains vast Islands meditate in velvet galaxies Clandestine spheres float across glassy fields of cosmic dew—chased by warriors of the Spiritquest The perfume of deep space beckons! Upon a cerulean Moon celestial fountains ignite into a frenzy sending ripples into the cosmos Within a communion of wizardry I stand in the

effervescence of empyrean fire and vistas of supernovas
Gateways within worlds spiral in the gravity of higher
consciousness Naked in multidimensional streams, shadows
bathe in echoes of love In a tapestry of amber horizons gather
the ancients—Avatars of the Sun, poised in immortal

 Arthur Crow is a writer, poet, and artist. His
work and expressions are mainly attributed
to the gothic/dark genre, including spiritual
romance and mysticism. Regardless of what
he is writing about, he is always passionate.
He is a student of art and science but a long
patron to the spirit world and paganism. His inspiration comes
from the depths of his beliefs, extending infinitely into realms
of fantasy and beyond.

When not writing, he is working in computers and graphic
art and completing his physics degree. In his spare time he
loves listening to music, surfing at the local beach, and
photography.

Dissolution
Sean Logan

Finch opened the door on his elegant new apartment. It was fully furnished, as promised. He admired the torn avocado-green couch, where he will soon spend his evenings watching the nineteen-inch TV and sipping the finest malt liquors—with his pinky out, because he's classy.

And there, three steps away, was the kitchen where he will be supping such delicacies as canned pastas or rice and beans. This was a modern kitchen. In fact, the single plug-in burner that sat on the broken stove was purchased from Target only a month ago.

And what was that earthy aroma? Was it the woodsy smell of mold coming from the bathroom? He would certainly be spending long evenings luxuriating in that rust-stained and mold-blackened tub.

Finch took it all in. It was more than an apartment, really. It was a monument.

It was a monument to every bad decision he'd ever made.

Finch took the backpack and gym bag that held the last of his remaining possessions to the bedroom, which didn't seem to have a door, but did have a John Tesh Live at Red Rocks poster. A fully furnished apartment indeed.

Finch switched off the bare overhead bulb, got in bed and wondered if this was hitting bottom. Could he start to rebuild now or was there a lower level he had to sink to first? Because that's how the story always went: the fuckup had to hit rock bottom before he got his shit together and went on to become the best damn equestrian skijorer this town has ever seen! So was this his rock bottom?

As he lay there feeling those bedsprings poking at his back and smelling the sweat and cigarette stink of the damp bed sheets, he certainly felt he could make a case for rock bottom status. But there were some twitching toothless methheads sleeping out on the sidewalk that could probably put up a pretty good counter argument.

A slight buzzing in Finch's brain reminded him that he'd forgotten to take his Seroquel. He fished the bottle out of his backpack and rattled it in the dark. One left. That was fine. He was fine. A-OK! Ship shape. Just a little memento from back when he was crazy. The Clozaril ran out two days ago. He could get a refill tomorrow; he had $32.78 in his pocket. But he liked eating even more than he liked being sane.

He went to the bathroom and swallowed the pill with a mouthful of water from the sink, which tasted a bit of seaweed.

As he lay back in bed he heard thumping and banging reverberating through the wall from the apartment next door. It didn't seem like there was a whole lot of wall getting in the way of the noise. It sounded like another of God's chosen was moving in. Finch had taken a look at that apartment before settling on his. That one was bigger but the rent was forty dollars more, so Rockefeller over there gets the luxury suite.

As the Seroquel did its thing, and Finch felt his head slowing down and getting heavy, he heard a scratching noise. It was faint but persistent, coming from the apartment next door, through the wall next to his head. It sounded like it was coming from *inside* his head, but that was not the case. That was almost certainly not the case.

Finch worked on his resume but gave up after half an hour. It was fine—Senior Director at a large pharma manufacturer, VP of Sales for a medical equipment startup, all good stuff. The problem was his personal references. He didn't have a single name he could put down. If anyone called one of his past supervisors, the best they'd say was that they thought he'd lost his mind. The worst they could say? Drove a company-leased car into a lake. Exposed himself during an offsite team-building exercise. Called a client a "panty-sniffing douche bag." There was probably more, he just couldn't remember. He wasn't always an asshole, he just went looking for life's outer edge and thought drugs might get him there. But they didn't. They got him here.

Finch threw on a clean dress shirt, swung his backpack over his shoulder, and headed out for some old-fashioned job hunting, the kind where you have to fill out an application rather than hand in a resume. As he opened his apartment door to leave, he saw his new neighbor's door opening, a girl with stringy black hair and pale skin, heading out. She jerked when she saw him and lurched back inside, slamming the door.

Finch was amused. He waited until she opened the door again, smiling and looking sheepish.

"Sorry," she said. "I wasn't expecting to see anyone. I don't know why, it's not like I'm the only one who lives here."

"Not a problem," Finch said. "I get that reaction a lot."

She laughed. She looked like she was in her early thirties, but probably looked mid-twenties when she was dolled up. She was in saggy Levi's and a plain white T, but Finch could picture her in a vintage black lace dress, Betty Page do, dark eyes, and bright red lips against that pale skin of hers. As it was, she just looked a bit tired, faint frown lines, crow's feet around the eyes. Finch noticed the tattoo on her right arm, a dragon surrounding a five-pointed star. She pretty cute, but he thought he probably looked pretty square to her. He may be a million miles away from a straight suit right now, but he was sure he still had some of that corporate stank on him.

"I'm your new neighbor," she said, and then rolled her eyes and swept her hand toward her apartment. "Obviously. I just moved in yesterday."

"Me too." He put out his hand. "I'm Finch."

She grabbed his hand and gave it a big up and down, exaggerated manliness. "I'm Suze."

There was a tiny pause between the "I'm" and the "Suze."

It was nothing, just half a beat, but Finch was certain she was lying about her name for some reason.

"So, how'd you end up in these parts, Finchy? You mind if I call you Finchy?"

"Hell yeah, I mind! Finchy? That's horrible."

"I like it. It's just like your name, only with pizzazz."

"No way. Finch is an awesome name. It's my best feature. That and my nose—I've got a pretty good nose. But Finchy? That sounds like the name of a cat with clumpy orange fur and half a tail."

"That's a pretty specific image, Finchy. Don't worry, you'll get used to it. So how'd you end up here? You seem kinda upscale for these digs."

Finch knew she'd be able to smell the office on him. "Actually, I'm a film director. I'm scouting locations. I'm trying to find a really shitty apartment for my next movie. A real hell hole. I think I'm getting close."

"Oh, a big time movie director, huh? So what's your movie called?"

"They Call Me Mr. Finch."

"Very nice. And guess what—I'm a movie director too. And you know what my movie's called? Guess 'Suze' Coming to Dinner. Bam!" She pumped her arm and threw a karate kick. "You see what I did there?"

"Sidney Poitier."

"Sidney motherfuckin' Poitier."

"Not bad, Suze. You're pretty sharp."

"As a knife, Finchy. Sharp as a motherfuckin' knife."

This was fun and all but Finch had to get out there and start humiliating himself looking for work. "All right, I'm going to let you get back to it."

"Get back to what, being sharp?"

"I guess. Stop by if you need to borrow a cup of sugar or something."

"You have a cup of sugar I can borrow?"

"No."

"Man, you're a lousy neighbor already."

"See you, neighbor."

"See you, Finchy."

Eight hours and fourteen applications later, Finch dragged his beat carcass back to his swinging new pad at the Lancing Arms Apartments. He jiggled his key into the lock on his door, which like the rest of the hallway was spotted with the black curlicues of taggers, trying to find fame in the one small way they could get it.

Finch went inside, had a bowl of canned minestrone soup and watched a few "reality" TV shows with good looking young people crying and yelling at each other until he was tired enough to go to sleep. It was all painfully boring. But he knew he had to embrace the boring. Boring was good. Boring was nice and healthy. He tried exciting and that didn't take him anyplace he was looking to get back to. Drifting a Carrera around a tight bend on Skyline Boulevard, the twin terrors of Grey Goose and white powder filling his head with electricity and warm water, misjudging his speed, wrapping the rear fender around a tree trunk and nearly snapping his spine—that was exciting. But it wasn't good. Sitting on the side of the road praying the tow truck would show up before the cops, the buzz slowly fading to agitation and exhaustion, counting up the thousands of dollars in damage that little joy ride cost. There was nothing good about it.

Actually, no. That was a lie. Everything up until he slammed to a crunching, jarring stop had been pretty damn good indeed. And that was the problem. It would be nice and easy to give up the bad behavior if it wasn't so much better than anything he knew when he was straight. The wind in his face, the tingling in his skin, roar of the engine, cool air like ice water in his nostrils—it sure beat a night on the couch watching *The Bachelor.*

But you have to pay for times like that. Finch figured he paid about double on average. If he had eight hours of flying high, he had sixteen of coming down, feeling like shit. If he had an especially joyous and carefree moment, he'd later feel depression twice as strong. And if he had a year of decadence, searching for the crazy extremes, he had two years of paranoia, jittery movements in the shadows, people's faces contorting into demonic masks, deep resonant voices coming from someplace inside his skull, tortured souls scratching at the edges of his dreams trying to get in.

That last one, he recognized, may not be universal.

Now, the price he was paying was boredom, and that was a fee he could afford.

Finch put his bowl in the sink and filled it with water. He went to the bedroom, and as he got undressed, he noticed something black around the edges of the ceiling above his bed, like mold creeping out from under the crown molding. He might mention it to the slumlord, but as far as health code violations in this complex went, it would hold a low place on a long list.

He undressed and got in bed, thankful that at least he didn't have bedbugs. As far as he knew.

Another day, another dozen applications and Finch landed himself a sweet gig slinging decaffeinated soy lattes at a non-chain café, making approximately eighteen percent of his previous salary. His first day behind the counter, he was reminded how exhausting it was to be on his feet for eight hours straight. But it was okay. He knew he was lucky to have a job at all. And he knew that a year ago he wouldn't have appreciated it. He was grateful that he was grateful.

Besides, that's how the story goes: the fuckup hits rock bottom, and then he pulls his shit together, gets a job, and goes on to become the best damn competitive ice fisher this town has ever seen!

After that first night on the job, Finch headed back to his apartment, pulling his inappropriately expensive suede coat tight around him. He turned up Wisconsin toward his apartment, and the street here looked strange to him. The dim light had a silvery quality and he wasn't sure if the sun was all the way down or not behind the clouds. The street seemed oddly still, like a plastic model, yet bristling with electricity around the edges. Maybe all that free coffee wasn't such a great perk after all.

He heard a rustling sound, like footfall on dried grass, from the sliver of space between buildings. It was too dark to see into the narrow alley, but if it was a person, he was skinny. And standing sideways.

He kept walking, passing a man in a long, slick raincoat and a floppy sou'western hat. The shadowed face under that

hat was twisting and contorting in ways that Finch had a hard time rationalizing. But he managed. Turns out the guy was just silently and expressively talking to himself. Anything else can be chalked up to a trick of the light.

Back at the apartment complex, Finch passed two women on the stairs. They were both in their early thirties, wearing T-shirts and jeans, their faces unmade, hair flat and greasy, one tall and blonde, the other short and brunette. They stared at him as they passed, turning their eyes more than their heads. He gave them his best I'm-just-a-harmless-friendly-guy-and-not-a-rapist smile. They looked at him like they were waiting for an apology. Who knows, maybe he owed them one.

At the top of the stairs, he passed another pair of slightly weathered young women who weren't thrilled to see him. He tried his smile again. It didn't work.

Suze was in her doorway at the end of the hall, leaning against the frame, the door pulled up against her so he couldn't see into the apartment.

"So are those your friends?" he said. "I don't think they were digging me. It's the shirt, right? It's after Labor Day and I'm wearing white."

She just stared up at him for a moment with an unamused expression. "Don't worry about it," she said and turned into her apartment, shutting the door and clicking the lock into place behind her.

"Okay," Finch said to the closed door, "I'll try not to."

Boy, I'm charming the pants off 'em tonight! he thought as he let himself into his apartment. Last time he saw his neighbor, she actually seemed to enjoy his company. A generous observer might even say she was flirting with him.

As he went to the bedroom to change, he noticed the blackness along the edge of the ceiling. It was beginning to drip down the wall from under the crown molding. He could get some bleach when he got his first paycheck. He might want to go ahead and get those prescriptions refilled as well. He was beginning to feel something like a deep dark hole opening up inside himself, the first rumblings of a voice coming from thousands of miles beneath him.

Yeah, he could spare a few bucks. Eating was overrated anyway.

When Finch got home the next day, he noticed that there was more graffiti in the hallway. He looked at the curling, totally illegible pen marks and realized that there weren't more of them, they had just gotten bigger, the lines continuing from where they had been, curving and swooping back on themselves, making the knotted-hair markings look like they'd swelled.

Suze opened the door to her apartment. "Oh, hey," she said, looking a bit scattered. "What are you up to?"

"Just acquainting myself with the local art scene."

She appraised the wall. "Yeah, it's like living in the MoMA, isn't it? These just needed a bit of embellishment."

"I saw. Did you do that?"

"I don't know," she said absently, looking at the swirling black marks.

"You don't know?"

She seemed to snap out of some sort of daze. "I don't know who did it."

"I was just going to put on some coffee," he said and held up a bag of Italian Roast. "This is what they give me instead of stock options. You want to come over for a cup?"

"Nothing helps me get to sleep like a big cup o' Joe. Fill 'er to the rim, Finchy."

She followed him inside and flopped onto his spongy old couch.

"Looks like you're in a better mood tonight," Finch said. "Last night it seemed like you didn't want anything to do with me."

Suze swung her feet up onto the cigarette-burned coffee table and aimed the remote at the TV, making herself right at home. "Yeah, you were acting kind of weird."

"What? Really?" he said. That didn't make any sense. He was acting normal. And he'd barely said two words to her.

"Hey, I've got some of these guys."

Finch was filling the coffee pot with water. He looked over and saw that she'd found his Seroquel bottle.

"Why do you have them?" she said.

"Schizophrenia."

She hitched a thumb at herself. "Bipolar, pleased to meet

you." Finch switched on the coffee maker and sat next to her on the couch.

"So you're crazy, huh?" she said. "Is that how you ended up here?"

"I'm *mildly* crazy, thank you very much. And that's part of why I ended up here. Addiction and bankruptcy were also up in the mix. Actually, I think I've got to give the lion's share of the credit to the addiction. The bankruptcy and the crazy, they followed the drugs."

Suze switched off the TV and pulled her feet off the coffee table. "For me it was gin more than drugs. Self-medicating, of course. Trying to keep the highs low and lows high. I wasn't diagnosed until I was sober. Then I spent two years in the nut house."

"Well, you've got me beat there. This place is as close to a nut house as I've lived in."

"It's a step up for me!"

The coffee maker started gurgling and coughing as it finished its business. Finch got them two cups.

"So how crazy did it get for you?" she said. "Tell me a good story, something that will make me look at you funny the next time I see you."

Finch flipped through his mental rolodex until he came to a good one. "I tried to conjure a demon once, how about that?"

"Oh, do tell!" Suze said, smiling and pulling her legs underneath her, readjusting herself on the couch to face him.

"Okay," he said, settling in, "I was going through a bit of a phase, wanting to suck every ounce of excitement out of life that I could, trying to take everything to its extreme. I was working then and had a lot of cash, so I was flying off to crazy places whenever I'd get a chance for one adventure or another."

"Like where? You ever hike up Everest?"

"I started to, actually. I didn't make it to base camp before I figured out that this was not my idea of a good time. Taking a Maserati GranTourismo 180 down the Autobahn was more my speed. That and a lot of blow. But I kept wanting to push it. I'd stay up days at a time. I totaled three cars in ten months, costing me most of what I made that year. I took half a sheet of acid and tripped for a week."

Suze looked impressed. "Wow, you were a bad boy."

"I was just really, really unhappy and I was looking for something to take me away from this stupid life. I mean, I know this now. At the time, I thought I was having fun. But anyway, I was reading a book by Aleister Crowley—you ever heard of him?"

"No," she said, but there was a little pause before she said it, like when she'd first told him her name.

"He was an occult figure, kind of a hero to me at the time. In this book he talks about a demon called Choronzon, the Dweller in the Abyss. He's the last big obstacle for a mystic. When you think you're ready, you call the demon. If you're prepared, if you've reached a certain spiritual evolution, he destroys your ego and you obtain enlightenment."

"And if you're not prepared?"

"He destroys you, completely. He's a demon of disorder and confusion and he's supposed to be this shapeless, formless entity. They also call him the Lord of Dispersion. If you call him and you're not ready, he breaks you apart and sends you into the Abyss. Into nothingness. You become nothing."

"But you thought you were ready?"

"I thought I was at the time, which looking back, in the clear light of day, is absurd. If he was real, I'd be dust for sure. But I thought all my drug-induced insights made me ready. It was the ultimate test, the ultimate extreme, so I decided to call him. I ate a bunch of mescaline and went out into the desert. When the drugs started to kick in, I drew a circle in the sand and put a silver bowl in the middle of it. I had a grimoire I got from a coke dealer I knew. It had an incantation. I tore out the page, started chanting the words and I spilled my blood into the bowl."

Finch opened his hand to show her the pink ribbon of scar tissue across his left palm.

Suze's eyes were locked on him, her mouth hanging slightly. "So what happened then?"

"Nothing. I lit the page and dropped it into the bowl in the center of the circle, which was supposed to call the demon. But he didn't come. The paper dropped in the blood and the flame went out. No big confrontation, just a cut up hand and sand in my shoes. But that's when I started to go a little … it's when I sort of lost my composure for a bit. All the psychedelics I'd been taking caught up with me at that point. I was seeing things out of the corner of my eye, strange people with twisted faces scuttling in the dark. I was hearing voices, and that's really fucking scary because those voices are coming from inside you but you really, genuinely feel like you have no control over them, like they're independent from you but inside your head."

"What did the voices say?"

"I don't know," Finch said. He'd started off thinking this would be a wild, crazy story to laugh over, but his voice was slow and deep, a weight on his chest and a burning starting behind his eyes. "I couldn't tell what the voice was saying, but it was scary. Everything was, that whole time. I was thinking that the demon was trying to get to me, that I'd called him and he just couldn't break through before, but now he was trying crack the surface of this world and take me. It was too much. It was really more than I could handle. I wanted to end … ."

Finch's voice was starting to quiver. He didn't know why he was telling Suze all of this. He didn't really know her at all. But she was listening and she didn't seem scared of him. She just seemed concerned. He continued, "I wanted to end it all. I wanted to kill myself before the demon could get me. But I couldn't do it. I didn't want to die."

Suze took his hands in hers. "I'm so sorry."

"No, it's okay," he said. "I realized I didn't want to die, and that's what it took to start getting better."

Finch couldn't look at Suze. He was staring at his lap, watching the way she caressed the back of his hands with her thumbs. He could feel her looking at him. He looked up and into her eyes and saw the sympathy they held for him. "I'm not crazy, you know."

She pulled him in and wrapped her arms around him. "I know."

"I'm not crazy."

She kissed him with a warmth and softness that seemed almost foreign to him. What he knew of intimacy, the coke-fueled flings in nightclub bathrooms and marathon stunt-fucking with HR assistants, it seemed like something else

entirely. She held him with a gentle strength that felt like she
was absorbing his flesh and soul and all his many sins.

They moved to his bedroom, navigating through the dark.
Clothes disappeared. They were together and one and he didn't
have a thought in his head, just the flooding electricity of the
moment.

And when they were done, she got out of bed, grabbed her
clothes and fled the room. Finch heard the front door open
and shut, and he was left to lay in a wash of exhausted peace,
marred only by the niggling question of why she had run off so
quickly.

Finch went to the bathroom, ran his head under the sink
and dried his hair with a dirty hand towel. He looked at himself
in the mirror, seeing his age and the darkness under his eyes,
and he was unsure of how he felt about that. He thought about
Suze and here he felt more certain. It felt like there might be
something real there. Maybe he had hit bottom and was on his
way back up now. Because that's how the story goes: the
fuckup hits rock bottom, and then he pulls his shit together,
gets a job, gets a girl and goes on to become the best damn
jazz xylophonist this town has ever seen!

Finch smiled in the mirror and almost believed it.

He grabbed a pair of sweats off the bathroom floor and
put them on. He went back to the bedroom. He turned on the
light and stared in horror at what he saw.

The wall above his bed, where he thought mold was
beginning to creep down, was now covered in squiggly black
lines. It looked like the graffiti in the hallway, marking halfway
to the bed in dense swirls and loops. He stepped closer and
saw that the lines seemed to form an intricate maze, like
something from a puzzle book. But who the hell had come
into his room and done this? Was it Suze?

Finch went back to the living room and saw dark coiling
lines in the corners of the ceiling he hadn't noticed before. He
opened the door to the hallway and just in the time since he
had come home, the graffiti on the walls had increased, the
individual tags mushrooming out, some connecting, nearly
filling the surface of the hallway in a twisted scrawl.

He sensed that the lines were continuing, getting longer as
he stared. If he looked at an individual line, he saw nothing.

But if he didn't focus on anything in particular, there seemed to be movement, the remaining blank spaces filling in. It created a crawling sensation, like the wall was alive with insects.

Finch knocked on Suze's door. "Hey, you in there?"

She didn't answer right away, so he tried the knob. It turned and he opened the door. The room was dimly lit with a ruby and gold Tiffany lamp, but even in the faint colored light, he could see that the ceiling and every wall was covered in tight dark lines.

Finch heard noise in the back bedroom. He crossed the living room to the bedroom door and eased it open.

"It's okay, you can come in," Suze said. She was standing in the center of the room holding a candle.

"What's going on?" Finch was feeling lightheaded, a jagged vibration around the edges of his thoughts. That dark hole inside him was beginning to open up, something rumbling down there.

"I'm sorry about this, Finchy," Suze said. "I didn't know you before. But … it wouldn't have made any difference. It wouldn't have changed anything."

"I don't know what you're talking about," Finch said. The voice inside him was speaking a language he couldn't understand.

"I don't want anything bad for you," she said. "But you have to finish what you started."

"What does that mean?" he said. He noticed a silver bowl on the floor.

"You weren't just supposed to spill your blood," she said. "You were also supposed to spill your seed." She tossed a crumpled tissue into the bowl and pulled a charred, stained piece of paper from her pocket. It looked like the incantation. But it couldn't be. Could it?

Suze touched the old sheet of paper to the candle flame and tossed the burning page into the bowl.

The voice in Finch's head grew loud and clear and bright and then disappeared. There was a swirling energy in the air, a cold breeze and a magnetic pulling.

"What did you do?" Finch said. "Suze? What the hell did you do?"

Suze looked at him with pity in her eyes. "I'm sorry," she

said. "There's no turning back. There never was."

Finch ran out of the room, to the front door. He threw it open, a gust of wind at his back, blowing into the negative space of the hallway. The black markings covered the walls completely now. On the far side of the hallway where this vast labyrinth ended, something was gathering. A dark, shapeless entity was growing and moving toward him.

Finch ran into his room, slamming and locking the door behind him. On the walls, the black lines were growing across the surface like a spreading stain.

A hole appeared in the front door, a pinprick that radiated outward, melting away from the center until it had dissipated completely. The black mass poured in through the doorway and toward him, destroying everything in its path that wasn't covered in black markings, the carpet and lamp and coffee table, all of it erased as it was engulfed by the cloud.

Finch backed himself into the far corner. He screamed but sound seemed to die in the swirling presence before him.

The cloud moved in. Impotently, he kicked at it, his foot dissolving, blood pouring from the stump, but only for a second as the shapeless mass pressed forward dispersing the blood as well as the flesh.

The pain was unbearable, a tearing, screaming fire as inch after inch of him was destroyed. But Finch felt something much worse than pain. It was worse than even death. As Choronzon overcame him, Finch felt what it was like to be nothing.

And like a mound of dust that thinks it's a man, Finch was scattered to the winds.

 Sean Logan's stories have appeared in more than thirty publications and can be found in *Black Static, One Buck Horror, Vile Things,* and *Once upon an Apocalypse.* He lives in northern California and enjoys reading, skateboarding, bad movies, and good tequila.

Touch
Gerard Houarner

Sarah missed Jeremy's touch the most.

"Can you pass the pepper?" she asked over the grilled salmon and steamed vegetables he'd prepared. The cookware and his dish were drying on the rack. Judging by the bottle, he'd already been on his third glass by the time she sat at the table by the kitchen window to pour her first.

Jeremy thrust the wooden pepper grinder at her, holding on to the head. The grinder turned, spitting out a dusting of pepper on the table. They used to hold things in the middle so their fingers would meet.

"Are you here?" she asked, twisting the grinder.

He reached across the glass table and pinged the empty wine bottle on her left with the end of the corkscrew. Without meeting her gaze, he stood and reached over to the wine rack next to the refrigerator, picked out another bottle. Pulled the cork.

As he poured himself another glass, she drained hers. He left the kitchen first, settling in the darkened living room. She went to the bedroom, packed, and left without waking him as he lay dozing on the couch, his glass overturned on the floor, wine staining the rug. Since he'd done such a fine job cleaning up after his dinner, she left her plate, the pans, and the empty wine bottles for him to pick up as well.

At least this time, she'd been the one to leave. She was finally learning the lesson Dad and her first, Bernard, had taught her.

Her mother was not happy to see her. "What did you do now, Sarah?" she asked, graying eyebrows trembling as she stepped aside to look up at her passing daughter.

"It's never the big betrayals," Sarah said, dropping a suitcase in the entry, rolling the carry-on through the dimly lit apartment into the second bedroom in the back. "It's the hundreds of little ones. Tuning me out when our friends are around. Forgetting what we talked about. Letting—"

"It's always the big betrayals," her mother said, her voice carrying clearly through the high-ceiling rooms.

Sarah stopped in the bathroom, did her business by the single vanity light still working, moved on through the living room to the kitchen where her mother had returned to her eggplant caponata and limoncello. The old florescent bulb flickered above them.

She felt for her name carved under the wood table before sitting at her place across from Mom. Rudy never carved his name to make something, or someone, his. He took them. He'd been the first to teach her about the little betrayals, pushing her aside trying to be Mommy's little boy, and Daddy's too.

If she'd sat across from Dad instead of Mom, maybe Mom would've been the one they buried. But she'd wanted him close, to smell his sharp aftershave and squeeze his arm in the morning, to have his voice vibrate in the hollows of her chest as he talked about the day at work. Too eager, too greedy. She should have sat across from him, where her name carved into the wood would have kept him anchored to life, to her, and let their bond grow.

Then they might have had to bury Mom to bring back the balance of three. Or Rudy. It wouldn't have mattered which. Later, in the bloom of what they were meant to be, when Mom wasn't needed, or Rudy's time to go out and make it on his own finally came, she and Dad would have been all that was left.

Sarah sipped from her mother's glass until her mother re-filled it from the limoncello bottle in the freezer, got another, larger glass from the cabinet over the counter, placed it in front of Sarah and poured to the top.

An empty niche in the wall by the kitchen entry held Sarah's attention. She sat perfectly still, like their furball, Brimble, used to before launching into a clawed, toothy leap. The dust looked like it hadn't been disturbed since Dad last picked up his keys and wallet.

She listened to the silence, thick as the dust, in the apartment, by the front door and hallway beyond.

"So what're your plans?" her mother asked.

Sarah's gaze drifted over the living room, picking out the old furniture, family pictures, decorator paintings, the snow globes and other holiday and vacation remnants barely visible in the gloom carved from darkness by the pair of ornate, low-wattage lamps with the same yellowed shades she remembered from childhood.

Family pictures crowded the mantelpiece. Her mother kept the altar to her daughter's childhood in Sarah's old room, as she did with Rudy in his. Their lives progressed on the mantelpiece, though with Sarah nothing much was displayed past college graduation. Rudy's twins encroached on her territory.

"I think your furniture's rotting," Sarah said. "That foam in your sofa cushions is dead."

"You want something to eat?"

She was curious where all her old CDs had gone, and if her baby clothes were still stashed away in a cardboard box in the back of her old room's closet.

"How's work?" Sarah said. She took a long sip, the citrus tang filling her, reminding her of Dad's smile as he watched her and Rudy playing video games while sipping his after dinner cocktail.

Her mother put the fork down. "Everything's work," she said. "What are your plans?"

Sarah took her drink and drifted into the living room. Rudy had bought her a flat screen to replace the old Sony. It was almost invisible on the wall. The latest Xbox with all the bells and whistles had been hooked up. Wireless speakers brooded in the corners like owls, watching over the space. Sarah imagined family fun.

She lingered by the mantle, squinting at the pictures, letting memories pass through her like a spring breeze. In the back, beneath a tipped-over holiday card, a glint of gold caught her eye. A wedding ring. Her dad's old ring.

She glanced over her shoulder. Mother was out of sight. She rearranged the pictures slightly. Picked up the ring. Put it in her jeans pocket. It felt warm through the cotton against her skin.

She missed Jeremy's fingers, the heat of his palm, in casual acknowledgement of her presence. Sometimes you needed that, so you didn't believe pictures could disappear from rooms and mantelpieces, and lives vanish, and three could slip down to two without the missing ever knowing they'd been alive. Dinner plates could float to you magically from the kitchen by simply wishing them to do so.

This was the touch he gave her hair when she looked particularly beautiful, and men and women were watching her, and he had to claim her in some way so the hits wouldn't keep on coming. The brush of hair would set off tiny bursts of scent from the hair spray, the perfume on the skin of her neck.

They'd give each a look that was a promise.

He hadn't pulled that touch out of the repertoire in a while. She wondered if Dad could have warned her that what she'd finally be driven to do was coming, or if he would have let it happen, been there when it did, sitting in the recliner, sipping limoncello, listening to her confess everything that had ever gone wrong in her life.

No. They would have saved each other.

"Are you here?" she asked.

"What?" her mother called out.

She envied her mother's loss, because it meant she'd once had something real. Not a mirage, like Jeremy. Or Bernard.

Sarah told her mother about her plans, and the conversation turned to Jeremy and the tiny little missteps they'd taken at some unknown junction that had put them on separate roads leading to very different destinations. Sarah didn't feel comfortable until her mother took over, talking about how it had been with Dad, and the old days when

everyone and everything had been easy and safe and full of life.
Dawn broke along the edges of the closed blinds. Sarah called
in sick. When she finally woke, she started calling around for
an apartment.

Her search for something cheap and convenient brought
her to a string of basement studios in private homes in the
outer boroughs. The ads forgot to mention how far out.

She took tours, drank in the smiles from owners liking
single females with steady jobs. One woman, old enough to be
her grandmother, showed her how the door from the
basement to the rest of the house was always open. She was
lonely, but proud.

The finished basement was as cramped and damp as any
of the others she'd seen. There was a carpet, all-weather. The
boiler was closed off in its own cinder-block shelter next to a
tiny bathroom with a plastic shower. An old refrigerator
grumbled, taking up as much space as the pot-sized sink and
counter. The microwave stood on a shelf over an aluminum
table for two set against the wall, the hot plate taking up the
other diner's space. The recessed ceiling lights looked too small
to light up the room.

But ground-level slit windows near the ceiling looked out
from three walls, through shrubs to blue sky. Light poured in
from the southern side, casting dramatic shadows. The bed was
a four-poster queen dominating the space, scarred from years
of service and moves. But the linens and pillows were piled
high, their soft pastels inviting the feminine into their embrace.
Nestled as it was in the earth, with the shine of a moon and
even stars a faint but persistent promise, the bed seemed made
for dreaming. It seemed to have a life of its own, separate from
everything around it.

Still debating the bed's overwhelming physical absurdity,
Sarah followed the old woman through the first and second
floor of a fully furnished but somehow still empty house. The
bedrooms on the second floor, even the old woman's, gave her
the impression of resurrected tombs in a museum, until she
stood in the room that had belonged to the woman's son.

His picture, in dress uniform, and the medal he'd earned
by dying, belonged to a small altar of other pictures, a pair of
baby shoes, a small trophy, a few toy cars on a side table. She

sat on the edge of the bed. It seemed like his was the only other room, besides the basement, that was alive, as if he might step through the door at any moment. It was clean, and the curtains were parted to let the light in. The scent of a man's musky cologne lingered in the air. She'd seen an old bottle of men's cologne in the upstairs bathroom, saw another, dusty one on top of the dresser. She liked that his bedroom was on the top floor, while she'd sleep far down below.

While the old woman walked around the space, pointing to the larger trophies and books and pictures hanging on the walls as memories spilled from her, Sarah took a loose, brass Eagle and Anchor Marine Corps dress button from a tray of pins, matchbooks, rings and other knick knacks on the side table.

She also took the basement studio.

Sarah drifted in and out of work as she set up her new life. "You haven't taken down the picture," her office neighbor, Carmen, said, a week after she'd had moved and everyone in the office knew she and Jeremy were not together anymore.

Sarah glanced at the cubicle wall before her where she'd pinned her father's old black and white picture with some friends. He looked happy, relaxed, like somebody she could talk to.

Carmen took down Jeremy's picture, a crinkled printout of a smiling portrait meant for a professional website. It had looked down on her from near the top of the cubicle wall. Carmen crumpled it into a ball and threw it in the garbage can.

"Thanks," Sarah said. "Guess I moved on so fast I didn't know I still had him clinging to me."

"Like a piece of shit stuck on your ass. Girls' night out Friday," Carmen said, pointing a finger at her. "The night is a lonely hunter."

Carmen's expression hardened. She started back to her cubicle. "You never had any inside things like that with Jeremy," she said, the sharpness in her voice freshly honed.

In her mind, Sarah heard the next line, "Maybe that was the problem," even if Carmen never spoke it.

She bit back the "screw you" response on her tongue, swallowing the bitterness of office politics, women's politics, the ballet of competition between women in the domain men thought of as their own. The finger-touching and the few other lost, intimate habits of her marriage were too cold, too long-buried, to offer as a defense of what was also dead.

She felt a touch of jealousy, thinking of Carmen. Stewart.

Later that night, after everyone had left, she went to Carmen's cubicle. Its walls were layered far beyond the limits of company policy with photographs, magazine pages, printouts dating back ten years. Feeling like an archaeologist, she peeled back the layers of Carmen's life, recalling backwater gossip and rumors.

It was the fast food cartoon figure toy, paint scraped, a tiny plastic finger missing from the waving hand, tucked behind an old printer buried under report binders on a corner table where, long ago, a child might have played, that caught her eye.

Maybe the story of an old boyfriend's visit, little boy in tow, long before Sarah had been hired and the company was just starting out, was true. She'd only heard it once, early on, before promotions and turnover swept away the last of the old guard survived only by Carmen.

The boy had been Carmen's son. The old boyfriend had custody because of what Carmen had been like, before her rebirth.

And just when life seemed about to take a turn for the best, something else had happened. The boy died. The father never returned to try starting up their relationship again.

Carmen stayed Carmen, in the same office, in the same life, paralyzed, rooted in place and person, while the world moved on around her. Stewart came along. Maybe he was a way out. Maybe he was a way to stay in place. Someone to balance the other side of a pair, waiting for a third to catalyze new and deeper connections.

"What are you trying to tell me?" Sarah asked the little plastic figure, the shadows of its history, the silence and gloom that was all that remained of the office.

She waited for the walls to speak, to rise to the defense of lives fighting to repair themselves, of office romances replacing lost intimacies and blood bonds. She listened for the fatherly advice of taking what you can get where you can get it. Find your own Stewart, someone said, inside her.

Sarah took the toy. Knowing what she did about Carmen took a little of the sting out of her dig. But the plastic figure was something more. She went home, put it next to the pictures of herself, her father, an old diary, candles, postcards, a half-empty bottle of Corona, her father's ring and the Marine button.

Ring. Button. Toy.

Three was a number that was more than an accidental, greater than coincidence. Three was the number that tipped a balance. Affirmed a reality.

The childhood trinity of mother, father, daughter had proven that. Things had been perfect, back then. As they might have been for Carmen.

Rudy's arrival had broken that perfection. He'd turned her into the sacrifice that cemented his bond to their mother. That was it for family.

As for men, Dad left first. Rudy the betrayer proved himself by not only by displacing her, but by moving on from their mother, as well, while still managing to remain her favorite with his gifts and accomplishments.

Bernard was next, and then Jeremy found another way to abandon her. That was the final proof. Men were all the same. No hope in men.

Three was the number she needed, but the nature of three had to be different. They had to belong together, like mother, father, daughter. But different. All different.

At home, there was only her and the old woman. That was comfortable. Balanced. Her altar, a territory marking, like carving her name under a table. Crowded with things from dead pasts, it was both an anchor to a new place, and a shield against ghosts of a future that would never break through to ruin the peace she'd found, at last. Like Carmen and her Stewart.

"How do you like it so far?" the old woman asked one Saturday afternoon, coming down with covered dinner plate. She always glanced at Sarah's altar, nodding her head at it, closing her eyes with a smile as if recognizing an old friend.

Sarah had covered the button with postcards sent by college friends she never saw, anymore, from far-off places she'd never see. In case of discovery, she had a story ready of a friend's brother who'd been a Marine, and how she'd had a crush on him, long ago. Sometimes, she even dreamed the story true.

"It's great," she said, as always. She didn't mind the free meals, especially since they didn't come with long conversations.

"New generation," the old woman said, setting the plate down on the table. "Always on the computer. Don't you ever get lonely?"

"Not really," Sarah said. "I felt lonelier when I was living with somebody."

"Yes," the old woman said, climbing slowly back upstairs, "it can seem that way, sometimes."

Sarah didn't bother telling her about the dreams that kept her company since she'd moved in. Though the moon hadn't swung by the windows, yet, and city lights washed out the stars, the glow from street lamps and the play of light and shadows on the walls as the occasional car passed in the street had been enough to touch her sleep, to wake vivid memories of what had not yet happened.

The thousand little groans and sighs a house could make in the night seemed to fill her sleep with voices. And though she couldn't understand a word, whatever the boiler's creaks and gurgles or the refrigerator's murmuring compressor translated to in dream was a comfort.

But it was the sheets, smooth and cool against her skin, holding her tight when she wrapped herself in them, squeezing her as she writhed and struggled in their grip, caressing her body as they draped over her when she found release, that made the dream true, that made her need to stay in bed, to burrow deeper into the dark, to the heart of the home she'd finally made for herself.

"Are you here?" she prayed every night.

Something touched her, through the windows, from the altar, the top of the stairs, the bed. She ached to embrace what held her, to touch something warm. She screamed, laboring to find the connection to what lay beyond her reach, digging into her flesh to find the missing organs that would bridge the gap between what dreamed promised and the waking world provided.

A glass breaking on the floor above answered her cry.

"Are you all right, dear?" the old woman asked, bringing

down breakfast on a day Sarah called in sick to work. "Maybe you should spend more time upstairs. Or I can give you one of the bedrooms, and you can have the run of the house. I wouldn't mind the company, you know."

The next day, Carmen looked her up and down. "You look like shit. You're partying way too hard after this last breakup, little girl. You need to pace yourself. Let me come along, pull your coat. Hey, we could even double date. With nice guys, for a change."

Sarah caught the glance at Stewart.

In the basement, Sarah sat on the edge of the bed and watched night fill the windows, shadows cross walls, a water bug creep across the oval of bathroom floor illuminated by a night light. She waited for the basement floor to sink deeper into the earth, for more than the old woman's steps to echo through the house above. She asked the depths beneath her, and their voices, what she should do.

A car passed. Shadows danced, for perhaps a moment longer than they should have.

She looked to the altar. Spread her hands across fresh sheets. Closed her eyes. She needed more than an altar commemorating the past, a marker declaring her territory. She needed an amplified speaker, a bank of floodlights sweeping the sky with a Bat Signal call for help.

Street fairs drew her. Garage sales, antique and consignment stores, estate liquidation auctions, Salvation Army and Goodwill became her hunting grounds. She searched for the small things, personal items perhaps still stained with sweat, oils, spit. Old, when she wasn't sure the item belonged to someone dead.

It seemed important that the things destined for her altar should come from dead people. Dead men. Her father's ring, the little boy's cartoon figure, a button from the landlady's Marine Corps son—they were like initials carved into a dinner table. These were the connections she felt herself drawn to, the anchors to the reality she was looking for. These were things from the absent, the missed.

She tore the altar apart, salvaged its three crucial pieces and dropped them on the mattress after a linen wash. Her body found each, pinned itself to their positions—elbow to ring, knee to toy, toe to button. She added new acquisitions—a gold tiepin, a broken pre-Accutron Bulova watch, a pair of frayed suspenders, a dingy white shirt, a few more rings, a tortoise shell comb, vintage machine-stitched striped and paisley ties, a wallet chain—after each wash. Her body outlined their shifting constellations.

The house groaned. Voices spoke louder, until she heard their foreign accents and strange languages clearly, though the meaning of their urgent whispering still eluded her. She sank deeper into the bed's embrace, as if the mattress was collapsing under the gravity of her desire, drawing her closer to its secret heart. The sheets slid over skin like water, held her as gently as leaves grasped passing mist.

Sarah reached for the only bond she knew. She bought her father's brand of after shave and the same cologne used by the old woman's son, and sprinkled both on the pillows. She passed along her mother's recipe for her father's favorite meal, buccatini ala carbonara, and scented the basement air by taking a few puffs from a small cigar late at night.

She fell deeper into the bed's hold, adding sheets and blankets until she was tangled in layers of fabric, trapped body heat raising sweat, her own perfume accented by the scents of memories. Skin prickled, and she shivered from subtle caresses and careless entanglements. She reached for solidity, groaned at the receding, collapsing walls surrounding her. From the vanishing smoke of her desire, she heard an echo. A twisted knot of sheeting poked her. She threw off the bed covers and stared at the tangled mess, feeling the tension in its locked mass.

Sarah pressed her hand against the mattress, leaving a hand impression in the bottom sheet. She filled the indentation with her hand. The mattress seemed to push up against her palm.

She wept, and from the other side, something cried out.

The voice was not her father's. The intimacy was not the same as what a child craved from an adult. It was deeper, richer, a promise of something greater.

Knowing something true was so close, but still beyond her reach, deepened her despair.

The old woman came downstairs the next morning and held her as if Sarah had lost a newborn. Sarah surrendered to her arms and lap. The old woman wept softly as she caressed Sarah's hair.

Sarah understood the old woman, her pain and bitterness. She heard the echoes of her weeping in her own mother's bitter voice over being left behind by Rudy. She felt the old woman's emptiness in the places her father had left deserted.

She saw the spark of the old woman's hope as it must have ignited long ago, when she sensed that her son had come home. It was what Sarah saw, in the shadows, in the temple of the boy's room, in the trinkets she'd collected.

She thought of the need for the balance of three so that the intimacy of two could be nurtured and grow.

She shouldn't have used her father's aftershave. It was a distraction from the son's scent.

When she returned to work, Carmen gave her a long look. She left the number for the company's Employee Assistance Program on Sarah's desk and left early.

Sarah threw the number away. Requested a vacation. Her supervisor also gave her the EAP number, granted the time off, and took her number promising to call.

She came home late in the morning. The house was warm. Curtains whispered with the passing of a breeze following her through the door. The old woman was upstairs taking a nap. Sarah took a knife from the kitchen, drew a hot bath, poured in the old woman's scented bath oils. She wished she could have lived all the years since her father died, still appreciating life's small sensual pleasures.

There seemed to be only one door she could open, one direction to take. She was willing. Standing on this side, alone, almost feeling what she needed, but not quite, was too much to bear. She wasn't a child, anymore. The balance of the three wasn't enough. And neither was the intimacy of a pair, in the flesh.

Sarah had to go someplace, become something else. Maybe then she'd find the salve to her ache.

She lay in the water. Closed her eyes. *Not yet,* she thought. *Wait until the water turns a little cold.*

Water rippled. Something brushed against the inside of her left thigh. Something craving warmth.

A short, sharp cry cut through the stillness.

Sarah waited, listening. Knife in hand, she slowly got out of the water. Shivering, she slipped into a thick robe, careful to hold the knife out against the closed bathroom door. She stood over the toilet, leaned forward, put her ear against the door.

Her sound of her breathing, raw and ragged, seemed to roar in her head, as if sustaining two souls instead of one.

Slowly, she opened the door. Peered up and down the hallway. Though it was the middle of the day, shadows filled the house and a slight creak traveled across cross beams above the ceiling, as if a weight had settled on the roof.

She waited for any sign of life, the old woman waking, a robber lurking.

"Hello?" she called out. Her voice seemed to come from the other side of shadows.

She went to the old woman's room. Pushed the door open with the knife point. The old woman lay wrapped up in tangled bed sheets, a foot and arm sticking out. Her chest was still, her head turned to the door. Her eyes were open, unblinking, her smile frozen, as if welcoming the embrace of someone long lost.

The house shuddered as if a train had thundered by.

Sarah dropped the knife. She took a deep breath of the old woman's sweetened perfume soured by shit and piss, pinched herself, ran fingers across the wood of the door jamb.

She was alive. Free. And so, she felt, was something else. Entering the world through the rupture of a death. Moving through the house, flowing downstairs, to the basement like black storm waters in a hurricane.

Sarah followed the shadows shuddering across the walls, floor and ceiling down to her place, her bed. Something picked her up and carried her the last few steps, set her down, gently, on the bed. The mattress seemed to break, like the surface of a still pool, and she sank. Her arms jerked up, and she sucked in breath, a scream exploding in her chest.

But what the bed had become flowed all around her, over skin and eyes and lips, and a thousand caresses and kisses blanketed her, each electric touch shooting through muscle and bone. Thoughts formed like tiny pools, and in them she glimpsed reflections of what was happening to her, but they washed away in the flood of sensation carrying her far from the stillborn scream and panic and any need for reason and explanations.

She held what held her, touched and was touched back. She kissed, and felt what contained her shiver and return the favor. She gave up what was inside, all that she was and had ever been, secret and locked away, and felt herself becoming a part of something larger, a thing needing her as badly as she had to have it.

She felt its surrender, the loss of whatever strange and incomprehensible thing it had once been. She surrendered herself, as well, as they both raced deeper into each other, touching, exploring, falling into undiscovered depths, creating new spaces, senses, sensations.

Sarah's name came back to her first. Through the word, the sound of it coming to her muffled and distant, she recognized her voice. Memories came. Her fingers closed around her father's ring. She let it go.

Three were needed, because one had to be sacrificed. Sarah, for her parents and Rudy. The Marine, for those his death had saved. Carmen's little boy, for Stewart and what that life might bring. Her father, for a deeper bond between life and death.

She remembered to eat. Bathe. In time, she called the police, reporting the old woman's death. She was reminded of the necessity to work, and the current of her old life started up again. It was a small current, nearly lost in the greater tides moving through her.

"I wish I had your vacation," Carmen said when Sarah came back to the office.

Sarah said all the things that needed to be said, to remain the image of what she'd been to others, to be safe in the world through which she walked. She took care of herself, of all that she had become. She held, and was held, by that reborn self. Not tightly, to choke or smother. And not so loosely that what was dear might slip away.

And she let nothing come close to breaking the company of two that was all she'd ever needed.

 Gerard Houarner is a product of the NYC school system who works by day at a psychiatric institution. At night, he writes, mostly about the dark. Publications include more than 280 short stories, four novels, and six story collections. He's also edited or co-edited three anthologies and serves as fiction editor for *Space and Time* magazine. To find out about the latest, visit www.gerardhouarner.com, http://www.facebook.com/gerard.houarner, or his board at http://horrorworld.org/msgboards/viewforum.php?f=76.

Neck Bolt Lynch Pin
Steve Vernon

My name is Captain Nothing.

I'm a super hero. All right, so there is really nothing super about me. The truth to tell, I'm just a big guy with a bad attitude and a poorly stitched-on black leather mask. I'm not really even sure if the word "hero" needs to come into play. I do try and get the job done when I am asked to, and sometimes when I am not.

I have very little personal pride and I will stoop to any means necessary to achieve whatever goal I decide upon and I am very hard to surprise having seen damn near everything there is to experience—which is why certain people call upon me whenever something remotely weird comes up.

Like right now.

I get to the hospital and the police assault team has already deployed itself. I'm talking wall to wall Kevlar and more gunpowder and blue-tinged testosterone than you could swing a fat dead tomcat at. I see blue and brass and badges and buckshot surrounding the confines of the children's intensive care ward.

Yup, there's nothing weird here, folks.

And then, right in the middle of it all, I see the big guy. He is long and tall and gangly like somebody had stuck up a scarecrow of a Harlem Globetrotter mascot on top of a totem pole standing on top of a stepladder mounted on a pair of rickety stilts. This guy has got more stitches on him than a team full of French Canadian hockey players and that flat slab of a head and those twin crackling neck bolts are a dead giveaway.

"Is that you, Frankie?" I ask.

I know who he is. I'm just being polite, is all. He usually stays up north, about six hundred miles beyond the frost line. He has built himself what he refers to as a bastion of seclusion—constructed from glacier bones, Precambrian granite, and the occasional fossilized grudge. I have visited him up there a couple of times—but Frankie isn't much for keeping company. I mean why else would you build yourself the ultimate man cave unless you really wanted to be left alone.

Besides, the cable reception that far north absolutely sucked.

"It's him all right," the police captain confirmed.

I looked around at the deployed forces. "Good thing you've got him outnumbered."

"Are you kidding me?" the captain asked. "Just as soon as we got word that he'd been sighted in the hospital, we moved in with everything we had."

Have I ever told you just how much I hate policemen? It's not anything personal, you understand. It's just the way some of them seem to have somehow transplanted a manual of bylaws and traffic codes in the gap between their ear holes, in place of a functioning cerebellum.

"Guilty until proven innocent, eh?"

"Look, you," the captain said. "My name is Captain Tony Cook and I'm in charge of this crime scene."

I took a look around. "What crime scene? He's just sitting there, as far as I can see. Are you figuring on giving out parking tickets?"

The captain stepped up and leaned closer. I could smell his cheap aftershave and the sour of his day-old sweat. He'd had something with garlic for breakfast yesterday and his teeth were the color of last year's lawn clippings.

I'm not saying it was pretty.

"Would you mind standing back a bit?" I asked. "I don't like to get this close on a first date."

He didn't much care for that.

"I'm in charge here," he reminded me. "You just got called in because you're the closest thing to a weird expert the department knows of but that doesn't mean I have to take any kind of sass off of you."

"Ooh, I'm trembling," I said. "Can I feel your muscle when you flex it?"

He glowered at me.

He did have a pretty good glower, but oddly enough I felt no cold surge of terror.

Then I turned back to Frankie. "Hey, big fellow," I called out to him. "Why don't you step away from that little girl that you are looming over? All of that shade you're casting is bound to stunt her growth."

You see, that was the thing.

Frankie was standing over the bedside of a little girl with more tubes in her than a fifty-year-old television set. As far as I could tell she couldn't have been any more than ten years old. I don't know what was wrong with her, and I don't know why Frankie was standing there like that—but my heart went out to that poor little girl and I was determined to see her to safety— no matter what Frankie said.

So I stepped a little closer, still trying to figure just how to play this.

I'm not saying that I had a plan or anything like that.

"The shade is good for her," Frankie said. "Too much sun can burn you."

I snorted at that.

"Have you been talking to that Transylvanian again?" I asked him.

I took another step closer.

"I don't know why you are doing this, Frankie. You know that this isn't going to end well."

"It never does," he answered.

Talking to Frankie was about as cheerful as talking to a depressed Eeyore in a postpartum slump. The man was about as bright and sunny as the wrong end of a condemned midnight coal mine.

"So why are you doing it?" I asked.

"It's my nature," Frankie said. "She called me here. That's how it always starts. Somebody little needs my help."

I decided to needle him a little.

"Like that little girl at the river?" I asked.

"That was different."

I knew it was different.

Frankie had been helping there too—only the story had told things differently.

Stories usually do.

"So what are you doing down here?" Frankie asked.

"I was called in as a consultant."

"Well, let me consult you," he said. "Did you happen to bring a gun?"

"You know how I feel about guns," I said.

"Let me guess," Frankie replied. "You don't believe in them. It figures. None of you heroes ever do."

"Oh, I believe in them all right," I said. "I just can't afford one, is all."

And then I let a slow smile creep out onto my face, angled just so that only Frankie could see me grinning.

"But I know where I can get one fast," I said.

I looked back over my shoulder.

"Hey, Cook," I called out. "Come here. He wants to surrender peacefully but he says that he'll only give up to the proper authority."

Cook almost tripped over himself stepping towards us. He had his pistol out and was aiming for Frankie as he strode manfully in our direction. He was packing a big manly .45 caliber Desert Eagle that a Freudian would have a field day with. I turned suddenly and caught the side of his pistol with my right bicep, knocking his gun arm off target. I followed through with a good left hook, catching him on the chin just hard enough to jar him as I reached over and caught hold of the fumbled .45 pistol.

He didn't let go at first, so I twisted hard enough to pull the knuckle of his trigger finger out of joint. I really didn't mean to break the finger but I heard the snap just the same. I caught hold of the pistol and jammed it into his ear, sticking another jab into his chin, just because I did not like the man.

"You tell your boys to back off now," I said. "You may think you're running the show, but I'm calling the shots—and the first one is going right through this ear and straight out the other."

It would have been a good plan if he'd only cooperated— but he tried to fight me, twisting away from my grip. He almost made it.

"Hold still," I gritted.

Cook was tough, I'll give him that.

I caught hold of his arm and bent it a little further than it was built to go.

There was another snap.

Cook whimpered a little but mostly kept his cool. Meanwhile the rest of the assault team kept angling for a shot but I just kept myself and Cook directly in front of Frankie, who was purposefully standing directly in front of the girl.

Hero complexes.

They're as contagious as the pox.

"Tell them to back off," I retold Cook, screwing the muzzle of the big Desert Eagle a little deeper into the large cop's left ear hole.

"Back off," Cook weakly barked. "Do what he says."

Only one of his men wasn't listening that well. He had himself a big loaded shotgun and was just dying to use it on one of us.

So I screwed the .45 Desert Eagle just a little deeper into Cook's ear until I felt the ear wax yielding to gray jelly.

"He's not listening, Cook," I said. "Tell him a little louder. That shotgun of his goes off, there's no telling who he'll hit."

"Put the shotgun down, Jones," Cook ordered.

"But he's going to get away," Jones argued back. "I can get him."

"I was in charge of this unit when we walked into this hospital," Cook reminded him. "This is a direct order. Now back away."

Jones started backing up.

I swear I heard a beep-beep-beep from behind his ass.

"Get him to drop that shotgun," I prompted.

"I can get him in the leg, Captain," a third assault team

member said, drawing his Sig Sauer handgun and pointing it my way.

Things were way too crowded in this hospital for my liking.

"Go for the good wound," Jones agreed, prompting his buddy. "Captain, we just can't let him get away."

"Good wound, my ass," Cook howled. "Listen, Kalanta, if you wound him in the knee, this masked knucklehead is bound to put a .45 wound in my skull. How good is that? Now both of you boneheads listen to me or I'll have you bounced back to beat cops before you can whistle Boots and Saddles."

Jones and Kalanta laid down their weapons and backed away.

Finally.

Frankie picked up the little girl.

A doctor spoke up nervously. "I can't let you take her."

His name tag read "Thad."

I don't really know if that was his first name or his last.

Frankie growled in reply, deep from within the rusty gearbox of his throat.

Dr. Thad's face paled to the color of his lab coat, which was bleach-bone white—but he still wouldn't back off.

"He might have a point," I remarked. "That girl is hooked up to an awful lot of tubes. Some of them might be important."

"I don't care if he has a point," Frankie said. "I don't much care for doctors."

"I don't much care for tactical assault teams, either," I replied. "But we're not going to get anywhere with you carrying that girl. So put her down and then let's get out of here."

"Go if you want to," Frankie said. "I'm still taking her out of here."

He wasn't going to change his mind, so we walked out of that hospital with Cook in the lead, followed by the muzzle of the Desert Eagle, followed by me, followed by Frankie and the little girl.

"You're not going to get away with this," Cook warned.

"I don't really want to get away with this," I replied. "I'd just rather get away with you."

"Sooner or later somebody is going to think too much and take a shot at you," Cook said. "It's bound to happen."

Frankie growled again.

The man had an awfully fine growl.

"Not before I feed you to him," I promised Cook. "And he looks awfully hungry."

Cook shut up.

We walked up to Cook's squad car.

"Keys," I said.

He handed them to me.

I climbed inside and fired up the engine.

"Needs tuning," Frankie noted.

"So now we know that Captain Cook here isn't much more of a mechanic than he is a cop," I replied. "Let's just get the hell out of Dodge."

I drove off with Captain Cook beside me and Frankie in the backseat with the little girl. He was singing to her now in a voice that sounded like something that had been torn from out of the working end of a rusty combine. I didn't like putting him back there with her, but I wanted Cook close enough to shoot, if I had to. I could see in the rear-view mirror that we were being followed by about twenty squad cars, a half-dozen police vans, one armored car, and eleven long-haired Friends of Jesus in a chartreuse microbus.

All right—so I made up the microbus.

There was still one heck of a hot pursuit in effect.

"You keep talking on that radio," I warned Cook. "Tell them not to follow too closely. They make me nervous; my trigger finger might slip."

He kept talking on that microphone like a man with a mission to spread the word of the gospel. They must have listened because I could see them falling back, just a bit, in my rear-view mirror.

"They're not going to stop," Cook warned me. "No matter what I tell them."

"I don't want them to stop," I told him. "I just want them to slow down long enough for me to get to where I'm driving to."

"So where are we going?" Frankie asked.

"It's a surprise," I replied.

Meaning I hadn't thought of anything in particular.

"How many of us three are going to be surprised when we finally get there?" Frankie asked. "I don't know about you, but I'm betting it's all three of us."

"Don't worry," I told him. "I've got a plan."

"Gee," Frankie replied. "I wasn't worried until you told me that."

"Oh ye of little faith," I answered.

We turned the corner.

I sped up a little, hoping to lose our pursuit.

"Almost there," I said.

And then I pulled up outside the All Saints Cathedral—as close to the front doors as I could possibly get.

"This is it," I said. "The biggest church in town. Stone walls and a solid hardwood door."

"So what have you got in mind?" Frankie asked.

"I was figuring we'd run a Quasimodo on them."

"I had a hunch you'd say that," Frankie replied. "Do you think it'll work?"

"Do you have any better ideas?"

We got out of the car and ran for it. Cook tried to stop us, but a well-reasoned argument with the butt of the big Desert Eagle gently applied to the back of his skull allowed him to see reason and to settle into an indisputable state of gently bludgeoned unconsciousness.

"Sanctuary! Sanctuary!" Frankie and I shouted at the top of our lungs. "Sanctuary!"

We were met by a priest who likewise accepted the same argument that had worked on Cook. There are some who might say that it is bad luck to pistol whip a priest at prayer— but I left him lying face down in the doorway like a holy doormat. Then, on second thought, we dragged him inside, slammed the door shut on the approaching squad cars, and we made our way to the altar.

"Do you got a name?" I asked the priest. "Or should I just call you Daddy?"

"My name is Father Zuma," the priest said.

"Zuma? Sounds like something from a *Lion King* movie."

"What do you want me to do?" Frankie asked.

"See if you can find me a bottle of communal wine," I told

Frankie. "All of this fleeing from the forces of the law is mighty thirsty work."

"Sacrilege," the priest muttered from the floor tiles.

"It's communal, isn't it?" I asked. "Last time I checked, communal meant share and share alike—and I sure hope you like to share, padre, because you haven't seen anyone guzzle wine like a twelve-foot dead man."

I pointed at Frankie when I said that, just in case the priest got confused between the two of us.

After all, I had hit him pretty hard. He still looked a little cross-eyed, which come to think of it might actually be his natural state.

"Is it working?" I asked.

Frankie took a quick peek out the closest clear window—which was just high enough for him to reach without needing to stand on tip-toe. The sun was beginning to sink and the dusky light made pretty pictures in the stained glass altar windows of the church.

"They've still got their cars parked and their pistols holstered." He told me. "Mostly they seem to be standing there and scratching their heads. Some of them are scratching other places but that's a little too vulgar for me to mention in a church."

That sounded pretty good to me. The last thing I wanted was a firefight in a house full of this many windows.

"There must a lot of good Catholics out there," I decided. "How about that wine?"

"He can probably find it faster than I could," Frankie said, pointing at the priest, who had just begun to find his feet.

"Sacrilege," the priest muttered again. I guess he liked that word but he stopped using it after I cocked the Desert Eagle significantly. Of course I really wasn't going to shoot a priest. I had some pride, and bullets were far too useful to waste on the likes of them.

He brought two bottles out.

He put them at my feet and backed away. Then he found himself a corner that must have looked safe and knelt down and began to pray.

"No need to say grace," I told him. "We'll drink this straight up. Words only spoil the bouquet of a good bottle of

219

bug juice."

I pulled the cork out and took a swallow. It was bitter and felt as if he'd baptized it down with water.

"Nothing worse than a cheapskate high-collared bartender," I said, taking another swallow.

Booze was booze, watered down or not.

"So what were you doing in that hospital?" I asked.

"Just what I told you," Frankie replied. "She called me in her dreams. When a child gets that close to the shadows she'll call out to them just like you might call out in a dark room and ask if anybody was there or not. She called out and I answered her."

He was rocking her in a cradle of bone and stitched flesh, humming a lullaby that was one part dirge and one part death rattle. I could see her breath, thin and wispy in the cold of the cathedral, like tiny ghosts circling about her slowly bluing lips.

"What's the matter with her?" I asked.

"She's got AIDS," he said. "They've been pumping her with chemicals, but all they did was buy a little time, and right now her credit is all run out."

I looked at her lying there in his arms. He looked a little like the world's ugliest nanny—but she seemed more than happy with his company.

"AIDS? I thought you got that from keeping bad bedroom company," I said. "What happened? Did somebody rape her?"

"Who knows," Frankie said. "Maybe her mother slept with the wrong fellow. Maybe her daddy had the bad luck to share needles with someone he shouldn't have. There are an awful lot of ways a person can catch it and if a baby is made while that person is accidentally catching it then that child is born with a head-start on death."

I shook my head in disbelief.

"She's so damn young," I said.

"Doesn't mean a thing," Frankie said. "Just look at the numbers. In 2008 more than two million people in the world had AIDS, and one out of every seven happened to be a child just like her."

"You've looked into this."

"It looks into me," he said. "Being made of death like I am I spend a great deal of life living in the shadow world of the reaper. Me and the boogey man and the closet monster and the under-the-bed creaker are generally called upon by those people who are living with one foot in the shadow and one in the sun. And mostly children call on me."

"Why?" I asked.

"I don't really know why," Frankie admitted. "Maybe they think I'm big enough and ugly enough and scary enough to chase off Death himself. Maybe they figure I'll introduce them to him, maybe get them on his good side. Maybe they just see me as some sort of stitched-together lynch pin keeping the flywheels of life and death from binding up against each other. Who knows? It's one of those unfathomable mysteries, the way that people who are mostly dying think a lot differently than people who are mostly living."

"Was that how it was for the girl by the river?" I asked.

Frankie looked away.

"She was different," he said. "Her daddy was doing things he ought not to be doing. She went down to the water with one thing on her mind. I just helped her get there, was all. Afterward I helped her daddy too—only not nearly as gently."

"Couldn't you have done that first?" I asked. "Couldn't you have let her live?"

"Some scars don't heal," he whispered. "I was doing her a favor, whether you believe it or not."

I believe a lot of things.

I believed what he was telling me too.

"At least it's in a church," I said. "Makes it holy, doesn't it?"

Frankie looked around at the dead statues and yellowed prayer books and the big brass crucifixes that hung on every wall.

"I don't like all those crosses," he said. "They look a little too much like so many windmills to me."

I looked up at the dead stone man hanging on the cross.

"Me too," I said.

"Sacrilege, sacrilege," the priest whispered.

"Shut up and bring us another couple of bottles," I said.

He scurried off obediently.

"How long do you figure?" I asked.

Frankie looked down at the little girl in his arms.

"Soon," he said.

I shook my head.

"I mean how long do you think they'll wait before they come in and get us."

Frankie looked away for a minute.

You've heard of a thousand yard stare? Right now Frankie had himself a look that was yearning past light years—like he had seen somewhere far down in the darkness, farther and deeper than any mortal man ought to look to—like he been that far and had himself a lifetime conversation with something down there that told him what grew in the shadows and ought best to be forgotten.

"They'll come when the sun rises," he told me. "They'll come and they will drag me away with crosses and torches and shotguns and clubs. They'll cut me into pieces and burn me with acid and maybe shoot me and crush the pieces between rocks and beat on them hammers made out of blessed silver. They will kill me in as many ways as is humanly and inhumanly possible—just the same as they have been doing for the last four hundred years."

He looked down at the little girl.

She was still now and the ghosts had stopped whispering at her thin blue lips and a few careless strands of blonde hair was lying across her closed eyes like someone's forgotten angel wings.

"They'll kill me and I will pass back into the shadows until some damn Tokyo grindhouse makes another movie and the Halloween factories pump out another hundred thousand masks and the dreams and nightmares of a billion sleeping children will rouse me from my shadows and I will come to their rescue and repeat this whole damned cycle one more time."

"Isn't there anything we can do?"

Frankie shook his head.

"It is the way that things must go. Night must follow and death must follow life and they are going to do just exactly what they would have done to me in the hospital and all that your rescue attempt has served to accomplish is to buy this little dead girl a few moments of peace to die alone and tubeless in the quiet of this church."

"That and a couple of bottles of watered-down wine," Frankie said. "That's all your sacrifice has bought for me."

He raised the bottle to his lips.

"Thanks for that, at least," he said.

And then he tipped the bottle for one long last swallow.

I watched the wine juggle down his throat.

There was nothing left to say.

We sat there and emptied the wine in the shadows of an empty church waiting for the biplanes of sunup to arrive.

 Steve Vernon is a storyteller. He is a hybrid author with both traditionally released ghost story collections (*Haunted Harbors, Halifax Haunts,* and *The Lunenburg Werewolf*) and independently released e-books such as *Flash Virus, Tatterdemon,* and *Sudden Death Overtime: A Tale of Hockey and Vampires.* There are *two* e-books full of further Captain Nothing tales—*Nothing to Lose* and *Nothing Down*—available in Kindle, Kobo, and Nook format. For more info, facts and recipes, follow Steve's blog at http://stevevernonstoryteller.wordpress.com/.

Puttyskin
Malcolm Laughton

We drove out of Glasgow and hit the narrow country roads. Passing though Balfron, the rain came on—the sky had been threatening, and now it gave full vent to its malicious promise. I pulled into the side, as the heavy rain pummeled the tarmac. Clouds, rain, sky, and horizon merged. There might have been nothing out there—no hills, no world, no day or night—just gray.

The gray looked like it would last forever—then moments later the rain stopped, and it was a spring day again. I looked to the rear, and saw big clouds billowing west, still pouring their furious waters into the earth—but to the east the skies were clearing.

We headed along country roads whose wet sheen evaporated in the sun—and drove until the road became a track, and then almost disappeared. We parked and got out. The land before us fell away into a glen inhabited by trees, gorse, and bracken.

"We seem so alone. And we're still hardly outside of Glasgow," said Rob. "Amazing!"

"You know it *is* amazing—in fact it looks like no one's

lived here since Neolithic times."

We pitched tent and gathered deadwood for a fire.

That night I suffered broken sleep. Rob proved a restless sleeper, constantly turning and shifting.

Morning broke, and we emerged into the early day. The fire still smoked in its hearth of stones. A small bird sang its wee heart out. The glen looked very green—and it pulled at me invitingly. I felt good—though something crabbed inside.

We walked down into the glen. There was a path of sorts—and we waded through torso-high fern, and elsewhere thick gorse scraped at us. Eventually we came out into the shallow floor where the trees were mostly silver birch—but one tree stood out: a big, old oak.

"They rot on the inside, and grow on the outside." Rob pointed toward the oak. "The really old ones."

I stared at it, feeling the pull stronger than before. The tree was a mingling of growth and decay—a life so old, it should have given up long ago, but couldn't.

"Anything else would've been dead by now," said Rob. "Look, the branches are falling off. There's holes in its sides. It must be *nearly* dead. Can you smell the decay?"

"Yon tree's been like that from before we were born. It'll be like that after we're gone." I looked into a big hollow in the trunk, full of darkness and a dank smell—like pushing my head into an old lung. I drew out. "Let's go on."

We reached the burn that flowed at the bottom of the glen. Its water dimpled over pebbles; and elders grew along its banks—weird, wastrel trees with bark like rotting skin.

We sat down. The skies were clear—the air sharp and clean except for the pungent drift of the elder scent.

"Do you see that over there?" asked Rob.

"What? Where?"

"On the other bank."

"I don't see anything."

"The mound."

"Mound, what sort of a mound?"

"Like a tumulus. A burial mound. A barrow. A lair. It's got a hole in it."

"Oh, right. I see it. Looks natural to me."

"There's stones at the front."

"So?"

"So they look like they're framing a doorway," said Rob.

"Are ye daft? That's not a doorway."

"There's a narrow slit between the stones. Look! Maybe it's a *boggle hole*."

"Boggle Hole? Natural feature," I said. "Anyway, we've been sitting here long enough. Let's stretch our legs. I'm getting uncomfortable."

"Let's to go over and have a wee peek," Rob asked.

But I rose, started to walk away, and Rob followed.

That night I *really* couldn't sleep. Rob was turning again, as if caught in the mesh of some vivid dream—and my mind kept drifting to the image of the tumulus: so I decided to get up and go outside the tent for some fresh air.

Outside, I saw early daylight—but what strange light. I looked up into a big yellow moon that had risen over the hills to the south—and I realized it was still night.

I was wide awake now—though the glen remained dreamlike—and against my better judgment, I set off downhill.

In the moonlight I could follow the windings of the ferny path. The bracken fronds caressed my skin lightly as I passed—but the gorse scraped and clawed with wicked glee. I reached the silver birches, their bark made of moonlight. Then I found the oak—a mass of black. At last I heard the bubbling burn, and as I stood under the elders, I saw the mound on the other side.

The mound humped darkly. The moonlight did little to illuminate its earthy body, but the stones of its mouth shone bright. The gape showed a narrow seam of black. I paused, feeling its undertow tug at me.

I was scared now.

"So, there's something *inside* the mound?" Rob asked as we neared the burn in broad daylight.

"Aye."

"But you didn't see what it was because it was dark?"

"That's right."

"And you didn't even cross the burn for a closer look?"

"No."

"So how'd you know there's anything there at all? And yesterday you didn't *want* to look."

"I don't know why I think there's something inside. There probably isn't really—and I'd like to prove that. But during the night, I felt something pulling me to it."

"To be honest," said Rob, "I want to go and look in the mound, as well. I've been dreaming about it in my sleep."

Soon we stood before the mound. It looked aberrant to the landscape, with its mouth-like hole blackly dark even in daylight. I caught a musty smell of earth and leaves—a den of old bones, and withering.

Rob got down on his hands and knees and peered in, close to the hole.

I wanted to look in, *to go in*. But I was too scared.

"It's not so scary," said Rob, as if reading my thoughts. Then he stuck his head full between the lips of stone.

"You'd better watch out, in case there's some animal in there," I said.

"I can't get a proper look, but there is something in there. Help me with these stones."

I shouldn't have, but I helped Rob heave away stones from the mouth, until it was big enough for Rob to crawl inside. *A bad idea*, I thought. And it was me who'd dragged him back here. I called out for him to stop. But there was no stopping him. Head, legs and feet—disappeared into the mound. I waited. I could hear the burbling of the burn, but here in the pit of the glen it was otherwise silent. Eventually Rob began to slither out backwards. He emerged hugging something. It was like a little man, the size of a very small child—its red-clay-colored skin wet from the rain storm.

I stared at it. Curled in a fetal pose, it rested on Rob's lap. I could only see its back. "It's not alive?" I asked. It was a stupid question. Of course it couldn't be. It didn't move. Or perhaps it was asleep?

Rob smiled indulgently, and turned it round so that I could look. For a moment, I thought that it might indeed be some living creature—mummified, or cocooned in a cast of clay—but it was an artifact of some kind. I was sure of that. Maybe it was a Neolithic god or spirit. Or perhaps it represented death and rebirth. But it wasn't alive. Except for the skin. *That* really did seem some sort of alive—with a slippery, but clinging, reddish, sucking, fleshly finish. Like wet putty. The earth from beneath the mound appeared to be stuck to it. The tumulus must rise from a clay bed holding the dank residue of decay-filtered water. I peered closer, to look at its face—but the red, wet, putty skin masked its features.

"What are you going to do with it?" I asked.

"Look after it. Give it a home. A place to live."

That night I slept a fragmented sleep—morbid disturbances welling in me. When finally I awoke outright, Rob no longer lay inside the tent.

I got up and went out into the night—big bright under the yellow moon. I could make out a hollow place on the ground I didn't remember noticing before. In it, very still, lay Rob. As I went toward him, I noticed another, smaller figure by his side. That of the wee putty-skinned man—*the boggle*.

I peered over the face of Rob, but couldn't make anything out. I peered closer. Then jumped back. His face looked wrinkled and sunken. Drawn by a repulsive fascination, akin the pull I'd felt before, I peered in close once more. His features were decaying—slowly, slowly going, turning autumnal like a litter of wet leaves. I put my hand to his face, and felt his skin—wet and putty-like, sticking lightly to my fingers. I pulled my hand away and little wet flakes came away with it.

I stood back. The dead silence of the night was broken by a rasping sound—the wheezing of old lungs. Rob was still breathing.

I turned to the figure beside Rob. It was, very slowly, uncurling from its fetal position. I saw features forming on its face. Shaking, I peered in close—I couldn't help myself; I had to look. As wet clay sloughed from its head, exposing fresh ruddy skin—the face of an old child looked up into mine.

Anger, not fear, now pulsed through my veins. That putty-skinned boggle was sucking Rob's years from him, sucking them away to revive a life that should have died long ago.

I paced up and down in a guilty fury. I'd taken Rob back to the boggle hole. It was all my fault. I had to save him. But I

229

didn't know what to do. I wanted to get a hammer and smash the boggle—but it had stolen some of my old friend into itself, so breaking it might harm Rob. The boggle hole welled up in my memory. *Underground*—the boggle should be *underground*. I reached down toward the boggle— and then drew my hands back. I couldn't touch that skin.

I ran to the car and opened the hatch. There was a spare groundsheet. I pulled it out and ran back to the boggle and threw the groundsheet over it. Then I rolled the boggle in the sheet, careful not to touch it with my bare hands. I hefted it over my shoulder—the burden felt heavy, but I'd cope—and headed down the glen.

At times I felt it wriggling on my back, but when I stopped I couldn't discern any movement. And it seemed to be getting heavier. At first I thought it might be fatigue, but as I struggled on, there could be no mistake—the boggle was getting heavier *and* bigger. I stumbled to my knees, and dropped my burden to the ground. Dragging it by the groundsheet, at last I reached the tumulus.

I heaved the boggle to the mouth of the mound. The boggle had grown to the size of an adult. At times I almost gave up, but I finally managed to shove the boggle fully inside at last, groundsheet and all, it was back where it had come from. I heaved and pushed stones and earth into the mouth, tightly, so that no hole appeared. I sat down, gathered my breath, and wept. I'd done my best. But my friend might still die. I just didn't know.

Day was breaking, as I began to climb back up the glen. I looked back just to check things.

The mound humped like a pregnant belly in the red of the breaking dawn. As I stared at the mound, a terrible thought seeped into my head: that I'd pushed Rob into the mound instead of the boggle. At first I dismissed the thought—how could I possibly have bundled up Rob instead of the boggle? But I couldn't shake the notion from my mind.

I went back to the mound and, after only a short hesitation, began to clear the earth and stones from the mouth. When the hole was big enough, I crawled within and came to a hollow place. In the blackness, an overpowering odor hit me— along with the sweet stink of the elders, and the fungal rotting of the oak, I smelt a bestial musky sweaty scent. I sensed the boggle sharing the dark. Panicking, I backed out—finding my way with my feet, pushing with my hands and arms.

Out in the light, I got up and turned to get away. But then I stopped. I had to look. There at the mouth, showed the top of a ruddy, putty-skinned head—birthing from the mound. I ran.

Panting, my lungs hurting, my throat choking on its own sore breath—I reached the hollow in which I'd left Rob. Catching my breath, I turned and glanced back down into the gloaming of the glen—I could see nothing that had followed. I walked up to the hollow. I stopped, and stared down into it. Rob had gone. I looked up, and all about. I saw the car still there, but no sign of Rob. I looked again into the hollow. There I saw the detritus of old leaves—an autumnal flutter in a light spring breeze. And I smelt again, in the air all around, the dizzying scent of musk, oak, and elder.

Malcolm Laughton lives and works in Glasgow, Scotland. His work has appeared in *Bards and Sages Quarterly*, Volume 5 Issue 2; *Deep Wood Publishing, Fantasy Friday; Dark Horizons, the Journal of the British Fantasy Society 57; Abandoned Towers Magazine 2 & 5; Whispers of Wickedness 16; Quantum Muse;* and *Wild Violet, Mystic Mist* issue.

The Second Carriage
Jonathan Templar

Danny had an "awkward" relationship with his dad. He was old enough to recognize this, too young to understand why.

At times they were like peas in a pod. Danny's dad would take him to the marina, and they'd sit eating ice cream cones and watching the boats, and his dad would get him to read the names, those exotic words written with a flourish along the hull. Dad would help if they were tough to decipher or beyond Danny's understanding (he'd had to deflect his son's attention from some of the less age appropriate slogans.) These were golden days, and the glow it gave to their relationship took weeks to fade.

Watching movies was great as well, his Dad would plonk Danny down in front of something made in the 1980s ("that's when it was perfect, Danno, it's been downhill all the way since then") and they'd share popcorn and Dad would tell him where he'd first seen the film, be it *E.T.* or *The Goonies* or *The Last Starfighter*, and how he'd brought the toys or the comic books or collected the trading cards. Danny would prefer his father's stories to the ones that were playing out on the LCD screen before him, loved to hear the passion in his voice, savored every moment when his dad was so captivated by memories of his own childhood.

But those days were rare, and often a cloud seemed to pass over his dad's head, a dark and foreboding cloud that would soon bring a downpour of bad spirits into the household. Then his dad would not smile or share stories; there would be no popcorn or ice cream cones. At those times Danny needed to be on his best behavior, needed to be careful, because his father's temper could be a dangerous thing.

It exploded at strange times but in familiar ways. Dad liked things to be *Just Right*. When they weren't *Just Right*, he tended to get a little upset. And then a lot upset. Danny had seen it over and over again, the quick descent from annoyance that something had been misplaced to a ferocious rage at everyone else's inability to keep things where they were *Supposed to Be*.

There had been a bad one at Christmas over the pattern of gold and green balls on the Christmas tree (*"One green, old gold, one green, one gold, how complicated can it be, Katherine?"* he had screamed at his wife whilst tearing the decorations down). That one had led to Mom and Danny eating cold chili from a tin for Christmas dinner after the turkey that had been slowly cooking had been hurled into the garden in a red rage. Mom had given him empty assurances that his dad was just feeling tired and needed "a bit of a rest."

The chili had been awful.

Shortly after this, Danny had been brave enough to ask his mom why it was that dad got so angry. His mom had given him a sad smile that he was far too young to translate.

"Your father had a difficult childhood, honey," she had told him gently. "When he wasn't much older than you are now his brother disappeared. You remember me telling you about Larry? Your uncle Larry? And it wasn't just Larry either. There were other children, two or three, I can't remember just how many, but they were all kids your father knew and played with. All of them just disappeared from the neighborhood, and nobody ever found a single trace of them, never knew where they went or with who. It was a very hard thing for your dad's family to deal with, and there were some very difficult times for him."

"Does Dad remember what happened to Larry?"

"No, but he still thinks about it an awful lot. And he worries about you as well." She kissed his forehead. "We both do."

She rubbed his haystack of blond hair and shooed him away to play with his toys. Danny was six years old, but he wasn't stupid. He knew when he'd been fed a line.

A few weeks later he was playing in the attic on his own.

This was a risky thing to do. If there was one place in the house that his dad was particularly paranoid about, it was the attic. Danny didn't know why this was; the attic was sparsely stocked with boxes and cases, the last remaining relics of his parents' previous lives they were loath to throw away and the few bits and pieces that family life could do without on a regular basis and were best hidden away from plain view. The Christmas and Halloween decorations, some of Danny's many, many paintings and drawings sent home with him from kindergarten. A few old filling cabinets kept stacked to bursting with bills and receipts that nobody would ever need to refer to again, until they were thrown out and suddenly became irreplaceable.

Danny loved it up there—the way the sunlight from the one round window hit the dust mites and made it look as if they were dancing for his benefit, the slightly stale but warm smell that contrasted with the pine fresh monotony of the rest of the house. He loved to take a book here and just curl up on a warm day, happily isolated, blissfully at peace.

That day he found the box of toys.

They were tucked away behind a chest full of his old baby clothes. Had the box been sealed he would never had the courage to poke at the contents, but the cardboard flaps sprang open as he pulled it to toward him and showed off the treasure inside.

They must have belonged to his dad. Danny pulled out a handful of action figures, some of them Star Wars, some more obscure, weird, blue see-through aliens and armored space men. They looked a bit primitive to Danny's critical gaze and he dropped them back in, unimpressed. There were a few others items: a green slinky far inferior to the one Danny owned, a small selection of handheld games that required you to navigate ball bearings over plastic ramps that might well have come from the Stone Age.

And a train set.

The train set lit a fire in Danny's imagination. He'd asked for a train set for Christmas a year or so back, a Disney one he'd seen in the local toy shop that had him panting with desire. But his dad had been resolute that there was no prospect of his owning a train set. "Forget it, Danno," he said. "There's no way on God's earth that you are ever going to have a train set as long as you are under my roof."

Danny had initially thought (*hoped!*) that this was a ruse to dampen his enthusiasm so he could then be suitably surprised come Christmas morning. But no, there was no train set waiting under the tree when the time finally came, and he had never raised the matter again.

He took the various parts out. It was an old fashioned set, metal pieces of track and delicate die-cast carriages. The engine had a switch on it that Danny eagerly flicked and the wheels still turned, the battery inside still functioned. It was very unlike his dad to discard anything without first removing the batteries but Danny didn't stop to consider that. It was still early afternoon, his dad wouldn't be back from the office for hours yet so the risk of getting caught rummaging up here was still slight. Danny took out a pile of track and started laying it out.

A pleasurable while later a circuit had been constructed on the attic floor. A simple one, a figure of eight with two tunnels on opposite sides of the route, two eight inch structures that Danny had yelped with delight at finding in the box. He stood, admired his handiwork and then put the train onto the tracks, hooking the single accompanying carriage to it. He turned the train on and off it went, whirring its way around the track in an electronic haze.

Danny sat and watched, hypnotized by the motion of the train. It took him a while to realize that something very odd was happening. Took him even longer to understand what it was.

The train was passing through the tunnel furthest from him and gaining a second carriage. It went into the tunnel with one, exited with a second. Then the suddenly expanded convoy would do a half circuit of the track, enter the other tunnel and exit back to its original number.

Danny watched this a half dozen times and it kept on happening. He was confused, but found it quite wonderful all the same.

Naturally he investigated, stopped the train in its tracks, lifted the new carriage up and examined it. It was the same as the original, painted red and yellow with tiny fixed wheels, the windows transparent plastic. There was something odd though, a feeling of electricity that ran through his fingers as he held it, as though somehow the tiny object was repelling him. He put it back down and reattached it to the other carriage. And thought, just for a moment, that he could hear something. A whisper, a sigh, a call to the very back of his consciousness that was just too faint to hear.

Danny turned the train back on. It ran through the tunnel and the carriage he had been fingering with curiosity vanished once again.

"Weird," he said.

He decided to put the train set away. And then things got even weirder. As he picked up the pieces of track and carefully returned them to the box exactly as he had found them he noticed a tiny piece of paper on the floor. It was brittle and yellow, as though it were very old. It had been folded in half, and Danny pried it open and read the tiny letters printed inside in faint red script.

"Please, tell him we're sorry!"

Danny tucked the paper into his pocket.

He thought about the train set a lot over the next few days, and the tiny message. There were a number of moments when he very nearly asked his mom, asked if she knew anything about it and the weird magic trick that it performed. Each time he realized that if he said anything it would expose him, reveal where he had been concealing himself when she thought he'd been reading in his room. The thought of her telling his dad and the inevitable meltdown that would lead to was enough to ensure Danny's silence.

As soon as the situation presented itself he crept up to the attic and got the train set out again. It was a weekend, his mom was busy downstairs and his dad had gone to the office and wouldn't be back until the evening.

Plenty of time to play, plenty of time to ponder the mystery of this amazing new toy.

Danny laid the pieces exactly as he had the first time, switched on the engine and let it roll. It happened again, the single carriage went into the first tunnel, came out with a partner, went through the next tunnel, came out alone. Danny watched for a while and then grabbed the convoy between tunnels.

The electricity was there as it had been before, a tickle in his fingertips where he touched the metal of the new carriage. Danny held it up close to his face, peered at it intently.

There was something inside. Almost too small for his eyes to detect but as he stared hard at the tainted plastic of the windows he could see there was something within the carriage. Something moving. He held it right up to his eye.

And then the sound that Danny dreaded more than any other roared through the enclosed rafters of the attic.

"What are you doing with my things?" It was Dad. He was at the top of the ladder, his face puce with rage, almost snarling at his son.

"I'm sorry; I was just curious," Danny said, ice in his veins.

His dad stepped up into the attic and swatted a box full of receipts to one side. He loomed over Danny like an evil giant from a fairy tale, blind to anything other than his own uncontrollable temper.

"I've told you to leave my things alone," he bellowed. "I've said that the attic is out of bounds and you said you understood me, Danny,"

"I know, Dad, I'm sorry. Please I'm really, really sorry."

"I'll have to teach you a lesson about respecting other people's property, Danny. I'll have to put you somewhere where you'll finally learn to behave yourself!"

"No, Dad, please!"

His dad towered over Danny, and Danny shrank away from him in terror. And as he curled up he tried to make himself as small as he could, make himself a tiny target. And it was working. His dad was getting farther and farther away, and Danny was getting smaller and smaller until he was too far away for dad to hurt him anymore. And then Danny slept.

He woke up on a hard floor that smelt old and damaged. It was neither hot nor cold, just sort of … *empty*. It was dark, almost too dark to see. Danny got up and saw that he was in a long narrow room, windows on either side that looked out into nothing but gloom. There were benches to either side, like pews in a church, but they looked like they were made of plastic and the seats were too shallow to be comfortable. The ceiling was low; half of it was covered in old faded paper, a tear in the middle where the rest had been pulled away exposing the rusty metal beneath. Pulled away so it could used to write a note. A note that Danny still had tucked into his pocket.

Danny realized he wasn't alone. There were three boys, all around his age, standing in a line staring at him. They looked odd. The one in the middle was wearing jeans, but they were tight and a very bright blue with white cloudy patterns all over. He had a baseball jacket with the sleeves rolled up and his hair was long at the back, almost to his shoulders and short on the top, almost spiky. He looked like one of the kids from *The Goonies*, and now Danny could see more of them so did the other two. Like kids from the eighties.

"Did you tell him?" the kid in the center asked.

"What?" Danny asked dryly.

"Did you tell him we were sorry? Can we come out now? We'll promise to keep things tidy this time, really."

A horrible thought occurred to Danny. "Are you Larry?", he asked tearfully.

"Please," his uncle begged. "Please tell him to let us out now."

From what sounded like a long way away, Danny heard the lid of a cardboard box being taped firmly shut.

And then there was only the darkness.

 Jonathan Templar has written a growing body of dark and speculative fiction, much of which has been included in anthologies from a variety of publishers, including the Bram Stoker-winning collection *Horror for Good*, and the highly acclaimed shared-world saga *World's Collider*.

Jonathan's steampunk detective novella, *The Angel of Shadwell*, was released in February 2013 by Nightscape Press, and his first collection of stories, *The Geometry of Hell*, will be published later in 2013.

You can find out more about Jonathan, including a full bibliography, at www.jonathantemplar.com.

Song in Absentia
Janet Joyce Holden

He knew it wouldn't be the same, and the differences were evident as soon as he stepped outside the vehicle.

Small tufts of grass pushed through gaps in the brickwork; the ivy had been stripped from the front of the house, and it all added to the feeling of emptiness. No laughter, no music drifting through open windows, and no other cars on the drive. Right now everything was closed up, locked down, deserted.

Alice was impressed. She'd gotten out of the other side of the car and stood alongside the guy from the estate management company. "Hey, your uncle had good taste."

Liam nodded, kept his own counsel, couldn't articulate how he felt right now as he looked up at the two-story sprawl of red brick and leaded windows.

She arched an eyebrow. "Well, are we going in, or just standing here?"

The other man fumbled with the keys, and at that moment Liam wanted to tell them to stop. He was off balance, overwhelmed by the silence and the barrier it had erected. The door looked like a mouth, all set and ready to swallow him, while the bright California sun conspired to make a brittle caricature of the exterior and give the lawn a sickly, unwelcoming hue. It all piled on and shook the foundation of his childhood memories, denied their integrity, as if the past had never existed.

But that was the accident talking. Its hunger, never satisfied, was creeping up on him again, surreptitious as always, quietly tearing into his psyche and unraveling the fabric of his life. Annoyed by his culpability he pushed it away and forced a smile. "Sure. Let's go in." *Let's enter the house of Terence Rhoe.*

The door opened easy and Alice was off like a racehorse, down a gloomy passage that forked left and right. "Oh, look at this."

Liam warmed to her voice and followed. He knew exactly what lay ahead, and when he emerged he gave a sigh of relief. The grand hall was backlit by huge windows that stretched from floor to ceiling, and directly before him—a sweeping cantilever staircase that curled upward. He remembered dashing up there as an excited little boy, and once more he took it all in—the grandeur, the stairway and wood paneled walls. The entire effect gave the room a welcome personality, and he used the effect to claw back some of his equilibrium.

Alice was staring at a large portrait on the wall, specifically at the signature scrawled at the bottom. "Oh, wow ..." She whispered the name of the artist as if impressed. Liam didn't recognize it; he had no clue, but just one look at the picture and his safety net evaporated, faded away like mist.

The estate management guy, Scott, was alongside him and he was smiling. "I can see the resemblance."

"Yeah?" His reply came out soft, distracted. He wandered over to the staircase as memories blossomed and he remembered the weird old guy with a beard and stringy hair, standing at the base of the steps. *Hey, kid,* the man had said, and he'd reeked of sweat and patchouli and Liam's mother had pulled him away, her hand a stiff claw on his shoulder. She hadn't liked this place from the moment she'd entered. Hadn't liked the stranger with the beard, or Uncle Terry for that matter. And in the background, echoing off the walls, the sound of piano, guitars, and laughter, on and on it had never stopped.

Scott and Alice were already on the move, heading toward another section of the house, and so he followed, while his mother faded and silent melodies accompanied him and tugged at his concentration.

Steps rang hollow on polished floors until they hit the carpet in the salon. No more pretty girls with long, skinny legs or guys with kohl-lined eyes that flitted like moth's wings. No smoke that had made his mother cough and exclaim—*Is that marijuana?*—while his father had shrugged and whispered an apology. No music, except for the aria playing in his head. The memory of his parents hurt, and once again he tried to shrug it off. Empty of the living, sure, but ghosts of the past were everywhere in this house, some more poignant than others, and it made him wonder if he had the guts to stay here.

They reached the kitchen. Scott was telling his girlfriend, "I had the fridge restocked, and there's a cleaning crew that comes once a week," but she wasn't paying attention. She was leaning over the sink, staring out the window.

"Aw, jeez." She sounded disappointed.

"Ah," the man said.

Eager for a distraction, Liam joined them at the window.

"I'd heard there were some issues with the pool, but ..." Scott trailed off for a moment. "Don't worry, we'll get it fixed."

Beyond the alarming rectangle of green sludge, the rear yard was no different from how Liam remembered. "How soon?" he asked. He'd had fun out there, way back when, before his parents had dragged him away, back on the plane and back home. *But Mom—who else has a swimming pool in their backyard, huh?* He'd been breathless with protestation at the time, and had regretted leaving that pool most of all, and it seemed almost sacrilegious now, to see it in a state of disrepair.

"I can have someone out here tomorrow."

He nodded, put it aside. And while the tour resumed he let Alice ask any further questions, and an hour later the keys to his Uncle Terry's house lay in the palm of his hand.

Death in absentia. Terence Rhoe—composer, hellraiser, rock god—had been missing for ten years, and both music and man had been pushed into a dusty, rarely visited corner of pop culture history. The estate was supposed to have passed on to Liam's dad, but an inebriated driver had taken care of that, and

Liam had emerged as the only living relative. He'd received $32.4 million after duties and taxes, plus the house, and he'd have given it all away to see his mom and dad alive again.

"What if this guy isn't dead?" Alice had asked on the flight to California. "What if he's just out there and he turns up on the doorstep one day?"

Liam had shrugged. "Then I give it all back. I don't care about any of this." He'd meant it, despite the initial euphoria when the numbers had come in, because he couldn't help feeling he'd assumed an insurmountable burden, not to mention his feelings still ran a little ambivalent toward a man cloaked in folklore and scandal, whom Liam's mother had seemed particularly wary of.

A couple of ingénues, they did the tourist thing. Hollywood and Highland, the Santa Monica pier; they went to Disneyland and Universal Studios. After that they attempted to assume the guise of others who lived in Beverly Hills. They tried some of the up-market stores and restaurants, all of them way overpriced. They managed to gain entry to the fancier nightclubs but they hated the atmosphere. They shopped at Whole Foods; they went to Vegas, blew through a horrible amount of money and felt guilty about it afterwards.

Alice joined a gym and took yoga classes; Liam continued to write and sell articles and spent long hours pacing the house, back and forth, inside and out. Looking for his uncle, his girlfriend had offered at one point, and relentless as ever she had continued to ruminate. "What if he's in the bottom of that pool? Do you think anyone has taken a look?"

In the end he excused his restlessness as a rather pathetic attempt to reclaim some of the better moments of his past. And lately he'd been sitting at an old upright piano in the study. Another memory. This one a particular treasure.

His uncle had been skinny and tanned and had looked nothing like his dad. "Can you play?"

"Sure I can." Just a kid, he'd been eager to impress.

They'd begun at the Steinway, and he had run through a few scales, back and forth, two hands, two octaves, followed by a stilted rendition of *Für Elise*. His uncle had laughed and patted him on the back, and at that singular moment the younger Liam really *had* wanted to play the piano and not because his mother had deemed it so. And when he grew up he was going to sit there like his uncle Terry, a glass of wine and a lit cigarette close by, so sophisticated while his hands ran languid and easy across the keys while others looked on and applauded …

He remembered why they'd moved onto the battered upright. "They all sound different, play different. You have to listen. Feel it in your fingers."

He'd complained. "It's so old." More than anything he had wanted to get back to that shiny, impressive Steinway.

"Sure it is, but this one is special." Smoke had curled lazy and mesmerizing from the ever-present cigarette. "Because the keys are made of bones." *Play for me, Liam.*

His mother had arrived at that point, brandishing an accusing finger. "You stop that. You'll be giving him nightmares." And once again she had hauled the young, impressionable Liam away. "They're made of ivory," she had whispered soon after. "Don't you go listening to him." And much too soon it was back home to a normal life where he'd dropped the lessons at the grand old age of fourteen and had never played a note since.

The memory was bittersweet, and now the piano was older still. The keys looked about ready to break apart, fractured like split fingernails and brown at the edges. He tapped them gently. Bones, his uncle had said. He smiled.

The pool water remained swampy. The guys who came to fix it told him it would take a while. They explained about filtering and 'shocking the water', and for a short time they were a regular presence out there in the yard.

Alice stood and watched them and complained about the chlorine smell. And complained some more when they stopped coming. "I think they're lying," she said when the reason for their absence had been given. "Their supervisor isn't sick. I think they've given up."

Liam figured it was becoming an obsession. Three times, now, he'd seen her standing at the bedroom window in the middle of the night, staring out into the yard, a pale, naked figure; a ghost like the rest. It freaked him out and he told her so.

"This house," was all she said.

In the weeks that followed, and despite the more eloquent
Steinway sitting in the salon, he kept going back to the study
and the old upright and its scuffed varnish and broken keys.
Listen, Liam. Just listen. And during the afternoons, usually when
Alice was at one of her classes, he sat there and reacquainted
himself. It wasn't easy, and although he'd remembered the
necessary fingering he was unable to coordinate both hands
like he used to. The scale of C major took him a week to
master and for a while he despaired.

He rummaged, discovered piles of sheet music stacked in
dried-up heaps against the wall, and yet more beneath the lid of
the piano stool. He remembered a little of how to read the
different notes and tempo and so he got to work, fingers
stretching across the tainted keys, groping for the right chords.

The task drew him in, stopped his aimless wandering. He
began to feel safe, huddled at the piano in the gloomy study,
shaded from the relentless daytime brightness by the eaves of
the house. Sometimes it felt as if the entire building was
folding around him, filling in the terrifying spaces, pouring into
the pits gouged open by the accident. It surrounded him like a
blanket and inspired fond memories of childlike wonder and
music and glamour; Dad and Uncle Terry embracing when
they'd first arrived all those years ago; the grins on their faces,
the backslaps and the laughter; the sound of his dad's voice
echoing through the grand hallway. Until the struggle with bars
and tempo, the ache in his fingers as they slid over the rough
keys—the ritual—let him shake loose his terrors of that awful
night and allowed him to wallow in happier times.

However, not to be outdone, reality fought back. Alice
complained he was becoming distant. He missed a deadline
and the subsequent article he delivered lacked his usual tidy
wit. But he no longer possessed the strength to apologize.
Instead he clung to the notion that Alice had been poisoned by
her disquiet; that the written piece had been up to his usual
standard and not the hasty pile of crap it actually was. Because
along that verdant, soporific path lay the pretence that

everything else was okay and he wasn't missing his parents; that he wasn't falling apart and the house wasn't getting under his skin.

Alice called the delinquent pool company and they told her she might want to get in touch with animal control; that there might be something alive in the water. She and Liam spent an hour outside after the call, they stuck a long pole in there, and a net, and wondered if it might be snakes, or turtles, or even fish. But with all the chlorine they were both of the opinion that nothing was alive in there and agreed the company had simply given up. And from then on whenever he looked outside, he gave in to the illusion that it wasn't a swimming pool at all. That it was a deep, dark pond, holding secrets that writhed beneath the scummy surface. He tried to ignore it and keep up his rituals and the art of sewing himself back together. But there was no denying Alice.

"I want to go back home for a while. And you should come with me."

"I thought you liked it here?"

"It's just …" she hesitated. "What if you sold this place? We could live down at the beach."

"No." It came out firm, resolute. He couldn't give it up. No way. Not yet.

He gave her his reasons, wasn't sure if she wholly understood, but in the end they made a deal. She'd go back home, they'd give it a month and then try and figure something out.

At the airport they embraced and she held his hand until the last possible moment. "Don't get too caught up in that place," she told him. "And stay in touch, okay?"

He nodded. He wanted to say please, don't go—but he couldn't help notice the look of relief on her face when they finally broke apart and she stepped into the security line. And when she finally turned a corner and disappeared into the terminal he felt gutted and raw.

The next few days felt odd, and he wandered, restless and despondent now she had gone. It was enough to kick him out of his former stupor and keep him on edge and in the end he knew she was right, that they'd be better off in one of those airy, pale-walled chalets along the coast.

Until the end of the month, then. He gave Alice a call, booked her a first class ticket.

He finished up the remaining freelance jobs he had, and began to fill the extra time by going through the minutiae of the house. All his uncle's belongings—tucked in drawers, hung in closets, stacked in cupboards—he hadn't touched it before because it had seemed disrespectful. Dead was dead, but missing, presumed dead was a whole other ball game as far as he was concerned. He and Alice had already discussed the over-stuffed wardrobes, the cars, the framed gold discs. You could sell it all to a museum, she'd said. But again, the irreverence, the blithe assumption; it had stuck in his craw and left him hogtied.

Even now he was careful, as if someone was watching as he began a thorough examination of one room, followed by another. *Looking for something, kid?* No, sorry, Uncle, I was just …

Gradually, he fell into a new routine. He dutifully kept up his Skype sessions with Alice, and when he wasn't rummaging through his uncle's cupboards he returned to the piano. His scales were improving, he'd gotten beyond *Für Elise* and was now attempting some Rachmaninoff, along with a few of his uncle's compositions, every one of them hammered out on the upright and its ancient bone keys.

Loneliness gnawed at him, and when the weekly cleaning crew arrived he followed them about and chatted, until they left and took all semblance of life with them along with their mops and brushes and polishers, leaving him alone once more, rattling through the house, as much of a ghost as his uncle, his parents, and those long-legged girls he remembered. Even Alice had resumed the guise of such, and there had been more than one night when he'd wakened and seen her standing by the window, looking out toward that awful, slimy pool.

Three and a half weeks into his month-long stint and he began on the study. He'd been methodical, had begun at the western side, and so it was only now he'd assumed the task of searching this particular room, even though he played the piano in there every single day.

The walls were lined with books—Homer, Nietzsche, Shakespeare, Dumas, Conan Doyle, Blake, Keats—the room packed to the rafters with should-reads. He traced his fingers along their spines and wondered how he'd only just decided to pay attention; that it had been the music and not the written word that had drawn him, and he heard his mother's voice. *I don't like this house; I don't like this room.*

Her words tugged at his attention while he continued his study of the shelves, until, looking up, he spied a keyhole. It was high up, and he needed a nearby stool in order to get anywhere close. It heralded an opening, so loud it pushed away his mother's misgivings, rekindled his boyhood delight, and he began a hurried search for the key.

He found nothing. No key. No clue. And as a last resort he brought a crowbar and a flashlight from the garage and ignominiously popped the lock.

For a moment the desecration overshadowed his curiosity. The wood was splintered and cracked; some of the books had fallen from the shelves and he was, therefore, feeling quite apologetic as he swung open the bookcase.

Beyond lay a dark hole. *I don't like this room.* He turned on the flashlight and saw the beginnings of a shallow space—and more shelves. He stepped inside and discovered more books. Diablerie. Sorcery. Demonology. Satanic rites. Some of them seemed particularly old; one of them was handwritten in a style of old English he could barely translate.

The surrounding gloom whispered to him, quietly berating him with the obvious, that there was, aside from the drugs, the fights, the bitter, well-publicized sound bites and DUIs, perhaps much, much more to his uncle Terry than he'd originally thought. The discovery excited him; it also curdled his stomach and offered a viable explanation as to why his mother had been so leery.

Amongst the discovery was a tattered folder of sheet music. The rubber band holding it all together came apart and he almost let the contents slip. Inside—more of his uncle's compositions. But why keep them hidden, when other similar sheets had been placed within easy reach?

The ancient tomes gave him the creeps and so he closed up the bookcase, propped it shut with the stool and took the folder over to the old upright. He picked out a likely candidate, what appeared to be a simple melody his rudimentary skills could cope with. *Adagietto*, it said, and so he tried to slow it down and not hammer so hard on the keys. Again and again, over and over, until he'd lost himself and his wrists ached and the melody sank beneath his fingertips.

"So what do you think?" his uncle whispered. "Talent is one thing, but need has to burn inside, until nothing else matters."

The hand lay heavy and sodden on his shoulder. Excess water dripped like a dull metronome on the rug. Liam's neck muscles twitched and he sat bolt upright, and for a moment he panicked, couldn't breathe.

Reason kicked in. It was dark outside and he must have fallen asleep at the piano. But the presence at his shoulder lingered and his heart began to hammer until it hurt.

Turn around. Goddamn it, you fool, turn around. And when he did he saw the bookcase had swung open; it had pushed aside the stool and the dark, yawning gap grinned wide and promised secrets and his missing uncle who had crawled out of the pool and was waiting in the shadows, wearing tattered flesh and wet, algae-ridden clothes.

It took him a while, but in the end he forced himself to stand up, walk to the bookcase and swing it back into the wall once more. He propped it shut with the much heavier desk chair and, disgusted with himself, he turned off the lights and went to bed.

But he couldn't sleep. Instead, he lay in bed, waiting, breath shallow, eyes focused on the ceiling. He tried to assure himself that everything was fine and he was simply spooked and he should try and relax and get some rest. Over and over, until the noise he'd been listening for finally arrived.

Thud.

Muffled, distant, his hackles rose and informed him it was the chair he'd left by the bookcase; that somehow it had been thrown aside and something had emerged and was standing in the study, or perhaps it was creeping up the stairs, hoping to catch him by surprise.

He sat up, swung his feet over the edge of the bed. His hand groped and found the crowbar. The cold metal in his curled fingers shocked him. He'd picked up the crowbar and brought it upstairs? Damn right he had.

He hauled on his jeans, fingers trembling. He dropped his phone twice before he was able to put it in his pocket. "This is stupid." The words came out tight and nearly choked him. Barefoot, on tiptoe, he headed downstairs, crowbar firmly in hand, across the hall where moonlight offered slanted blocks of pale illumination across the polished floor. And all the while his ears kept up their vigilance. No more sound, but that didn't mean anything. They, it, whoever—what if someone had broken in, a thief? And what if they were armed with something more deadly than a twisted piece of metal?

He took a deep breath and he counted—one, two, three—and gently pushed open the study door. The chair had overturned, the bookcase lay open; in the dark the hole beyond was a powerful draw, but he didn't enter the room until his eyes had flitted back and forth, over and over, looking for signs of movement.

"Wuss," he scolded. He stabbed at the light switch and blinked. Everything seemed innocuous, banal, inert, except for that narrow, yawning chasm. He barked out a laugh. "That you, Uncle Terry?" He listened, his head cocked, and after mustering the necessary bravado he stepped forth, his manner overly deliberate, a false smile on his face.

Close up, he could see the beginnings of shelves inside his uncle's secret library, nothing more. Until his vision took a turn into the darkest corner where the angle of the wall seemed askew. He frowned, puzzled. On this particular approach it appeared as if there was a gap …

He stepped forth, his hand reached out and discovered thin air. The shock made him recoil. He backed off, picked up the flashlight he'd left on the desk, switched it on and re-entered the fray. And there it was. So intent on the books and the folio of music, he hadn't deciphered the play of light and shadow and had failed to notice the narrow stairwell behind the shelves that led down …

Play for me …

A hazy circle of light pushed ahead of him as he took one step, followed by another, while reason argued for an expeditious retreat. But the mystery had him by the nose and led him onward, down a narrow single stairwell that creaked underfoot. At the bottom, a left turn and a passage that, if his sense of direction wasn't askew, would take him outside and into the yard.

He heard a melody, soft and easy it emerged from more practiced fingers. A thin strand of smoke curled upward. "You see, music is transcendental, Liam. This house, everything I own, is paid for by those who want freedom, who want to be liberated."

"I could never get the hang of it," said his dad. "But Liam here ..."

Memories flew from him, resonated in dark space. His breath was coming up short, his lungs were constricted and it took a deliberate effort to draw air. The corridor bowed outward, and via the flashlight he could see part of the ceiling curved, dipped low, and ran on as far as he could see and he thought about the pool. He stepped carefully to avoid a pile of rags on the floor, and he heard the creak of leather and a choking sound and he realized he was no longer alone.

She came out of the ceiling, her hair a slimy, dripping rope. There was a horrific stench of wet rot and he gagged and dropped the flashlight.

"Play for me." The words were a ribbon that slid down his throat.

He tried to run. Two strides and she pulled him backward and he fell. Her arms were thin like cable and they curled around him and wrenched the crowbar from his fingers. He could hear breath whine between his lips as she twisted his head. He could feel her on the inside, too, gliding along the staves of memory. Above him the house closed in; it had been a trap all along.

"Play."

He struggled, lunged forward, and for a moment his fingers brushed against the flashlight and a hazy circle danced across the wall where a figure was strung up, withered arms outstretched, crucified.

His uncle's shriveled head lolled, his eyes cracked open.

Liam tried to scream but she'd bound him further, constricted his chest, and she patiently rode him while he bucked and writhed. And in the end he couldn't breathe and had to stop. She began to tug and pull on his thoughts, stealing them away, intent on doing more damage than the accident had ever done. "Please," he gasped. "It's all I have left." But it didn't matter.

Helpless, he lay there inert while she feasted on him. The flashlight died and he thought he could hear his cell phone ringing, and for a little while the horror of darkness and a thin strand of hope danced together and mocked him.

And now she was on the move, hauling him up, binding his arms until they lay outstretched, every muscle and tendon at their limit; his chin lifted, his back arched. And while he fought the agony, she slipped by and dove deep.

"Everything I own ..." whispered his uncle.

"Liam."

She was moving him again. His shoulders screamed in protest. But it felt different this time and the voice was no longer inside his head.

"Liam, it's okay. You're dehydrated and they're taking you to the hospital."

Alice. It was Alice's voice. He drew breath and his throat hurt. He blinked, tried to focus. "What—?" The word tumbled forth on a bed of broken glass.

"I guess you found your uncle's remains. They say he's just a pile of rags, and you tripped—"

"No," he began. He was being lifted and his head spun. "No, wait." He tried to sit up but he couldn't. Red and white light hammered on his retinae, and he heard a man's voice telling him to relax. But they had to go back. That thing—

A jolt, and more disorientation. His vision cleared and the flashing lights stopped, and he recognized the interior of an ambulance. They'd strapped him to a gurney and the doors were closing.

He raised his head toward the female paramedic along with him for the ride. "He's alive," he told her. "He's still alive."

The vehicle began to move. He lifted his head a little further, watched the woman check the bindings at this ankles and wrists. She leaned over, pulled the strap across his chest.

Tighter and tighter until he coughed.

"I know," she whispered.

The surroundings grew dark and her skin turned gray. She climbed aboard the gurney and straddled him, and began to hum a melody he could barely remember. Her lips pulled back and became a familiar gaping hole, and his memories, his life, poured in.

Author of *Carousel*, writer and multimedia artist. She grew up in the north of England amongst a startling juxtaposition of dreary, soot-covered walls and mysterious bluebell woods. Surrounded by weaving mills, the coal mine, an abattoir, and the gasworks, escape often meant climbing the hills where the sky opened up, the larks sang, and the land bore hilltop follies, Roman roads, peat bogs, old battlefields, canals, black-faced sheep, and ruined churches. It was a fertile bed of dreams and ideas. It's where she grew up, it's what she lived and breathed, and it's who she is—soot, sheep, bluebells, and all.

Meepy
Brent Jenkins

They laughed at him. He tried to ignore it.

They spat at him. He didn't react.

They called him names. They threatened him. He kept walking.

The boy was new at his elementary school, and he hated it. The teachers were mean. The kids were meaner. He had been going there for a month, having moved with his mother following his parents' divorce. Every day he tried his best to ignore their taunts. Pay them no mind. Don't give them the satisfaction. This sounded good, but the truth was he was too scared to stand up to them. Their words hurt. Every day made him a little sadder, a little more depressed. The boy had decided he would run away, escape this place, at the end of the month.

But it turned out there was no need, because one day he started seeing Meepy, and Meepy changed everything.

The first time he appeared was during math class. The boy had nodded off during the teacher's boring lecture, and when he opened his eyes, there was Meepy mocking the teacher. He comically mimicked the woman's every movement and mannerism. Wagging his finger like an angry cartoon mother every time she emphasized a point. Drawing funny and vulgar pictures on the board whenever she wrote out a math problem. All the while, the stick-figured jokester smiled at the boy, letting him know that this was for him. The boy snickered under his breath.

He came across Meepy again the next day in the cafeteria. As the boy stood in line, he saw his enchanting new friend behind the counter. Meepy, with his big blue head and body made of sticks. Meepy, with his painted-on smile. Meepy, with his bright, circular eyes. He was dressed like one of the lunch ladies: apron, hairnet, and all. Every time the next kid in line would come up, Meepy would do a little jig and shovel slop onto their trays. But when one of the bullies reached him, Meepy dumped the slop not onto his tray, but on top of his head instead. The bully didn't seem to notice and went on down the line looking like he had decided to dunk his head in a pig's trough. Meepy smiled at the boy—he was always smiling. The boy laughed.

And so it went on like this for weeks. The boy would go to school looking for Meepy. Meepy would always show up, but never quite when the boy expected. Sometimes he would be doing goofy exercises in gym class. Sometimes he would chase the boy around during recess. The boy saw him in the classroom, on the bus, in the halls. Meepy had even started showing up outside of school, occasionally at the boy's own house. But it was always a surprise, a wonderful surprise the boy looked forward to every day.

Meepy made him laugh. Meepy made him happy. Meepy made everything else matter less. He was the boy's special friend, a magic person—or *thing*, really—that only the boy could see. The boy loved Meepy.

One day, toward the end of school, the boy went to the restroom and found Meepy upside down in the toilet. His big blue head, usually a balloonish, round thing, had been stuffed inside the bowl. Despite his scrunched up smile, Meepy did not look happy.

"What are you doing in there, Meepy?" the boy asked.

"Tommy did this to me," his special friend answered. Tommy was one of the kids that often bullied the boy. "That meanie beat me up and stuffed me in here. Now I'm sad. Just a tad too sad to play with you, lad."

This made the boy angry.

"Hurt him for me," Meepy told the boy. In the past, Meepy's voice had always been a high, goofy thing, like that of a cartoon. But now his tone became very deep and had an uncomfortable rasp to it, like sandpaper scraping across dry skin.

"Hurt him for *us!*" said Meepy.

The boy liked that idea. It was one thing to bully *him*, but to hurt Meepy like that, well … well the boy loved Meepy, and he would make sure Tommy knew never to do that again.

When school was out and all the kids were walking to their busses, the boy found a brick on the ground and picked it up. Once they reached the walkway near the bussing lane, he snuck up and hit Tommy in the knee with it. The bully fell down in agony. The boy could tell that he wanted to get up and pummel him for such an offense, but all Tommy could do was lay on the ground and hold his bloody knee, crying.

As the boy stood over him in satisfaction, he saw Meepy standing outside the fence that lined the other side of the bussing lane. Two big thumbs up, he gave the boy. "Great job, kiddo!" he yelled in his once again normal, goofy voice.

The noise that had been the idle rumbling of bus engines began to shift. The vehicles started to move, and would be coming around the corner any moment.

He looked at Meepy, who stared intently, urgently back at him. Even with his obscenely large smile, the boy could tell his friend had something terribly serious in mind. Something he was trying to communicate to the boy.

The first bus swung around the corner of the building, and suddenly Meepy's message was clear. *Push him in front of a bus!* Meepy was telling him without saying it. The boy understood, and he wanted to do it. He hated Tommy, who had been a chief contributor to his misery. He wanted to make Tommy hurt really bad, maybe even *kill* him. It would be so easy. The busses would be driving by merely a few feet from the boys. Only a single railing separated the driving lane from the walkway on which they stood. All it would take was a simple *push*.

But the first bus drove by, and the boy didn't push

Tommy. Then another bus passed, and he still could not bring himself to do it.

While this was happening, he looked at Meepy. The vision of his friend was repeatedly interrupted by the passing of busses, but in the spaces between, when the boy could see Meepy, Meepy was angry. Angry at the boy. Angry *beneath* the smile. In each successive, flashing vision, the blue-headed stick man looked more furious. *Is his head turning purple?* the boy wondered. Then the last bus passed, and Meepy was gone.

The boy got in big trouble over the incident. His mother was livid when she found out what he'd done, and she grounded him for a long time. He spent most of this time in his room, torn between two regrets. He felt a moral guilt about what he had done to Tommy. Hurting people was bad, he knew. But he also felt another guilt, this one perhaps stronger. It was the shame of disappointing Meepy. He had let his best friend down. He had made him angry. And for some reason, upsetting Meepy made him feel worse than upsetting his mother. He wanted his friend to be happy, so the two of them could laugh and play together. After all, he did love Meepy, and knew that Meepy loved him back.

But there would be no more laughing or playing for weeks—Meepy stopped showing up. The boy was very sad. He hated life without Meepy, and wanted nothing more than for his friend to come back. He hadn't seen him since the incident with Tommy, and the boy wondered if he had made Meepy so mad that he might *never* return.

Then one day, while the boy was in his room, he heard something at the window, perhaps a rock hitting it. He walked over to it and what he saw, of all things, in the tree outside his room, was Meepy. *Meepy!* His greatly missed friend was sitting on a branch, waving at the boy and smiling. Not a trace of anger was on his face. The boy waved back as he lit up with excitement.

Meepy, his body consisting of sticks, looked like just another one of the tree's branches, albeit with a blue balloon stuck on the end of it. As the boy was thinking this, a squirrel ran up Meepy's body and snatched his head right off. The furry little creature scurried up, down, and around the tree with Meepy's big round head in his teeth. The trademark smile on

Meepy's disembodied head had changed to an O of shock, and his headless body ran all about the tree in pursuit of the thieving animal and the bounty in its teeth.

This scene was about the funniest thing the boy had ever seen. He doubled over in delight, his face hurting from laughing so hard. He told Meepy how silly he was, but doubted his friend could hear him.

When Meepy finally retrieved his head and popped it back on, the 'O' became a smile again. He then gestured to the boy to open the window. The boy happily did so. Meepy crept through the opening head first and stood up, but had to stay hunched over to avoid the ceiling. *Was he this tall before?* the boy wondered.

"Well howdy doody, dude!" Meepy greeted him. "Thanks for lettin' me in. I was really losing my head out there!"

The boy giggled. "Hi, Meepy," he said softly so his mom wouldn't hear. "Where have you been?" Then, before his friend could answer, "I'm so sorry, Meepy! Sorry for not doing what you wanted me to do to Tommy!"

"Oh, it's okie-dokie, kiddo! I went cuckoo about that for a minute, but now it's okie-dokie. You know why it's okie-dokie?"

The boy didn't know.

"Because I know you'll never do it again. You'll never disappoint ol' Meepy again, will ya buddy?"

"No!" answered the boy. "I'll never let you down again!"

Meepy did a little jig while his head spun around a few times, causing the boy to giggle some more.

"Super-awesome-marvel-errific!" Meepy shouted. "Then we have something super-duper important to talk about, squirt. Come closer."

The boy came forward. Meepy whispered in his ear.

"You know why I've been gone, kiddo? It's because your mommy found out about me. She found out about Meepy and she didn't want you and me to be best buds, so she locked me up in the shed in the backyard. She tied me up with a rope and did bad, bad things to Meepy. She *hurt* Meepy. All so me and you couldn't play together anymore. Can you *believe* that? Sorry to tell you, buddy, but your mommy tied me downsies and gave me the frownsies, just so best buds couldn't play aroundsies. Righty-roo, she did."

This story saddened the boy greatly; he started to cry. At first he couldn't believe Mommy would do such a thing. But then he remembered the million or so times she had kept things that he wanted away from him. She was *always* doing that, as a matter of fact.

Besides, had Meepy ever lied to him before? He thought not, and so he decided he believed Meepy. He trusted his friend.

"There's something we have to do," Meepy continued, after a moment's pause to let his story sink in. "Something that will make it so we can play and laugh as much as we want.

"We'll be together forever!" he promised.

This sounded wonderful to the boy, who grinned with pure adolescent joy. "Okay, Meepy! I'll do whatever you need."

"Wowza! That's turbo-tremendous-ultra-stupendous! Tell you what, I have to go now. But stay awake, squirt, 'cause I'll be coming back later tonight, after your mommy's asleep. Then we'll carry out Operation Together Forever, okie-dokie?"

"Okie-dokie, Meepy," said the boy. "I'll wait for you."

His friend then made his goodbye and slipped out through the window. The boy was happy, ecstatic even.

When Meepy came back, it was a little after midnight and the boy's mom had been asleep for an hour. This time he just came crawling right out from under the boy's bed while the boy was sitting on it, as if he had been under there the whole time. Stuck to his head were a pair of dirty underwear, a plastic army man, and a few old Doritos that the boy had dropped down there who knows how long ago.

"Hi-ya!" Meepy said.

"Hey." The boy laughed at the silliness stuck to his friend's head.

"Are ya ready to carry out this evenin's top secret mission?" Meepy had changed his voice to imitate that of a southern military general the boy had once seen on TV. "Are ya ready to perform Operation Togethah Forevah, sah-jent?"

"Yeah," said the boy.

"Ah cain't hear yoooou!"

"Sir, yes sir!" the boy nearly shouted, while stifling a chuckle.

"Well that's just dandy, sah-jent," Meepy said, still in his southern military drawl. He shook loose all the junk that was on him and then continued. "Fust thang's fust, we gotta infiltrate the base. I'm talkin' 'bout the garage. How's about ya lead us there, sah-jent. They's somethin' in there we gonna need to complete our mission."

As they left his room, they passed by his mom's closed door. Even though she would sleep through anything—his mom had started taking sleeping pills every night since the divorce—he still stepped carefully to lessen the creak in the floor that was always there. He noticed the floor didn't creak for Meepy.

When they entered the garage, Meepy went to the wall where the boy's mom kept her gardening tools.

"This one, buddy," he said, pointing to a pair of hedge clippers. Meepy had dropped the southern military accent. "This is what we need."

The boy could barely reach it, but he managed to grab the tool as instructed. His mother had always forbidden him from touching the tools that hung on the wall, and he could see why. It was heavy, and the two long blades looked really sharp. He wasn't sure what Meepy had in mind with hedge clippers, but he chose not to think about it. He chose not to question Meepy.

"Now," Meepy said with a wink, "back upstairs, squirt."

The boy went first, clippers in hand. His friend followed. Judging by the smile on his face, one would have thought Meepy was having a blast, or looking very much forward to what was going to happen next.

Once they reached the top of the stairs, Meepy pointed toward the mother's room. The boy gulped, crept over to the closed door, and hesitated. He looked back at his pal.

"Together forever," Meepy reminded him. His warm, friendly face assured the boy.

The boy opened the door and slowly entered. His mom was snoring loudly, as always. With his happiest smile, Meepy tiptoed in behind him, leaving the door open so they would have the light from the hallway to work with. The boy stood uncertainly three feet from the foot of his mom's bed, each hand gripping one of the hedge clippers' handles. He was starting to get a bad feeling about what Meepy might want him to do. He found himself, for the first time, becoming scared, dreadfully wishing he had not put himself in this spot. Again, he looked back at Meepy. Again, his magical friend encouraged him to proceed.

"Come on, pal," he said. "We're almost there! Just climb up onto Mommy's bed."

The boy gulped once more. "And then what?"

It seemed to the boy that Meepy's smile grew longer and curled up in an even more pronounced way.

"Then just a little *snip snip snip* with the tool there. After that, Mommy'll be in heaven and we get *to laugh and play and be silly all day, forever and ever and ever I say!*" He sang this last part.

The boy was not amused. But still, in his childish way, he found this promise intoxicating. He carefully climbed up onto the bed, next to his mom. As he looked at her, a tear broke from his eye. He realized in his heart that his love for her was too strong, even if she *had* kept Meepy tied up in the shed and away from him. He couldn't do what his friend was asking of him. He simply couldn't kill Mommy.

The problem now was Meepy, who was standing next to the bed, watching. The boy was afraid of what Meepy might do when he broke his promise and let his friend down again. In fact, he was starting to think Meepy wasn't really his friend at all. Maybe Meepy was a bad person, a bad *thing*. As he knelt on the bed and thought this over, he became terribly certain of it. Meepy was evil.

"Well, what're ya waitin' for, buckaroo?"

The boy was terrified, but suddenly remembered what a hedge clippers' true purpose was anyway—cutting sticks and branches of course—and at that moment, he did a thing of tremendous bravery. He turned and lunged toward Meepy, chopping madly with the tool. The blue-faced stick man was too close to the boy to have any real chance at escape. The clippers snipped his torso with ease, bisecting him. And as his top half began to fall—the smile on his face again an O now— the boy snipped again, this time slicing right through Meepy's neck.

As the severed head went rolling, the boy's momentum carried him off the bed, crashing to the floor next to the disjoined pieces of Meepy's body.

After lying frozen in exhaustion and fear for a moment, he rolled onto his back and saw Meepy, fully reformed and towering over him.

He supposed he should have known that he couldn't really kill Meepy, at least not with a simple gardening tool. And this newly put-back-together Meepy was horrifying. He was much larger than before. The sticks of his body were thick and covered with thorns. His head was now a bright, reddish purple. Gone were the simple facial attributes the boy had come to know. They had been replaced by the ugly, hellish features of a demon.

"*I guess playtime's OVER!*" Meepy screamed without screaming it. The words were only in the boy's mind, yet they made his head hurt. The voice had reverted back to the sinister, raspy cadence the boy had heard once before. The terrifying creature he used to call a friend leaned down, putting his face inches from the boy's.

"*You should have been a good boy and done as Meepy asked!*" The words physically pained the boy's ears, as if needles were being poked into them.

It was obvious that his mom couldn't hear a thing; her slumber was undisturbed. The boy wished more than anything that she would wake up. He wanted to scream, but even if he could muster up the strength to do so, he doubted she would wake.

Wide-eyed and scared out of his mind, he stared into the face of this unspeakable being. Meepy's head was twice as big as he'd ever seen it. And where there had been a painted-on smile before, there was now a gaping orifice filled with a hundred sharp, rotting teeth.

Meepy held the hedge clippers in his hands. He opened them up and positioned the two long blades around the boy's neck, pinning him to the floor.

"*You worthless shit! Listen to me! You WILL kill her, or I'll take YOUR head off right now, and then torture Mommy until she begs for death!*"

The boy was too terrified to do anything but cry. He laid there, staring up at the monster on top of him, afraid to move. Meepy's mouth twisted up into a grotesque mockery of his usual smile.

"Think I'm scary now? Just disobey me one more time and you'll see the REAL me, kiddo! That is, right before I kill you. You and Mommy!"

The boy continued bawling. Meepy opened the clippers fully and then quickly snapped them back together, stopping right before the blades would have sliced through the child's neck. This brought out a guttural cry from the boy, who was finally spurred into action.

"O-o-okay, Meepy," he stuttered. The boy realized, with great despair, that he had no choice. Did he want Meepy to kill both of them, but torture his mom first? Or did he want to give Mommy a quick, hopefully not-too-painful death? The lesser of two evils.

Meepy released the hedge clippers from around the boy's neck and dropped them to the floor. The boy sat up, grabbed the tool, and reluctantly crawled back onto the bed with his snoring mother. She slept on her back, and so the boy straddled her torso, opened up the clippers, and placed them around her neck as Meepy had just done to him.

He looked over at Meepy, who was once again smiling at him in his simple, blue-faced form.

The boy turned back to his mother, who snored away under the instrument of her death, blissfully unaware, off in dreamland somewhere.

"I'm so sorry, Mommy," the boy whispered through his tears. "I love you."

He leaned forward, gave his mother a tender kiss, and then sat back up.

Snip.

He'd done it. The clippers fell out of his hands.

He watched, stunned, as her eyes flew open and her hands shot up to her nearly-severed neck, from which a crimson river flowed. The boy, in utter, paralyzing shock, fell backward off the bed.

Meepy was on top of him again.

Meepy, who had never been able to actually touch anything.

Meepy, who had only been able to make the boy see and hear things.

Meepy, who, in order to become more real, had needed only for the boy to be a *good* boy—a boy who kills.

And he had. The boy had finally been very good, indeed.

Meepy was straddling the boy, and finally, just for the fun of it, he showed him his true face.

The boy went instantly mad.

The nefarious being put his stick hands in the boy's mouth and pulled at the corners, stretching it open severely. He lowered his head and squeezed into the boy's impossibly wide-stretched cavity. After he had gotten it all in, he continued climbing inside the boy, stick limbs disappearing into the child's mouth.

Once fully inside, the boy sat up. Or, that is to say, Meepy sat up.

For Meepy had spoken true when he promised the boy. They would be together forever now. Meepy and the boy could play as much as they wanted. Only from now on, they would play the kind of games Meepy liked to play. The kind of games where people got hurt.

The boy stood up, giggled, and with a big, shining smile on his face, he walked out of the room, down the stairs, and out the front door.

He couldn't wait to find someone to play with.

Brent Jenkins (1983–2041), though just now bursting onto the literary scene, has already won the Bram Stoker award for Short Fiction an astounding zero times. He only recently began writing. "Meepy" is his first published work, but he's confident many more will follow. He graduated from the University of Georgia in 2006 and has since been trying to figure out what he wants to be when he grows up, a quest that's found him working jobs ranging from corporate slave to poker player. He is a lover of movies, tennis, beer, philosophy, professional wrestling, Braves baseball, and all-around good times and good people. Mr. Jenkins currently resides in the Atlanta area.

The Black Father of the Night
David Schembri

Translated from the original Finnish

From trunk to branch, shrub to root,
Their bones we will grind to mix with flour,
Their claws we will bind, their throats be slit,
They will hang and drain for an hour.
Through the night they fly, through the dark they run,
They are the hardest to catch, but only for some,
We are quick, we are hungry, and we work and we bite,
Oh, how we feast—how we feast on this night ...
                            —the song of Vrant and Kull.

Viborg, Finland, 1901.

Night crows called ominously from the roofs of smoke-cottages.

Darkness settled. The winds began to gust and the local merchant in the watchtower shivered with unease. The crows always sing their most foreboding songs in the time between Christmas Eve and Christmas Day. When young hearts are filled with joy, an unknown dread dwells in the small hearts of the wild—local hounds howl at the moon more so this eve. The merchant beats his drum. Townsfolk finished up their business and hurried indoors, seeking refuge from the snow and the night.

Not all obeyed the watchman's advice. Little Markus, his pink feet within wooden clogs, wandered about in the snow-covered cobbled streets. He stood beneath the glow of one of the street lanterns, gazing up at the star-filled sky; *when will the gift-giver be soaring?* His ears flexed suddenly to distant footsteps; his mother called through the cold, "Come inside at once!"

The watchman's drum echoed. Wrapped in a large shawl, Markus's mother approached. "Come, Markus!" She cuddled him into the warmth of her garments.

Markus wanted to stay to see the gift-giver fly, yet he was seduced by the comfort, ever devoted.

She walked him back down the street toward their home. "It is so cold! Why must you wander? Neither brave, nor smart … you will come to ill!" she complained as they reached the gate.

"I was watching, Mumma. Tonight he might come?"

They entered the yard; frozen rose bushes lined the fence. His mother paused, hiding her anger behind her closed, thin lips.

"Mumma? I am not naughty, or bad? He will give to me this time?" he whimpered.

She knelt and looked into his big eyes; a smile did nothing to stop his sorrow.

"Maybe, my dear," she said as tenderly as she could. "He goes through much toil, this night … many houses … many children … over moon, through stars—"

"But I've been good, Mumma!" Markus cried as he fell into her arms.

"I know you have, my dear," she whispered into his neck. "Listen to me. Come morning, if your stocking stays empty, fail you not the one thing you have."

"What be that?" he cried into his little hands.

"Me."

Leena embraced her son in the cold before taking him to warm by the fire.

Markus woke to merry strains of old Christmas rhymes echoing from the town's square. Snowflakes fluttered past his parchment window, creating dancing shadows on his bedroom wall—it had to be a worthy sign. He flung the blankets aside and leapt from his bed, hope alive in his heart as he took the stairs two at a time, his mind imagining the possibilities of what the gift-giver might have brought: toy wagon, wooden horse, candy … something *new*, something *his*. A toy that would allow him to play with the other children, share in their laughter and friendship, not watch from the hedges again. It *had* to be his turn to receive from the gift-giver.

Markus's shoulders slumped. His stocking, hung with such belief above the fireplace the night before, was empty.

Markus cried as he fell to his knees. Leena ran from her stove. "My dear, you have risen so early." She cradled him. "There, there …"

He bawled into her chest, his tears wetting her garment.

"Look, Mumma has something for you." Leena eased her trembling son back, fetching something from her dress pocket as she did so. He watched through his fingers, confused. Leena held in her hand a toffee she had bought from the market the day before. She placed it in his little palm. "Here. Say now, my son, for my ears to hear … you do not need *his* gifts?"

"Naughty … I am!"

"No, no, you are not. You are a sweet boy!" She embraced him again. "You *are* good, dear Markus!"

His mother stroked his hair. The toffee had begun to melt in his grasp. "Other boys and girls get his gifts!" he cried. "Why not give unto me! The others tease, Mumma."

"Whence the tears have dried, pain slips away in its stead," she said determinedly. "Settle into my arms, my love, it is your one painless place."

Beneath the wooden beams of Markus's bedroom, Leena sang her son to sleep with a lullaby, the same one her mother used to sing to her. Leena always held back her tears whenever she sang it, but her dear little boy loved it so. His deep, slow breaths made her sure he was fast asleep, and she blew out his candle, gathering her coat. Being as quiet as a mouse, she tiptoed down the old stairs. Venturing out with a determined pace, the dark of Christmas night swallowed her.

The drumming from the watchman's tower echoed through the streets and trailed her into the dense mountain forest like prowling movements. The late chill ate at her skin, the snow dragged at her feet, and the shadows ruled the secret path, but nothing would preclude her ... the nightjars and rainbow bugs fell silent. A foul noise drifted on the wind, igniting her fear and quickening her heart. She scurried down the secret path, dread chilling her marrow.

A wave of heat swelled through Leena's shoulders as the little voices swirled around her, voices she hated, voices that still troubled her sleep. They'd mocked her when she was little, and they would persist until she shed tears. As she walked, she drew nearer to the creatures she had not seen for many years.

Their wicked songs lingered and strayed from the path into the twisting wood. She followed them, trying to control her fear. A rotten smell threatened her nose. Their foul little bodies were moving up ahead in a small clearing. Leena shifted a branch or two to feast her eyes on their camp. A fire was alive and cracking. Around it they danced.

Sickly songs spilled from their cracked lips, their black teeth like rotten candy against the orange glow of the fire. Their naked skin, darkened by years of chimney ash, their bony limbs, their dangling sex; their small leather belts, with a sheath strapped to each that housed their rusty little daggers. They were the father's helpers, wretched and grim. One was named Kull, the other named Vrant, and together they sang and chanted: "We will pluck them, we will skin them, we will boil them in a stew; we will herb them, we will brew them, and on their flesh we will chew!"

Mutilated night crows and hares lay dead around the fire. A large cloth sack wriggled and bulged. *A naughty child.* Leena's heart raced.

The little murderers, she thought as her mind wandered back. When she was not yet seven, she'd first spied on them. Once they had beaten a poor child until he died in the weeds. Year after year, Leena tried to put a stop to their evils, but her courage always faltered. Instead, she would cry and watch from the shadows ... her young eyes witnessed them rip arms and legs from children and gut them whilst they still had the strength to scream, their bodies trembling as their brief lives drained onto the forest floor. Their breaths reduced to tiny gasps, as death took them away, leaving in their place a feast for the dirty monsters.

Leena cleared her throat and stepped into the clearing, her face hot with outrage. They stopped their prancing by the flames, crouched over their dead, and began to pull the feathers and bite the fur. Melodies hummed from their lips, and one even grunted and shat in the earth.

Their little eyes darted with annoyance, but they kept about their work and sang again as if no disturbance had been brought. "We will cool them, we will cut them, we will serve them with bread. We will turn them, we will sauce them and bite off their heads!"

Leena stepped further into view, her heart quickening. "A demon spat onto the waters, and out you both came." She glanced at the moving cloth sack, and they hunched over it, guarding it like wolves over fresh prey. They hissed at her, drool stringing through their rotten black teeth.

"Not tonight!" she yelled.

"Ours! Our right! Our catch!" they spat in unison.

"Release the child, or joint from joint, I will undo you both!"

She stepped closer to their wretched bodies—she was not a little girl anymore. She towered over them, and knew in her determined heart that she could crush them.

Kull and Vrant laughed, mocked, and spat at her feet. They circled her, and sang a rhyme that used to send her crying to her mother.

> *Oh, Leena, Leena—Leena the small.*
> *You have the legs of a pig and the face of a troll.*
> *You are weak, you are ugly; you are nothing at all.*
> *Leena, Leena—how we love to watch you fall.*

"Free the child!"

"Ours!"

Vrant stormed in front of her and snarled and spat. He pulled out his dagger and thrashed it across her bulk. A sharp pain struck her thigh and she lost her balance and fell on her rear.

"You are not welcome, you filthy little whore! I will drain

you. I will eat you! My teeth through your skin like a saw!"

Vrant's dagger raised, its point destined for her gut. A thrash from the darkness sent him cowering by Kull. A tall and large figure entered the clearing, wielding a pointed staff, and through its beard came a vexed gruff. Vrant and Kull trembled in the blackness of its shadow as the fire gave hints of its form. "Father?" they both trembled. "Always, we honor you!"

"Be silent!" the father yelled in his deep voice. "Take your feast into the dark! Be off with you!"

Leena got to her feet, nursing her stinging wound. It was long, but she chose not to let it burden her. "The child! The child!" she protested.

"Ours to take!" claimed Vrant and Kull.

"The sack will remain!" the father ordered.

They both looked up at him with the eyes of sad hounds. "But, Father?"

"Your birds and your hares shall rest within your wretched arms. The child will live to steal bread another day … perhaps another will lay in bad luck's bed next year, but not this night."

Vrant and Kull snarled and sobbed, gathering their raw feast, and scurrying into the dark woods, cursing as they went. Leena hurried to the sack, her fingers trembling as she untied it. A young girl not much older than Markus was inside. Screaming and kicking out of her cloth prison, she ran back to the way of the town.

"Little monsters, how could you still let them prey on the young?"

He stood over her in silence, his face shrouded in shadow. "They have their uses."

"They are vermin!"

"They are loyal … and they only ask for one night to feast … this night."

"How dare you grant it!"

"Leave now … I have a fire to feed and some warmth to gain," he dismissed. Turning his back on her, the woods then swallowed him.

Leena rushed after him but said nothing; she wanted to talk face to face, not gasp and chase him for answers.

The moonlight shined over his hidden, wooden cottage, which rested by the roots of the mountain. Smoke billowed from its little chimney, and night crows called from nearby trees. Attached to the cottage was his workshop, and across the way, through a yard of overgrown shrubbery, was the stable.

The noisy slumber of Sleipnir caught her ears; the father's eight-legged horse, mistaken by the townsfolk as a group of reindeer. Sleipnir was menacing to feast eyes upon, but was easily tamable with a gentle stroke to the mane and a bucket full of carrots.

The father, although not acknowledging her chase, entered his cottage, leaving the door ajar. When Leena shut the wooden door behind her, the familiar scent of rum and dusted timber caught her cherry nose. The cottage looked as she had remembered. The boards were recently swept and the roof beams were clear of any cobwebs. She stepped down the dark hall, boards creaking beneath her feet, and into the dimly lit living room. The father was warming his large hands by the open fire, his staff resting on his armchair. "Nothing to my ears, have you to say?" she asked her father.

"I see you still service other men in their beds."

"What choice do I have? I need to bring shelter and warmth to my son."

"Away with you."

Leena stepped closer. "Why do you ignore him? He is your child!"

"Poison, his very body. He is the symbol of my flaws. I am mending my ways. Split asunder it will be if I chose to grant him."

"Punishing him for your own evils? Hate me if you must, but how dare you neglect him. He longs to have the treasures that are anointed to the other children at Christmas. A gift? A blessing? He is lonely, father. He feels worthless!"

"If this is why you have come, then leave," he said, turning around. "If he is feeling such a way, then as a mother, you have failed,"

"How dare you!" Leena stomped over to him and smacked him across his wide face.

He did not retaliate. He stood frozen, clutching his throbbing cheek with his large hand. He stared at her with wild dark eyes. His stare granted a stab of pity for him, but the longer she looked, the more she despised.

273

"Unto the pit of a pig, lays a neater place." She looked him up and down, hands on her hips. "The townsfolk claim you as a god. *The gift-giver; a saint?* Songs to end of songs, they would sing. Little do they see the swine, the old man, the one who used to call himself my father. The one who filled me with his seed."

"Stop this."

"You scared hog, in a beard and dress. Hiding behind myth, surrounding yourself with the filth you call your helpers. Teased and tortured I was, for years when I lived here, and you did nothing! Mother was the only one who cared."

"You will not speak of your mother!" the large man yelled.

"Why not? Ignorant was she? About your evils? The evils in my bed?"

"No! She had no knowledge!"

"You are so sure of this? This place is small, father." She teased in the cruelest voice; the anger was fuming in her, giving her strength. "There is no silence here, nowhere evils can hide. Mother heard you, breathing and panting. To you it was honey, but to her it was venom. She heard my pleas, but feared to do anything. That is why she dived into the river of death—"

"You little whore!" He backhanded her, knocking her to the floor.

Cheek throbbing, blood soured her tongue. He kicked into her ribs and flipped her onto her back. She tried to rise but he slammed his boot down on her left hand. It hurt, her wrist straining beneath his weight. Her right hand was pinned with his other boot as he leered down at her, triumphant.

"Let me up, Father!"

"Your mother was taken by the blizzard, and that is the end of it!"

"If that comforts you, then believe what you wish. But it is knowledge to us both that she ran out into that storm, willing it to swallow her!"

"You little witch!" He stamped his foot into her belly.

Leena gasped.

"Leave!" The father stepped back to his place before the fire. Trembling with anger, he held his large hands again before it. "Leave and never return."

Leena struggled to her feet, gathering the blood thick in

her mouth. She spat on his armchair with malevolence. He marched over to her with thundering steps and gripped her shoulders, forcing her against him. "How dare you!"

"In hell, may your flesh and veins be torn!" She turned her face from the stench of rum and spittle that fouled his beard.

The father groaned; he had never forgotten the smell of her hair, her breath, her sweat—it always aroused him. "I can grant a cure for loneliness to the boy"—he pressed his face to hers—"I, a man of great gifts."

"No ..." she whispered, his stink and words suffocating her fragile spirit. "Please, stop."

His tongue snaked out of his mouth and stroked her ear lobe. The sound of his bubbling saliva and the heat of his tongue forced her to dry retch.

She struggled to free herself but was held in place.

"You should never have come here."

He threw her to the floor.

Leena tried to get to her feet, but the weight of her father was upon her.

What would become of the emptiness in his little heart? Markus sweated in his bed, stirring and muttering in troubled slumber. He called for his mother. She answered him from down the stairs. He rushed to her, finding her resting before the dead fireplace. It was cold in the house; he could see his breaths. A layer of smoke billowed from the starving coals.

He went down to her and she was weak with red cheeks. He huddled within her arms and found warmth again; a warmth that would never fail him. A fast heartbeat drummed into his ear from the inside of her chest and an unwelcoming smell stung his nostrils. "Have you come to ill, Mumma?"

"Maybe for a time," she breathed. "Rise up from despair, my son. I will be well again soon."

"Where have you been, Mumma?"

She let out a trembling breath and uttered, "To see the gift-giver ..."

"You did?" He rose from her embrace. "Found for me a toy, Mumma?"

"No. There are no toys there in his evil place." She cupped his face. "Promise me now, my son, you will *not* long for his gifts again. You must hate him, now. He is wicked. He is evil, and so too are his servants."

Markus's eyes welled. "That cannot be true, Mumma."

"It is, my love. It is time for hate now, not tears."

"Why?"

"Because we know the truth that they are wicked, and when the time is right, we will seek them out."

Markus stared at his mother, disbelief trembling his bottom lip.

Leena took Markus's cold hand and placed it over her belly, whispering, "Feel it, it is a-growing. We must wait until your sibling grows, my dear … together, the three of us will enter the cursed lands of their forest. We must wait and be angry for many years, until you have the hands and strength of a man, and be not of a child.

"The wicked ones will be frailer with their souls decaying, and they *will* lose the war that we will beset upon them."

Markus cried into his mumma's arms; her hard and cold words were unfamiliar to his little ears.

"There, there, my darling." Leena returned some tender tones to her voice. "Your poor little mind does not understand, but it will in time and so will the mind of the newborn. In the dark of one future Christmas Eve, the gift-giver and his wretched servants will be cast into the river of death."

She stroked his hair as he cried further into her bosom. "Then your sibling will craft with you, care for you as you take the name of 'Nickolas,' and be forever more the man of great gifts."

David Schembri has been published in several print anthologies and magazines since 2006, and his first novelette, *The Unforgiving Court*, will appear shortly in the Chaosium anthology *Undead & Unbound*.

Muralistic
Matthew Warner

The mural in the children's play area of Augusta City Library normally featured what you would expect. A cartoonish cow stood in a field bordered by a split-rail fence. But today, a shadowy figure with wings walked on the horizon.

"Huh," Gerald said as he noticed the addition. He rubbed a hand across his stubbled cheeks and looked down at his one-year-old son. Parker had pulled Thomas the Tank Engine off the shelf and was murmuring something about a fire truck. "What do you think of that, buddy? It looks like a pterodactyl."

"Fire truck," Parker said and then abandoned the train for the toy kitchen in the corner. He ran with both hands up in the air and squealed with excitement. Beyond the play area, other children buzzed as they waited on couches or read picture books.

A mother seated nearby said, "It looks like a what?"

Gerald glanced at her tight-fitting tank top before forcing himself to look up at her face. "A pterodactyl. You know. A dinosaur? But it doesn't quite fit in with the cow. And it's too small."

She leaned forward to glance at the wall. "That's pretty cool."

Again, Gerald tore his eyes off her. He reached out to pull up the back of Parker's shorts where they had fallen to expose his diaper. The mother didn't notice Gerald's attention, however—or if she did, she didn't care—because her little girl was approaching the other adult in the room.

He was a bearded black man who often sat here during the wait for Mother Goose Story Time. Like now, he always occupied the rocker beside the Lego table. He scowled at a laptop computer balanced on his knees. Gerald had never identified a corresponding child, but he never doubted that Laptop Man, as he thought of him, had one within the crowd of roaming toddlers. No one in their right mind would otherwise hang out here before nine o'clock on a weekday morning.

"Tracy, honey," the shapely mother said. "Don't bother him."

Tracy had placed a hand on Laptop Man's arm and was peeking at the computer screen. He stopped typing to look at her.

"Tracy," the mother said.

But then the librarian interrupted, announcing Story Time was about to start. Gerald grabbed Parker's hand and led him away. The mother and little Tracy walked directly in front of them. Gerald was careful to keep his gaze elsewhere.

Back home, Gerald told his wife about the mural. He finished with, "The woman next to me didn't know what a pterodactyl was."

He must have betrayed something with his smile, because Eileen raised an eyebrow. "The woman 'next to me'?"

"Tracy's mother, apparently."

Crossing her arms, Eileen leaned back in her chair. It was the high-backed executive chair she'd brought from Staunton Medical Center when she moved her office home. A two-thousand-dollar laser printer—another trophy from SMC—hummed behind her as it printed out a patient's file.

When her other eyebrow raised, Gerald shifted uncomfortably where he stood. "What?"

"You know what. I can tell from the look on your face what she is."

"And what's that?"

"Young and attractive."

"Honey—all right, that might be so, but that doesn't mean I'm gonna cheat on you."

"'Doesn't mean I'm gonna cheat on you' … what? You left a word off the end of your sentence, Gerald."

He put his hands on his hips. "And what word is that? 'Yet'? 'Doesn't mean I'm gonna cheat on you *yet*?'"

"No. 'Again.'"

A beat passed in which he just stood there, staring at her. Down the hallway, Parker smashed something in his bedroom.

What do I have to do? Gerald thought. *It's been more than a year, and I still can't live this down.*

Eileen turned back to her desk. "I have work to do."

He left her to it.

After Parker went to bed, Gerald spent the evening alone in the master bedroom. He sat leaning against the headboard, reading a magazine about video games. The baby monitor, on the night stand, was up too loud. When Parker shifted in his crib, it sounded like thunder. But Gerald liked it that way so he wouldn't feel alone.

Eileen finally came to bed at about ten. She put on her nightgown, brushed her teeth, and climbed between the sheets without a word.

"We need to talk," Gerald said.

She grunted and rolled away from him.

"I want to make things better," he said. "I was thinking, now that we're both home and I'm taking care of Parker full time, maybe we should have another baby."

She rolled back to regard him. "You remember why I moved my office home?"

"To keep an eye on me. So I don't misbehave again."

"'Misbehave.' That's not a serious enough word. Parker 'misbehaves' when he draws on the sofa with a ballpoint pen. What you did was an utter betrayal that stabbed my soul."

Gerald slapped his magazine down beside the baby monitor. "So why are you still with me?"

She rolled away again. "That's a good question."

The artist responsible for the pterodactyl had returned overnight to paint over the previous image. The figure was twice as large now, having flown halfway down the cartoon fence toward the camera.

Gerald stared at this, but his mind was occupied. *Why can't she forgive me?* And the answer was always, *Why should I expect her to?*

Luckily, the mother with the magnificent body had taken little Tracy elsewhere today. Maybe to the pool, where mommy could sunbathe and …

Stop thinking about it, moron.

Laptop Man sat on his rocker in the corner as usual, scowling at his computer screen. The machine must have been giving him fits, because he was grumbling under his breath— something about 'them' and 'those messages.' Probably a spam virus.

Parker stood at the Lego table, smashing two blocks together. "Broken, broken," he chanted, sounding on the verge of crying. Gerald gently took the blocks from him and showed him how to fit them together.

If only other things were as easy to fix.

After feeding Parker and putting him down for his midday nap, Gerald pulled out the makings of baloney sandwiches for lunch. Eventually, Eileen emerged from her office and sat down in the breakfast nook. Her arms were crossed, and her eyebrows were bunched together. Gerald recognized that posture; he called it the "powder keg look." He'd seen it all too often. It was best to tread lightly when the powder keg look was out, but that would make for a mightily uncomfortable meal.

He braced himself. "How's work today, honey?"

"Just fine, *honey.*"

He stopped in the process of slathering mayonnaise and took a deep breath. "Okay. What did I do now?"

"Your computer. I've been looking through your browser history. I know what websites you've been visiting."

Gerald stared at her, a dozen excuses rising to his lips and falling away. There was no use denying it.

"You know what hurts the most, Gerald? You promised you were through looking at them."

"I've only done that a few times."

"Oh?"

"And it's still not the same thing as an affair."

"How is it not?"

"Because I don't even know who those women are. It's just entertainment."

Eileen stood up. She looked old and drawn. "I'm too angry to talk to you." She began walking toward the stairs, back to her office. When Gerald opened his mouth, she held up a hand. "No. Just ... tomorrow. Let's talk tomorrow. We need to make some decisions about our marriage."

Her voice broke on the last word. She covered her mouth with one hand.

Gerald watched her go until she left the room. A moment later, his knees buckled. He lay full length on the kitchen floor until he was sure he wasn't going to be sick.

They didn't see each other again all day. Gerald passed her closed office door a couple times and heard her sobbing. When he knocked, she told him to go away.

Parker woke up, and Gerald set him in front of the TV to watch his favorite *Bob the Builder* DVD. Then he took his computer out into the garage. It was the one Eileen gave him as a peace offering when they completed marriage counseling.

He destroyed it with a sledgehammer.

He slept on the couch that night but left the baby monitor in the bedroom with Eileen. It was only fair since he'd watched Parker all day. He wondered who would take care of their boy when they broke up. And how soon would that be?

I wonder if I have an addiction, he asked himself as he tried to get comfortable on the old cushions. They still bore faint stains from Parker's adventures with the ballpoint pen. *Would she buy that?*

"It's not my fault," he whispered into the living room's darkness. But the only thing that answered was the ticking of the grandfather clock.

His thoughts drifted to the library mural as he fell asleep. He thought now the enlarged pterodactyl reminded him of a thunderbird from American Indian mythology. He'd read about thunderbirds in a video game's documentation way back when. Some regarded them as a psychopomps—couriers of souls to the afterlife, like the Grim Reaper. Why would anyone paint that in a children's play area?

Odd that it would appear in the days preceding the explosion of the Gerald-and-Eileen powder keg. Or maybe not so odd.

Thoughts of thunderbirds flitted through his mind until they flowered into a dream.

Gerald was standing in the children's play area at the library. The room was dark except for a spotlight illuminating the mural. A man was painting over the old pterodactyl image—and Gerald could see now that it was indeed a thunderbird. The thunderbird was partially in human form, a black shadow with feathered wings hanging off its outstretched arms.

The painter wore a black suit over a black shirt with a black tie. Black fedora hat. Black sunglasses. Black skin. He used a black paint brush to slather black paint onto the wall.

When he saw Gerald, the man turned to him. He removed his sunglasses to reveal black eyes with no whites. He smiled, showing black teeth.

The thunderbird stepped out of the mural.

   "Wake up."

Gerald opened his eyes. For a moment, the person sitting at the foot of the couch was the thunderbird. He gasped.

"Gerald?"

He sat up, the afghan falling off him. Morning sunlight darkened the circles under Eileen's eyes.

"You didn't sleep?"

"No," she said. "I don't know what we're going to do."

"Honey, it was just a website. That's all."

Her fists bunched in her lap. "Don't *tell* me it was just a website. Don't tell me you're not still looking at every woman who walks by. Don't tell me you're not still thinking about *her.*"

"I haven't talked to her in over a year. I'm still loyal to you."

She looked away. Tears glistened on her cheeks. "Yes. But you don't want to be."

The words rose to his mouth, the ones he'd settled on last night: *I have an addiction. It's not my fault.* They might give him a way out of this.

Instead, he said, "You're not being fair."

"Fair. Were you fair when you committed adultery?"

"Were you fair when you snooped through my computer?"

"I wouldn't snoop if I trusted you."

He looked toward Parker's room. Hopefully, their son would wake up, and they wouldn't have to continue this conversation.

"I've tried," he said. "I've tried hard."

"No, you haven't. If you were trying, you wouldn't still be visiting those websites."

"There's nothing wrong with it. We used to visit them together, if you'll recall."

"That's not the point. You made a promise to me, and you broke it." She got up and trudged into the bathroom. "Marriage is all about promises."

There seemed nothing more to say.

They ate breakfast in silence, except for talking to Parker. It was the most uncomfortable meal they'd had since the day she discovered his affair.

After washing the dishes, Gerald loaded Parker's diaper bag with extra items for the day: a water bottle, a Tupperware of Goldfish crackers, and his baseball cap for protection from the summer sun. But when he beckoned Parker to sit in his lap so he could put his sandals onto him, Eileen entered the room. She hadn't unclenched her fists all morning.

"Why don't you leave him here?" she said. "I'll watch him. You go on."

Gerald gaped. "Don't you have to work?"

"I'm taking the morning off. Go on."

He stared at her, noting how she glanced at the coat closet, where their suitcase was kept.

He set Parker down. The boy immediately ran off to his

room, hollering, "Fire truck! Fire truck!"

Gerald stood up slowly. He wanted to ask if she'd be here when he got back. But he was afraid he already knew the answer.

"I'll be at the library," he said.

He couldn't help hanging his head as he plucked his car keys off the table and headed for the door.

When he left, he drove the vehicle that didn't have Parker's car seat. Eileen would need it.

He went to the library's magazine room, figuring it would be a good way to pass the time until Eileen finished whatever she needed to.

Maybe she really was just taking the morning off, sitting with Parker as he watched Sesame Street. She was breathing deeply, like he was now, and planning how they would save their marriage.

And maybe pigs played chess.

It was almost nine o'clock. Mother Goose Story Time would start soon. He'd spent so many mornings singing "Twinkle, Twinkle" and "Little Red Wagon" that it felt strange not to be down there with Parker now.

He hesitated, stood up, and headed for the elevators. As he rode down to the children's area, he told himself he wasn't secretly hoping the shapely mother would be there.

Stop lying to yourself.

Okay, it wasn't a secret hope at all. If Eileen was leaving the house and taking Parker with her, then why shouldn't he flirt? Why shouldn't he do something crazy?

The play area was full today. Toddlers swarmed between the Lego table and bins full of blocks. Laptop Man sat in his rocker, occupying space and scowling at his computer. Little Tracy unconsciously touched Gerald's leg as she passed on the way to her mother.

Gerald made eye contact with the woman. He smiled and stepped toward her before he knew what he was doing.

Then his vision snagged on the mural.

The thunderbird had approached as closely as it could without emerging from the picture like in the dream. It was huge, the size of a full-grown man. He saw now its wings weren't feathered at all but were membranes of skin, like a bat's. They covered half the wall, obscuring the cartoon cow and fence. Gerald watched the children, but no one seemed to notice the figure.

Laptop Man slammed his fingers on the keyboard. "Messages. I don't want them! Can't they understand that?"

The sharpness of his voice dampened the children's chatter. Alarmed, little Tracy turned in her mother's embrace.

Gerald started forward again, but this time not to talk to the shapely mother. Maybe he could help the man and stop him from scaring the kids. After all, as Eileen pointed out, he certainly knew his way around computers. He looked over the man's shoulder to see the monitor.

It was blank.

Laptop Man kept typing anyway. "No, no, no. Not that one either. No!"

He slammed the lid closed.

Gerald looked up at the mural again. *A bad omen.* It had been getting closer all week. He'd assumed, deep down, that the thunderbird was here to warn about his impending divorce.

Still mumbling, Laptop Man began to rummage through his carry bag.

Could the thunderbird be here for a different reason?

More people were arriving for the morning program. Gerald glanced at a mother and toddler walking toward him.

It was Eileen and Parker.

Eileen's face was red and puffy from crying, but she was smiling. "Gerald," she said, hardly able to talk. "I love—"

Parker broke away from her. "Daddy!"

Laptop Man found what he was looking for and pulled it out. It was a gun. Not just any gun, but one of those one-handed machine gun things from a bad Sylvester Stallone movie.

He aimed it at Parker.

The shapely mother screamed.

No.

Gerald leapt for the gunman as he fired, spoiling his aim. The air exploded with gunshots. They were deafening in the tiny play room. A line of holes appeared in the mural. They strafed straight at the thunderbird, stopped at the edge of it, and reappeared on the other side.

Gerald was faintly aware of screams and commotion as he fought for the gun. Laptop Man drove the muzzle into Gerald's stomach and fired again.

Crashing pain. Couldn't breathe.

The gunman pushed him away. Gerald rolled onto his back.

"I told you!" the man screamed. "No more!"

He disappeared with his gun into the library aisles. Parents shielded their children as he passed. A second later, there was another burst of gunfire.

"Oh my god," someone said. "He killed himself."

Eileen appeared in Gerald's field of vision, kneeling over him. She said something, but he couldn't make it out. She seemed too far away. She held Parker under one arm like a sack of potatoes. The boy was shrieking but in one piece.

"I'm so sorry," Gerald said, but he couldn't hear himself.

The mural was visible over his wife's shoulder. The thunderbird had disappeared.

Then Gerald was gone too.

Matthew Warner's publishing credits span a variety of formats, although readers mostly know him through his horror novels and short stories. Dramatic works include films from Darkstone Entertainment based on his screenplays, plus a radio play and stage play premiered by theaters in central Virginia. Warner lives with his wife, the artist Deena Warner, and sons Owen and Thomas. Readers can visit him at matthewwarner.com.

Awaiting Redemption
Maurice Broaddus

The Nuer word for "thousand" meant "lost in the forest," Alang once explained to the missionaries, for that was what you would be within a number that high. The cramped quarters smelled of sweat-drenched, dirty bodies and the stink of dying hope. Alang awoke to the flies buzzing too close to her ears, the itch marking their passage along her skin. Hate flared hotly inside her. Her thigh throbbed with fresh bolts of pain when she shifted, so she kept still. Along the inside of her leg, she traced the raised column of flesh serving as her brand. Counting the shadows, Alang shivered in the darkness. She was lost in a forest of her kinsmen.

Alang was ten years old.

The roadless plains surrounded the village, speckled only with acacia shrubs and long-horned cows, emaciated and hump-backed. The sun-baked, tawny landscape differed very little from her home village, Wunlit. The square, mud and thatch huts with round, uneven roofs mirrored those of her home, but there was no confusion. During the dry season, her people migrated to the camps by the river. Camps of grass-roofed and mud-walled houses set among palms and thorn bushes that proved uninhabitable during the wet season. With the wet season upon them, they wandered

back to Wunlit. They never expected their kinsmen to turn on them.

Alang closed her eyes. Gunfire, angry rapid drumbeats punctured the tranquility, leaving an acrid smell, like burnt hair. She covered her ears to block out the screams. She thought of the village elders who clung to the old ways. They taught that a bit of the blood of the person put to death was thought to be in the slayer and had to be bled out by an earth priest. Ridiculous in this age of space shuttles and the Internet; seen doubly so once she joined the world of the missionaries. Though there was little room for Jesus in the Sudan, and the idea of the spirits of the dead haunting their butchers pleased her.

The blood of the Wunlit men muddied the plains. She was an alien in these lands, no better off than the cows who miserably chewed the passing tufts of grass.

"You are a little scrawny thing? Won't be able to do much work. Too willful. I can see it in your eyes." A tall, reedy figure bedecked in robes spoke with a voice much like the bleat of goats. His hands snapped shut on her face like a crocodile's jaw, turning it from side-to-side in inspection. Lust glinted in his eyes. "You'll do I suppose. I've broken stronger."

Serving was her religious duty, he told her, though she was too impure to read the Qur'an for herself. She knew his kind. For him religion was a tool he re-shaped into his own image to vent his cruelty and hate. He probably knew less of the Qur'an than she did. His dagger sliced her Arizona Cardinals Super Bowl XLIII 2009 Champions shirt, still stiff with dried blood. Wearing only her Nike running shoes, one size too small, she lowered her head, not allowed to cover herself. He touched her in a familiar way, but she would not taste shame no matter how he tried to force feed it to her. She never hid her scars. They told the story of who she was, a map to her soul.

"Call me Master. You aren't fit to say my name." He raised her head to meet his gaze. "Your only hope for redemption in the after world is through obedience. For you, the road to heaven is under your master's foot."

Alang refused the God he worshiped.

Escorted to a dirt-floored room, Alang shivered in the shadows. Shards of light pierced the slats, enough to see her

Master doing the only work he enjoyed doing himself. Three mounds rested along a shelf carved from the earth itself. Ants scrabbled in streams, busy about their day's work. Her Master made quite the show of scooping many of the squirming red bodies into a clay cup. He covered it and set it on a tray next to another cup with a pestle leaning against its side. Once satisfied, he turned to her, and with a nod, two men grabbed both of her arms.

"Will you call to Allah?" he asked.

Alang said nothing.

"Struggle all you want, but soon you will see the mercy and benevolence of Allah."

Her Master stuffed the tiny ants into her ears and then sealed them with a mixture of pebbles and beeswax. Alang screamed. He held up a scarf before her, delighting in his evangelistic endeavor, and then bound her head. Rope lashed into her hands and feet. Gruff hands shoved her to the ground. Hot tears soaked the scarf. The ants marched along her ears. They bit into her, their stings like nettling spears jabbing her brain. Alang lost track of the minutes, hours, days. She only knew that she screamed and cried until she had no voice.

Gripped by a dark fever, a mix of bloodlust and greed, her kinsmen rose up. Neighbors, some of whom she'd known all her life, buoyed by service in the name of the God of the missionaries. They were no different, only waiting for an excuse to turn their blades to their tribal rivals. In the end, they were all earth priests. Purging her kinsmen, no longer deemed human, but dogs meant to be snuffed out of their misery. The bodies of her fellow villagers piled in front of a church. The blades of her kinsmen dulled on the bones of her family. She hid within the pile for a week, lost in a forest of her kinsmen. The blood of hacked limbs and bodies riddled with bullets pooled beneath her. The susurrus of low moans and tears a reminder of her need to be strong. To never forget. By night she slipped away to find water and scraps of food and by day she dreamed of bones being dragged away by dogs. Or maybe it wasn't a dream. The moans eventually ceased. Only their echo haunted her.

And one night, they returned and she knew she'd never see her village again.

Large hands tugged Alang to her feet. She was too weak to resist. The scarf pulled free, the sunlight pummeling her eyes. Her Master's wife stood before her.

"Will you call to Allah?" she said.

"O Allah! You are forgiving and you love forgiveness, so you too forgive me," Alang said in a coarse whisper.

"Good. Now mark her so that she does not 'get lost.'"

Alang did not see the hot iron until it passed between her legs. At its touch, her legs gave out and consciousness soon fled.

The brand hurt less now. She palmed a sharp rock during her first days' labors, finding comfort in its sharp edges. She sliced a bar across the brand, forming a cross much like those worn by the missionaries. Her scars were a map to her soul and she was an earth priest for her new land. Today she washed her Master's hands before he dined. Tomorrow, she'd begin preparing his meals, only a matter of time before she became one of his concubines. She imagined grinding glass into his food, the shards tearing up his insides until he spewed them up in choking coughs. A mess she'd be all too happy to clean up. Or one day she would be strong enough, fast enough, to plunge a cooking utensil into her Master's throat and free the blood of the slayer to cleanse his soul.

They both awaited redemption.

Maurice Broaddus has written hundreds of short stories, essays, novellas, and articles. His dark fiction has been published in numerous magazines and anthologies. He is the coeditor of the Dark Faith anthology series and the author of the urban fantasy trilogy Knights of Breton Court. He has been a teaching artist for more than five years, teaching creative writing to elementary, middle, and high school students, as well as adults. Visit his site at www.MauriceBroaddus.com.

The Cat in the Cage
Nicole Cushing

The cat batted the thick, orange extension cord with his soft white paws, catching it in his teeth, gnawing, oblivious to the fact that Sheila planned to use it to hang herself.

"Stop it!" Her voice cracked. Her face flushed. Her mind reeled, still catching up with the new reality. Doug did it this time, after years of threats. He really left. Said he couldn't stand the stench of booze on her breath anymore. Since giving up drinking never worked for long, she decided to quit breathing instead.

Suicide (as a daydream, a temptation) first latched onto her in middle school and, like a lapdog, never left for long. The urges came and went over the years, but (unlike the men in her life) didn't wander far. Sometimes accompanied by well-thought-out plans, but often not. Once or twice she'd even started writing the note, but always discarded it. This time she decided not to bother. Writing a note slowed her down and invited doubt. She didn't want doubt. Not anymore.

For decades, she'd just wanted to shut off the hurt in her head. She'd just wanted *peace*. The move from the city was supposed to help, but didn't ("geographical cures never do," her AA sponsor had lectured). A suicide cure just might, though.

She'd never before worked up the moxie to go *this* far. She didn't need the cat messing around, distracting her. Truth be told, she didn't need the cat *at all*.

But he was legally in her care. Well, maybe not "legally." It wasn't like adopting a child or anything. She hated it when the animal shelters called getting an animal "adopting" one. She'd been adopted (not from an animal shelter, but out of a foster home). She didn't like the comparison.

But her sponsor had told her that a cat would help, so she got one. Her sponsor had told her to do a bunch of other shit, too. Shit that came out of the big blue book they read out of at meetings. Pray to a god who wasn't there. Apply the twelve steps to all her affairs. Give up her own will to that of the group. Nope. Nope. Nope. She couldn't do it. Not any of it.

Get a cat? Yes. She could do *that*. Of all her sponsor's suggestions, taking in a stray made the most sense. It didn't require her to duck her head in the sand like a faithful, unquestioning ostrich. It required no prayer; the only time she'd have to spend on her knees was in front of the litter box. Better than begging for help from an imaginary friend. Better still than praying to the porcelain god while puking up gin and ramen noodles.

And for a while it worked. Sure, he got into everything. Jumped all over the place. Knocked over more lamps than she ever did while tipsy. She hated him. But he was warm and fuzzy when she was cold and clammy. He had this endearing, meek meow that sounded like a bird. The good behavior "calming collar" she'd bought for him at the pet store had a pleasant odor. The package said it gave off mother cat pheromones. She didn't know if that was true or not; to her it just smelled like lavender. Nice to whiff when she cuddled him. She loved him.

We always hurt the ones we love. She hurt the cat by drinking.

They weren't all full-fledged benders like this past week. Just little slips, sometimes. But they never ended well. She'd forget to scoop out the cat poop for a few days, and then the poor thing would resort to shitting in the house. Or she'd forget to feed him, and he'd start to get aggressive. Scratching her. Biting her. Sometimes on the face.

She had scars from the last time. They were the only thing that cut through the blackout to remind her of what happened. She imagined herself a latter-day Hester Prynne, the scarlet bite mark etched in her forehead, stigmatizing her to all feline society as a neglectful owner.

So her addled brain constructed a new syllogism. She couldn't stand the guilt after coming to and realizing she'd accidentally starved the cat. If she got drunk, she'd accidentally starve the cat. Therefore, she couldn't get drunk.

It worked better in theory than in practice. Her sobriety had been hanging by a thread and then snapped. She drank last night because Doug said he'd had enough of her. That's what he said. He'd "had enough" of her reclusiveness. Her distance. Her frigidness. Her drinking. Her letting herself and the housekeeping go. The place hadn't been uncluttered (let alone *cleaned*) in months.

He said he had to go "clear his head" up at his brother's house in Muncie. They had no children together (no strings, no one to hurt by separating), so he could do that. After he "cleared his head" for a month, maybe (*maybe*) he'd be back.

She looked up at the ceiling for the heavy hook she'd spied earlier, but got distracted by cobwebs. She almost stopped what she was doing to take a dust mop and clear them away. She didn't like the idea of people coming in and seeing stuff like that. Dirt. Disorganization. Flaws. People would talk if they saw the house in this condition.

But she couldn't keep everyone out, forever. Not if things went as planned. She'd have to be willing to let go of her need to control everything. In a month, give or take, Doug (or someone) would find her. Then the A.A. people would stand in church parking lots, smoking cigarettes, and gossip about her death. Some of the meaner ones might even pass on rumors about the coffee stains on the counters and the carpet gone too long without vacuuming. So what? She could tolerate being gossip-fodder if it meant an end to the misery.

The cat rubbed against her leg, forcing her glance downward. He looked up at her with big, yellow-green eyes and let out a timid squeak. He knew her moods. He had to know she wasn't wanting to cuddle, but tried to suggest snuggle-time anyway.

She bent at the waist and scowled. "Am I going to have to put you in your cage?" It wasn't an idle threat. There was, in fact, a cage (big enough for the cat to jump up on plastic ledges and play with catnip-laced toys; big enough for his bowls and his litter box.) But, facing facts, it was still a cage.

Doug didn't like calling it a cage. He called it the "kitty condo." He was always sugar-coating shit ("just a month away to clear my head").

The cat flinched and went back to playing with the extension cord.

She let him do that, for now. It would keep him busy while she got the ladder. It didn't weigh much, but its bulk made it hard to maneuver while she was still hung over and clumsy. It lurched too far to the right, knocking over a heap of mail that had accumulated on the coffee table. She didn't bother cleaning it up. It didn't matter anymore.

Nothing would matter, soon.

She spread the ladder's legs and tightened the hinges to keep it in place. Then she turned to get the cord.

The cat looked over his shoulder, caught in the act as he bit and clawed at it for all he was worth. She sighed and lurched toward him.

He ran, taking the cord with him down the hallway, into the kitchen, dragging it against the linoleum.

"Get back here!"

He scattered four paws on the floor in quick bursts of energy, slipping and sliding. But the heavy cord weighed him down. He could drag it away, but only so far. She caught up with him, grabbed him, but he twisted in her grasp. She didn't *mean* to shake him, but in her haste that's just what she did. He swiped his paw against her cheek. Another scratch.

"That's it. I'm done."

She picked him up. More scratches and bites as she trucked him to the unused dining room; the room he had all but taken over. Stray litter and crumbs of cat food were scattered over the hardwood. She winced and threw him in the cage. Home incarceration in the kitty-condo. She closed the latch, locking him in for good measure, and retrieved the cord.

She went back to work, trying to remember what the

website said about making the noose. In the end, she did the best she could. Improvising, like she always had. Throwing something together and hoping it worked. She hung it from the hook where the planter had hung before she'd killed the fern. She experimented with it to see if it might bear her weight. It seemed sturdy.

It took some doing to get the knot tied so that it'd actually *stayed* tied. The noose wasn't perfect, but it didn't need to be. It just needed to do the job. She placed it around her neck and for some reason she wasn't sure of, started sobbing.

The cat let out a squeaking, brittle meow. She looked down from her perch and saw him in the next room, his eyes and voice coordinated in a campaign for release. *Let me out and I will love you*, he seemed to be promising.

But no one had kept their promises. Her mom hadn't when she chose crack over groceries. Doug hadn't when he left. The cat hadn't when he scratched.

She inhaled, took one last look at the mess her house had become (the mess her life had become), and kicked the ladder out from under her, falling a short distance before catching. The drywall cracked, sprinkling dust into her eyes; but the ceiling held. The noose tightened, crushing the breath out of her, swelling her throat.

But she didn't die; not right away.

Her heart raced and she wished she'd drunk some more before she'd tried this but she knew she would have fucked up even more if she'd been totally trashed. The cord burnt and her lungs wanted to breathe, even if she didn't and her chest felt like it would burst from the blossoming ache, but it didn't. Not yet. She felt herself flush and she just wanted it over. And it would be, soon but not soon enough.

The cat spied her swaying and made shadow-boxing motions, like she was just a big toy teasing him into pouncing. Only he couldn't, not after she'd locked him up.

Then (*only* then) as she swung from the noose did she look down into the cage with bulging, teary eyes, and see his empty bowl.

Nicole Cushing is the author of the acclaimed novella *Children of No One* (DarkFuse, 2013) and more than twenty short stories published in the US and UK. Her work has drawn praise from Thomas Ligotti, John Skipp, and *Famous Monsters of Filmland* magazine. She lives with her husband in Indiana.

A Mean Piece of Water
Mary Madewell

Love the river, her father had said. *You've gotta love her, and you've gotta show her you love her. If you don't, if you don't take the time to romance her, she'll turn on you. Never let the water turn on you, Ren. Never turn your back on her, and always show her a smile.*

They went fishing together in a small rough boat. Her father rowed them out to his favorite spot in the dim morning fog, grunting with each stroke, his sweat mingling with the living scent of the water. Ren dangled her fingertips in the river as they went. The water clutched at her. She smiled, whispered I love you, and the water let go. Ren giggled.

Don't lean too far, her father said.

She moved back to the middle and watched as he baited her hook with a wriggling worm. It continued to wriggle even after being impaled, twisted, and impaled again. Ren felt faintly sick, but her father smiled down at her so she cast her line just like he said. The worm disappeared with a distant plop and she felt better.

The day wore on. The sun rose in the sky but the fog never burned away, only got a little lighter. Ren's bobber never dipped below the surface of the water, and soon she slipped her rod into the coffee can full of rocks her father had brought in case she grew tired. Her father told her again not to lean too far, and then he told her again. Ren went back to the edge to look, to dangle her fingers, to smile. The surface moved lazily, swirled slowly around their boat. The river flirted. Ren wished to pet it. Beneath the sleepy surface she could see swift shapes darting through the depths, ignoring her hook, swimming lower and lower until they rested on the sandy bottom which was far too deep to see. Yet Ren could see it. The river showed her.

Soon her father's warnings had lost their good nature. Sternly he told her again not to lean so far over the side.

We'll tip over, lose all our gear. You want to swim home?

Ren thought *yes* but she knew it was the wrong answer.

No, Papa.

Okay then. Stay away from the edge.

He began to reel in his line with quick, stiff movements. Ren was sorry she'd made him angry, but more, she was sorry they had to leave. She looked down to see farther than she should be able to, and gave the river a last smile, a final touch of her fingers.

As though made to sink, the boat slipped to the side. Too easily it dumped Ren into the river, and then her father and all their gear. It was gone in a moment, their rough wooden boat. Her father shouted for her but she had already gone under. The river held her in watery arms, filled the space around her with air so she could breathe, hid her from view. Ren's father could swim like a fish through tar or brine, and he shouted her name and dived under to find her. The river made a face for her so they could play. It winked a watery eye. Smiled with watery lips. Ren laughed as she sped to the bottom. Too far down to see. The river winked, stuck out a shimmering tongue, blew wet bubbles that floated in her air pocket. It did what it could to distract her. Ren let it. Soon her father's muffled shouts quieted. No more splashes echoed from the surface.

After a time she grew sleepy, and she slept in the deep, and when she woke up in her own bed her sobbing mother held her too tightly. Her father hadn't come back from the river. Ren had been found asleep on the banks as dry as summer straw. She cried until her eyes burned, sorry for her poor papa, sorry that she'd let the river take her down to play.

That night she lay awake. Her chest ached and her eyes ached, but somewhere in her belly a fire burned. What had he said? He said love the river, and never turn her back on it. Ren thought hard. Her poor drowned papa hadn't smiled at the river when they put out in their rough boat. He hadn't trailed his fingers in the water or whispered that he loved it. Maybe he knew he'd done something wrong. Maybe he meant Ren shouldn't be sorry when the river took him. Maybe he was leaving her in the protection of a friend.

Something about it didn't feel right. Something tickled the back of her mind, whispered like the river that she wasn't where she needed to be, to keep looking. Ren decided she'd keep looking. The tickling stopped and she went to sleep.

She was forbidden to go to the river alone after that, so she snuck down at night while her mother lay in the arms of her whiskey dreams. Ren looked. She smiled at the river, whispered that she loved it, and then dove into the inky water. Sometimes she left her clothes on the bank and swam like a regular girl, working her arms and legs until the muscles were sore and her breath came ragged. On those nights she snuck home early to dry her hair before her mother woke.

Other times she jumped in fully clothed, to talk and play with her closest friend, her only friend. The river filled a pocket with air so she could breathe. It propelled her upstream to see the city lights reflected on the water. It took her downstream to see the place where it opened to the ocean, melted with it, so the two became one. The river whispered of the ocean her lover, but Ren didn't understand what it meant, so it merely floated her home on the surface so she could lie on her back and watch the stars pass. Ren looked. Whenever the tickling wrong started up again she pretended to seek some greater answer until it went away, but in the deeper place she knew she'd made a choice.

She chose the river.

Her mother's stare grew hard. Ren spoke so much at night that she had little left to say during the day. She was put into a special class, but still fell asleep at her desk too often. Her mother didn't speak to her about it, only removed Ren from school altogether as soon as Ren was old enough. Ren was overjoyed. Now she could spend more time at the river.

The days melted together. Winters were hard for her, but she could still sit on the ice for brief periods of time to be with her friend. Spring, summer and fall she barely came home, and then once she was old enough to understand that her mother could hardly bear to look at her, Ren stopped coming home at all.

She built a lean-to on the riverbank and slept inside on the ground. The river gave her fish, washed them ashore so she didn't need a pole and hook. Ren cooked them over a crackling campfire. Once a deputy picked her up for vagrancy but after the sheriff remembered who she was she was let go, and they left her in peace after that. In season she sold fish to the market, to the restaurants, to tourists, and after just two seasons she had enough for a boat. A few more seasons and she traded in the cheap, trim rowboat for a houseboat that had suffered a fire, whose owners only wanted it gone. It floated, that was the important thing to Ren. The rest could be rebuilt. The river helped her, told her what to do, because it had seen many things since it woke up and knew much about boats and much about people, and it filled Ren's head with tales about both.

It was a hot summer day the first time she saw the man. She lay on the deck of her boat, transfixed by the faint wrinkles and valleys on the water that belied the seeming stillness. She had the place to herself for once. Tourist season had started but they didn't come out when it was so hot. Ren lay on the baked wooden planks with one arm over the edge to trail in the water. She wished she could swim, but she'd spent the night and morning in the river and her skin needed some time in the sun. The river whispered that she should come in anyway, that it wouldn't let her get wet, but Ren shook her head.

Soon enough, she said with a smile. *I have to eat too.*

I'll feed you, it whispered. There was a movement as of something big and heavy rising, and a trout appeared. It floated on the surface as though held there by an invisible hand. Ren smiled and scooped it up.

Thank you.

Can you swim now?

I have to cook it, silly. Ren laughed and went inside. Her boat had been a wreck when she got it, but she worked hard on it, gutting and practically rebuilding the entire structure. It had a small kitchen, a bathroom with a shower worth the entire cost of the boat as far as she was concerned, and a bed to sleep in. She hadn't slept in the bed once in the last four years. In the winter the boat had to sit in dry dock. During the freeze she slept in her old room at her mother's. Neither of them enjoyed the company, but Ren left before her mother got up in the mornings and mostly came in after she'd gone to bed at night.

She'd filled the gas tank exactly twice. A show for the docking crew. Otherwise she merely floated. The river took her wherever she wanted to go.

When she reappeared on the deck a man was there, standing on the shore like a blaze, as though the bright sunshine were no more illuminating than moonless dark. Ren's breath caught. She wiped the grease from her fishy fingers onto the seat of her shorts and wished she'd thought to comb her hair that morning. He stood at the bank not fishing, simply smiling at the water, taking in the fresh air.

Romancing the river, Ren thought.

Please swim now, the river said plaintively. Ren shook her head. *You must, I want you to.*

No. Look at him. Who do you think he is?

His sandy hair was threaded through with brilliant red. He wore jeans and a crisp white t-shirt with no shoes, and Ren felt a small shock at the sight of his bare feet. She wished he were close enough to touch.

Come to me. I need you. NOW.

The boat sped up so fast Ren stumbled into a wall. It broke through her trance. She clung to the wall, staring wide-eyed at the water and at the man who had finally noticed the lurching boat. For a moment he wore her father's face. Good-naturedly telling her not to lean so far. Then it was gone, and a pair of perfect blue eyes speared her from across the water. Ren let go of the wall and half-raised a hand in greeting, still entranced despite the danger. Just a man. Just a beautiful man to break a spell, no more than that, but he crashed through her glass house and sent the shards of her delusions flying. For that she found him mesmerizing.

The boat began to spin in the water, to turn her away from

the bank and the blue eyes. She started to take a step, circle the
cabin so she could keep him in sight, but another little nudge
sent her crashing back into the wall. Her eyes closed, she clung
to the spinning craft, her stomach in revolt. She thought she
might be sick.

When she opened her eyes she faced the opposite bank.
The river had brought the boat downstream as it spun. The
man had disappeared around a curve. Despite the danger Ren
knelt on the deck so the river could not mistake her glare.

What is wrong with you? Don't ever do that to me again.

I don't know what you mean, the river replied innocently in its
usual soft whisper. *I only wanted you to come play.*

You almost knocked me off the boat, making it lurch like that.

*Sometimes I can't keep my currents in line. I'm sorry. You don't
seem to mind when I'm taking you upstream to sell fish in the city.*

Yeah, but ... Ren faltered. Her anger began to give way to
caution. The image of her father's face on the stranger flashed
before her again. Her mother was a waste drowning in a bottle.
There was no one left to be brave for her.

This wasn't a current. You didn't want me to look at that man.

I don't know what man you're talking about.

*That's not true. He stood on the bank just upstream. You didn't
want me to look at him, because you think I will like him more than I
like you.*

I do not lie.

The river's voice hardened but grew no louder. In fact the
next words were so faintly spoken Ren had to lean closer to
the water's surface.

*I do not notice men because I am eternal, I am the fog and the rain
and the lashing sea. My currents run from snowy peaks to the wide ocean,
and I am in the ground, and in the sky, and in all things. I am in you,
too. All living beings are made of me, and they are slaves to my will. Does
the wind lie to the leaves? No. It does not deign to notice that which is
caught in its wake, because the wind goes where it will and does not care
for the notice of men. I am like the wind. I am eternal. You dare to
question me?*

Ren shivered. Her face had gone pale. She remembered
the first time she'd seen down to the bottom, how the water
had been cloudy and then it wasn't. Their trips to the city, to
the ocean. She remembered being held on the surface so she

could watch the stars. Diving to the bottom and then climbing out without so much as a single drop clinging to her hair.

She looked around herself, then. The houseboat that was her home. The remains of her meal. Even her clothing, such as it was, had been paid for with fish from the river. Ren didn't know the first thing about real fishing, because she'd never had to do it. Her entire life depended on the river's good will. It was as if, suddenly, she had given up everything all at once rather than the slow compromises she'd made over the years.

The tickling returned to the back of her head but it wasn't a tickle any longer. It was a fist, and it was punching. Each strike brought back another picture of that day. Her father's delight in taking her out in the little rough boat. His easy nature. How he put her worm on without being asked. The way his panicked screams had been muffled by the water while the river held her down, waiting for him to tire and drown.

She wiped tears from her cheeks.

I'm sorry. You're right. I'm sorry.

Thank you, Ren. Come play now. No need to worry about that man again. I see that he's left the bank and gone home.

Ren wanted to ask how the river could see him now but it couldn't see him before, but she held her tongue. Maybe if she could make an excuse, dock and get to town, maybe then she'd have a chance, but not today. Today was too soon. It would be suspicious.

She slipped into the river and the familiar peaceful silence surrounded her. The river held her with firm hands. Ren tried to kick, to swim, but it took her to the bottom. It didn't bring air. Ren's throat began to burn. Her lungs ached. She thrashed, panicked, her eyes wide.

Then, she had air. She gulped it down, threw up some of the water she'd swallowed, gulped again. The river still held her but its grip was lighter.

Next time I ask you to come play what will you do?

Ren coughed. She sobbed a little.

I'm sorry. I'm sorry. I'll play. I'm sorry. Please don't hurt me again.

Are you hurt? Oh dear, that's too bad. Maybe you need to get some rest.

Instead of cradling her at the bottom in a pocket of air, the river propelled her swiftly upward and dumped her on the deck of her boat like a discarded toy.

I can't sleep with you?

I think you should sleep alone tonight. See how it feels. I've always been alone. You think that man with the blue eyes will stay? He's already on his way home. He didn't even wait to see if you were okay, that's how much he cares about you. I take care of you. I would never leave you.

You would never let me leave you, either, Ren thought, but she was careful not to let her face belie her doubt.

Please? I don't think I can sleep up here.

No.

After that no amount of pleading would elicit a response. Ren splashed her foot in the water, she shouted, she paced on the deck. She told herself it was to reassure, to convince the river that it was still her only friend, but in her heart something vital was breaking. Ren had been so wrong for so many years. Facing it now was all but impossible.

Her boat was held fast in the middle of the river, no longer allowed to approach either bank. At last she went inside and lay on the bed for perhaps the second time since she built it against one wall of the cabin. The sheets smelled like mildew but everything on the river smelled like that after a while. Ren took deep breaths, soothing her wounds, and soon she fell asleep.

When she woke it was dark. The boat was still in the same place, there in the middle of the water, and the river still refused to speak to her. Ren stared at the expanse of water. It moved lazily on top as it always had, hiding the danger beneath slow water, and she wondered for the first time if the river could see both its start and its finish at the same time. If it was down by the ocean romancing a new little girl, could it still sense what Ren was doing here? It wasn't away tonight, certainly, not the way it held her boat still.

She shook her head at the distance to the bank. She wouldn't make it farther than a single leap away from the deck. There had to be something else.

Ren went back inside and lay on the bed again, but this time she lay awake.

The next morning she opened her eyes to a distant whisper.

Wake and come out. I'm sorry. Wake and come out to me.

Ren bounded out of the cabin and dove into the water with a grin. Watery arms wrapped around her in a hug.

You see now.

I do. I missed you. It was difficult to sleep.

I know. Promise me you won't fight me again?

I promise.

Ren swam all day. She laughed in her air bubble, floated on her back to stare at the clouds, splashed with the geese who got too close. It was like the old days. For lunch the river served her up a fresh trout and Ren went inside the cabin to cook it. After several moments she came out, her face pale, one hand clamped over her wrist.

You're hurt.

I cut myself. It's deep.

Oh no, oh no. Get your first-aid kit. You have bandages.

Blood seeped between Ren's clamped fingers. Her cheeks were pale. It had taken all her resolve to plunge the knife in deep enough, and now that the cut was made, she knew she didn't have a lot of time. The river would know if she wasn't in danger. Would it let her die rather than let her get help? Ren almost wished it would.

She held the wrist to her stomach. Her T-shirt blossomed and grew a deadly red rose. Ren slumped to the deck. It didn't hurt as bad as she'd imagined. She pulled one hand away from the slash and watched the blood spurt out with wide eyes. In a way it was beautiful, like her river, flowing down and across her lap.

Get the first aid kit. You have to get up.

Ren held her arm over the boat's edge and let some of her precious life pour into the water.

The boat lurched so fast Ren fell off. She splashed into the river, but it dumped her back onto the deck even as it sped her and the boat toward town. It beached her beside a popular seafood restaurant that boasted waterfront seating, but by that time Ren had lost consciousness, so she didn't have to suffer the insult of seeing land-loving tourists in loafers and khaki shorts crawling all over the deck she'd sanded and varnished herself.

The emptiness woke her. It was still, and there was no murmur of current against rocks, against rushes, against earth.

She woke in a soft hospital bed that smelled of antiseptic, her mother weeping in a chair beside the bed, and just as she had when Ren was little her mother held her hand too tightly.

Ren whispered something but her mother wept too loudly to hear it.

What? What was that?

I said, it was my fault. I'm sorry, Mom. It was my fault Papa drowned.

Oh, Brenda.

Her mother's head shook as if to deny it but Ren didn't need her to believe, she only needed her to hear.

A nurse came in and brought her a pitcher of water and a plastic cup. Ren stared distrustfully at the liquid for a long time. It didn't whisper to her but she didn't like the look of it. She thought it moved wrong. She put it down and refused to drink. At last they gave her water in a bottle shipped in from two states away. Her mother carried in a case of bottled water and helped her bathe, because Ren wouldn't turn the shower on. She couldn't stand the sound.

Even after they had moved away, when their new house sat baking beneath a saguaro sun and her mother's whiskey dreams were as forgotten and faded as Ren's old lean-to, Ren had to leave the house whenever her mother washed the dishes. The sound of running water frightened her, and it hurt her heart. She didn't know what was more terrifying; the promise of a whisper, or the idea that if Ren smiled and told it she loved it, no answer would come.

Mary Madewell is a freelance writer and artist living in the Pacific Northwest. She loves video games, animals, nonfiction about Einstein, horror, and vegan pizza. Her fiction has appeared in *Lenox Avenue*, *Devil's Work*, and *Intracities*. She is married to writer CJ Hurtt.

Kitty
Gary McMahon

The party is over. Only the usual stragglers remain. There's me, my wife Jane, Ted and Lizzie from across the street, and Benedict. There is always Benedict—that drunken oaf never knows when to leave.

"So it goes something like this—" Benedict pauses to take another drink. His eyes are watery; his cheeks are flushed. He's been drinking whisky all night and it never agrees with him.

"Oh, come on. You're making this one up." Lizzie giggles. "I mean, there's no such thing as Here Kitty."

Benedict grins. He puts down his glass—it's empty now. "Seriously it's true. I heard it from a friend. Somebody he knows had a cousin who knew someone it happened to." His voice is slurred.

I sigh and raise my eyebrows.

Jane moves closer to me on the sofa, clasps my hand. It's the first time she's touched me all night. She's always been easily frightened.

"Anyway," says Benedict, "the story goes that there was once this woman who loved cats. Hated people, but loved cats. She took in strays, fed all the cats in the neighborhood. They called her Here Kitty, because that's all you ever heard in the

307

evenings: this old woman leaning out of her doorway, shouting '*Here, Kitty, Kitty,*' calling in one of her pets for its supper."

Everyone's gone quiet, listening to his tale. We've already spoken about Bloody Mary, Candyman, the Hook—all the usual urban legends. But this one is new; none of us has ever heard it before.

"So one night she gets really drunk and falls down the stairs. She breaks both of her legs, or her spine. Something like that. The cats start creeping over to investigate. One by one, they come out of all the rooms in her house, and they sit on her. All of them. On her chest. Her face. When finally she's found, a few days later, she's dead. But it wasn't from the fall. Oh, no; the cats killed her. They smothered her to death."

I glance at my watch. It's past two a.m. We should go home. We really should go home.

"When the police searched her big old house, they found all kinds of weird shit. Cat suits, stuffed cats, cats' bones and skulls … and a cat mask. It was made from the pelts of some of her dead pets. She'd cut them up and stitched them together, made some whiskers out of fishing line, and there were photographs of her wearing the thing. In each one she was just standing there, naked except for the mask, and looking into the camera. Creepy."

He grabs his glass, realizes it's empty, and puts it back down. The room is silent. Nobody speaks or even moves.

"A couple of weeks later the killings started. Some of the local kids who'd tormented her while she was alive started turning up dead. They all had wads of cat fur stuffed into their mouths; giant hairballs. Their throats were slashed—several cuts, in a row. Like claws. Then it just stopped. They say that if you stand in front of a mirror and say '*Here, Kitty, Kitty*' she appears behind you, wearing that mask. She'll kill you with her claws."

His story now finished, Benedict rises unsteadily to his feet and goes looking for more whisky. The rest of us just sit there, looking at each other, until Lizzie starts to laugh.

"Fucking idiot," she says, standing and crossing the room to put on some more music. "One last dance for the road, eh Dan?"

I stand and walk over to her. She's swaying from side to

side, her crotch thrusting forward. Pearl Jam's *Black* is playing loudly. I ignore Jane's slit-eyed gaze and slow-dance for a while with Lizzie, too drunk to care that someone might suspect it's the same song we play whenever we make love.

Jane brings it up while we're walking home. She refuses to hold my hand. I'm stumbling a little—too much vodka, taken neat. She walks a couple of paces ahead of me, as if refusing to acknowledge that we are still a couple.

"What the hell was all that about?" Her voice is low, angry.

"What do you mean?"

She stops and turns around, folding her arms beneath her breasts. "Back there, with Lizzie. The two of you looked like you were making out, not dancing. Could you have been more obvious?"

I stand in the street, swaying. My head is swimming; my thoughts are blurred. I can't quite remember what it is I'm supposed to have done. "I have no idea what you're talking about. It was just a dance."

"I know you've been having an affair, Dan, but please, out of respect, don't rub my fucking nose in it." She turns around and marches off along the footpath, swinging her arms like a pretend soldier.

By the time I get home she's already in bed. The bedroom door is locked and there's a pile of sheets and a pillow on the floor outside the room. I pick them up and go back downstairs, unsteady on my feet. I make up a bed on the sofa and settle down for the night, my head spinning and images of Lizzie, naked, hanging in the air at my side. I try to masturbate, just to release some pressure, but I've had too much to drink.

I close my eyes. Dream of cats prowling the house, looking for something …

Next day is a Sunday and I don't have to go in to work. Jane's already out and about by the time I wake up—she's left a note saying she'll be back later that evening, and that I shouldn't expect to sleep in our bed.

I make a bacon sandwich and drink three or four cups of coffee. My mouth tastes stale; my eyes keep trying to shut. I watch some football on TV, getting up only for coffee refills and to snack on salty junk food. There's another match on straight afterwards, so I start to watch that one too. I keep trying to think about Jane, and how I badly handled the situation last night, but my head is filling with pictures of Lizzie's thighs.

When the phone rings at four p.m. I know it's her.

"Hello," I say, gripping the handset tightly.

"Are you alone?"

"Yes. She's gone out. Won't be back till late."

"I'll come over, then, shall I?"

She puts down the phone, not even waiting for my answer. She already knows what it is.

She knocks on the door fifteen minutes later. When I let her in she goes upstairs without even speaking, and walks directly into the master bedroom. When I get there she's already taking off her clothes. Her skin is smooth and pale; she has on the underwear I chose for her in a mail order catalogue. It's cheap and tacky; a whore's costume. I love it and I hate it and it makes me want her.

"Listen," I say, calmly closing the door. "I'm not sure if we should carry on doing this. Jane … she knows what's going on."

Lizzie smiles. I've always loved that smile. You know when someone says that a smile can light up a room? Well that's it; that's Lizzie's smile down to a tee.

"Ted knows, too. But he doesn't mind. He gets a kick out of it, actually. He keeps asking me about what we do, how we do it, and if your cock is bigger than his." She smiles again, teasing me. "It is, just for the record." She lies down on the bed and makes crude come-to-me gestures with her hands.

"I'm serious. This was … fun. It's been great. But it was never mean to be for keeps." I stay where I am, at a safe distance from the bed.

"Oh, I know that, honey. We never said we'd fall in love. This is just sex—great sex. It's something we weren't getting from our partners. Where's the harm in that?"

I think about Jane, and the fact that her sex drive has dipped dramatically since we found out we couldn't have a baby. It's as if sex, to her, is simply a means of procreation. She receives little pleasure from the act; it's just a way of producing babies.

"Come on, Dan. Don't leave me high and dry." She bares

her teeth. It looks like she's snarling. She reaches across the bed and presses a button on her mobile phone. Mood music: *Black*, by Pearl Jam.

"I'm not sure, Lizzie … it just doesn't feel right anymore. Not now that people are getting hurt. *Jane* is getting hurt."

"You should've thought about that earlier, baby. Before we started. Why the hell did you think that nobody would get hurt? Jane's soft, like a little kid. It was always going to be her. Ted's always known about my little adventures. He leaves me to it, as long as I don't bring home any diseases."

The reality of what we've been doing hits home, but it's far too late. I'm already caught up in some kind of middle class game, involving sex and status and competition, and things have suddenly become real.

"I'm sorry," I say, moving towards the bed. "This has to end." My mouth is saying the right words but my body contradicts them.

"That's better, baby. That's right." She sits up, reaches out, and begins to unbutton my trousers. I'm still not sure how I get from one place to the other, but within seconds I'm down on the bed beside her, and then I'm *inside* her. I stare deeply into her eyes, looking beyond the colors. I've never noticed before how much like cats' eyes they are. Green, narrow, and filled with a sense of slyness that borders on the psychotic.

When she leaves I take a hot shower, to clean off the smell of sex. My skin feels thin and greasy, as if it might split if I rub too hard. I stay under the scalding jet of water for a long time, promising myself that this will not happen again. It's over; things are different now. The game has ended in a draw.

I step out of the shower and dry off in front of the mirror. The glass is steamed over; I can't see my reflection but I know it's there, under the gray layer. Of course it is. Where else could it possibly be?

Feeling stupid yet oddly panicked, I clean a patch of the glass with the edge of my hand. Staring back at me is my own wet face. I'm there. I am still here, no matter how thin and insubstantial I've begun to feel.

I drop the towel and take a few steps towards the mirror, leaning into the glass. I stop when my face is a couple of inches away. I hold my breath to stop the glass from clouding over again.

I say it as a joke, or perhaps as a challenge. I don't know. I'm not sure of the reasons. But I say it, that's all that matters.

"Here, Kitty, Kitty."

Nothing happens. I don't expect anything to, but somewhere deep inside I'm disappointed. There's nobody standing behind me in a cat mask, displaying big, sharp claws. The house is silent and empty; there isn't a sound that cannot be accounted for.

I finish drying myself off and return to the bedroom, where I dress in some fresh clothes—the other ones still smell of her, of Lizzie, so I push them to the bottom of the washing basket.

When Jane comes home it's already dark. I can see the streetlights coming on through the window, and I watch quietly as a taxi pulls up outside our house. She climbs out of the car with a couple of shopping bags, pays the driver, smiles and says something to him, and then walks down the drive to the door. The taxi driver waits until she's opened the door, and then he drives slowly away.

I wait for her to come into the room.

"We need to sit down and talk," she says, taking off her coat without even looking at me.

"I know. I've been ... stupid." I look down at the floor, examining the pattern on the carpet. For the first time I think how ugly it looks—how ugly the entire house is, and the street we live on. Maybe we should sell up and move: a new start, a clean break. It might help us to move closer together.

"More than that," she says, picking up her shopping bags and heading for the kitchen. "You've been so much more— and a lot less—than that, Dan."

I don't know what else to say, so I just stand there, looking at my feet. My shoes are ugly, too. The clothes I'm wearing don't suit me; I remember that Lizzie picked them out for me weeks ago, sending me the link to an online menswear store. I told Jane that I bought them cheap in a sale.

I sleep on the sofa again. Try to sleep, anyway.

Neither of us has eaten dinner—it didn't seem appropriate to sit down at the table together and make small talk. The conversation we need to have is close, but it isn't quite close enough. We have to wait until it feels right before we can even begin to take things apart. Then we might be able to piece our relationship back together.

I glance at the clock on the mantelpiece: 2:20 a.m. The house is silent, holding its breath. I can't even make out the usual sounds of creaking pipes and settling timbers.

I get up and go into the kitchen, open the fridge and take out a can of beer. The sound when I pop open the tab is much too loud, a gunshot inside the room. I take a few mouthfuls and return to the living room, sit down in the armchair by the window. The curtains are open. I look out at the street. The only light still on in any of the houses belongs to Lizzie and Ted. I wonder why they are still up, and what they are talking about. Maybe the conversation Jane and I need to have has stopped off over at their place first.

I finish my beer and stand up, leave the room. I climb the stairs, holding on to the handrail. At the top of the stairs, the bathroom door's open wide but the light is off. I pause at the doorway and look inside, catching sight of a face in the mirror. It isn't me … but it is me, too. I look different somehow; my features are arranged in a way that I only partly recognize.

I turn away and walk along the landing.

When I reach our bedroom door I stop and just stand there, wondering if Jane is asleep. I doubt that she will be awake, not at this hour; she has never been a night person.

I open the door and take a step inside. The curtains here are open too—which is unlike Jane; she always enjoys her privacy, especially while she sleeps. Sickly streetlight leaks through the window, illuminating small areas of the room to make them look unfamiliar.

The woman kneeling on the bed isn't my wife—she is naked, and I know Jane's body well enough to recognize that this isn't her.

I don't feel afraid, but I should. The only emotion I experience is one of profound regret.

"Lizzie?" My voice sounds heavy; the question drifts slowly across the room like a gas.

The woman on the bed slowly shakes her head. The cat mask tilts first to the left and then to the right. It looks old, shabby; some of the stitching is coming loose and the catgut whiskers are crooked and bent. A few of them have snapped off halfway.

"Who are you?" I don't really want to know. What I do want to know is what has happened to Jane, and where she is. You never miss people until they're gone; you don't realize what love is until it's no longer there. I glance down and see something small and pink poking out from under the bed. It might be part of a hand. Or it could simply be an object we've stored under there, and the dim light is making it seem like something else entirely. Something it isn't.

"Please. Where is she?" My legs are trembling. I feel the hot rush of urine sliding down the inside of my leg as my bladder opens.

The woman on the bed stirs; she slides her legs from underneath her buttocks and stands up, her heavy breasts shifting, her thin, graceful body moving languidly, and with a strange feline grace.

She is facing me across the room. I stare at her, still unable—or perhaps unwilling—to move. There's nowhere to run, anyway; I always had this coming. It's been waiting for me for quite some time.

The cat mask tilts a fraction to one side, an inquisitive movement. The large glass eyes catch the light and shine like gemstones. Her skin is smooth and pale, almost like flat, white fur. Her fingernails are at least six inches long, and filed to sharp points.

Something about my eyesight adjusts, and I realise that this woman could in fact be Jane. Now that she's standing up, her body looks more like my wife's body, and the questioning posture she's adopted is somehow familiar.

Is it her? Is it Jane, taking revenge?

Jane … Lizzie … someone else. In truth, I'm not entirely sure who it is. Nothing is certain. Only the fact that she's here, in our room, and something bad is about to happen.

I don't say anything else. I know what's coming.

"*Here, Kitty, Kitty*," says the woman in a high-pitched, child-like voice.

Then she rushes quickly and lightly toward me, swinging her claws.

Gary McMahon is the acclaimed author of seven novels. His short fiction has been reprinted in several "Year's Best" volumes. He lives with his family in Yorkshire, where he trains in Shotokan karate and likes running in the rain. He can be found on the Web at www.garymcmahon.com.

Mister Whisper
James A. Moore

No one really expected the plan to work, but it did. Four men, all of them lifers with absolutely nothing to lose found themselves on the outside, and they made the most of it.

The thing of it was, they had absolutely no idea what to do with themselves. Sure, they'd all dreamed of escaping, thought about what they might like to do if they managed to get out, but at the end of the day, they never thought it would happen. The likelihood was right up there with little green men landing on the lawn of the prison and telling them they were all going to the land of Beautiful Nymphomaniacs.

And now they were stuck and hating it. That was all right. They wouldn't have to hate it for long. Lewis was behind the wheel of the delivery truck and he knew how to drive a big rig with ease.

He also knew the roads in the area, and most importantly, he wanted to get well the hell away from the prison before Cotton found out he was gone. That was what this was all about. They were lifers. They didn't have much left that they could be afraid of, but they had Cotton and that man was hands down the scariest bastard they'd ever met. He'd proven just how bad a single man could make the lives of each and every man in that delivery truck at one time or another. They hoped to never see that vile, crooked grin of his again.

Lewis intended to make sure of it. There were probably roadblocks set up, but he managed to dodge them if they were there. In short order he had them out of Collier County and well on their way to freedom. Just as soon as they found a good spot for it, the group intended to dump their vehicle and head in different directions. They had no special affection for each other, and they had their own plans. They'd discussed those plans a hundred times, but those plans changed as much as the weather, so it wasn't really like they could do much to hurt each other down the road.

Of course, if he had the opportunity, Johnson planned to kill the others. He didn't know that the situation would arise, but if it did, he'd end them quickly and very violently. There were plenty of areas where a few bodies could fall and no one would notice. Had they found even half the people he'd killed over the years, he'd have been in line to get a lethal injection.

They were not, as a rule, good men. That was why they were on the run.

The best of plans tend to fall apart. That was why Kragel said they should play it loose. Turned out the little bastard was right, but the law of averages said he would be eventually.

The simple plans tend to fall apart too. The idea was to avoid getting caught, and that ripped at the seams pretty damned fast after they crossed the state line. It should have gone smoothly. It might have gone smoothly, but Chambers looked out the passenger window of the truck and the first face he saw was a cop who was maybe more alert than most of them. He recognized the escapee's face. Luck of the draw, really, because Chambers was about as plain looking as a man could be.

The cops turned on the flashing red and blue lights, and rather than pull over Lewis sideswiped the squad car and sent it off the road and into a ditch. The likelihood that the cops were injured was small, but it damned sure put their car out of commission. Sadly, that didn't mean their radio wasn't working and it also didn't mean that the truck hadn't been made.

There was no point getting upset. Sometimes you just have to adjust to the situation. That was what Kragel said and the others agreed.

It was Chambers that suggested the subdivision. Most of the houses there were two story jobs, and they had garages and places where the truck could be ditched. It wasn't like they were hiding a tractor-trailer, just a little four-wheel job. Lewis slid it in next to a Winnebago that had seen better days, and from the road you couldn't even see it from behind that mountain of a vehicle.

All they had to do was get one of the cars from the garage and maybe grab the family inside to keep them company. A few family members tucked in the trunk and they could be on their way with a little extra security to get them where they were going.

The house they picked was a nice brick job and the sliding glass door leading from the back yard was unlocked. Everyone stayed outside except Johnson. Johnson was pretty, and as an added bonus he was good with his hands if things went wrong. None of them were prepared for any sort of fire fight, so it was best to have one person see what could be done, and Johnson was willing to be that one person.

If they'd known, they might have done things differently. Sometimes you find out the unpleasant truths a little too late to do anything to change them.

Lenny Johnson was not a good man. On his best days he could fake it, but not for long. You can pretend to be someone else, but eventually the truth leaks out around the corners, where the varnish we cover ourselves with is thinnest.

There were exactly three people at home, two young boys and a little girl. The oldest boy looked to be around twelve. The other two, obviously his siblings by family resemblance, were no older than five.

The oldest boy stood up fast when he saw Johnson, his eyes wide and a worried expression on his face. Johnson knew the look well enough; the kid knew he'd screwed up. He was supposed to lock the doors, to watch out for his little siblings, to make sure that no one who wasn't a family friend came anywhere near them, because strangers were dangerous people. Everyone knew that.

Johnson's parents had never taught him that when he was younger. They taught him other lessons about what a pretty face could mean to the right strangers.

Johnson decided with exactly one look that the oldest boy needed to know how important that lesson was. He stepped close and brought his knee up into the boy's jaw. Bones shattered and the kid flopped backward and crashed into the living room table. His head bounced hard and his eyes rolled up into his bleeding skull.

That was all that Johnson needed to know about the kid. He was no longer an important part of the equation. The two younger ones stared at him with wide, frightened eyes. He grabbed them up and practically tucked them under his arm as he headed for the garage. They squirmed and started to scream, but he ignored them for the moment.

Sometimes suburbia made life almost too easy. That simple fact had allowed him to get away with far more than most people ever guessed. It was only a matter of minutes for him to get what he wanted and what he needed. What he needed was car keys. There was an SUV in the garage. What he wanted were weapons, duct tape and cash. The master bedroom offered up two pistols from the closet—some people have no idea what security actually means—and close to fifty dollars in cash from the dresser near the entrance of the attached bathroom. The duct tape was in the garage, along with dad's tools. There were a few weapons there, too. By the time Johnson left the garage—backing out the SUV, he had two kids trussed up in the back seat, tape on their wrists, their ankles and over the squalling mouths, the cash in his pocket, and one of the pistols jammed in the small of his back. It was loaded. He checked.

The other three climbed in the car in short order, all three taking the time to stare at the kids with goggle eyes.

"You, uh, you do that sort of thing before, Johnson?" Chambers eyed the two kids a second time and his eyes lingered.

"You don't need to know about me. I don't need to know about you. Let's get the fuck out of this town."

They drove away moments later.

After they'd left the house, the oldest boy of the family carefully climbed to his hands and knees and started across the living room, heading for an old wooden chest that sat near the front window. The piece was in lousy shape and quite old, having survived both World Wars and a few dozen skirmishes before that time. It had been in most of Europe over the decades, and the contents had changed little over that time. A few minor changes, but always minor.

His fingers shook as he reached for the lock. It fought but only for a moment. The blood on his fingers seemed to work as a lubricant. He knew that, too. He had been warned by his parents that the trunk should only ever be opened if there was a good reason. They had also told him that there must always be a sacrifice offered. Normally the best sacrifice was a few drops of blood.

Thin arms shook as he lifted the lid and the hinges of the old trunk squealed in rusty protest. They had never been oiled. Never once.

He looked inside the trunk and stared down at the wooden figure inside. The old carved face leered back, wooden eyes shining with a dull merriment that sent fever chills of fear down the boy's spine, despite the pain swimming through his ruined face.

He spoke as carefully as he could, the words minced by the broken teeth and bloodied lips. "We need you, Mister Whisper."

The words were slurred.

Mister Whisper did not care. He heard. He understood. He woke up.

They made it out of the state three hours later, moving along a back road that barely existed. The pavement was pitted and cracked and in extreme disuse. There were no road signs worth noticing, and the occasional crossroad they ran across was even less like a sign of civilization and more like a deer path than the stretch of road they were occupying.

The children had cried themselves to sleep well over an hour earlier. Chambers kept staring at them. Johnson never said a word. Kragel leaned over the two sleeping children at one point and stared with hard eyes at Chambers until the man finally looked away and nodded, the message received.

Kragel had his own set of morals and they were a lot closer to the norm than Chambers would ever be. Kragel didn't like to speak about why he was in prison. He was friendly enough, but he was also quiet in that way that made clear he'd have no problem with dropping a few more bodies. Not even Cotton liked fucking with Kragel. Well, maybe he did, but more than one person had noticed that he wasn't as likely to mess with the slim redhead as he was with others.

The car was quiet when things started going wrong. The radio was working fine, but there were no stations to pick up that weren't offering either farm reports or long sermons on how to avoid Hell. None of the men were farmers and they had already survived enough Hell to know they didn't want to go back, so instead they drove in silence.

Lewis took another turn on another road that made no sense to the rest of them and they were okay with that. The man hadn't managed to get them lost so far, and no more cops have come anywhere around them.

The farms were fading away and the trees were cropping up again.

Johnson shook his head. "Where we headed?"

Lewis let a slow grin spread across his face. The smile never reached his eyes. It likely never had. He was that sort of guy. "Woods here are old and privately owned. There's maybe four or five cabins back in here, near a little lake." He shrugged. "I figure it's cold enough there won't be anyone using them. We can get a little rest."

Johnson nodded and the other two agreed as well. The children said nothing, but the young boy opened his eyes and looked past Kragel's face, stared at the gray skies above and the moving branches of the trees, and then closed his eyes again with a small, satisfied sigh.

The left rear tire of the SUV blew out with a thunderous report, and Lewis fought as the vehicle tried to slew itself off the road. The sound of the axle grinding and breaking was impossible to miss.

Kragel reached out and grabbed the kids, pulled them to him and stopped them from free-falling inside of the vehicle as the entire thing shuddered and jumped and bounced to a screeching halt. The engine let out a rude noise and died. Both kids were decidedly awake when it was over with, and both of them had wide, alert eyes.

Chambers frowned as the two children exchanged an odd, conspiratorial look. He might have asked them something, but their little faces were still covered in duct tape. Instead, he opened his door and started to climb from the vehicle. Someone needed to see how bad the damage was.

The two kids in Kragel's arms pulled closer in on themselves and closed their eyes.

Kragel looked toward the children, puzzled by the sudden action, so he missed the way Franklin Chambers died. But he heard it. There was a series of snapping noises, muffled and wet, like cooked chicken being pulled apart at the joints, and then Chambers fell face first to the ground.

Of course in this case "face first" was only an expression, as Johnson realized when he looked at the fallen man.

Chambers lay on the ground and twitched, his legs shuddering and his one visible hand doing a nervous, pointless dance in the growing pool of blood surrounding his torso. From the area where the neck and the shoulders joined, there was a gaping, wet wound with jagged edges and spluttering flows of blood that continued to slop across the aged asphalt. Johnson looked at him from the half opened car door, as he too had planned on seeing what was going on outside of the SUV. Lenny Johnson was not a shy man, and he'd certainly seen more than his fair share of blood over the years, but looking at the still moving, headless corpse of a man who'd been sitting behind him in the car for the last few hours took him by surprise. He let out a noise and shook his head, and almost closed the car door on his leg as he slammed it shut.

Then he let out a proper scream of pure panic.

There had been no sounds, or explosions. There had been no axe-wielding maniac. A giant bear hadn't come along and taken off the man's head. Chambers was dead and there was no noticeable cause for it. The sheer shock value guaranteed a scream. For the moment he forgot all about the gun in his waistband.

Then he remembered it. His face grew calm and he reached for the piece and checked the safety even as the other men in the car screamed questions at him.

He looked at Lewis. "Chambers is dead. Something got him. It won't get us."

Lewis looked at Johnson and started to nod. Then he flinched. His eyes flew wide and he let out a tiny mewling noise.

Johnson turned his head so fast that something hot flared in his neck as he pulled muscles. The pain was sharp and sudden, but he saw something from the corner of his eye as he squinted against the unexpected pain. Whatever it was, it was long and thin and gangly and looked wrong. That was the only way to put it, really. It looked wrong. So much so that Johnson's teeth clenched and he all but snarled. Stay in prison long enough and a good snarl is a better response than occasionally screaming in fear.

He opened his eyes all the way, looked around and saw nothing. Whatever he had spotted was gone.

"What the hell was that?"

"Freakiest looking old bastard I ever saw," Lewis said. His voice carried the faintest note of shock; though much less than what Johnson was feeling. On the other hand, Lewis hadn't seen what had happened to Chambers.

"Can we go anywhere in this thing?" Kragel's voice was thin and reedy and Lewis damn near jumped out of his skin. He'd managed to forget all about the man in the back seat and the kids, too.

"No way in hell." Lewis shook his head and his bottom lip jutted out. "Not a chance."

Johnson stared at the woods around them. The day wasn't done with, not for at least another hour, but the trees and hills around them hid away a surprising amount of sunlight.

"How far to those cabins you were talking about?"

"A good three miles. And I don't think there's much between here and there."

Johnson nodded. That was probably a good thing in some ways. "We need to get on the move. Make sure you got the other gun and let's see what we can do about getting to shelter."

"What about whatever's out there?" Kragel's voice again. The man was thinking hard, trying to consider the logistics of the two kids and how they were going to get to the cabins or much of anywhere else with the little ones weighing them down.

Johnson's eyes assessed the two young children, and then he answered Kragel's unasked question. "Leave 'em."

"They're just kids." Kragel's voice was annoying on most days, but now it was worse, because the words he was saying were exactly the sort of words that could get them killed. They couldn't afford to have consciences.

"They'll slow us down. Leave them here or maybe you'd like to stay with them."

"Man, fuck yourself. That ain't the way it's done. I have kids of my own."

"Yeah? Been taking care of them while you've been locked up?" Lewis's voice was harsh. He stared hard at Kragel for all of ten seconds and then averted his gaze. Kragel was still a scary bastard, squeaky voice or no.

Johnson shook his head and looked at Kragel through half-lidded eyes. "We're going for the cabins. You want to take the kids, you carry them. You want to find the cabins; you do it on your own. We aren't waiting."

Kragel stared at the two kids, both of whom were looking back at him with wide eyes. "So I'll catch up." He couldn't do it. Couldn't leave two kids alone in the woods. They'd be dead in no time. Especially since there was something out there that had already killed Chambers.

Johnson shook his head and gave off a sort of half smile that was not at all pleasant. "Suit yourself." A moment later he was out of the ruined SUV and heading in the direction the vehicle had being aimed in before everything went wrong. He carefully stepped around the remains of Chambers and he did his best to look everywhere at once while he was at it.

Lewis stared at Kragel for a second and then shrugged with a sheepish grin before following. Kragel watched them go and shook his head.

He hadn't been paying much attention when they turned off the road. He'd been dozing and half-dreaming about the life he wanted to make for himself instead of doing anything remotely helpful. No one to blame but himself. Daydreams tended to be better than the reality, that's all.

He looked at the kids. They weren't really struggling, but the little girl was moving like she really had to take a leak.

"You have to pee?" He looked at her and she nodded so

hard he thought it might fall off. He tore the tape on her hands and ankles. It was sort of loose anyway because Johnson was smart enough to know that little kids couldn't exactly bust out of the stuff without being noticed. "I got your brother, okay? So go pee and come right back."

She nodded and then pulled at the tape on her mouth. The goo left behind left a cob-webby residue on soft skin that was red and irritated from the glue compounds. He winced just a bit. He hadn't thought that the stuff would hurt the kid.

"Don't go anywhere, mister. Mister Whisper is out there."

"Mister Whisper?" Kragel frowned.

The little girl nodded solemnly and then half-ran for the closest tree, her hands already pulling at her pants to get them out of the way. Modestly made her hide behind the tree's trunk. Fear made her peek around the edge of the tree to make sure her brother was still there.

And while she was urinating, she heard the sound of Mister Whisper moving through the tree limbs far above, just barely making any noises at all as he hopped from limb to limp. She looked up in time to see his face peering down at her. She stared at the familiar face, not used to seeing it moving. Mister Whisper smiled down at her for a moment, his eyes quietly letting her know that she would be safe. He turned his head in that way that always made her think of a bird, and waved his impossibly long fingers at her as his smile grew wider and wider.

Then he was gone, moving far too fast for a person, taking chances that would have had her terrified for any member of her family.

But not Mister Whisper. She had been told the stories by her grandmother and her father alike.

Mister Whisper was a member of the family, yes, but he was more than that. He was like the tooth fairy. He was special.

She finished her business as best she could with nothing to wipe with, and then she pulled her pants back up and moved toward the stranger who was holding her brother.

The man looked at her and frowned. He was a nice enough man, but he smelled bad and he had tattoos on his arms, pictures of creepy things like spiders and skulls. "Who's Mister Whisper?"

She stared at him with wide eyes and tried to figure out the best answer for that. "He's my family's …" She struggled to remember what her father had told her. "Protector." She smiled, proud of herself for finding the right words.

The man frowned and looked nervously around them. Then he started pulling the tape from her brother's hands. "Okay. It's your turn to pee."

In the distance a tree branch creaked and several pinecones dropped from their resting places in a small shower of needles. The little girl couldn't help but smile a little.

Daddy always said that Mister Whisper liked to "play with his toys, like a cat plays with a mouse." She'd seen what the mean man had done to her older brother. For that reason alone she didn't feel a need to warn the man that Mister Whisper did not always play nicely.

The winds were picking up and the cold was sinking in as the sun lowered. It would be damned cold soon and none of them were exactly dressed for the weather. Johnson lamented not taking the time to look around earlier. Maybe he could have come up with a coat or something.

Too late now, any way you looked at it.

The trees were mostly barren, the cold season was on them and the leaves had fallen easily a month earlier, leaving skeletal things that rattled and rustled in the wind. Yeah, that shit wasn't making his skin crawl.

Lewis coughed into his hand and looked around nervously. Both of them were walking at a solid clip and both were feeling their months of relative inactivity.

"What the fuck happened to Chambers?" Lewis's voice was low and winded.

"Don't know. I just know I don't want it happening to me."

"I didn't look closely, but it looked like a shark had taken his fucking head off, Johnson. What the hell could have done that?" Lewis's voice was shaking a bit. He'd been calm enough earlier, but now he was starting to sound like he might become a problem. Johnson considered the pistol in his belt but left it alone for the moment. Whatever had happened to Chambers still had to be considered, and if there was something out there that wanted to take a head off, he wanted the odds in his favor. If that meant dealing with Lewis, he would deal with the man.

Johnson looked at him. "Yeah? So what did you see? When you got all freaky earlier, looking in the trees."

Lewis shook his head and tried not to remember, but the image was there, bold and bright and locked in his mind. The last time he'd seen anything that fucked up he'd been dropping acid and didn't know it. College, what could you do? Only now he wasn't dropping anything. His mind was as clear as it could be. No one had slipped him anything. No one could have. The only food or drinks they'd had come out of cans and bottles they'd snagged at a rest stop a while back and came fresh as could be from the vending machines.

What had he seen? Nightmares were made from what he'd seen. "Had to be my imagination. It was only for a second and I guess we were all a bit freaked out, right?"

Johnson coughed and then spit a wad of phlegm at the ground. He was still eyeing the woods around them with a healthy dose of paranoia. "So humor me. Tell me anyway."

"It was an old man. Well, maybe old. I don't know, man. All I saw was a nasty looking face with a nasty looking smile and a body that looked all wrong."

Johnson stared daggers. "Do better than that. Whatever you saw, maybe it was real. Maybe it's what fucking tore Chambers' head off. So maybe you should just try really hard to remember."

"When I was a kid I saw one of those puppet shows, like they had in the Middle Ages, the ones with the famous puppets." He thought back. "Punch and Judy, I think. Anyways, the face I saw looked a little like the Punch doll. It had a big nose and a pointy chin and dark little eyes." He shook his head. "It doesn't sound all that creepy, but it was. The body was all wrong. It was too long and too thin. Thin like spider legs thin. And the old man, he had white hair, long and scruffy."

"So you saw a skinny old man?"

"No." Lewis shook his head. "I know it sounds like an old man, but it wasn't an old man. It wasn't … It didn't look like an old man. It had features like it should be an old man, but it was too healthy for that."

Johnson nodded like maybe he understood, but Lewis didn't think he did. He didn't think it was possible to describe what he'd seen properly. All he knew was that the thing had freaked him out.

He looked around the woods and scowled at the thought that they might be outside when the sun went down.

Johnson must have been thinking the same thing because he asked, "How much further?"

"Can't be long. We been walking for a while and it's got to be close."

That was about as useless an answer as he'd ever heard. He let it go for all of the same reasons as before.

Behind them, the trees rustled and sighed in the growing wind. Because his skin started crawling, Johnson looked around and studied the way they'd come. He felt like someone was watching him, and he hated that feeling. Over the years he'd gotten very good at knowing when he was being watched. His folks had taught him that lesson early on.

There was nothing in the road. Even the wrecked SUV was lost in the distance, hidden by trees and curves in the path they'd followed. But there was something … .

Johnson closed his eyes for a moment and stopped walking. He took several deep breaths and then opened his eyes again, looking at the shadows along the side of the road, the dark places between the trees, where the sort of thing that could rip a man's head off his shoulders might hide. He bit back a sudden shudder at that thought. Maybe he was a little more freaked out than he wanted to admit, even to himself. It was one thing to be tough in prison, and another to be safe in the middle of the woods. His hand found the pistol and he let it. Fuck everyone and anyone else. He was getting out of this in one piece.

Something in the woods shifted. He saw it, a flickering thing that moved high in the trees, higher than anything that size should have been. And the trees moved with that sudden motion. Not a lot, just the tiniest little bit, but it was enough to catch his attention.

"Something."

"What?" Lewis looked his way with a frown on his face. He was normally frowning, but it was more pronounced now.

Johnson kept his voice as calm as he could. "There's something up in the trees. Up high."

Lewis craned his head up and started looking, trying to see if he could spot anything. He was smart enough to see where Johnson was staring and to look from there outward. "I don't see anything."

"Neither do I. Not now, but I did."

Something laughed out in the woods. Not someone. Johnson would have bet on that, because the sound wasn't human, but it was definitely laughter. His skin tried to pull itself up his neck and back as he heard the sound, and the fine hairs on his arms stood on end as he listened to the racket echo across the trees.

"What the fuck?" Lewis's eyes were wide and his mouth trembled.

"Maybe an owl?"

"No fucking owl I ever heard."

The wind whipped up into a frenzy and the trees creaked as they swayed, the ground seemed to hiss as the leaves shivered and danced between the trees that sighed and groaned.

And goddamned if something didn't seem to move between the trees again. The motion was a flicker there and gone, but it was enough for Johnson. He aimed at the spot where that darkness seemed to jump and he fired three times. If any of his bullets hit anything at all, he couldn't have proved it.

Lewis let out a scream and jumped back from him like his ass was on fire. He stared wildly at Johnson and reached for his pistol, but stopped himself when he realized he wasn't the target of the gunman's efforts.

"You lost your fucking mind?" Lewis shrieked the words.

"I saw it again, damn it!"

"Saw what?" Lewis's face was red with anger, his eyes half-bugged from his face.

Before Johnson could answer, a tree came crashing down to their left.

Both of them heard the groaning noise and looked in that direction. They watched the tall, thin shape tremble and shudder as the violent snapping reports erupted from near the base. The tree shivered as it crashed across the road leading to the cabins and bounced twice before it settled.

"Good job, asshole! You killed a fucking tree!" Lewis was screaming, but he was half-laughing, too.

Johnson wasn't laughing. The tree was nowhere near where he'd been aiming.

He was about to point that out when something came out of the woods and ran right for them.

It was fast, no two ways about it. His eyes tried to keep up with the shape but he may as well have tried to keep pace with a bullet. The shape was vaguely humanoid, he could make out that much, but it was also wrong on an elemental level. It was too thin, too tall, and too pale.

He had enough time to register the grinning face, the long, leering smile and the dark eyes, and then it was running past and Lewis was yanked off his feet. He staggered backward, his hands flailing in an effort to keep his balance. He failed. The man took four steps backward and fell as surely as the tree had fallen.

Johnson stared at the man for a moment, stared at the shape that vanished back into the trees and took aim at the retreating form, but he stopped himself before firing. It would have been wasted. Whatever the hell had just ripped past him was already gone.

Then Lewis screamed again, a different sort of noise this time. This wasn't panic or humor or fright. No, the noise he made was pure pain., undiluted and unexpected.

Lewis's hands covered his face in an instant and he screamed a second time as lines of red stained his fingers and then dribbled past.

"Lewis? What happened?"

Lewis's only answer was another scream as he started kicking his feet, and the blood flowed faster past his fingers. For just one second Johnson was tempted to go to the man's aid, but then he caught himself. Helping Lewis meant leaving himself open for whatever the fuck had just torn into the other convict.

In the distance, where he'd seen the thing vanish a moment earlier, something waved in the air near a tree. He squinted and looked closely, not daring to move any closer.

What he saw looked like a hand. It had a thumb and four long fingers with long, wicked looking nails. The thumb and forefinger, both too long and too pale, dangled something and let that something wave like a flag.

Just as soon as Johnson focused on the waving item, it dropped from the fingers that held it. His eyes tracked the object as it slipped toward the ground, pale and painted red. It had holes cut in it. No, not cut. They were supposed to be there. It looked like cheap Halloween mask as it flopped heavily into the leaves, but Johnson knew better.

There was too much weight and blood, and the texture, well, that was the one that gave it away. Human skin has a certain texture to it that he could make out even from a distance.

Lewis's torn face hit the leaves just as Johnson fully comprehended what he was looking at.

He knew good and fucking well why Lewis was screaming.

Then the laughter came cutting through the air again, even as Johnson backed up, horrified.

He stopped backing up when he ran into something too solid to move. What should have been behind him was nothing but road. He knew that because he'd been walking on the road for a while now and there was nothing to impede the way except for poor, screaming Lewis to his left and the tree ahead of him.

Johnson started to turn, his hand moving, already preparing to take aim at whatever was blocking his access.

The hand that grabbed his wrist was cold, the skin dry, and the nails on the impossibly long fingers dug into the flesh of his arm like fish hooks into the upper pallet of a properly hooked trout.

The pain was bright enough to make him draw in a breath as he looked down at that hand, at the dark claws digging in, at the pale skin that made his own flesh look several shades darker in contrast. The hand was connected to a long arm that was as pale as a corpse, and he looked up the length of that arm until it met the rest of the thing standing behind him.

The face was looking down at him seemed inverted. He saw the smiling mouth full of long yellowed teeth, and the hooked nose and the long chin, and the eyes, oh, the eyes that were so dark, almost a perfect contrast to the too white flesh around them. An old man, was that what he'd thought of when Lewis described the thing? He was wrong, so very wrong.

It wasn't old. It was ancient. But oh, so very vital. More alive than it should have been. Then should have been possible. It was alive in ways that made no sense, but he could feel that vitality, that life essence. It radiated like heat despite the cold grip that held him.

The smile grew broader. The eyes narrowed. The face leaned in closer, close enough to kiss. To take a big bite of his face like a starving man biting a juicy apple.

The voice was a whisper, a sighing of the wind through the trees and little more than that, but he heard the words as clearly as could be. "You've been very naughty, haven't you, Lenny?"

He had just long enough to wonder how the thing could possibly know his name, before it took that big, juicy bite from him.

The sun set all too quickly, and the two kids settled together in the back seat of the SUV, while Kragel contemplated the situation he found himself in. Depending on how you looked at it, he had nowhere to go but up. Well, up, or dead.

He didn't want to go back to prison, but if he did, it wouldn't be any worse than what he'd already been through. The kids were the thing. He couldn't do it. He couldn't leave them in the middle of the woods. No one would find them. If he left them in the car they'd probably die of exposure. Maybe not, but they were little kids, and he couldn't take that chance. He wasn't in Laura's life, or in Tommy's, but he'd never forgive anyone who left them alone in the cold and he couldn't make himself leave the kids he was with.

After the sun went down and the darkness crept in closer, he let himself drift into a fitful sleep. Exhaustion does that after a while. He closed his eyes and leaned against the locked back door and fell away from consciousness.

He woke up when the noise started. His eyes flew wide open and he stared at the ceiling of the car, his body tensed and his mind alert.

There were no crickets to sing to him. It was too cold for that. But the wind offered a lullaby instead, hissing incoherent words and crooning with the accompaniment of the trees that swayed along.

The children were gone. That was the thing that he realized first on a conscious level. The kids he'd been watching were gone.

That got him sitting up fast. He looked around and saw that the doors were still closed. The vehicle still tilted at a strange angle.

"Hey, kids? You out there?" He looked around the interior of the SUV, feeling a little foolish in the nearly complete darkness. His eyes had long since adjusted, however, and he should have been able to see them if they were nearby.

Finally he shivered a bit and then opened the locked door, slipping out into the cold night to see if he could find them. There was no sign of them.

There was no sign of the road, either. Not even the smallest path to indicate that anyone had ever walked on the pristine land where the SUV now sat. The land was unfamiliar. There were trees, but not like any he'd ever seen before. The grass grew deep enough to hide his ankles, but no bugs made noises, no animals chattered in the night. The silence was almost overwhelming, save for the sound of the wind and the trees.

From the corner of his eye he caught a slip of paper pinned to the windshield, held in place by the wiper. He stared for a solid minute, puzzling at that. Like everything else it felt wrong.

Finally he reached for the paper and read what was written there in a tight, delicate script.

Dear Sir,

I do not know your name, only that you were kind to the children I am charged with protecting. For that reason I shall be kind to you. The police will not find you. Not where I have left you. Search and you will find food and water. You will find no roads to travel, but with effort you might someday find a path. This is my last kindness to you.

Mister Whisper

Kragel stared at the note and then folded it into his pocket.

Impossible. No way the man could have moved the van without him waking up. But despite his excellent night vision it was too dark out to actually try investigating, and he was relatively safe for the moment. He was cold, and he had no blanket. After a brief consideration he decided that he would wait at the SUV until morning and then he would head out in search of the road. He had no idea who Mister Whisper was, and he didn't much care, but he would find his way in the morning. With that thought in mind he climbed into the back seat and locked the doors, feeling only a little foolish at the gesture.

Mister Whisper told the children stories the entire way home, and he had them laughing with delight on occasion and shivering with the cheerful joy of a good scary yarn on others. By the time midnight came around, they were at home. He opened the door and ushered them inside, where their parents were waiting.

As was tradition in the family, the parents did not look at Mister Whisper, not while he was awake and moving. There was no guarantee that he would take offense, but the Fae had their own ways and it was best not to take chances. When both of the children had been greeted properly, their mother took them by their hands and led them to their bedrooms after they bid their father and their protector a good night.

The father spoke softly, "Thank you, Mister Whisper. Again."

"It's a debt I gladly pay, young William. You know this." The voice was beyond soft. He lived up to his name in that way. "How is your Timothy?"

"Mending, thanks to you."

"A small charm. He'll be fine in a day, should he remember not to dance. Also, keep him away from cats for a while. They'll find his odor offensive."

"He smelled fine to me."

"You, William, are not a cat. Trust me on this."

"The men who did this?"

Mister Whisper smiled. William could see his teeth from the corner of his eye. "They will bother no one else."

"Denise wanted to know about the car …"

"Like the men, it will bother no one else." Mister Whisper's long-fingered hand set a small bauble on the table. It was a tiny glass jar, and inside was a swirl of color that resembled little as much a forest at night. "Keep this well, William. Lock it in the trunk with my shape. I rather like it."

When William risked looking up, he was alone.

Without another word he walked over to the trunk against the wall. The lid was still raised, and when he looked the carved shape of Mister Whisper was where it belonged again, not missing like it had been when he and Denise got back from their trip to the neighbors. Ten minutes was all the time they were gone, fifteen tops, and look how quickly their world had changed.

He shivered at the thought of what he had almost lost. He'd call the police tomorrow; report the truck in his backyard. That was all he'd have to do to get past what could have been a true nightmare. His fingers carefully arranged the old wooden doll in the case and then he set the bottle on the ground of the trunk, near the wooden hand.

He mouthed the words "thank you" one last time and closed the lid.

Mister Whisper did not answer.

He seldom did.

In hindsight, it was possibly for the best.

 JAMES A. MOORE is the award-winning author of more than twenty novels, thrillers, dark fantasy, and horror alike, including the critically acclaimed *Fireworks, Under the Overtree, Blood Red,* the *Serenity Falls* trilogy (featuring his recurring antihero Jonathan Crowley) and his most recent novels *Smile No More* and *Blind Shadows* (with coauthor Charles R. Rutledge). He has also recently ventured into the realm of young adult novels with his new series *Subject Seven*. In addition to writing multiple short stories, he has also edited, with Christopher Golden and Tim Lebbon, *The British Invasion* anthology for Cemetery Dance Publications.

Writer's Block
Thad Linson

The man stood in the middle of the deserted street as dusk settled, looking around for any signs of life. There were empty cars all around him, some wrecked, some simply abandoned. He noticed a blood streak on the driver's side window of a Honda Accord and an open door of a Ford Focus next to it. Down the street another car sat with its lights, on and just at the edge of the beams he saw flickers of movement.

"Oh, no," he said.

He began to discern figures coming toward him, moving slowly, arms outstretched. As they got closer, he could tell there were hundreds of them, all in various stages of decomposition. He heard a droning sound and realized it was the moaning of the living dead. When they reached the intersection that was roughly a half-block from him, one of them broke out of the ranks and ran at him, like a sprinter coming out of the blocks.

"For pity's sake," the man said. He raised his hand toward the zombie with the palm out. "*Stop!*"

The runner came to a halt fewer than ten feet from the man, trying to give him its best puzzled look despite half its face being gone. It reached for the man, who promptly snapped his fingers at it. He pointed at the zombie, wagged his finger at it, and shook his head. The horde behind the runner had stopped in mid-shamble, confused.

"There's this beautiful setting, and you're what comes out of the dark?" the man asked. "You're not supposed to be here. Go on, get out of here, take a break; do whatever it is you guys do in your downtime. Smoke 'em if you got 'em."

The runner turned around and began to walk away. The horde didn't move. "Go on, piss off!" the man yelled.

The horde began shuffling off in different directions. The runner stopped and looked at the ground. It bent down and picked something up. The man saw it was a finger. The runner sniffed it and then put it in its mouth.

"Really?" the man asked. The runner looked back at him, gave a halfhearted shrug, and went on its way.

The man closed his eyes, bowed his head and began to rub his temples. When he opened his eyes, he was seated in front of his computer in his home office. He looked at the words on the screen and frowned when he saw the word zombie. He hit the delete button and pushed his chair back from the desk. He sighed, got up and left the office. As he entered the kitchen, he found his wife sitting at the table watching a small TV that was on the counter. He opened the fridge and grabbed a can of Coke. Popping the top, he sat across from her.

"So you're blonde today," he said.

"Yes. It's the new hot thing again," she said, not looking away from the TV.

He took a sip of Coke and stared at the can. After a couple of minutes, his wife looked at him and read his face. His brow was furrowed, eyes in a slight squint, a frown that was so deep the edges of his mouth almost rested on the table. She sighed.

"Story not working?"

"Not in the least. I thought I finally had something, but it turned out to be damn zombies. Can you believe that? Everybody and their mothers have done zombies to death."

"Were they fast or slow?"

"What does it damn matter? They were fricking zombies!" He lifted the can toward his mouth. "Both," he said and took a drink.

"Maybe you should stop writing scary stuff and try

something else. Some science fiction, maybe a mystery. Ooohhh, I know. Urban fantasy is really big. Maybe you could start a series about a wizard detective or something."

"You're really not helping right now. You do realize that, don't you?"

"It's not like I said you should write what I write."

The man choked on the drink he was taking, not quite doing a spit take, but some Coke dribbled down his chin as he stifled a cough. He got control of himself and wiped his chin with the back of his hand.

"You mean about all that frilly stuff like hope and love and whatnot? Not a chance."

"You used to write about hope."

"No, I used to give my characters hope just so I could take it away from them, which made the emotional impact of what was happening to them even stronger."

"So your characters are now hopeless instead."

"I didn't say that. Hopelessness has become too … numbing. All the apocalyptic books and movies, especially the movies, have such deep hopelessness that you can't like or cheer for any of the characters because you know it's a waste of time since they're going to die anyway."

"Those characters always struggle to survive in the face of overwhelming odds. That struggle provides the character hope. Living provides hope. Hope provides a sort of dignity that helps define that character."

"But you need fear to drive that struggle, not acceptance of your fate." He pointed at the TV set. "Look at these jackholes, for example. First there was only one guy who wanted to skydive from a plane that was almost in orbit. He wanted to do it because he was afraid of it and wanted to conquer it. Now there's nine more who want to join him. They even want to do tricks and crap on the way down. They're not afraid of doing it anymore. It's just become something else to do."

"The news said these guys haven't had a bad dream in a few weeks. How long has your writer's block lasted?"

"I'm not blocked. Nope, nothing here is blocked. The words come just as easy as they used to. It's the freaking stories that don't want to freaking go where I want them to freaking go."

"I can tell you're blocked. You're not cursing like your usual self."

"Well, pardon me all to hell."

"Of course, your cursing is what attracted me to you." The man looked at his wife who smiled and got up. "I'm off to write some more frilly stuff. I hope you solve your blockage soon." She left the kitchen.

"Sarcasm isn't sexy, you know," he called after her.

He sat a few more minutes and then sighed and got up. He went back to his office and sat at his computer. He stared at the screen, watching the cursor blink. There and gone, there and gone, there and gone. After a while, he shook his head and turned his focus from the screen to his office. His eyes roamed over the huge bookcases on one wall, scanning the titles hoping to find some inspiration.

Clowns, he thought. *Clowns are scary. Nah, been done before. Witches. No, all I see when I think of witches is the cute redhead and her pretty girlfriend from* Buffy. *How about an offbeat superhero named Major Ennui? Been done. Something out of Native American folklore. Done. Aliens. Done, and better than I could ever do. Ghosts, the devil, a plague. Done, done, really done.*

He glanced at the action figures to the left of his computer. He reached out and picked up a swordsman and an orc. He had the swordsman stand on his keyboard and the orc on his desk. He had the swordsman point his sword at the orc.

"It is the end of all your schemes, vile creature. You and your kind will bother the men of this land no more."

"No, my army has come to kill all humans. Orcs shall reign supreme."

"Umm, what army?"

The man had the orc look behind it. "They're coming. In fact, they're just beyond that hill."

"Lying filth! Time to for you to die!"

"Ahem," a female voice said.

The man threw the figures down on his desk and looked up to see his wife standing in the doorway. "*What?*" he said. She made a typing motion and smiled. He mocked her with a typing motion of his own. She laughed and went back to her office. He glared at the open door for a few more seconds and then went back to staring at his blinking cursor. He finally reached out, put his fingers on the keyboard and started typing.

When he did this, he found himself in a large warehouse. It had makeshift walls set up on one end to create living quarters for whatever was there. He saw a group of people standing around a table that had at least twenty guns on it. A woman in a skintight leather outfit was putting magazines in her semiautomatic handguns. To her right stood a big man, well over six and a half feet tall, wearing only a pair of jeans. An alarm sounded and everyone looked around. The woman chambered bullets in both her guns and the shirtless man pointed to two other men.

"Protect the cubs!"

As the two men ran towards the partitioned section of the warehouse, the shirtless man began to change. Bones and muscles grew, sinews and tendons popped, his face elongated, hair sprouted everywhere and he grew another foot in height. The werewolf flexed its hands, its claws growing to more than half a foot long. The werewolf looked up as dozens of ropes dropped from the ceiling and men in black combat uniforms began rappelling down them, firing their weapons. More people changed into werewolves and started attacking the men as they hit the floor. The woman fired her guns as her werewolf companion reached out, pulled a man off his rope and bit down hard on his combat helmet. The helmet cracked and the werewolf jerked its head back, taking the other man's head with it in its jaws. Blood pumped from the decapitated body as it fell.

Another of the attackers got close to the woman and knocked both guns from her hands. She reached out, grabbed him by the edges of his Kevlar vest and pulled him towards her. She opened her mouth and hissed at him, showing her elongated canine teeth. The man began to scream but it was cut off when the female vampire bit into his throat and pulled her head to the left, tearing his throat to shreds. She dropped the man and did a cartwheel to where her guns lay, picking them up when her hands were on the ground and landed on her feet, firing both guns. A bullet hit one of the warehouse windows, shattering the black painted glass. Sunlight streamed in and caught both the vampire and her werewolf companion in the rays. They shielded their eyes from the sudden appearance of the bright light, but nothing happened to the vampire. At least, nothing that the man liked.

"Whoa, whoa, whoa, *whoa*," the man said. "Everyone hold it one damn minute!"

Calls of "cease fire" rang through the warehouse and within seconds everyone was looking at the man. He walked over to the vampire and werewolf, looking at them from head to toe.

"Are the two of you ..." the man said, his face contorting as he tried to not say the next word. "Sparkling?"

The female vampire looked up at the werewolf, who, scratching his chin, had suddenly found the most interesting spot of nothing on the wall to look at. She rolled her eyes at him and looked back at the man.

"Well, we were waiting for everyone to arrive, so I was playing with his little girls. They wanted to make their daddy a card, so we ... we used some glitter, okay. Happy now?"

The werewolf reached into a back pocket of his jeans, pulled out the card and showed it to the man. The werewolf's lips were pulled back and it looked like he was smiling. The card had all different colors of glitter on it and said "Good luck, Daddy!"

"Oh Katy Kee-rist," the man said, closing his eyes and reaching up to rub the bridge of his nose with his right forefinger and thumb.

He opened his eyes and stared at his computer screen, making sure he had actually written what he thought he had. He started hitting the delete button, harder and harder, until he was banging on his keyboard with his fists. He finally stopped and looked at the ruined keyboard. Plastic pieces were all over, and the "f" button had landed next to his orc figure. He unplugged the keyboard and dropped it into the trashcan next to his desk. He then got up and headed for the kitchen again.

His wife was there, cooking dinner. He got a beer from the fridge and opened it. With a big sigh, he sat at the table. He took a long pull from the beer and stared out the window that was above the sink. He then looked down to find a new keyboard, still new in its box, sitting next to his place setting.

"What happened?"

"I found myself in the seventh circle of young adult hell," he said, and then took another pull on the beer.

His wife looked at him, concerned. "What did you write about?"

"You. Really. Don't. Want. To. Know."

"Oh. Okay." She paused to gather her thoughts. "The news reported that ninety-six percent of the people they polled have gone without a nightmare for almost two months now."

"What's the margin of error?"

"Four percent."

The man sighed. "What you're saying is bad dreams are now a thing of the past. Wonderful."

"Two months. Isn't that when your ... never mind." His wife turned back to the stove.

"When I developed my writer's block. Yes. I admit it. I have writer's block. Most of the time I just sit there and stare at my screen, hoping the words will pop up on their own. But they don't. It's only been the last couple of days that some ideas have started to come back and I'm able to get a story going. But the story takes on a life of its own and just doesn't go where I want it to go. So I wind up deleting everything."

He finished his beer. His wife went to the fridge, pulled another one out, opened it and set it in front of him. He gave her a small smile, which she returned. She sat in her usual chair opposite him.

"There's something I've never asked in all our time together," she said.

"Shoot."

"Why fear? What makes you want to scare people?"

"Fear is such a primary emotion. Fear affects so many of the things you say and do. I want to talk to that cute girl over there but I'm afraid to, so I don't. And because I don't, we don't get married and have a child who grows up to cure some big disease. Or I'm afraid to tell my boss what he needs to hear, so the company goes under because I don't."

"Aren't those extreme examples?"

"The results may be, but the reasoning isn't. Fear can define you. Ask someone who's agoraphobic. But it's our response to our fear that can really set us apart from one another. Take the military. You'll always have some soldier freeze in battle, while another soldier will go above and beyond to save his buddies' lives. It's how you handle the fear. Those two soldiers can be the exact same at every other time except for that moment, and it's how they handle their fear in that moment that they'll be remembered for and how they're defined."

"So what about love? Am I wasting my time with my writing?"

"No, you have a beautiful way with words. Love is just too difficult to describe. Fear is tangible. Love isn't. But I can say that feeling love doesn't always conquer fear. I should know. I was so scared to ask you to marry me, scared to spend the rest of my life with someone."

"But you did. You conquered that fear. One more question before dinner, though. What scares you now?"

The man hesitated. "Being alone," he said in a soft voice.

She got up and walked around the table to him. She bent over and gave him a soft kiss on the cheek. He reached out, took her hand and smiled.

"I think I see the wheels starting to turn. What was it your mentor said?"

"Don't write about what scares other people. Write about what scares you."

She released his hand and went to the counter and started making their salad. "So I guess this means a late night of writing."

The man got up and went over to help his wife. "Actually, I think the world can go one more night without being afraid."

Thad lives in a house in central Ohio that has way too many books and comics. He's had stories published on the Necon E-books flash fiction page and on Horror World. He finds writing about himself in the third person very awkward and never knows what to say.

The Miracle Material
Abra Staffin-Wiebe

The landfill is safe. I think. Even Tupperware frightens me now. The sight of a discarded teddy bear moves me to tears. I wonder if Meredith's teddy bear still lies abandoned on her bed, held under siege by the ever-glowing blue stars that decorate her bedroom.

I tell myself that Meredith is safe and happy. We came from the sea, the scientists said—when there were scientists. What could be more natural than for us to return to the sea? I tell myself that she is safe and happy within the bosom of the sea.

I know I lie.

Wherever Meredith may be, however she feels, she is not my little girl anymore. And it is all my fault.

Well, not all of it. Once we brought the bluflex up from the Mariana Trench, the end was inevitable. But the loss of our children … that was my fault.

It was a deep and lovely blue. It glowed. It sparkled and shimmered. It resisted all extremes of temperature and stress, but it could be molded into any shape when submerged in seawater with an electrical current running through it. It was even non-toxic.

When I brought the bluflex doll home to Meredith, I was happy that she loved it so much. She took it to school for her "What My Parents Do" presentation. I was delighted when she told me that all the other third graders were jealous of it.

I saw the marketing possibilities.

My employers, Oak Leaf Products International, already had bluflex in production for use in building material, shoes, jewelry, food containers, and electronics components. It was the miracle material, an organic compound that needed nothing more than time and seawater to reproduce under the same environmental conditions as existed in the Mariana Trench. We had a lock on the national market, but we knew that our competitors overseas were racing as frantically as we were to find new ways to exploit bluflex's amazing properties.

Because it was my suggestion, I was put in charge of the toy division. I used the extra money to buy a house by the sea. That summer I was glad I had done so.

A hundred people died in the city during the heat wave. Sales of air conditioners made with bluflex insulation soared.

I worked ten-hour days, but I was always glad to be home again. Meredith was usually heading to bed when I got home, so I didn't get to talk to her much, but she said she loved living by the sea. She seemed content. She had the entire collection of bluflex toys, and she loved them all. Everybody loved bluflex.

The demand for bluflex was so high that our R&D division focused its efforts entirely on finding a way to speed up bluflex's natural reproduction in a lab environment. It wasn't cost-effective to mount another expedition to the Mariana Trench, and the population that we had wasn't reproducing nearly fast enough to keep up with the demand.

The week they succeeded, Oak Leaf Products International held a party for all employees and their families. I noticed that every child wore bluflex clothing or carried a bluflex toy. I only smiled, a drink in my hand, when parents told me that their children refused to go anywhere without their bluflex.

God help me, I only smiled.

Meredith loved her bluflex snorkeling mask and flippers. She spent more and more time in the sea. Even though it was fall, the worldwide heat wave had not abated. Everyone either stayed inside their air-conditioned homes or went swimming.

From our house, I watched Meredith swim with her friends. I had never seen so many children without parental supervision at the beach, but they all seemed to be happy and healthy. And they all wore bluflex snorkel masks and fins.

I remember when the icecaps started melting. It was December, and it was ninety degrees in the shade. Oak Leaf Products donated a hundred bluflex air conditioners to the homeless shelters, but there were still so many deaths that the city council mandated immediate cremation.

There were rumors of plague, but sales of bluflex products remained high.

I was in the basement with the plumber when Meredith told me she would be gone overnight for a farewell party for a few of her friends. Our basement was flooded. I had noticed puddles growing in the basement a couple of months ago, but now the water was knee high. It smelled like the sea, and I could've sworn I saw movement in the water.

I asked Meredith if her friends' parents would be chaperoning.

She was quiet for a moment, and then she said, "We won't be alone. Don't worry, I'll be fine."

In the darkness of the basement, the bluflex bracelets she wore shimmered brilliantly. Their reflection in the water made the basement alive with small gleaming lights.

After Meredith left, I gave the plumber some excuse and retreated to the sanctity of the kitchen.

Heat waves shimmered above the beach outside. They distorted the light of the setting sun until ripples of red, gold, purple, and blue ran across the sand. The children on the beach looked as though they were swimming in a teeming sea of color.

The plumber told me that there was nothing he could do. I offered him a drink, and he took me up on the offer. When he set his toolbox on the table, I noticed the bluflex logo printed on the side, and I smiled. Over a cold beer, he told me that the water table was rising.

"You should consider selling before it gets worse," he said. "A lot of other people are."

"I can't," I told him. "My daughter loves the sea too much."

He finished his beer and left without saying anything else. I stayed sitting at the kitchen table, in the dark, drinking and watching the beach. Even though all the windows were closed, I could smell the sea.

There was a bonfire on the beach. At first, I thought the small lights around it were sparks cast by the fire, but as my eyes adjusted to the darkness, I saw the truth.

They were children.

Children wreathed in glowing, sparkling bluflex. I watched them dance, watched the pulsing beat of the light. The colors seemed to respond to each other. They never did that in the laboratory tests. I told myself that I was only thinking that because I was drunk, but I kept watching until just before sunrise.

The sparkles gradually clustered together, stopping near the edge of the water. Three dancing lights kept moving out until I could barely see them. I half-thought I was imagining them, until they flashed brightly enough to leave an afterimage on my retinas. Then the mass of sparkles on the beach flared in return, and I was blinded. When I could see again, the sparks of light on the beach were dissipating.

The sea was dark.

I stayed sitting in the kitchen until I heard the front door open and close. Soft footsteps padded down the hallway. I got up and turned on the light in the kitchen. The footsteps paused.

Meredith stood in the darkened hallway.

"Meredith," I started to say and then stopped.

She didn't say anything.

"I'm selling the house."

After a moment, she continued towards her bedroom. I could see the bluflex bracelets she wore sparkling to each other long after I lost her form in the darkness of the house.

I returned to the brightly-lit kitchen, threw out the empty beer bottles, and then went to bed.

The next morning, I put a for-sale sign in front of our house. Despite the flooding in the basement, I had an offer within the week.

"The heat isn't good for the wife," the man who made the offer told me. "They say it feels cooler by the sea. And Junior just loves to go to the beach."

Although the air was oppressively hot, goose bumps raised the hair on my arms. Junior stood next to the kitchen windows, watching the beach. He didn't respond to his father's assertion, but the bluflex yo-yo that spun from his fingers glinted.

Meredith was not happy.

She didn't try to change my mind, but she was subdued for several days. She fondled her bluflex bracelets constantly, as if she needed their reassurance.

I did not try to keep her from her friends on the beach, despite what I had seen. I suppose I was trying to hide the truth from myself, trying to convince myself that I'd misinterpreted what I'd seen through the haze of alcohol.

They were only children, after all. It was natural for children to enjoy the sea. And it was good for Meredith to have so many friends. The number of children who visited the beach tripled during the months it took us to prepare for our move.

Also, I didn't need to feel guilty about drinking in front of her when she wasn't there.

Our new home was twenty miles further inland. Inside, with the windows closed and the air-conditioner humming, it was impossible to smell the sea. I found that a great relief. Meredith quickly made new friends. She was gone playing with them for most of the day while I was at work. She would show up for dinner, her skin glowing a healthy brown against the blue of her bracelets, armbands, and necklaces. After dinner, she would leave again.

I never met her friends, but all the children ran wild during that long, hot Indian summer. A teacher died from heatstroke in January, and the schools were closed temporarily. Most school buildings were old and could not be fully air-conditioned. It didn't seem to bother the children, but a number of teachers became ill. Once the heat wave had subsided, the government promised, schools would be reopened. Scientists were working on the problem. They thought electromagnetic radiation might be among the causes.

The heat wave was finally over, but there are no schools.

One day at work, I came across a lab technician crying at her desk. She told me that her son had run away. He hadn't come home last night, but she didn't notice until breakfast. He spent so much time at the beach, she had just assumed … but all his bluflex toys were gone, so she knew he wasn't coming back. She forced a smile and asked me how Meredith was doing.

I realized I didn't know.

That night at dinner, I asked Meredith if she would like to see the place where we tested and molded bluflex. I was gambling that she'd be interested. Once I had her attention, we could talk. We would spend more time together, grow closer. I hadn't been paying enough attention to her since I'd become absorbed in developing and marketing bluflex toys. We hadn't done anything together, just for fun, in almost a year. I had neglected her, and she had become a stranger to me.

I took her in on the weekend. I could show her around, get a chance to talk to her, really talk to her, and at the same time, I could check on some tests that I'd left running on Friday.

I had set up a special lab room in a sealed environment, solely to reanalyzing any compounds that bluflex might exude. The correlation between the toys I had suggested and the strange behavior of the children who owned them was too strong to ignore. The tests I was running were not only for the standard toxins. We had tested for those before. I was looking for mild hallucinogens, mood-altering chemicals, organics … anything. Anything other than the standard diatomics and carbon dioxide. Anything that would explain what was happening to our children. Anything that would give me an enemy I could fight.

The children were not the only thing I should have feared for, but they were all I could see.

I showed Meredith around the building and explained what the testing and manufacturing processes were. The sparkle in her eyes and the glints in her bracelets both brightened.

I didn't explain the special lab. I didn't want my own daughter thinking I was a crackpot.

I left her in the hallway outside the lab, telling her I'd only be a moment, and went into the adjoining room to check the results of the gas chromatography tests. They were all normal. From the time the tests had been set up, there had not been one suspicious molecule in the air of that room. Not one.

I was studying the charts when I caught a movement in my peripheral vision: a door opening. I looked up, through the one-way glass that stood between the lab and the instruments I was using, and saw my daughter.

She hesitated just inside the door but then began to explore the room. I shook my head and studied the gas chromatography. Her presence would not mess up the results. There were no results.

I turned back to the stream of information presently coming in from the room. And stared.

The readings were far from normal. They were so far from normal that my first thought was that they must be wrong. There were high levels of organic chemicals I didn't recognize, a few psychoactives I did, and insanely high concentrations of carbon dioxide. Meredith! I bolted out of the chair, ready to run to the lab and drag her out. I expected to see her gasping for air.

She was leaning over one of the vats of bluflex. She reached out her hand to brace herself against the side of the vat, and a brilliant light filled the room. When my vision cleared, Meredith was standing beside the vat. The bracelets on her wrist showed only subdued sparkles. Meredith's expression shifted to normal surprise so quickly that I hardly caught a glimpse of her previous expression, but a glimpse was enough. There had been worry and suspicion there … and an anger as deep as the sea.

I bundled her home as quickly as I could. I tucked her into bed, careful not to touch any of her bluflex ornaments. I kissed her on the forehead and left her to her dreams.

Her hair smelled like the sea.

When I recovered the data from the gas chromatography tests on Monday, I was stunned. Everything was completely normal until Meredith entered the room. The abnormal readings lasted for only a few minutes. The last abnormal reading was the one I had been staring at the instant before the flare of light. After that, the readings had returned to normal levels. There was no transition period, no time for the molecules to disperse. They were simply gone. I couldn't shake the conviction that the results showed a sentient, hostile reaction. The bluflex in the lab had somehow known that it was under observation. The bluflex that Meredith wore hadn't—until it was warned.

I took my findings to the president of Oak Leaf Products. I explained that we had to recall all bluflex products from the market immediately. Ten minutes later, I carried out the contents of my desk in a cardboard box.

On the drive home, I turned on the radio to hear experts discussing the continuing heat wave and the projected disappearance of the polar ice caps.

When I got home, Meredith was out. I packed our essentials into the car, being especially careful to leave behind anything containing bluflex. That ruled out a lot. For the first time, I appreciated the endless meetings about new bluflex products that I had been forced to sit through.

I drank some courage and waited for Meredith to come home. I knew I would regret what I was about to do, but I had no other choice.

When I heard Meredith's footsteps in the hall, I got up with dread in my heart. She was surprised when I bent to give her a hug hello. Had it been that long since I hugged her simply to show my love and welcome her home?

However long it had been, this hug had no such innocent motivations.

My arms went around her and held her immobile. She didn't say anything; she just looked at me. She didn't start fighting until I removed the first bluflex bracelet. Then she fought.

It was over quickly. Once the last of her bluflex adornments hit the floor, she stopped struggling. She must have guessed what I was planning, but she didn't try to run away. She didn't reproach me. She just stared at the abandoned mound of sparkling, shimmering bluflex.

I drove as far inland as I could go. I kept the windows rolled up and the air conditioner blasting, but the smell of brine followed us, swimming through the air currents.

At the end of the second day, I rolled the windows down.

The air was clean and wholesome, smelling of fresh-turned dirt.

The wind felt cold on my cheeks where it crossed the wet tracks of my tears.

Meredith had visited the place where we were going, but not in many years. When my parents were alive, we made the pilgrimage to their mountain cabin every summer. After they died, the visits stopped too. I wasn't able to bring myself to sell the place. I was too attached to it, an attachment for which I was now grateful.

I stopped in a little town at the base of the mountain to buy supplies. Meredith was sleeping. I covered her up carefully with a car rug and entered the small grocery store. I was debating whether I should buy more than just the fixings for peanut butter and jelly sandwiches when I saw a mother and her two boys. The boys were bored, as all boys are when taken grocery shopping by their mothers. They were playing with their yo-yos.

Their bluflex yo-yos.

They must have noticed me staring at them, because they looked up. Their bland, incurious eyes summed me up and dismissed me. They returned to their discussion of the best superhero and super-villain. Through the entire encounter, their yo-yos spooled evenly from their fingers in perfect synchronicity, twin lights gleaming in chorus.

I bought enough dried and canned supplies to feed an army garrison for six months. When I went to the register to pay, I noticed a bulletin board covered with 'missing child' posters. There were so many sheets of paper that when the wind blew they danced like seaweed at high tide.

Before I carried the supplies out to the car, I turned to confront the woman whose boys I'd seen. I knew it wouldn't do any good, but I had to warn her.

"If you want to keep your children," I said, "take away their bluflex toys and stay away from the sea." I lowered my voice. "If you can."

The woman's eyes widened with fear. I felt a spark of hope, until I realized that it was me she was afraid of.

"Boys," she said, keeping her tone level, "come here. We're leaving."

She headed toward the door, the boys trailing behind her. I couldn't let them leave, knowing what I did.

"You don't understand," I said.

The boys stopped and looked at me. "You can't stop us," one of them said. Their eyes were dark, as unreadable as the depths of the sea.

In desperation, I grabbed for their yo-yos. If nobody else would listen to me, if nobody else would do anything … I would. The yo-yos spun away from my fingers, swinging away from me in perfectly symmetrical arcs. The boys turned to follow their mother. The rhythm of the yo-yos never skipped a beat.

I stepped forward.

"Hey!" the clerk shouted at me. "Get out, and leave those boys alone!"

I was defeated.

The cabin was fairly low on the mountain. I unpacked the car and woke Meredith. She was hesitant, at first, as though she was suffering from culture shock. I kept my keys in my pocket and my eyes on her. She didn't bolt. During her tentative foray into the trees, she found the swing her granddad had put up for her.

After some false starts, she remembered how to use it. I left her with an easy heart. She was pumping her arms and legs awkwardly but with growing enthusiasm, and her face bore the closest thing to a smile that I had seen from her in more than a week. I thought we would be safe here, maybe even happy.

I should have remembered the missing child posters.

The next month made me grateful we were safe on the mountain. Safe! I should have known better.

Low-lying cities were flooded as the massive icebergs melted. Thousands of people died in the heat. Millions more lost their homes and their livelihood to the hungry sea. And their children. I cannot forget our lost children, because it was my fault we lost them.

Refugees swarmed to the mountains, bringing their most prized possessions. They brought bluflex with them, and the sea followed at their heels. Even the smell of the pines could not mask the salty brine that the breeze carried up the mountain. Though the last of the icebergs had melted, the sea level continued to rise. Worldwide, governments admitted that they were baffled.

I was not surprised when Meredith disappeared. I had lost her to the sea, or given her away, many months ago. I thought I had found her again. I had hoped I could keep her. But hope was a fragile mist that the wind from the sea easily dissolved.

When I called to report her missing, I only got an automated service that took my information, and the line went dead before I was finished. I didn't bother trying to call back.

On my drive down the mountain, I saw two end-of-the-world signs, four refugee families huddled together under a tarp for shade, and one enterprising man building a houseboat. I wonder where he is now? I hope he's doing well.

At the grocery store, I saw the woman who had been there with her children the last time I bought supplies. She was alone, and her grocery basket held only single-serving microwave dinners. The dark circles under her eyes told me all I needed to know. I don't think she recognized me. I did not talk to her.

I did not talk to anyone. The man behind the register talked about selling the store and moving. The basement was flooding, and now his house, further up on the mountain, was having water problems. I looked around the store, and I had a revelation.

There were bluflex toys near the register and bluflex containers scattered around the store. Bluflex was everywhere. It wasn't safe.

The sea was coming for its children. It had taken our children, but that was not enough. That was why it kept rising. It would not stop until all the bluflex was back under the sea.

I bought as much food as I could load into the car and drove up the mountain. I didn't feel safe. I knew that the global warming would continue until the bluflex was safe beneath the sea. And there was bluflex everywhere. It was the miracle material. It would not all be returned to the sea until the whole world had drowned.

I sat in the cabin, and I didn't feel safe. I could smell the sea.

I was sitting on the porch one day, drinking, when a garbage truck rumbled past me up the road to the landfill on top of the mountain. I drank a lot. Drowning my sorrows, as they used to say.

I hate the phrase. The sea has taken everything else from me; it cannot take my sorrow.

I remembered my parents complaining about that landfill when they built it. Despoiling the beauty of nature, they said, but it was a barren mountaintop that didn't attract tourism, so the town council had voted to put the landfill there. I didn't see much beauty in nature those days, but the landfill.... The landfill would be my salvation.

It was at the very top of the mountain, and it should be safe. Nobody ever threw bluflex away.

I waited until the road up the mountain flooded. I listened to the radio, but all that I could pick up was old radio shows punctuated by news bulletins listing the latest flood disaster areas and designating refugee shelters. The mountain was never among them.

I heard the bulletin when the town at the foot of the mountain flooded. I waited to hear that the top of the mountain, my part of the mountain, was a designated refugee haven, but I never did.

It was forgotten. I liked it that way. I could be alone with my booze and my old-time radio shows. I had no fondness for the human race. We had done this to ourselves with our desire for more, new, better.

I had done this.

I slowly moved my belongings to the landfill. I never saw anybody. From the top of the mountain, I could see for miles. Most of what I saw was water.

Each trip, the land diminished.

Finally, all my possessions were moved. I spent most of my time sitting in a broken lawn chair, drinking and listening to The Shadow. The Shadow knows.

One day the radio went dead, so I just sat and drank. I watched the seagulls. They flew in great wheeling flocks across the sky. The ocean had settled. I lost no more ground to it.

A month after the radio went dead, I drank the last of the alcohol. I spent a week scavenging for half-empty liquor bottles and going through withdrawal.

Without the soothing blanket of booze, I started to think

again. Meredith was gone, but was I really alone in the world?

The seagulls could not be the only survivors. They flew away from the landfill and returned days later. There must be other land nearby.

I stopped looking for alcohol and started searching for a boat, or at least an engine.

The landfill is safe, but safety is not the most important thing in life. I saw a column of smoke in the sky this morning, far off to the east.

As soon as I have finished building my boat, I will set out towards that signal. The sea cannot stop me. I would dare it to do its worst, but it already has. It took my home, my job, and my child. It took my entertainments and my addictions.

It could not take my hope, because hope cannot be drowned, not by alcohol and not by the sea.

If I survived, there will be others. I will find them. And one day, we will take back our land from the sea, and our children will play in the grass.

 Abra Staffin-Wiebe has sold stories to publications including *Jim Baen's Universe* and *Tor.com*. She specializes in optimistic dystopian SF, modern fairy tales, cheerful horror, liquid-state steampunk, dark humor, and heartwarming grotesqueries.

Discover more of her fiction at her website, http://www.aswiebe.com, or find her on the social media site of your choice.

The Lilac Hedge
Rose Blackthorn

Yarrow grew up surrounded by flowers. She was named for a flower, as was her mother, Viola, and grandmother Lily. Her most intense memories were of hours spent in the garden with her grandmother. But not all her memories were happy.

She was an only child, and although she loved her mother, Viola, intensely, they had never spent much time together. Yarrow's father left when she was too young to remember him, and she never knew why or what happened to him. Her mother met another man and married him. Viola then spent most of her time doing what she supposed would please him. She kept her hair long and full, makeup flawless, and wardrobe stylish—at least as much as she could afford. She was kind to her quiet, intense daughter but in an absentminded way. Whenever possible, she traveled with her new husband, a long-haul truck driver who owned his own rig.

"The only way to make money," he always said, "is to keep this rig a'rollin'." He lived by that creed and booked his runs back to back whenever possible.

"For better or for worse," Viola would say to Yarrow. "That's what marriage is, Ladybug." Then she would pack up Yarrow's clothes and toiletries and drive her daughter over to her parents' place to stay for a while.

Grandma and Grandpa never seemed to mind. They were very fond of Yarrow, always happy to see her, and willing to keep her for as long as their wandering daughter asked. Grandpa would take Yarrow's battered suitcase filled with clothes for the next few days or weeks, and Grandma would take Yarrow's hand and lead her into the kitchen, where homemade bread had invariably just come out of the oven.

In the summer, Yarrow spent her time in the fields, helping with the weeding and watering of Grandpa's vegetable garden. She caught pollywogs and water snakes in the cattail-rimmed pond in the far pasture and played with the kittens that lived and hunted mice in the hay barn.

If it was autumn, she helped bring in the harvest and then washed and prepared the vegetables for bottling. She used the old cane rake to scrape yellow and brown leaves into piles and stand with her hands out for warmth as Grandpa used a pitchfork to toss them in the old barrel he used to burn them.

In winter she built snowmen and forts in the front yard, or used an old broom to break off the glistening spikes of icicles that clung to the eaves. But the spring was her favorite time of year at her grandparents' place.

In the springtime, in the evenings, they would sit out on the back lawn near Grandma's rose garden. Grandpa would light a couple of candles to draw any biters, as he called mosquitoes. Grandma would bring her crocheting, which she could do in the deepening darkness by touch alone, and the elderly couple took turns reminiscing about the old days.

In the spring of the year that Yarrow would turn thirteen, Grandma inherited some old china, an antique wooden rocker, and five stunted lilac bushes from her only brother. Emery had died a widower estranged from his children, and he had lived all his life in the house where he and Lily had been born. The items he left to his sister had been left to him by their parents.

As soon as the ground was soft enough, Yarrow helped dig the holes to plant the old crooked lilacs. Grandma had in mind a kind of hedge, so she placed the bushes a few feet apart along the edge of the back lawn.

"Emery always cut them back every year," she said, using the garden hose to water the newly transplanted bushes. "But I think I'll let them grow a bit. The blooms on these bushes were always the sweetest smelling; but I imagine it'll be a year or two before they start putting out flowers again."

"Why is that?" Yarrow asked curiously. She sat on the grass, picking dirt out from under her nails.

"It's the shock of it," Grandma answered, dropping the hose on the ground and walking over to turn off the water. "These bushes are so old, older than I am, older than my mother was. They came from Ireland with my grandfather, and they've been planted in the same ground for decades. Moving to a new place, putting down new roots, you have to expect them to take a while to recover."

Yarrow nodded thoughtfully, gazing at the stunted tangles of limbs. There were a few new leaves beginning to open on the twig-ends, but all in all, the bushes looked rather sad.

"We'll just make sure to keep them watered," Grandma said, pausing to tuck an errant strand of pale hair behind Yarrow's ear. "And keep the weeds out. In no time, these lilacs will be happy as ever."

Over the course of that spring and into the summer, Yarrow took special care of the lilacs. As Grandma had supposed, they didn't put out any buds; but they were soon covered in heart-shaped healthy leaves. Yarrow built little earthen dams around each bush, so that the water would stay near the roots rather than running off into the lawn. She carefully removed any other plants, either grass or weed, that sprouted too close, so that nothing would take away nutrients from the transplants.

In the summer, Grandpa took her fishing up in the hills. Between them with their simple bamboo poles they caught three trout and three carp. In years past, Grandpa had always thrown the carp back. "Not good eatin'," he would say, and leave it at that. But this time he kept them. When she asked him why, he just smiled, his hazel eyes twinkling behind his black-rimmed glasses. "You'll see. It's a surprise for your Grandma."

Grandma came out to meet them when they pulled into the yard, and to compliment them on their catch, whatever it might be. When Grandpa revealed the newspaper-wrapped carp with a flourish, she raised one eyebrow. "Since when do you like carp?"

Grandpa shook his head. "Not for me, Lily. They're for your lilacs."

It was the strangest thing Yarrow had seen in her life. With a solemn feeling of ceremony, Grandpa cut two of the carp in half and then dug holes next to each lilac bush, being extra careful not to hit any roots. He put a portion of carp in each hole, an entire fish for the center bush, and filled them back in with dirt.

"Is it a funeral?" Yarrow finally asked when all was done. She'd had a goldfish when she was five, but when it died her mother had flushed it down the toilet.

"It'll feed the roots," Grandpa said, nodding his head sagely. "Used to do that with your Grandma's roses, if they were lookin' sickly. Turns the trick every time. You'll see, those lilacs will grow like gangbusters now."

Grandpa was right. By the end of summer, the bushes were lush and healthy, and reached out to each other as though to embrace. They'd all grown at least a foot in height, and the center bush more like two feet. When Viola came to take her daughter home, back again from a long stint on the road, Yarrow looked wistfully at the lilacs.

"I'm a transplant, too," she whispered to them before getting in the car, "But every time I get roots down, I'm dug back up again."

Fall and early winter were spent with her mother that year, but not long after Christmas Yarrow began to notice the telltale signs. Viola checked the mailbox every day, sometimes two or three times, to be sure she hadn't missed a letter from her husband. She rarely left the house, waiting for a phone call from him. She was kind and patient as she always was to Yarrow, but it was obvious her mind was elsewhere. On a cool blustery day in March, Yarrow came home from school to find her suitcase packed and ready to go.

Viola dropped her off with a kiss and a squeeze, and spoke to Grandma for a few minutes while Grandpa helped Yarrow with her suitcase and then was gone. After putting her clothes away in the old painted dresser, Yarrow went out to check on the lilacs.

The bushes were covered in bright new leaves, and they seemed taller and fuller than she remembered. Going up on tiptoe, she noted tiny little round bumps circling most of the twig-ends. Yarrow smiled to herself; there would be flowers this year, she was sure of it.

She quickly settled into her old routine. It was late enough in the year that the snow was mostly done, but before most of Grandma's garden had put out any flowers. Cheerful purple crocus had opened beneath the kitchen windows, and daffodils and tulips were beginning to push skyward, their stiff sword-like leaves already standing proud. The peonies had produced large round tightly-closed buds the size of a baby's fist. In the weeks to come they would open into multipetaled flowers of a deep burgundy red.

In April, the weather warmed, and it rained. Sometimes the rain was soft and whispering, gently falling to the thirsty ground. Other times the wind blew, thrashing the trees and bushes wildly, while the rain hammered down from a thundering sky. Yarrow loved the soft spring rain, but was anxious and uneasy in the angry spring storms. It was during such a thunderstorm that she first saw the shadowy figure crouched beneath the lilacs.

"Grandma?" she asked after staring out the window for a while. Lightning arced, a hard brittle crash following only a second later, and the thunder rolled for what felt like forever. Outside the back window, water fell from the roof in a miniature flood, and for a moment Yarrow felt as though the house was underwater. Everything outside rippled and flowed, making it impossible to be sure of what she was seeing. But still, a shadow nestled beneath the lilacs, and she just knew it was looking back at her.

"What is it, dear?" Grandma asked rather absentmindedly. Grandpa had gone into the bedroom to take an early afternoon nap, and she was crocheting lace onto the edge of a pillowcase, the small silver hook darting in and out of the threads like a hummingbird's beak.

"There's someone in the back yard," Yarrow replied, and her voice shook just a little.

"In this weather?" Grandma said, looking up now, her hands falling still. "Who is it?"

Yarrow shook her head, turning back to gaze out the window. "I don't know."

Grandma set her handwork aside and got to her feet. She crossed to the window where Yarrow perched, and leaned forward until her nose almost touched the glass. "Where?"

Yarrow pointed, and said, "Beneath the lilacs."

Grandma searched the yard intently and then stepped back. "I can't tell anything with this rain. Stay here." She left the girl at the window, and went around the old secretary and the bookshelf to the back door. When she opened it, the sound of falling water swelled. Yarrow imagined this was what it would sound like at Niagara Falls.

Thunder boomed and rolled, and the rain actually increased, making its own attempt at thunder across the shingled roof. Grandma called something through the screen door, which she had not opened, but the world outside was so noisy Yarrow couldn't tell what. She looked back out the window, just in time to see the shadow crouch lower into a kind of misshapen bow, and then it turned and seemed to melt into the center lilac bush.

When Grandma came back into the family room, Yarrow asked breathlessly, "Who was it?"

Grandma shook her head and smiled gently. "No one there, dear; just a trick of the wind and the rain. Don't you worry about it." She sat in her chair again, going back to her lace-making, and hummed softly under her breath.

Yarrow stared at her for a moment and then looked back outside again. The shadow was gone.

When the storm finally subsided, and the sun peeked out again, Yarrow went outside to check the lilacs. If there had been any tracks in the soil, the heavy rains had eradicated them. It was just a muddy soup now. Every leaf and twig in the yard glittered as sunlight sparkled off the raindrops clinging to everything, and Yarrow smiled when a rainbow began to form east of the house. Her anxious foreboding was allayed by the beauty of the late afternoon, but she didn't forget about the shadow that had stared back at her.

As the days and weeks passed, the weather got warmer and the spring rains subsided. Flowers bloomed everywhere. Grandma's wild roses were covered in bright-yellow blooms from near the ground to the top of the arching canes that reached seven feet before dropping back down to the earth. Her heirloom roses were blooming as well, planted in even rows behind the house and kept weed free as a matter of course. There were yellow roses, and white, and several shades of pink and red. Yarrow's favorite was pale lavender in color; the small bush only put out a few flowers each year, but also didn't grow many thorns. A dense row of irises followed the verge of the driveway, and the oddly shaped flowers with beards, as Grandma called them, showed pale blue and variegated gold and even some that were so dark a purple as to appear black. The snowball bush to the side of the hump-roofed cellar was weighed down with heavy blossoms, but the flowers that pleased Yarrow and Grandma the most were the fragrant pale purple lilacs. The five bushes transplanted the year before fairly drooped with the weight of them all. The scent of the flowers filled the yard, and Grandma kept her bedroom window open to let the smell into the house as well.

Yarrow noticed the shadowy figure near the lilacs many times, but always from the corner of her eye. Whenever she turned her head, it would be gone; a frustrating game of hide and seek. After Grandma's reaction to Yarrow's worries during the storm, she didn't bring up these fleeting visitations to either of her grandparents. Instead she tried to come up with a way to get a better look at it.

She tried sidling toward the bushes without turning her head, she tried looking away and then back quickly, she even tried lying on the grass beneath the graceful drape of flowers. Nothing worked, although she often got the overpowering feeling that the shadow was watching her, as it had done through the downpour. Finally she'd had enough. "If you won't play fair, I won't play at all."

Surprisingly, that did the trick. The center bush trembled, and then shivered, and Yarrow jumped back. A face, thin and angular, appeared between the heart-shaped leaves and heavy flower clusters. It was a boy, perhaps a year or two older than she, with unruly black hair and lilac colored eyes. And he was smiling.

"Who are you?" she asked and then flushed at the rudeness of her tone. He had startled her, though.

"I am Irial," he said, with a strange fluid lilt to his words. His voice was deeper than she had expected, and the teeth his smile revealed were very white and sharp. "I wondered how long before you'd speak to me."

"You've been watching me," she said quietly, but it was still an accusation.

"You helped me to feel at home," he replied, moving a little closer, a little further away from the lilacs. "I wanted us to be friends."

"Where do you live?" she asked, and was not surprised by his answer.

"In the lilacs."

Feeling a little odd to still be standing while he was crouched beneath the lowest branches of the center bush, she knelt down in the grass and sat on her heels. Grandpa was out in the vegetable patch, and Grandma was kneading bread dough in the kitchen. For the moment, they would not be disturbed. "How—" she started self-consciously, and twisted a lock of her pale blonde hair between her fingers. "How do you live in the lilacs?"

He moved closer still, revealing porcelain-smooth skin and slightly pointed ears that showed through his tangled black hair. His fingers and hands were unusually long and slender, like the twigs and branches of the bushes behind him. "How do you live in a house?" was his answer.

"But everyone lives in a house!"

"I don't."

Stymied, she nodded. "How long have you lived in the lilacs?"

"All my life," he said, and reached out one long-fingered hand to her. "Where do you go when you're not here?"

Without any thought, she put her hand in his. It was smooth and cool, like touching a sapling. "I go to live with my mother. Then, when she gets tired of me, I come back here."

"You're so pretty—how could she get tired of you?" he asked, tugging gently, and she moved closer to him.

"She's married. She likes to go on the road with her husband." She ducked her head, trying to keep her long hair from tangling in the heart-shaped leaves.

"If you lived with me," he whispered, his cool breath

against her cheek, "I would never send you away. I would keep you with me, always." He smelled like the lilac flowers.

"I can't live with you," she said, closing her eyes when he put his thin strong arms around her. His kiss was sweet but sharp, and she felt dizzy.

"You could live with me forever," he said, pulling her even closer.

"Yarrow! What are you doing in the dirt?" Grandma called, and there might have been fear mixed with the anger in her voice.

Yarrow pulled back from Irial, her hair tangling in the branches above her, as though the twigs were trying to hold her there. Grandma grasped her shoulders and pulled her back away from the bush. Yarrow caught a glimpse of her new friend still crouched beneath the leaves, holding long strands of her blond hair between his slender fingers.

"Go back in the house and get cleaned up," Grandma said, her voice low. "You've got grass and dirt stains on your pants."

One look at her face, and Yarrow didn't bother to argue. She turned and ran back to the house to change her clothes. Grandma stayed in the garden.

After she'd cleaned up, Yarrow went into the kitchen. Grandma was punching down and kneading a fresh batch of bread dough, and flour floated in the sunlit air like pollen on a breezy spring day. Without looking up from what she was doing, Grandma said, "I want you to stay away from the lilacs, sweetheart. They don't need the constant attention now like they did last year."

"You want me to stay away from Irial?" Yarrow asked, and Grandma flinched as though she'd been stuck with a pin. "Did you know he was here?"

Grandma stopped what she was doing, her hands still buried in smooth dough. She sighed, and turned to place the lump of dough in a bowl and spread a towel over it so it could rise. She rinsed her hands in the sink, and finally turned back to her granddaughter as she dried her hands on her apron. "I didn't think he was still with the lilacs."

"Still?" Yarrow asked. She sat on the little stool at the end of the counter and waited.

"I met Irial when I was just a little younger than you are

now," Grandma confessed. "When my brother, Emery, found out about him, he started cutting the bushes back. When he did that, Irial went away. After all these years, I thought he was long gone."

"What is he?" Yarrow asked, remembering his cinnamon kiss.

Grandma shook her head, her faded blue eyes full of a mix of emotions she couldn't convey. "I don't know, sweetheart. But I know he can be dangerous. I want you to stay away from him. Promise me?"

Yarrow nodded, remembering his smooth long-fingered hand holding her own.

Late that night, Yarrow got out of bed and crept silently through the house to the back door. Because it was warming up, Grandpa left the wooden door open with only the screen latched, to allow a cooling breeze into the house. Beyond the heirloom roses at the edge of the lawn, Grandma stood near the lilacs. Bright moonlight shone off her long white hair falling unbraided and loose down her back. She wore a pale pink nightgown which clearly revealed her age-rounded shoulders, stooped back and sagging bosom. Before her stood a dark-haired figure. He seemed taller and older than he had to Yarrow earlier in the day, as though he had aged years in just a few hours.

"You can have me," Grandma was saying, holding out her liver-spotted hands. "But leave my girl alone."

The dark figure shook his head. "You ran away from me, Lily. Your time is done, and Yarrow's time is just beginning."

"You can't have her!"

He glanced past the old woman and met Yarrow's eyes. "Her choice is her own, Lily. You can't make it for her."

Yarrow stealthily returned to her bed, not wanting her Grandma to catch her spying, or even worse guess at why she was out of bed so late. But she wondered what it was that he wanted, and why it would be so bad to give it to him.

At the beginning of June as the lilac blooms began to brown and wither, Yarrow helped Grandpa trim off the dead florets. As they worked their way around the five bushes, she occasionally caught glimpses of Irial through the dense leaves. He never said anything, just gazed at her solemnly. It was clear to her that Grandpa couldn't see him, but the way Grandma watched to be sure they didn't cut anything back too far, it was obvious she could.

When her mother called a couple of weeks later to say Yarrow was coming home, Yarrow did her best not to sound disappointed. She loved her mother but preferred to stay at her grandparents' house. And she wanted to talk to Irial again, but under her grandmother's protective gaze had been unable.

In August, after Yarrow's fourteenth birthday, they got a call with bad news. Grandpa had apparently suffered a heart attack while working in the yard. By the time the ambulance had arrived, it was too late.

Viola immediately drove to her parents' house, where her mother waited alone. When they arrived they found Lily sitting in her wingback chair with her current piece of handwork in her lap. Her hands rested limp in the folds of cloth and embroidery floss, and she stared vacantly out the back window at the lilac hedge.

While Viola spoke to her mother, holding her lax hands and trying to get an account of what had happened, Yarrow went out the back door to look at the lilacs. They had been butchered; Grandpa's hedge trimmers and hand clippers lay abandoned on the grass amongst a scatter of branches. The hedge itself which had grown to over seven feet in height since being transplanted had been hacked down to perhaps four feet. Lying beneath the lowest branches, appearing skeletally thin and pale, Irial gazed up at her with eyes that had changed from lilac purple to the brown of the dying florets.

She crouched down so she could see him more clearly. "What did you do?" she whispered.

"He tried to kill me," Irial breathed, reaching out for her with one bone-slender hand.

She raised her hand and touched the tips of his fingers gingerly. He still felt cool and smooth, yet somehow not as substantial. "You killed my Grandpa," she said, more statement than question, and he pulled his hand back from her as though her touch burned him.

"It was his life or mine."

Yarrow shook her head and stood up, backing away from

the carnage.

"I'll be here," he said, and began to fade back into the shadows beneath the remaining leaves and branches. "When you want me, I'll be here."

Yarrow watched until she could see him no longer, and then she turned and went into the house to comfort her Grandma.

No matter how many years passed, there was nothing quite like a late spring evening, with the scent of blooming flowers on the breath of dusk. Yarrow sat quietly within her enclosed garden, the light of a candle lending a muted glow to hollyhock and delphinium, corn flower and freesia, peony and rose. The tulips were nearly done with their blooming, waxy leaves still standing proud and healthy. Sweet peas were climbing the lattice she'd supplied for their use. But with all the beautiful colors and scents, it was the lilac that ruled this May eventide. She took a deep breath of the perfumed air, remembering the events of her youth that had brought her to this moment.

After Grandpa's death, she had stayed with Grandma. Lily never spoke of what had happened the day her husband died, but she spent time every day near the denuded lilac hedge. Two years later, on the anniversary of her husband's death Lily was found unresponsive lying on the grass, a bouquet of heirloom roses she'd been cutting clutched to her chest. Since Viola was her only child, everything had been left to her. But there was a trust set up for Yarrow when she turned eighteen, and included in her bequest were the five antique lilac bushes.

Yarrow had grown up and finished school. She'd had her share of suitors, but none could compete with the memories of that summer before she turned fourteen. Now she had a little house with a yard of her own. She spent time planning and planting the different flowers she remembered and loved from her childhood. But her favorite part of the yard was the back corner where she'd transplanted the lilac bushes. For two years she'd let them grow untrimmed, and now they stood ten feet tall and laden with sweet smelling blooms. She had done her research, and surrounding the lilacs was a low wrought-iron fence. She didn't know exactly what Irial was, but she guessed he was some kind of Irish fey. And one thing all the books and folklore agreed on was that fey could not cross iron. Now that the lilacs were untamed, she wanted to make sure he stayed put, until she was ready.

Tonight, Yarrow waited until the last glow of sunlight had faded from the sky. She was wearing a pale purple silk shift, and her hair hung long and slightly wavy down to her waist, still the same pale gold shade it had been when she was thirteen. When the moon rose above the house to cast its glow into her garden, she got up from her bower and crossed the grass to the far corner.

Irial stood before the transplanted bushes, his lilac-colored eyes watching as she approached. His unruly black hair and clever smile were just as she remembered. "I've been waiting for you, Yarrow."

She nodded, stopping outside the ring of the ornamental fence. "I wanted it to be perfect."

He held out his long-fingered hand to her, as he'd done before years ago, but did not reach across the wrought-iron. There was a clear invitation in his light eyes.

Yarrow thought back to that late spring day, when she had taken his hand and been pulled into his arms. She remembered his sharp, sweet kiss and stepped over the fence.

Rose Blackthorn lives in Eastern Utah with her boyfriend and two dogs. She spends her time writing, reading, beading, doing wire-work, and photographing the surrounding wilderness. An only child, she was lucky enough to have a mother who loved books and has been surrounded by them her entire life. Thus instead of squabbling with siblings, she learned to be friends with her imagination and the voices in her head are still very much present. She is a member of the HWA and has published genre fiction online and in print with Necon E-Books, Stupefying Stories, Cast of Wonders, Dark Moon Digest, Buzzy Mag, and the anthologies *The Ghost IS the Machine, A Quick Bite of Flesh, Fear the Abyss, From beyond the Grave,* and *Horrific History,* among others

About The Editors

Christopher Jones lives in Toronto. *Eulogies II* is his first book as an editor. He can be contacted at chrisinthecellar@gmail.com.

Nanci Kalanta is the owner and editor of HorrorWorld.org and HW Press. She has edited and published *Eulogies: A Horror World Yearbook*, *Laughing Boy's Shadow* by Steven Savile, *Sparks and Shadows* by Lucy A. Snyder, and *Blood Born* by Matthew Warner. Nanci lives in the foothills of the Blue Ridge Mountains with her husband of thirty-two years and two cats.

Tony Tremblay has been a fan of horror fiction since he was a child, when his father gave him a biography of St. Augustine to read in the hopes that Tony would seek the priesthood. Instead, after finishing the biography and then progressing onto the Old Testament in the Bible, Tony decided he wanted to write horror fiction. Almost fifty years later he began to write in earnest, and his first published story was "An Alabama Christmas" in Horror World in 2011. Since then he has had several genre stories published in various anthologies and has completed his first horror novel. Tony is also a reviewer of horror and genre novels for Horror World and *Cemetery Dance* magazine.

Tony Tremblay never became the priest his father hoped he'd be, and he lives very happily in New Hampshire with his wife and two grown children.

Printed in Great Britain
by Amazon.co.uk, Ltd.,
Marston Gate.